Dear Reader,

A lot of you will, I'm sure, be thinking about your summer vacation now. So whether you're planning to sit in the sun by a pool, have a sporting holiday or just laze around at home (*my* favourite form of relaxation!) I hope reading *Scarlet* will be part of your holiday fun.

This month we are proud to offer you: the first award-winning novel by Julia Wild; critically acclaimed author Jill Sheldon's third *Scarlet* romance; a peep into the glitz and glam world of international tennis from talented new author Kathryn Bellamy; and a skilfully woven second novel, with a delightful Scottish background, by Danielle Shaw. As ever, we hope there are stories to suit every mood and taste in this month's *Scarlet* selection.

I always seem to be asking you questions – and here is another! Are four *Scarlet* books a month enough? Would you like to buy more?

I am very grateful to all those readers who have taken the trouble to complete our questionnaires and/or write to me. We are very grateful for your comments and we *do* act upon them.

Till next month,

Sally Cooper

SALLY COOPER,
Editor-in-Chief – *Scarlet*

About the Author

Danielle Shaw was born in Watford, England. She studied fashion and design at the London College of fashion and then joined The Royal Opera House, Covent Garden.

In 1967, Danielle moved to Geneva, where she met her Swedish husband, and worked in various kindergartens. She returned to the UK and set up her own school.

Danielle is interested in reading, music, theatre, the local countryside and gardening. She also likes to exercise and swims three times a week. 'Above all, though,' says Danielle, 'I much prefer to write!'

We are delighted to encourage Danielle to write and to offer you this, her second book for the *Scarlet* list.

Other *Scarlet* titles available this month:

REVENGE IS SWEET – Jill Sheldon
DARK CANVAS – Julia Wild
GAME, SET AND MATCH – Kathryn Bellamy

DANIELLE SHAW

MARRIED TO SINCLAIR

Enquiries to:
Robinson Publishing Ltd
7 Kensington Church Court
London W8 4SP

First published in the UK by Scarlet, 1997

A copy of the British Library Cataloguing in
Publication data is available from the British Library

ISBN 1-85487-956-1

Printed and bound in the EC

10 9 8 7 6 5 4 3 2 1

CHAPTER 1

'Two weeks, Andrew! You're going away for two weeks? But we've only just celebrated Christmas and New Year! Isn't there snow enough in Scotland for you?' Jenny's hazel eyes blazed with anger and her cheeks flushed scarlet as she regarded her brother.

Startled by the sudden change in his sister's voice, Andrew Sinclair busied himself uneasily with papers on the desk, while Stevie, who was taking the minutes of the meeting, anticipated a verbal explosion.

'Well?' demanded Jenny.

Andrew, opening his mouth to speak, was abruptly silenced by the ringing of his telephone. Grabbing the receiver, he held it tenaciously like a lifeline, hoping for a moment's respite from his sister's obvious disapproval. The relief on his face gave way to anxiety and replacing the receiver he moved swiftly towards the door.

'Andrew?' Jenny enquired, her voice losing its earlier sharpness. 'Is there anything wrong?'

On his way out, Andrew replied numbly, 'It's Fiona, she's got a temperature. Mary's called the doctor; she thinks it could be meningitis.'

1

Meningitis! Children died of that, didn't they? Only last week there had been a case in the paper. Alarmed, Jenny thought anxiously of her niece. At six years old, Fiona was the youngest of Andrew's three children and the baby of the whole family. She and Cameron had been godparents and Jenny loved her dearly. Nothing must happen to Fiona!

Closing her notebook, Stevie turned her wheelchair to face Jenny. 'Any other time I'd say he was saved by the bell, but not today.'

Jenny poured two cups of coffee and handed one to her PA. The two women worked well together although hiring Stevie had been another occasion when she'd done battle with her brother.

'You can't be serious about employing a cripple!' he'd demanded.

'I don't need her legs, I need her mind and business acumen. Have you read her CV?'

When he was forced to admit he hadn't, Jenny had ignored Andrew's disapproving looks and Stevie had joined the Sinclair team. There could be no excuses about disabilities or wheelchair access either. Their late father, William Sinclair, had himself spent his last years at the family business wheelchair-bound, and as a result the offices and corridors of Sinclair Tartans were more than able to cope with Stevie's streamlined machine.

To Jenny's satisfaction and Andrew's despair, Stevie negotiated each obstacle with admirable ease and dexterity. Even now it still amused Jenny to watch Andrew's face as the wheelchair ploughed tracks into his office carpet. The expanse of deep pile in Sinclair

2

colours was Andrew's pride and joy. He never said anything, just glowered with annoyance.

Rubbing at the flattened pile with the toe of her shoe, Jenny watched thoughtfully as the bright-coloured tufts sprang upright once more. Perhaps she had been a bit sharp with Andrew. His sheer hard work and determination had certainly helped Sinclair's through the recent recession. But the start of a new year meant they must continue to make similar progress and not go sauntering off on holiday!

Jenny sighed and tugged at her strawberry blonde hair, smoothing it back into place, where it was tied at the nape of her neck with a black velvet bow. Determinedly she turned to face Stevie.

'It's imperative to keep ahead of the market and I refuse to let Sinclair's lag behind its competitors. If Andrew goes away we run the risk of losing valuable business. Anyway,' she said, taking Stevie's empty cup, 'he won't go now if Fiona is ill.'

Andrew's absence from the office left Jenny with a heavy workload and by the end of a long afternoon she was both surprised and delighted when her sister-in-law rang inviting her for supper. At least she wouldn't have to worry about cooking tonight. Mary was an excellent cook; her ample proportions bore witness to the fact. Yet despite her size she was always elegant and well dressed.

Tonight was no exception as Mary, in fine cashmere skirt and silk blouse, met her at the door along with a wonderful smell of herbs and spices. Fiona, to Jenny's surprise, came bouncing along the hallway to meet her.

'Fiona, I thought you were poorly! Why aren't you in bed?'

3

'She should be, only she wanted to wait up to see you. Hurry away to your room now, Fiona, we grown-ups want our supper.'

Before obeying her mother, Fiona gave Jenny a warm hug.

'Well, what's wrong with you? You don't look too bad to me.'

From the top of the stairs, Fiona called down, 'I've got chicken spots, look!' With her words whistling through the gaps in her front teeth, Fiona lifted up her nightdress to reveal a mass of tiny red blisters.

Mary turned towards Jenny. 'Well, thank heaven it wasn't meningitis, at least. But have you had chicken pox, Jennifer?'

'Why, yes, I had it when I was small. It was awful, all that dreadful scratching and cold calamine lotion dabbed everywhere.' She shuddered at the memory and was grateful for the drink Andrew handed her as she entered the dining room.

'You look as if you could do with this. Sorry to have left you to hold the fort, especially when there's so much going on.'

Relieved to find no hint in Andrew's voice of their earlier disagreement, Jenny took a generous gulp of the refreshing Sancerre. She might have the quick temper associated with people of her colouring but she also hated atmospheres. Life was too short. She'd often heard of families having rows followed by long silences, only to be brought together by unforeseen tragedies.

By inevitable association the most recent tragedies in Jenny Sinclair's life came into her mind: the death of

4

her dear father – the result of a wasting and debilitating illness – and the sudden departure at Christmas of her fiancé. After six years, and without warning, Cameron Ross had abruptly ended their engagement. It had been so sudden, in fact, that Jenny was still recovering from the shock and even her family were unaware of the circumstances. Swallowing hard, she was glad of the diversion when Mary called them to the table and Jean and Iain, the two elder Sinclair children, joined their parents and aunt for supper.

After a short while, and feeling more relaxed as a genial atmosphere pervaded the room, Jenny enquired after Jean and Iain's studies and the latter part of the evening was spent discussing Morag and Miss Tandy.

'They've both had the most dreadful colds,' Jenny announced.

'I'm not surprised,' Mary retorted. 'I really can't understand Mother-in-law and Tandy wanting to stay in that cold, grey house with only an electric fire for heat. And goodness knows why Tandy has put up with her for so long. It's always raining on the west coast, too.'

'But Conasg is the family home,' Andrew broke in tetchily, running his hand through his thick sandy hair. It irked him to hear his mother and her companion referred to in such a way. 'It can't have been easy for her when . . .'

Jenny thought he was going to say, when Father died. Instead he continued softly '. . . keeping the mill running. It was only her stubbornness and canny head for business that kept us all going at the time.'

Silently Jenny agreed with her brother's statement,

and she wondered what Morag Sinclair would say if she could see the blazing log fire that burnt in the grate, in addition to the central heating. Not for Mary were there layers of thermal underwear and thick sweaters. No wonder she could get away with wearing silk on such a cold night.

'Jenny – more wine, or some brandy?' Andrew stood by her side, for once his stomach not hidden behind his desk. Like his wife, he was putting on weight. Too much rich food and too little exercise.

'No, thanks, Andrew, but if you'd just add some soda water to this drink? Don't forget I'm driving and I must be going soon. I had some ideas for Sinclair's this afternoon and I'd like to work on them before going to bed. Perhaps we could discuss them next week?'

Going to fetch her coat, Jenny was oblivious to the furtive glances cast in Andrew's direction by his wife and older children. In the hall, however, she was startled to find an anxious and bleary-eyed Fiona sitting on the stairs.

'Have they asked you yet?' Fiona whispered. Seeing her aunt's look of bewilderment, she added, 'Please, you will say yes?'

Her whispered plea came to an abrupt halt as the sitting room door opened and Fiona looked up into her father's anxious face.

'What's this you have to ask me?' Jenny enquired.

Andrew and Mary looked shamefaced. It was Iain who broke the silence.

'We wondered if you'd look after Fiona . . . while we're away.'

'You mean to say you still intend to go?' Jenny surveyed them all in utter disbelief.

'Please, Auntie Jen,' pleaded Jean. 'We're so looking forward to it.'

'Yes, especially as Dad has booked for two weeks!'

Andrew flinched visibly at his son's remark. He remembered Jenny's outburst that morning.

'You see, you've had chicken pox,' Mary continued, 'and Dr McAllister said she won't be infectious for long. Andrew says you can take her into the office – after all, there'll be no one else there . . . will there?'

Jenny thought of Andrew's palatial office and became aware of a small hot hand, clutching tightly on to hers. She studied Fiona's round, freckled face, curtained by two thick auburn plaits, and became transfixed by the intensity of the child's pleading dark brown eyes. Cameron's eyes had held that same intensity when he'd . . . Jenny shuddered and turned towards her brother.

'What about the backlog from this morning's meeting? Isn't there a trade fair too? You know you never miss those, Andrew.'

This was one question Mary couldn't answer, and Andrew's reply left Jenny speechless.

'Well, you've got Stevie, haven't you? Surely you of all people must realize how efficient she is!'

Stunned and unable to believe her ears, Jenny found herself sitting on the stairs with a warm, spotty body curled on her lap. Surrounded on all sides by Sinclairs, there was nothing for it but to concede. She would however make one condition.

'Very well,' she replied flatly, 'but if I'm to look after

7

Fiona *and* take responsibility for the office and the trade fair, Andrew must promise to consider my proposals for Sinclair's on his return.'

It was Andrew's turn to feel the focus of five pairs of eyes as they turned towards him with an air of expectancy.

'I agree,' he said reluctantly, thinking only of the respite from family pressure and the chance of two weeks' skiing ahead.

There were whoops of joy from Jean and Iain and a wet kiss planted firmly on Jenny's cheek by Fiona, with the request for Auntie Jen to take her to bed. At the top of the stairs Jenny surveyed the delighted quartet still standing in the hallway. It annoyed her to see Mary's smug look of satisfaction as she calmly said to Andrew, 'There you are, I told you Jennifer wouldn't mind.' The thing was, Jennifer minded very much indeed.

A jumble of thoughts raced through her head on the journey home. Would she be able to cope? Fiona was usually a well-behaved child and, after all, Stevie would be there to lend a hand – she couldn't wait to tell her of Andrew's 'compliment'.

Leaving the bright lights of Edinburgh and its busy city streets, the main problem, Jenny presumed, would be her proposed business plan, and that needed prompt attention. Now, with only two weeks to complete it before Andrew's return, she was determined to make sure he kept to his part of the bargain.

After what seemed like an eternity Jenny pulled into her driveway, where the day's anxieties and flashes of inspiration gave way to tiredness and contentment. Mary, she thought, could keep her large city house where theatres and shops compensated for the long hours Andrew spent at the office. Jenny was happier here in East Lothian, and her cottage with its pantiled roof and tiny windows seemed to welcome her home.

'Yes, I will cope.' She sighed sleepily. 'I'll make a list before going to bed.' At the top she wrote 'calamine lotion' and 'cotton wool' and at the bottom 'MOTHER', in large capital letters. By the words 'business plan', there was a series of question marks.

CHAPTER 2

An air of expectancy filled the large Edinburgh house. Mary and Jean rushed back and forth with numerous combinations of ski and après-ski wear. The baggage allowance was already exceeded, and Andrew was pacing the floor refusing point-blank to pay for any excess. Iain meanwhile tried on his new ski boots for the umpteenth time and, taking up his batons, practised slalom manoeuvres along the hallway.

'Iain! Will you not do that, you'll ruin the carpet!' Andrew's tone was one of exasperation. 'Mary, where's Fiona? Is she ready yet? I told Jennifer I would be there half an hour ago.'

'Coming, Daddy,' came the voice from the landing, and Fiona came bouncing down the stairs, auburn plaits swinging and chicken pox glowing.

Andrew, anxious with all the confusion and seeing his baby minus her front teeth and face full of spots, was suffused by a sudden pang of guilt. Fiona certainly looked a picture, but none any artist would care to paint. 'Ready, then?' he asked, hugging her warmly.

Fiona nodded and handed her father a small holdall. It was open and inside he recognized her most treasured possessions. Despite constant teasing from her brother and sister, Fiona would go nowhere without them.

'I just hope Auntie Jennifer's going to have room for all this,' he said, taking his youngest child and her luggage to the car.

'*I* just hope Jennifer's cottage is going to be warm enough,' Mary called, appearing with yet another armful of clothes. 'You will remind Jennifer to keep the child warm?'

Andrew remained silent. Jennifer's cottage was not Conasg House.

Sitting by the fire, Jenny watched flames flicker and envelop logs of apple and fir. The apple was from the gnarled old tree that had once stood at the bottom of the garden, and the fir was the remains of her Christmas tree. She felt strangely melancholy. It was like setting fire to part of her life; soon there would be nothing left but ashes.

Since Christmas she'd spent a good deal of time thinking of Cameron and wondering what would have happened if he hadn't broken off their engagement. But 'what if' and 'if only' were futile words. She and Cameron were no longer an item and she only had herself – or according to Cameron, Sinclair's – to blame for that.

Stabbing angrily at a glowing log with a brass-handled poker, Jenny relived Christmas and New Year. Christmas had been spent with Cameron's sister Triona and her husband at their rambling old vicarage. There the crumbling masonry had echoed to the sounds of gurgling babies and jovial adults, interspersed with the constant monotonous thump of bass from teenage bedrooms far off. And, while appreciative of Triona's hospitality, Jenny and Cameron had been relieved when the time came to depart.

Standing on the doorstep clutching the youngest of her brood, Triona had smiled broadly as the baby's chubby hands had reached eagerly in Jenny's direction.

'See how she adores you, Jenny; she doesn't want you to go. You've been such a help. I don't know what I would have done without you over Christmas.'

Disentangling tiny fingers from her hair, Jenny had noticed Cameron's disgruntled look and heard him mutter under his breath.

'And what's got into you, little brother?' Triona teased. 'You look as if someone's taken away your favourite toy.'

'Hasn't it occurred to you, as this is my last stint of leave for a while, it would have been nice to have had Jenny to myself instead of finding her constantly monopolized by endless streams of children?'

'But, Cameron,' Jenny broke in, 'we've only been here for three days.'

'Take no notice of him, Jenny,' Triona said, blowing a raspberry on the baby's neck so that she chuckled gleefully. 'Being the youngest of the family, Cameron was always spoilt – and when he couldn't get his own way he sulked, just like he's doing now. So just take heed, Jenny, and remember that when you're married and have wee ones of your own.'

'Hmph! Chance would be a fine thing!' Cameron flung back at his sister as he took Jenny's bags to the car.

'And just what is that supposed to mean?' Jenny

asked, watching him switch on the ignition and clumsily engage first gear.

'Exactly what it implies. How can we have children when we're not even married? I take it you still want children, Jenny?'

'Of course I do. We both do. We've talked about it often enough, haven't we? Ever since we became Fiona's godparents.'

Cameron threw her a sideways glance. 'And how long ago was that?'

'Six years. But what's that got to do with it?'

'That's how long you've been saying you're going to marry me.'

'Well, I will; it's just . . .'

'Just what?'

'Just that it wasn't easy for Mother after Father died . . .'

'But your father's been dead for three years . . .'

'And you were away at sea for so long that we just didn't see each other . . . then of course there's Sinclair's.'

Cameron laughed bitterly. 'Ah, yes, Sinclair's. I wondered when that was going to come into the argument.'

'I wasn't aware we were having an argument.'

Ten minutes later, having ignored Jenny's last remark, Cameron turned the car precariously into the gravelled driveway of her cottage, narrowly missing the gatepost.

'For goodness' sake, Cameron! Do you realize you nearly broke the . . .?'

'Oh, yes.' He sighed sarcastically. 'I realize only too

well. And, speaking of breaking, I am breaking off our engagement.'

Stepping from the car, Jenny stared at him incredulously.

'But only minutes ago you were talking about getting married.'

Cameron walked with her to the front door, then, putting her bags in the porch, turned and cupped her face in his hands. For once the familiar warm brown eyes were cold. 'Jenny,' he whispered, kissing her forehead with icy lips, 'aren't you forgetting something? You're already married . . . You, my dear, are married to Sinclair's!'

Numbed, Jenny watched him walk back to the car. 'What about Conasg?' she called lamely. 'You were supposed to be coming to Conasg House with me for New Year. You even said you were looking forward to the peace and quiet of a Sinclair gathering.'

'Yes.' Cameron nodded ruefully, climbing back in his car. 'But you forget, I'm not a Sinclair . . . and never shall be.'

Through misted eyes, and calmed by the aromatic woodsmoke, Jenny sat up with a jolt as a sudden noise broke the silence. This time it was not the sound of Cameron's sporty hatchback departing angrily but the purr of Andrew's BMW drawing up outside.

The car door slammed and Fiona went running down the path before Andrew had time to stop her. He'd fully intended to carry her indoors wrapped in the blanket as instructed by Mary. Now it lay on the cream leather seat with the array of Fiona's treasures that had spilled from the holdall as he'd negotiated the twists and turns in the road. Gathering the contents together, Andrew looked about him in the darkness. The place was so remote, and it still bothered him that Jenny chose to live here.

'Come along, Daddy, I need my slippers,' Fiona called chirpily, already sitting in the chair by the fire.

'Well, I see you've got yourself nicely installed,' Andrew said, producing slippers like rabbits with large floppy ears. He was pleased to see the fire – he could at least report back favourably to his wife on the question of warmth.

'Jennifer – er – Mary and I . . . we're really grateful to you for helping us out. In fact, I think Fiona's actually pleased she's got chicken pox and isn't coming with us.'

Fiona who'd already said goodbye to her father, was rummaging in the bag for her book. She looked up in her aunt's direction. Yes, her Daddy was right, and she announced brightly, 'We're going to have a lovely time together, aren't we, Auntie Jenny? I can be *your* little girl while Mummy and Daddy are on holiday, 'cos you haven't got one and Uncle Cameron's gone away too and . . .'

Andrew froze as he walked towards the door, 'Sorry, Jennifer.'

'It's all right Andrew, don't worry. Out of the mouths of babes, as they say.' Jenny watched as Andrew's gaze fell on the photograph of Cameron, which she still had standing on the mantelpiece. 'Besides, Fiona's probably just what I need at the moment.'

The scene at the airport was one of chaos, and it seemed to Andrew that half the country were going away. Mary groaned at the lengthening check-in queues sprouting skis from every angle. They weren't the easiest things to carry at the best of times. She watched Andrew and Iain perch theirs precariously on suitcases. Pausing for a moment to survey the snake-like meanderings across the terminal, Mary was thankful that Fiona at least had been spared this ordeal.

In an adjoining queue a younger man stood with two small girls, one fair-haired and blue-eyed and the other with olive skin, deep brown eyes and a mass of dark curls. Distressed by the swirling mass of impatient bodies, noise and luggage, the children cried and clung to their father. Then, recognizing a familiar face walking down the line towards them, they relaxed and released their grasp. An elegant woman dressed in black and scarlet ignored their outstretched arms.

'Now what's all this fuss? Don't cry, darlings, Mummy will be back soon. She's only going for a little holiday.'

The accent was strong and Mary, recognizing it as Italian, studied the woman discreetly. Numerous heads turned in the same direction, including that of Mary's immediate neighbour who voiced her thoughts openly.

'Poor little things! Fancy leaving them behind like that. She might be a stunner to look at . . . but she's no blooming good as a mother!'

Mary, filled with a sudden pang of guilt, turned towards her husband. 'Andrew, go and ring Jennifer and see if Fiona's all right.'

Hesitating just for a moment, Andrew realized there was little point remonstrating with his wife. He left the queue in search of the nearest telephone.

'Fiona's perfectly all right,' he said five minutes later,

hurrying back. 'She's had a good night's sleep and Jennifer's giving her breakfast in bed.'

Jean looked towards the two small girls, who had now stopped crying, and retorted angrily, 'I bet they don't get breakfast in bed. In fact they look as if they've been dragged out of bed. Do you think that man is their father? Poor thing,' she continued, startling her mother with her vehemence, 'no wonder he looks embarrassed, with everyone staring at *her*!'

At sixteen, Jean was constantly bemoaning the fact that she thought her parents old-fashioned, yet deep down she was glad her own mother would never embarrass her by parading like the woman in scarlet and black. Why, she looked just like a . . . Jean shuddered, unable to say the word even to herself.

Her brother, on the other hand, couldn't take his eyes off the glamorous Italian. At seventeen, Iain Sinclair was beginning to take a keen interest in the opposite sex, and when the dark eyes flashed in his direction he simply melted.

'What a stunner,' he whispered to his father. 'Pity we don't have any like that at the academy. I wouldn't mind studying for my highers then.'

Aware of Mary's penetrating look of disapproval, Andrew merely nodded. The woman was indeed beautiful and she knew it. She also knew, as she shook a mass of jet-black hair about her shoulders, that she was playing to a full house.

'Gosh, Dad! Do you see she's boarding the same flight as us?'

'Quiet, Iain!' Mary hissed angrily. 'People will hear you!'

17

At the departure gates, Gina Hadley bade an over-dramatic goodbye to her children and fluttered her eyelashes at her audience.

'*Ciao*, Celestina. *Ciao*, Emily. Be good, my darlings.'

Her attempt at a loving farewell to her husband, however, was less convincing, and in response, Paul Hadley simply replied softly, 'Goodbye, Gina. Have a nice time.'

Fortunately he was out of earshot when Mary's neighbour added to her earlier caustic remark, 'There's no doubt about the sort of time *she'll* be having!'

CHAPTER 3

To Jenny's surprise the weekend went all too quickly, and she delighted in Fiona's company, playing games, reading books and eating toasted teacakes by the fire.

'It's like a picnic indoors,' gasped Fiona as Jenny produced the old-fashioned toasting fork that had once belonged to her grandmother.

Later, freshly bathed and dabbed with calamine lotion, like a giant marshmallow dusted with sugar, Fiona snuggled next to Jenny in the big double bed. Quietly she watched her aunt study the trade fair catalogue and then looked at her picture book until overcome by a fit of scratching.

Concerned that Andrew and Mary shouldn't return to find Fiona covered in chicken pox scars, Jenny announced thoughtfully, 'Fiona, if you promise not to scratch, I'll give you a special treat. Now, what would you like?'

The child thought deeply. Toys, books, dolls? No, she had all those. What could she think of as a special treat? Suddenly her eyes widened excitedly. 'I've got it, Auntie Jen. I know what I want! A picnic, a proper outside picnic like the one in the book.' Fiona pointed to the pages in front of her. It had been that evening's bedtime story: a mouse was having a picnic with her friends in a wood.

'Very well, you shall have your picnic, but later, in the summer. Now you must try to stop scratching and go to sleep.'

'Will there be mices and will there be pwimwoses?'

'Yes, I expect we'll find mice and primroses, but you'll have to be very good and very quiet.'

Kissing Fiona on the forehead, Jenny switched off the light. She too was tired, and the trade fair catalogue and her plans for Sinclair's would have to wait.

With aunt and niece sleeping through the alarm, Monday morning began badly. To Jenny's despair Fiona refused to leave for the office without all her treasured possessions, and from the moment she arrived at Sinclair's the phones rang constantly. It was late morning before she even noticed the thank-you gift of flowers and champagne sent by Andrew.

'Hmm,' she mused, examining the bottle of Bollinger. 'That's all very well, but it isn't exactly going to help me get through this backlog of paperwork, even if it does ease Andrew's guilty conscience.'

After lunch Fiona came in search of attention. She had played quietly in Andrew's office during the morning but now wanted Jenny to read to her. Reaching for the book, Jenny dislodged the trade fair catalogue. The trade fair! It had completely slipped her mind! Partly because Andrew had left a note saying not to bother if there wasn't time – he knew how she hated crowds and trade fairs in particular – and also because he would see Bill Freeman himself on his return.

The difficulty was, Andrew had been at school with Bill Freeman, it was the old boy network in operation, and Andrew was perfectly happy to let things continue as before.

'That's just it,' she murmured, flicking through the catalogue, 'I'm not!' Jenny shook her head and shrugged. 'Sorry, Bill,' she announced, and called through to Stevie, 'Feel like reading a story about a mouse on a picnic? Only I really must get going if I'm to get to this extravaganza before they pack up for the night and go home.'

Stevie smiled and positioned her wheelchair so Fiona, still clutching her favourite book, could climb on to her lap. Collecting her phone and briefcase, Jenny hurried for the door.

'Call me if you need me,' she said.

At that precise moment Paul Hadley needed something or someone, only he wasn't quite sure which. Like Jenny, his day had begun badly, and the frantic search for Celestina's school uniform – hampered by the debris left in the wake of Gina's departure – was swiftly followed by a tearful Emily hunting for her nursery apron. Now his thoughts turned to more urgent matters . . . work! He desperately needed to find some!

With Gina constantly trotting all over the place, he'd decided someone had to look after the girls, but things had happened far too quickly and, declining his last assignment, there had been little choice but to part company with Baynham's and work from home. The problem, Paul realized, studying his reflection in the mirror as he left to fetch the girls from school, was convincing someone to employ him.

As he watched Cele and Emily skipping along, posters for the trade fair caught Paul's attention. If the neighbour could have the girls for an hour, perhaps he could put in an appearance. Just one contract would make all the difference . . .

'Thanks, Helen, you're an angel,' Paul shouted across to the neighbour as he ran indoors. Confronted once more by the hall mirror, he was reminded again of his crumpled appearance. His long blond hair flopped untidily across his forehead and troubled blue eyes stared back at him, expressing their deep concern.

'Well, Paul Hadley, a change of shirt and comb through your hair won't come amiss, will it? No wonder people were staring at the airport: Gina done up like a dog's dinner and you looking like something the cat dragged in!' Giving a wry laugh, Paul left his reflection to search for a clean shirt.

Long before he reached his wardrobe realization dawned. Knowing Gina, there would be none ironed. His only hope was the laundry room. There he was greeted by a pile of ironing and clothes tumbled everywhere across the muddied quarry tiled floor. Paul sighed. Even the door of the washing machine gaped open, its mouth seeming to spew forth a tangle of shirts, blouses and socks. The problem was, what was clean and what was dirty? All the whites were the same dingy grey, and the coloureds . . . Even Paul, with his designer's eye, was at a loss to describe those.

From the dark cavernous interior of the washing machine, he tugged at a bundle of fiendishly entwined sleeves and, checking his watch for the time, grabbed the first available shirt. Plugging in the iron, he smoothed the stubborn creases and watched in horror as rusty brown water leaked from holes not clogged with melted fabric.

'Damn you, Gina!' he cried in desperation. 'Damn you! Damn you! Damn you!' Like sludge on a clear blue sea, a dirty stain seeped across the back of his shirt.

With time at a premium and finding no other suitable shirt, Paul ironed the collar and front panels and fetched his jacket. The result was far from satisfactory and the fabric felt warm and moist against his back. Walking through to his study, the only room in any semblance of order, he took stock of the situation.

Paul knew only too well what he wanted, but what did Gina want? From the surrounding chaos it would appear she didn't want domesticity and motherhood. Yet before she'd married Paul, Gina had said it was all she'd ever wanted. Had she, he wondered, or had she just chosen him as a ticket to freedom? Reflecting on their first meeting at the local *trattoria*, Paul's mood changed from anger to sadness.

It had been a whirlwhind courtship, beginning with the photos he'd taken of Gina and her friends on their day off and ending with marriage and the birth of Celestina twelve months later. Life had been idyllic until Emily was born – Gina's religious beliefs having ruled out birth control. Then, quite by chance, when Baynham's had offered Gina a modelling assignment, everything had changed.

Reversing into the parking bay, Paul recalled how that first job for Baynham's had heralded disaster.

From that moment a life of glamour had beckoned Gina and she had followed it, ever eager and hungry for more, leaving behind all thoughts of religion, her children and her husband. Paul's concern for Cele and Emily was of little consequence, Gina refused to co-operate, and the end, when it came, was inevitable. Paul had no choice but to resign – his only hope now was the trade fair.

'Paul! How are you? I haven't seen you in ages. How's that gorgeous wife of yours?'

The firm grasp of Alistair Jennings' hand greeted Paul as he paused by the list of exhibitors. Paul shook his hand warmly but had no desire to discuss his private life now; it was too painful. Instead he changed the subject, told Alistair he was working from home and asked his advice. Alistair bit his lip and looked around the room thoughtfully.

'You could try Sinclair's. I overheard Jenny Sinclair making some enquiries earlier this afternoon.'

'Sinclair's? I don't think I know them, do I?' queried Paul.

'You must do . . . Sinclair Tartans . . . old family firm? A bit old-fashioned if you ask me, but weathering the storm of recession and doing reasonably well,' Alistair continued. 'The funny thing is, Andrew Sinclair normally attends these affairs but I gather he's not here . . . besides, he always uses Freeman's.'

Paul looked dejected. Freeman's were strong opposition. 'How do I get to meet Andrew Sinclair, then? Can you introduce me some time?'

'Not unless you want to wait another two weeks, and if you don't mind my saying so, you look desperate now. I must say, Paul – I've seen you looking in better shape.'

Paul felt uncomfortable; his clothes were shabby and he ran his hands through his unruly hair. Alistair as usual was immaculately turned out. Alongside him Paul felt the contrast even more pronounced and was anxious to get away. Quickly he added, 'Well, if you can't introduce me to Andrew Sinclair perhaps you can point out this . . . Jenny . . . that is, if she's still here?'

Paul followed Alistair's gaze as he scanned the crowds, stopping on two women deep in conversation. The taller of the two, with dark hair and eyes, made Paul think automatically of Gina, and his heart sank.

'There you are, Jenny Sinclair – the one in the black skirt and tartan jacket. Have a word with her. I'm sure you'll find her a real soft touch compared to Andrew. Now, if you'll excuse me, I'm meeting a client.'

Patting Paul's arm, Alistair turned and reached for his briefcase.

'By the way,' he called, 'we must get together for a drink some time. Don't forget to give my love to Gina.'

Alistair's words were lost on Paul as he studied the slight trim figure with hair like burnished copper. He was just so relieved. The last person he wanted to think about was Gina. His only concern now was not to lose sight of Jenny Sinclair in the crowds.

'Mrs Sinclair?'

Heading for the door, Jenny stopped in her tracks. Her head ached and her feet were sore from the constant trampling of feet. It was also getting late and there was still the prospect of Fiona for almost another two weeks. The last thing she needed now was to be confronted by yet another smooth-talking salesman. She turned sharply.

'Actually, it's Miss Sinclair!'

Paul stood in embarrassment, duly corrected. 'Miss Sinclair, I apologize. I wondered if you could spare me half an hour of your time? My name is Paul Hadley – I'm a designer . . . Alistair Jennings suggested I might be able to help you.'

At that precise moment Paul didn't have a clue if he could help Sinclair Tartans but, deciding it was worth a damned good try, he extended his hand in Jenny's direction.

Accepting Paul's hand, it was Jenny's turn to be embarrassed. Cautiously she studied the man, who gave the appearance of having slept on a park bench. He was certainly no sales rep, but what had she to lose?

'Ten-thirty tomorrow morning, Mr Hadley,' she replied sharply, giving him her business card. 'I'll tell my assistant to expect you.'

Paul watched her go in disbelief, then realized the time. He would be late fetching the girls and they would be wanting their tea.

'We'll go for a pizza,' he told himself, walking to the car park, 'and I'll cook a proper meal tomorrow. Tonight, Paul Hadley, you've got shirts to wash and iron and a suit to press!'

Jenny found Fiona pushing Stevie round the boardroom in her wheelchair.

'It's role reversal,' Stevie whispered. 'I'm the baby, she's the mummy.'

Jenny smiled and gathered up Fiona's belongings.

26

What would Andrew say? Endless rows of wheel marks criss-crossed the magnificent red, green and blue plaid. Never had the carpet seen so much traffic.

'Well, Stevie, I think it's going to be Marmite soldiers and bed by eight tonight. I'm exhausted. Andrew can keep his trade fairs.'

'How did it go?' enquired Stevie. 'Any luck with the reps?'

'No – but I met Worzel Gummidge and he's coming at ten-thirty in the morning. Actually I think he said his name was Paul Hadley.'

Fiona listening intently to the conversation, gazed at her aunt in wonderment. Had she really met Worzel Gummidge? And was he really coming to the office tomorrow? Amazed and delighted, she couldn't wait to see!

CHAPTER 4

The next day found Paul in control, with no intention of being late for his appointment. He found his one decent suit still in the polythene wrapper from its last visit to the cleaners and washed and ironed a shirt without mishap. Thinking back to the previous day's disasters, he was aware Jenny Sinclair had noticed his crumpled appearance. Today he would show her he could at least look presentable. To complement the dark navy-blue suit he selected an Italian silk tie, one of Gina's many peace offerings. There, he had to admit, she had good taste.

Once more finding himself in front of the hall mirror, Paul wondered if he should have had a haircut? Probably, he thought, pushing his hair away from his forehead, but as he chose to wear his hair longer . . . He shrugged his shoulders; it was too risky now and he was convinced the nearest barber had once worked on a sheep-shearing station. No, he decided, he would face Jenny Sinclair as he was. Although still uncertain if he could offer her constructive advice, he knew he would make sure of one thing. He must remember to call her Miss Sinclair.

If Paul was surprised to find Jenny's PA in a wheel-chair he didn't show it. He was too engrossed in the photos and brochures that surrounded him as he sat in the outer office. His first impression was of an old-established family firm – with good marketable products – in need of a little updating. The difficulty was, some of these families were so set in their ways and resented change. Paul studied the portrait on the wall and decided to gauge the situation carefully. Andrew, Morag and Jennifer Sinclair presented a truly formidable trio.

At ten-thirty precisely Stevie directed Paul to Jenny's office, where she stood waiting to greet him. Yesterday evening, having agreed to this meeting, she had been strangely apprehensive. Now, if Paul had been astute enough to mask his surprise at Stevie's wheelchair, Jenny did likewise at the change in Paul Hadley's appearance. Today there was no sign of the Worzel Gummidge that had so intrigued Fiona on their way home, nor could she fail to notice the particular emphasis he'd placed on calling her Miss Sinclair when he'd arrived.

Sitting opposite Jenny, Paul in turn studied her discreetly. Her suit was neat and elegant and his artist's eye recalled the two-piece she'd worn yesterday: the black skirt and subdued tartan jacket. Today her jacket was black but the revers and her skirt were tartan. A clever idea of combining two suits to create four different outfits. Gina would never consider such a combination. She much preferred the outrageous and to draw attention to herself.

Dispensing with preliminaries, Jenny came straight to the point.

'Sinclair's are an old family firm, Mr Hadley, and we have some excellent products; however, I do think it's time to move forward and look to different markets. So . . . do you think you can help us make that move?'

Taken aback by her forthright request, Paul was startled. It wasn't quite what he'd been expecting. 'I'm sure I can, Miss Sinclair, given some time and research, plus of course details of past products manufactured under the Sinclair label and . . .'

'Good! I can give you all those,' Jenny said abruptly. Calling through to Stevie for coffee and getting up from her chair, she led Paul through to the boardroom. 'All the information we need is in here.'

Paul followed to where shelves were lined neatly with books, files and samples. An embossed tartan volume caught his eye.

'Take whatever information you require, Mr Hadley, as long as you return it by Friday. Then . . . perhaps you can come back a week today with some ideas?'

A week! In stunned silence Paul took the coffee Jenny handed him and watched the steam rise from the gold-rimmed green cups. A week! He'd never been asked to produce anything so quickly. It would be impossible to complete a thorough project in such a short time. Paul's mouth went dry. How could he explain the difficulties involved? He needed this job but he also needed more than a week if he was to do it successfully.

Sipping her coffee, Jenny said thoughtfully, 'Of course I don't expect a complete project . . . just some rough ideas will do. I'm sorry, Mr Hadley, I should have explained fully at the beginning. Andrew – my brother – and I have opposing views on which path Sinclair's should be taking. With Andrew away I see this as my opportunity to change our designs and hopefully get my mother on my side before his return.'

Paul was intrigued and remembered the photo of the formidable trio hanging in Reception. So the elderly woman who had looked so dour was Jenny Sinclair's mother, and no doubt Sinclair's matriarch. While the cat's away the mice will play, Paul mused and concluded that the mice in this instance were Jenny and Morag Sinclair.

Finishing his coffee, Paul studied Jenny cautiously. This petite, feisty-looking woman was offering him the chance of a lifetime, but it also meant he could become embroiled in a battle between brother and sister. He grinned. What the hell? It was a chance he just had to take.

While Paul contemplated family feuds, Jenny placed brochures and books on the table for his perusal. Picking up the embossed tartan volume that had earlier caught his eye, he opened the pages carefully.

'Would it,' he asked softly, 'be all right if I borrowed this?'

Jenny hesitated. It was, after all, one of Andrew's prized possessions. The book told of Scottish clans and their descendants, giving in minute detail the history of each family. It was always Andrew's intention to study it carefully, in the hope that he would find direct connections with the present lairds. To date, not having much time for reading, he hadn't, but Andrew – and Mary too – felt sure he would find them one day.

'Yes, take it,' Jenny said quickly before changing her

mind, 'only do please take special care of it and return it by Friday.'

As Paul carefully placed the book and other documents in his briefcase, the door to the boardroom opened slowly. Both Paul and Jenny looked up, expecting to see Stevie. Instead, a curious and wide-eyed Fiona peeped surreptitiously into the room. Her look changed to one of complete and utter disappointment when she saw Paul.

'Oh!' She faltered. 'Are you really Worzel Gummidge?'

'Fiona!' broke in Jenny, desperate to silence her niece.

'No,' smiled Paul kindly, walking to where Fiona stood transfixed in the doorway. 'Why, did you think I was?'

'Well, you don't look like him,' whispered Fiona, casting a furtive glance at her aunt, 'but Auntie Jen said she met him yesterday and he was coming to see her at half-past ten. Wasn't that when you arrived?'

Paul and Fiona turned in Jenny's direction as she felt the colour rise in her face. Her once pale cheeks flushed with embarrassment. What could she say? Fiona, sensing something was horribly wrong, hurried away to the sanctuary of her father's office.

'I'm sorry . . . Fiona's my niece, I'm looking after her while Andrew and his family are away.'

Subconsciously Paul ran his hand over his hair to smooth down his slightly ruffled appearance and smiled quizzically, as if awaiting further explanation. None was forthcoming. Sensing Jenny's confusion, he added softly, 'I have two girls of my own, you know; they have a wonderful sense of imagination and never fail to amaze me.' Smiling, he closed his briefcase and held out his hand. 'Don't worry about the books, I'll take good care of them and return them on Friday. Goodbye, *Miss* Sinclair.'

Numbed to the quick, Jenny could only watch after him in silence. He must have realized she'd referred to him as Worzel Gummidge as a result of yesterday's meeting. He'd certainly looked unkempt then, but today, well, he was much smarter and . . .

'But not smart as in naval-smart,' she whispered softly, walking back to her desk. There, opening the top left-hand drawer, she removed the silver-framed photo of Cameron in full naval officer's uniform. At one time she'd always thought his dark brown eyes had been smiling out at her. Now she wasn't so sure; they appeared mocking and cruel. Feeling a shiver run through her body, she replaced the photo and closed the drawer just as Stevie appeared in the doorway.

'So that was Worzel Gummidge,' said Stevie breezily. 'A dishy sort of Worzel Gummidge if you ask me.'

'Don't you start, Stevie! I've had enough from Fiona for one day.' Explaining the whole embarrassing scenario, Jenny continued, 'I don't mind confessing, I just wanted that enormous carpet of Andrew's to swallow me up and take me out of here. Goodness knows what Mr Hadley must have thought.' She looked through to the boardroom at the vast expanse of tartan as if willing the edges to curl up and whisk her away. Instead it was only Stevie's lips that curled and broke into a smile.

'I'm sorry, Jenny,' she laughed, 'but I think it's hilarious.'

Jenny's face remained flushed and confused.

'Oh, come on, it's not that bad. Besides, Mr Hadley looks as if he's got a sense of humour. He's got very nice eyes.'

Jenny hadn't really noticed but thought they were probably blue. She usually only noticed brown eyes, and then simply to compare them with Cameron's. She felt a lump in her throat as tears pricked her eyelids. She'd started the week determined to forget Cameron and stand up to Andrew. Now everything seemed to crumble about her.

Stevie spun her chair round to face Jenny head on. 'Besides,' she said reassuringly, touching her arm, 'he probably doesn't even know who Worzel Gummidge is, so don't worry.'

'I wouldn't bank on it,' came the reply. 'He's got two children of his own and probably reads Worzel Gummidge to them every night!'

Jenny's voice brightened slightly. She thought of Fiona and the bedtime stories. She hadn't seen the child since she'd fled in the direction of her father's office. Poor Fiona. It couldn't be easy for her with her parents away and the chicken pox still causing discomfort. She was also probably hungry and wanting her lunch.

Fiona sat on the floor of Andrew's office surrounded by her toys and books. She hung her head when her Aunt entered the room and Jenny could see she had been crying.

'I'm sorry, Auntie Jenny, was I rude to the man? Mummy says it's not nice to be rude . . . but you did say Worzel Gummidge and I thought . . .'

The large brown eyes filled with tears once more and she sobbed, 'If you're cross with me, does that mean we won't have our picnic?'

Jenny sat on the floor and cradled Fiona in her arms. She stroked the thick amber hair that they'd plaited so carefully that morning, reassuring the child softly that everything was all right. It was just a slight misunderstanding. Grown-ups often said one thing and meant another. She would explain to Mr Hadley when he returned on Friday and of course they would still have their picnic. They would go when the primroses were in bloom.

CHAPTER 5

For the rest of the week Jenny quite forgot about Paul and the embarrassing reference to Worzel Gummidge. It was Fiona who reminded her as they drove into work on the Friday morning.

'Isn't the man coming today?'

'The man?' enquired Jenny, who was busy negotiating the bend in the road. There had been snow in the night, leaving large drifts. 'What man?'

'The man who borrowed Daddy's books.'

The car swerved slightly, Jenny's concentration interrupted. Fiona had missed nothing. She'd obviously seen Paul with the books and she also knew the value Andrew placed on such volumes. Fiona was right, Paul Hadley had promised to return the books today. More importantly, Jenny wondered, would he also bring some ideas to keep Sinclair's operating in a very competitive market?

By lunchtime, with no sign of Paul and still with her shopping to do, Jenny left strict instructions for Stevie to check the books should he arrive in her absence. There was no need to panic yet – after all, they had said Friday, and the office didn't close until five o'clock.

Returning to find Stevie and Fiona having lunch, Jenny's enquiring look was met with a definite shake of the head. Anxious not to draw attention to the situation, Jenny took a parcel from her basket.

'Here you are, Fiona, a present for you as you've been so good this week. I've hardly seen you scratching at all. It's to use indoors until we can have the real thing.'

Fiona's eyes opened wide as excitedly she tore away the paper to reveal a blue and white doll's tea set.

'Oh, Auntie Jen, it's lovely,' she cried, and ran to give her aunt a hug.'

'Don't I get a hug too for giving you lunch?' Stevie asked, and was promptly rewarded with a wet kiss on the cheek.

'P'raps we can have a tea party this afternoon?' Fiona said, looking at the two women earnestly.

Jenny, desperate to get Stevie alone to enquire if there had been any news at all from Paul, realized that with Fiona around it wasn't going to be easy. Quickly she removed her Paisley shawl and handed it to her niece, then she took a packet of shortbread from her shopping.

'Here,' she said, 'take these. You can use the shawl as a picnic rug and we'll have the shortbread with our tea. Run along now and get it all ready for us. Stevie and I have a great deal of work to do. We'll come in at four o'clock.'

Relieved to see Fiona disappear with a mission in mind, Jenny turned to Stevie. 'Well?'

'No sign of him, I'm afraid. No telephone call, nothing.'

'Nothing! Well, call me the minute you hear anything
. . . anything at all,' Jenny demanded.

During the afternoon it was hard to concentrate.
Jenny's thoughts kept returning to Andrew's precious
books. She'd allowed Paul Hadley simply to take them,
yet she suddenly realized she knew very little about
him. If he didn't bring the books back how could she
find him . . . and what would Andrew say if he returned
to find empty spaces on his shelves?

Jenny stood anxiously at the office window. It was
already dark and there were few people in the square
below. No one stopped or spoke, looking so miserable,
pinched and drawn, wrapped up against the icy chill.
Seemingly they had only one thought in their minds;
that of going home. Jenny too would soon have to be
thinking of going home. Worrying about Paul's non-
appearance, she'd even forgotten Fiona's 'tea party'.

A screech of brakes in the car park below caused her
to peer through the enveloping gloom. And at that
moment no one could have been more relieved to see
Paul emerge from the car, with the same briefcase that
had carried away Andrew's books. Not only did he
appear harassed, but there also seemed to be some
confusion coming from the rear of the car.

Two small girls sat in obvious distress and Paul was
trying to reason with them. Looking first at his watch
and then in the direction of Jenny's office, Paul hesitated before helping his children from the car.

'Miss Sinclair, I really must apologize for being so
late. My neighbour promised to fetch the girls from
school but she had a call to say her mother had been
rushed into hospital. I then offered to take her, it being

38

the least I could do as she often helps me with the children. Then of course I had to go to the school myself and . . .'

Relief flooded Jenny's face. 'Don't worry, Mr Hadley, at least you're here now, but I have to confess I was getting a little anxious. I'm sure you could do with a cup of tea after all that rushing around.'

Paul nodded and sank into a chair. He'd been dreading her reaction to his tardiness. So far their business relationship – brief though it was – had been somewhat bizarre. Unlocking his briefcase, he was aware of Jenny's gaze watching his every move as one by one he placed every object he'd borrowed on her desk.

Checking everything, Jenny observed that each item Paul had taken was now carefully wrapped in tissue paper. She was duly impressed.

'Did you find them of any help?' she enquired, and was further amazed to hear his response.

'Yes, very much so! I intend to prepare a file for you this weekend, ready for next Tuesday . . . as you requested.'

His statement was almost questioning, as if he half expected her to say she'd changed her mind about the project. To his relief she voiced no such objection, making only some comment about Stevie and tea. Puzzled by Stevie's non-appearance, Jenny walked to the door and looked into the corridor.

Paul coughed. 'I think she may have taken my daughters to the cloakroom. Coming straight from school and in such a rush, I'm afraid there wasn't time.' He looked embarrassed. Already this week there had been more than one occasion when he'd realized it wasn't going to be that easy trying to work from home and look after the girls at the same time. To his surprise Jenny seemed unperturbed. She'd had Fiona with her all week at the office and was becoming quite used to the ways of small girls. Besides, she announced, she was quite capable of making tea herself.

Paul watched Jenny reappear with the tray. There was no sign of tartan today. Instead she wore a plain woollen suit of dark green with a contrasting blouse. The subtle colours reminded him of autumn heather. How well they complemented her colouring. She also looked far less flustered than at their first meeting. Paul looked about him thoughtfully. Unlike his own study, here everything was arranged so neatly. For a brief moment he was envious of the quiet calm in Jenny's orderly office.

That, Paul had already decided, was to be his next task: to organize the corner of his bedroom where he had his 'study' if he was to produce something worthwhile for Sinclair's. Gina had long since taken over their bedroom; she claimed she slept better on her own and only occasionally wanted his company. He'd been deeply hurt at first but as Gina became increasingly volatile, craving more clothes, more holidays and more excitement – in what she constantly referred to as her boring life – he became thankful for the separation.

While Jenny unwrapped the books and Paul drank his tea, the moment's silence was broken by children's laughter.

Alarmed, Paul stood up quickly. 'The girls! I hope they haven't got into mischief!'

Jenny recognizing Fiona's delightful, gurgling laughter, headed in the direction of Andrew's office, closely followed by a deeply concerned Paul. They opened the door to find three small girls sitting on the floor, with Fiona's new tea-set neatly laid out on Jenny's shawl. On the small plates were shortbread biscuits and, in the cups, orange juice.

'I waited for you but you never came,' said Fiona, admonishing Jenny for her non-appearance. 'So Cele and Emily are having tea with me instead!'

Jenny and Paul stood silent and motionless, while Celestina and Emily glanced anxiously towards their father. Paul looked worried, his gaze searching the room for damage, but, finding none, he relaxed.

'You really shouldn't be in here, you know . . .'

Fiona broke in confidently and in one breath announced, 'I invited them and this is my daddy's office and we are having an indoor picnic 'cos Auntie Jen is going to take me on a proper picnic soon.'

Not knowing what to say, Paul looked in Jenny's direction. Was Fiona being precocious or was she just protecting his daughters? Certainly the girls had sensed concern in their father's voice. They remained quiet and still.

Something about the youngest child touched Jenny. The poor thing looked terrified seeing this unknown women standing there with her father. Her lower lip trembled as if she was going to cry.

'Well, I'm sure that's very kind of you, Fiona?' Jenny said gently, 'but it is getting a little late for a picnic today. Another day perhaps? I'm sure Mr Hadley is waiting to take the girls home, I expect their mummy is waiting to give them their tea.'

41

All three girls looked at Paul but he said nothing. It was far too complicated to explain. Instead he helped them gather Fiona's tea things together and led them to the door.

'Until next Tuesday, then, Miss Sinclair. Have a nice weekend. Goodbye, Fiona, and thank you for looking after my girls.'

As they reached the end of the corridor Fiona ran after them. Jenny watched as she handed over the remains of the shortbread but was unable to catch any of Fiona's whispered conversation with Paul. He just looked back at Jenny and smiled.

'What did you say to Mr Hadley?'

'Oh,' Fiona replied nonchalantly, 'I just said you didn't think he was really Worzel Gummidge and perhaps he'd like to come on our picnic!'

Jenny found herself blushing and was glad there was no one to see the colour spread across her cheeks. To save further embarrassment she determined to keep Fiona safely tucked away when Paul Hadley returned the following Tuesday.

CHAPTER 6

'Grannie is on the phone,' Fiona's voice called into the garden.

Jenny was kneeling beneath her new apple tree, clearing away dead leaves from small green shoots that pierced the rich brown earth. Kicking off her wellingtons, she ran to the phone. The contrast between the crisp morning air and the warmth of the kitchen caught at her throat.

'Jennifer, are you all right? Your voice sounds quite dreadful.'

'Yes, I'm fine, thank you, Mother, I've just run in from the garden. I wasn't sure quite how long Fiona had kept you waiting on the end of the line.'

Allowing her daughter to catch her breath, Morag Sinclair explained that she'd not been waiting long at all. In fact she'd been having a most interesting chat with her granddaughter! Morag laughed. 'I gather you and Fiona have been having quite an eventful time together. By the way, how is the chicken pox?'

'Oh, coming along nicely, hardly any scabs left at all now. Fiona was really quite poorly at first but she's been so good about everything.'

43

Jenny felt it inappropriate to criticize Andrew and Mary for going away; Morag on the other hand had no such compunction. In her book business and family came before holidays.

'I think Andrew and Mary should be thankful they have you to call on, Jennifer, particularly as Fiona says it's been a very busy week at the office.'

Jenny, wondering what Fiona had been telling her Grannie of the previous week's events, preferred to change the subject.

'Mother, I thought I might drive over and see you on Friday evening and bring Fiona too, if that's all right. I'm working on some ideas for Sinclair's that might interest you.' At this stage it was neither the time nor the place to mention Paul Hadley, especially as Fiona was once again within earshot. It would be better to show Morag in person, not try to gauge her reaction at the end of a telephone line.

Morag's voice brightened. 'That would be lovely, Jennifer, and it also sounds very intriguing. I shall get Tandy to make some of her special shortbread for Fiona.'

To Morag it seemed an age since she'd seen Jennifer and Fiona, yet it had only been New Year. Since then she'd found the endless rain and short daylight hours of early January particularly depressing. Followed by colds that had been difficult to shake off, she and Tandy had been getting on each other's nerves. It would be nice to think of Conasg House ringing to the sound of voices – especially young ones – next weekend.

Fiona, who had been listening to the conversation,

danced excitedly about the kitchen. She loved going to Conasg. The large, grey stone house with its antiquated furnishings and dark passages meant adventure and was so totally removed from her parents' Edinburgh house. For Jenny, further coherent conversation with her mother was out of the question. There was only time for Morag to enquire if Andrew had telephoned.

'I've had one very quick phone call,' Jenny replied, 'but the line was poor and Andrew didn't say much, other than that they were having a great time and there was plenty of snow.' With Fiona's excited chatterings, she couldn't quite catch Morag's comment but was sure it was something about all the snow that had fallen in Scotland during the past week.

Andrew and his two eldest children were indeed having a great time. The same, however, could not be said of his wife. On their very first day, misjudging a ski-tow, Mary had landed badly and sprained her wrist. The sprain, though only slight, meant being confined to the hotel. There, in the combined pool and sports complex, Mary had to make do with indoor exercise.

The only other occupant of the pool, she discovered, was an elderly English widow on holiday with her middle-aged son. With no intention of skiing, she made no secret of the fact that she was there merely to keep an eye on him. To date, Phyllis King had managed to keep her son Gordon from the clutches of undesirable females, and she fully intended to see it remained that way.

'The trouble with Gordon,' Mrs King confided, as she and Mary shared a table for tea on the second afternoon, 'is that he's too vulnerable as far as the opposite sex is concerned. It's not Gordon they're interested in, you know, it's his money. My late husband left him a great deal. Besides, as I said to him, at fifty-four, what does he want with a wife? Surely his mother should be all the company he needs?'

Mary, not knowing how to respond, poured milk into her tea.

'Gosh, that looks disgusting,' she said. 'It's what my mother-in-law would call thin.'

Her elderly companion snorted in agreement and stabbed aggressively at the teabag in the glass mug. Her attempt at drawing more flavour from the already depleted teabag was in vain.

'I told Gordon to pack some tea bags,' said the irate mother. 'I should have known better . . . it's always the same, he never listens to me!'

'Don't worry, Mrs King, Andrew and I always take plenty when we travel. I'll bring some to your room later.'

'That's very kind of you, I must say. Now I insist you call me Phyllis. I feel sure we shall become great friends if we are to spend our afternoons together.'

Mary shuddered at the thought and eyed the twisted arthritic fingers placed on her hand in a gesture of friendship. 'Please God', she murmured beneath her breath, 'my wrist heals soon!'

The quiet of the tea discussion was shattered by a woman's laugh. Mary recognized it instantly. She and Phyllis turned to see Gordon walking through the doorway with Gina. Withdrawing her hand from Mary's, Gordon's mother clutched at the arms of her chair until her knuckles grew white. Dumbstruck, she watched her son struggle with Gina's skis.

'Gordon, you are a perfect darling,' Gina pronounced loudly. 'Perhaps I shall see you later, yes?'

'Not if your mother has anything to do with it,' Gordon, thought Mary.

Over dinner, describing her day's activities – or lack of them – Mary made special reference to Gordon's return with Gina and his mother's subsequent disapproval.

'But you've got to admit, Mum, she really is gorgeous; even Dad couldn't take his eyes off her today!'

Iain winced as Jean kicked him under the table and Mary cast a withering look in Andrew's direction. Nursing a bruised ankle, Iain determined to get his own back. 'Well, I think Gina's a bit of all right!' Turning to Jean, he added, 'Anyway, what about Philippe, your ski-instructor fellow? I bet you've got the hots for him!'

'Iain, please! What will people think?' Mary looked anxiously about the dining room. Her worries were unjustified. No one had overheard their conversation as all eyes were on the door. Gina was making her entrance.

Gone was the bright turquoise and pink ski-wear of the afternoon and in its place exquisitely cut velvet trousers and a black and gold top. Gina resembled a tigress on the prowl. Phyllis King watched anxiously as she slunk across the floor in search of her prey. Where would Gina pounce?

Gordon made as if to stand, ready to offer Gina a chair, but bony fingers dug into his wrist. 'Sit down, Gordon,' she hissed. 'Don't make a fool of yourself.'

Gina's cat-like eyes fluttered only briefly at Gordon.

There would be no kill at that table tonight. Instead, hearing someone call her name, she headed for the far corner of the room.

'Philippe,' she purred. 'Where have you been? I'm quite cross with you for neglecting me. Have you been making all those young English girls fall in love with you?'

'Can I help it if they do, Gina? Anyway, they are nothing compared to you.' Philippe laughed and raised his glass to her with a knowing look.

Mary watched hurt and disappointment surface in Jean's face and realized this dark, swarthy Romeo must be Philippe the ski-instructor.

'There you are, you've lost him now,' quipped Iain, only adding to the pain and humiliation Jean was already suffering. 'He doesn't like English girls, he prefers hot-blooded Italian ones!'

'I'm not English, I'm Scottish!' Jean remonstrated, pushing back her chair. Stunned, her parents watched as she left the restaurant.

'Andrew, I suggest you have a word with your son!' Mary said sharply, following close on the heels of her daughter.

After some persuasion, Jean emerged red-eyed from the bathroom. Mary put a comforting arm around her daughter's shoulders and sat with her on the bed. 'Jean, you mustn't get so upset. You know what they say about ski-instructors. Oh, I know they all look gorgeous in their red sweaters, with their golden tans, but they're all Romeos, ready to break the hearts of innocent young girls like yourself.'

Jean blew her nose on a tissue and reached for yet

48

another from the box beside her. Deep down she knew her mother was right but this was to be her first holiday with no small sister tagging along. A holiday where perhaps romance would blossom and flourish. Her friends at the academy had been so jealous when she'd told them of the forthcoming holiday. She'd already confided in her diary how attentive Philippe had been, how he'd whispered gentle words of encouragement when she'd stumbled and how he'd put out his hands to help her. Gazing into his eyes, Jean's heart was lost. No matter what anyone said, she was in love with Philippe!

'It's not fair,' Jean sighed, 'she's so beautiful, I don't stand a chance, and Iain's being such a pig! Still, it's only because Gina ignored him at lunchtime. She was more interested in Dad and Mr King. It's obvious why she fancies older men; they're the ones with the money!'

'Jean!' Mary gasped, wondering what on earth had happened at lunchtime. She was certainly keen to find out. She'd been so looking forward to this holiday, yet somehow it seemed doomed from the onset.

Mary assessed the situation. First there had been Fiona's chicken pox, then the sprained wrist and now . . . Well, what was there now? A love-struck sixteen-year-old and her husband and son – and no doubt most of the other male guests in the hotel – infatuated by Gina Dintino. They had hardly been here five minutes and Mary was already sick of the name. No matter how she felt tomorrow, sprained wrist or not, Mary determined to join her family skiing. But before then she must remember to take the promised teabags to Phyllis King.

Approaching the room, Mary heard raised voices, or

at least that of Gordon's mother. 'Gordon, do you hear me, I absolutely forbid you to have anything to do with that woman? She's nothing but a trollop! Think of your reputation and the business.'

Mary didn't wait for Gordon's reply. Instead she crept silently away to rejoin Andrew and make a few suggestions of her own.

The next morning, cloudless blue skies and sunlight glistening on dazzling white snow soon dispelled memories of the previous night's upsets. Mary passing the tea bags to Phyllis King at breakfast, whispered quietly, 'Don't worry, I'll keep a discreet eye on Gordon for you.'

The twisted fingers accepted the package graciously, and knowingly acknowledged Mary's comment. 'Thank you, my dear . . . thank you.'

Walking away to complete the Sinclair Quartet, Mary wondered if it wasn't perhaps a little unfair even to think of spying on Gordon. With such a domineering mother, the poor man probably deserved a bit of fun and freedom. In her mind's eye Mary pictured Gordon with his mother on one side and Gina on the other. What a dreadful combination! But she decided Gina was perhaps the more dangerous of the two.

Joining the queue for the ski-lift, Mary determined to find a more suitable companion for Gordon. She scanned the most likely-looking candidates and, lost in thought as the agony aunt of the ski-slopes, missed the arrival of Gina and her entourage. A mixed party of glitterati, dressed more for a fashion shoot than a day's skiing gathered to one side.

They talked excitedly together in a mixture of languages. Mary discerned French, German and Italian as well as English. It was only when they joined the queue that it became clear Gina and company would not be accompanying them today. From what little French and Italian Mary understood, she realized the group had decided to go skiing off-piste instead; it would be far more exciting. Mary breathed a sigh of relief. Today Gordon and her husband would be quite safe.

CHAPTER 7

Hoping he'd taken all the necessary information from Andrew Sinclair's books, Paul sat at his desk surrounded by rough sketches and scribbled notes. Only time would tell, of course, and he remembered the anxious look on Jenny's face when he'd arrived late, and the subsequent meeting with Fiona.

Smiling, he murmured, 'Worzel Gummidge,' and reached for a pencil, remembering Fiona with her lisp and missing front teeth, not forgetting the parting gift of shortbread and her whispered invitation. How defiantly she'd protected Celestina and Emily too. If only his daughters could be half so confident. He hadn't been cross with them at all, just concerned that they'd gone into Andrew's office uninvited.

Today the girls were installed in the dining room. Seeing their father busily sketching, they'd asked if they could draw too. Paul gave them some of his special paper and found pencils and crayons before explaining the importance of his own work. He knew they would sense his concern and remain quietly occupied until lunchtime.

After lunch the girls chatted and showed Paul their

drawings. He was encouraged to see that he appeared in most of them. There were pictures of him taking the girls to school, swimming and dancing, plus their recent walk in the park. Admiring their efforts, Paul saw Cele push a picture to the bottom of the pile. 'What's that one, Cele? Let me have a look.'

Cele's face became anxious as reluctantly she pushed the drawing towards him. Paul studied the picture thoughtfully but said nothing. On the plain white sheet of paper there were triangles – presumably mountains – with a female form standing between two peaks.

The mass of black hair and blood-red mouth could only be Gina. Stick-like objects protruded from her hands and feet, Cele's attempts at drawing skis. What concerned Paul most was that the whole drawing had been scribbled on. Doubtless this was why Cele had looked so worried. It was Emily who broke the silence.

'We didn't like it so we drawed all over it! Mummies shouldn't go away and leave their little girls. Fiona's mummy left her too, which wasn't nice 'cos she had spots.'

Paul had indeed noticed Fiona's spots but thought little of it as Cele continued the conversation. 'Yes – but Fiona said we can go on her picnic when she's better. You will let us go, won't you, Daddy?'

Grateful for the diversion from the disturbing picture of Gina, Paul was hesitant. 'I don't know, it's not up to me to say. It would appear it's Fiona's auntie who is arranging the picnic. We can't just invite ourselves.'

'But we're not,' echoed the girls. 'Fiona invited us and you too, when she gave you the biscuits.'

Fiona, handing over the shortbread, had been most insistent with her invitation, which was why Paul had looked back at Jenny in amusement. She'd also assured him he wasn't really like Worzel Gummidge, 'though her Aunt did think his hair was a wee bit long and untidy!'

Smiling ruefully, Paul thought that, whatever else happened to Sinclair's, they need not worry about their survival. If Fiona Sinclair joined the firm in later years, their success would be guaranteed! 'Come along,' he said turning to his daughters. 'Let's get our coats. We could do with some fresh air and exercise.'

Wrapped up against the cold January weather, Paul led the girls through the main shopping centre to the park. There they ran in and out of the bare tree-lined avenue to the swings. Paul pushed them both, watching their brightly coloured scarves billow behind them as they soared higher and higher, hearing their laughter fill the air.

'Stop now!' Emily's request was abrupt. 'I don't want to go higher. I might go over the treetops and into heaven.'

'Whoever gave you that idea?' enquired Paul.

'My friend Gemma at nursery. Her grannie has just died and she's gone to heaven – that's in the sky, isn't it?'

'Well . . . I don't think you need worry about that,' Paul said reassuringly, helping her from the swing.

'Is Helen's mummy going to die?'

'No! Certainly not!' He replied in answer to Cele's question about their next-door neighbour. 'Helen's mummy has only broken her leg, but I expect she'll be in hospital for quite a while.'

'P'raps we can draw her a get well picture?'

'That sounds like a good idea to me. Now, girls, I think it's about time we went back for some tea and Fiona's shortbread.'

On the way, Cele and Emily chattered excitedly about the pictures they would draw. They liked Helen Craig, the retired schoolteacher who had knitted their bright woollen hats, scarves and gloves. Helen's house was cosy and welcoming and she never shouted at them, not like Gina. That night the girls prayed for Helen's mother to make a speedy recovery, partly from genuine concern and partly from selfishness. If Helen had to keep going to the hospital, they couldn't go to her house!

With the girls bathed and tucked up in bed, Paul sat alone with his thoughts. As on so many previous occasions, the hurt was still there. Gina had been gone a week and hadn't telephoned once. At bedtime there had been the usual awkward questions about mummy coming home, and as usual he could only reply that he didn't know. He never knew when Gina was coming home, yet she always rang the moment she became bored.

The Sinclair file lay open on the desk. Paul picked up a pen and jotted down some ideas. They were all sound possibilities but nevertheless lacked that something special. Jenny Sinclair would be expecting that same 'something special' from him. He could hardly return to her office with the predictable run-of-the-mill ideas he'd seen in the shops on the way home. Ties, rugs, scarves and comb cases had been done a hundred times before; Sinclair's deserved better than that. For a moment he thought of ringing her, but realized it was Saturday evening. Besides, remembering the engagement ring on her finger, he assumed she would be spending a cosy evening at home with her fiancé.

Numerous sketches later, Paul succumbed to tiredness and climbed the stairs. On the landing he switched on the night light and peeped in to check on both girls. Emily's duvet was already in a heap on the floor, casting a mountainous shadow on the wall. Paul thought of Gina. Why wasn't she here? Here to see to stray arms and feet protruding from the bedclothes, or to arrange the vast array of soft toys in their currently required order of merit. Removing Emily's thumb from her rosebud mouth and disentangling Cele's fingers from her mass of dark curls, Paul kissed them both and crept towards the bedroom door. Only then did his foot catch something between the two beds.

In the dim glow of the nightlight Paul discerned a check tea-towel, some plastic mugs and a container each filled with scraps of paper. Trying to rearrange the disturbed objects, his attention was drawn to the scraps of paper.

'Girls, you are brilliant!' he whispered, and hurried back to his desk.

With Stevie given strict instructions to keep Fiona out of mischief, Jenny welcomed Paul's return to her office. Their greeting, as before, was formal, with Paul as anxious to show Jenny his new ideas as she was to see them. There was now only a short time before Andrew's return.

'I'm afraid they're only rough sketches,' he said apologetically, placing the folder on the desk. 'But I'm convinced there is something here that will interest you more than the others.'

Paul watched anxiously as Jenny leafed through numerous pages of drawings and notes. 'From the information you gave me, Miss Sinclair, I'm well aware you've tried the usual gamut of tartan goods and clothing, all of which I appreciate are high quality. But the department stores and shops are already full of them . . .' He paused for a moment; Jenny had reached what he considered to be Cele and Emily's flash of inspiration. A delicately detailed drawing of a sprig of gorse, set within a shield and tartan border.

'I thought you said these were only rough sketches,' she remarked, picking up the sheet of paper and studying it closely. 'This one clearly isn't, although I have to confess, I don't quite see the significance.'

With no intention of telling her he'd sat up until three in the morning to finish the sketch, Paul replied modestly, 'I got carried away with that.'

With new-found enthusiasm and all thoughts of tiredness forgotten, he'd been oblivious to time. It had been just like the old days at Baynham's.

'The idea came from your brother's book,' Paul explained. 'Gorse is the badge of the clan Sinclair. Its origin is French . . . from Comte St Claire in Normandy.'

Descended from the French – did Andrew know that? He'd never mentioned it before. In fact Andrew wasn't at all enamoured of the French. She wondered if that was why he'd never spoken of it. Poor Mary, no Scottish laird, just a French count! Jenny smiled. Paul, oblivious to her amusement, was too busy laying drawings across her desk.

'It's January now, isn't it? But think of summer . . .'

Jenny looked puzzled. 'Summer?'

'Picnics!'

'Picnics?'

'Yes, a range of upmarket picnic and tableware, using the gorse as the main emblem. Of course you can still incorporate the tartan, but make it less heavy for summer. The scope is endless. Start with the fabric – you still have the mills, the looms and the workforce. Go on from there, incorporate it in homewear, household linens, bedding, anything . . .'

Paul laughed enthusiastically. 'Everyone associates Scotland with the thistle . . . but this is the House of St Claire!'

'The House of St Claire?' Jenny looked into Paul's eyes, trying to read his thoughts. They were blue, as she'd expected ages ago . . . but they were so fired with enthusiasm. 'Go on,' she urged.

'The House of St Claire . . . a complete new range of products,' he said, placing an even more detailed design of a shield in her hand.

'The House of St Claire is more suited to a new range of products and after all you're only going back to the original family name. Just think of it . . . gorse embroidered on crisp white linen or cotton could look so fresh for the summer. Thistles and tartan can be a bit old-fashioned.'

He stopped short. 'I'm sorry, I didn't mean to be

rude.' Jenny was wearing her tartan suit, adorned by a traditional thistle brooch.

'That's all right, no offence taken,' she said, 'but what happens after summer? The season is so short, you know, particularly in Scotland.'

'Exactly!' replied Paul, delighted at the prospect of short summers. 'So what happens in Scotland in the autumn?'

'Grouse-shooting?' she answered, as if in response to a teacher's questioning.

'Right, grouse-shooting!' He beamed. 'Now look at these!'

She was almost expecting a gold star for her correct answer. Instead Paul handed her more sketches of hampers and accessories. The crisp white linen made way for soft heather colours and wider bands of tartan, but there was still the ever-present gorse emblem.

'Are you suggesting we go into the food market?' Jenny asked dubiously. 'Mother and Andrew would never agree to that.'

'No! You send the hampers stocked with the non-perishable House of St Claire merchandise to the food companies. They supply the rest, either to the retail outlets, or the estates themselves who are holding the shoots. It's much too risky to start dealing with food!'

'Thank heavens for that,' she sighed.

'I'm sorry . . . you don't like the idea.' Paul stopped short. 'You shouldn't have let me ramble on so.'

Jenny was intrigued. Here was a totally different Paul Hadley from the person she'd met little more than a week ago.

'No! Please go on,' she reassured him. 'I think it's a great idea. As you say, the potential is enormous, I can see that. I particularly like the House of St Claire emblem, too; you've drawn it so beautifully. In fact it's just what we need. A complete change in direction from our usual lines, and we must move with the times. The idea of following through the seasons is such a good idea too. Just think of Christmas, there's so much scope!' Jenny thought of her sister-in-law and continued, 'Women always want things to match in the home according to the seasons.'

'I'm glad you said that and not me.' Paul added, 'Although I have to admit I thought it. I didn't want to insult you twice in one day.'

He looked at her, waiting for a reaction, and was relieved to see her smile. At the same time a shaft of wintry sunlight broke through the heavy grey skies, casting golden glints on her hair and in her eyes.

Collecting the papers together Jenny's hand brushed accidentally against his. Paul moved away, sensing her embarrassment, but his eyes never left her face. Jenny felt strangely uncomfortable.

Regaining her composure, she continued quickly, 'It's certainly an unusual idea but can I ask, apart from Andrew's book, what inspired you?'

'Your niece and my daughters!' he replied matter-of-factly.

'Fiona and the girls?' gasped Jenny. 'But how?'

'Well, since last Friday the girls have been playing at picnics, and I found paper shapes of sandwiches and shortbread on their bedroom floor.'

Jenny laughed. 'And the House of St Claire emerged just like that?'

'Just like that,' replied Paul. 'By the way, how is Fiona?'

As if on cue, Fiona crept round the office door. Paul held up two neatly folded drawings. 'These are for you,' he said.

Fiona looked nervously in Jenny's direction.

'You may come in, Fiona.'

Stepping forward, Fiona took the pictures with a quick, 'Thank you.' Then, with a whispered, 'I like your hair!' she was gone to retreat behind Stevie's wheelchair.

'What's wrong with Fiona?' Paul enquired.

'I'm afraid I told her not to disturb us.'

'Oh, dear! Then I hope I haven't got her into trouble.' Paul stroked the back of his neck, where his hair had recently curled. Fiona had missed nothing; she'd obviously noticed his haircut.

'No, that's all right.' Jenny smiled kindly. 'I'm not such a complete dragon, you know. In fact I'm especially fond of Fiona and I'm taking her to see her grannie – my mother – this weekend. I think the poor thing could do with some fresh air in her lungs after being cooped up in the office with me for almost two weeks. She's like me really . . . adores the wildness of the west coast . . . so we can run wild together. In addition to that, I have to confess I have an ulterior motive, Mr Hadley. If I get Mother on my side this weekend, then Andrew won't be such a problem. I'll ring you on Monday with a progress report if you like?'

Paul nodded thoughtfully. He was keen to have Morag Sinclair's reaction but at that moment could only visualize Jenny and Fiona like two Highland ponies, copper manes blowing in the wind, galloping free along a desolate west coast shore.

CHAPTER 8

On Friday evening Jenny and Fiona left the cloudless skies of Edinburgh and headed for the west coast. Fiona chatted incessantly, clutching the drawings Paul had given her from Cele and Emily. Though far from complimentary, depicting her missing front teeth and red spots on her face, Fiona was delighted with them. She couldn't wait to show Grannie and Miss Tandy, especially as they depicted in minute detail her plaits complete with Sinclair ribbon bows.

'Are we nearly there?' she asked for the umpteenth time.

'I'm afraid not, Fiona, we've a wee while as yet. Why don't you try and sleep for a bit, otherwise you're going to be very tired tomorrow?'

Folding the drawings and placing them carefully in her pocket, Fiona soon nodded off and Jenny was left to contemplate the coming weekend. Since Paul had first suggested the House of St Claire project, her head had been buzzing with ideas. Now all she had to do was convince her mother to agree to it. With Andrew's imminent return, there was so much to discuss in so little time.

Casting a sideways glance at the sleeping Fiona, Jenny turned in the direction of the Connel bridge. Then, as if on cue, the heavens opened and the rain poured down in dense grey sheets. Across Loch Etive, visibility was virtually nil, but to Jenny it didn't matter; from here she knew the route so well. After the next bend in the road she would be able to see the distant lights of Conasg House, home to three generations of Sinclairs.

Fiona stirred as the car came to a halt and three figures stood in the light of the open doorway.

'Hello, Grannie,' she said sleepily as Hamish, the gardener and odd-job man, lifted her gently from the car, 'I've so much to tell you. My friends – '

'Tell me tomorrow, dear,' said Morag kindly. 'It's long past your bedtime. Let Tandy get you some nice warm milk and tuck you up in bed and I'll be up to see you in a wee while.'

Fiona allowed herself to be carried upstairs and Morag turned to embrace her daughter. 'Jennifer, I'm so glad you could come, yet by the looks of you . . . you could do with something a bit stronger than warm milk! My dear, you look exhausted.'

Following her mother through to the sitting room, Jenny noticed not the familiar electric fire but blazing coal and logs.

'Tandy thought you might be cold,' Morag said, as if reading her mind. Then, unbuttoning the neck of her heavy-knit cardigan, she added, 'Personally I don't feel cold at all . . . but as Fiona's been poorly . . .'

Jenny smiled as she sipped the whisky Morag offered. The cut crystal sparkled in the firelight and she felt suddenly warmed by the amber liquid. She knew she always felt and looked more tired when she was cold.

Morag, in her usual layers of woollens, needed no additional warming aids, but she did allow herself her nightly glass of whisky. It was, as she frequently quoted, her 'one and only extravagance'.

'So, Jennifer – you've got some new plans for the business, have you? I'm glad someone has . . . Andrew seems not to care what happens to us.'

'I don't think that's quite fair, Mother. Andrew worked incredibly hard helping Sinclair's through the recession.'

'Hmph!' retorted Morag somewhat unkindly. 'And just exactly how is going away to Switzerland for two weeks going to help Sinclair's? Why, at New Year both Andrew and yourself were complaining of a heavy workload and the need to forge ahead.'

'I know, Mother, and these past two weeks – even with Fiona – I've . . .'

'And that's another thing! How could Andrew even consider going away when Fiona was so poorly? Mind you, I expect it was more Mary's doing. What your poor father would say at such extravagance!'

Putting down her glass on the old oak chest, Jenny walked towards the diminutive figure reclining in her father's favourite armchair. There, sitting on the floor, she reached for Morag's pale and wrinkled hand.

'Mother,' she whispered softly, 'we're not going to starve, you know.'

'Maybe not,' sniffed Morag, 'but nevertheless he should still be here!'

Reminded of the fact Andrew had always been Mother's favourite, Jenny sighed wistfully. 'Well . . . he isn't, so you'll just have to make do with your daughter instead.'

With an uncharacteristic gesture, Morag stroked Jenny's sleek copper hair, where it hung loose about her shoulders. 'You must forgive me, Jennifer . . . but January has been a particularly depressing month. You know, I think we've had rain every day, and I've been trying to clear out your father's study.'

Jenny looked up, startled. Morag hardly ever went into Father's study. She'd always insisted it should remain just as it was when he died.

'But you always said . . .'

'I know,' broke in Morag, running a finger along the threadbare tapestry of William's armchair, 'but I thought . . .'

'You thought what, Mother?'

'I thought perhaps I should start using it for myself. Tandy's always scolding me for cluttering up the dining table and my bedroom with papers.'

At the mention of her name, Miss Tandy opened the sitting room door.

'Fiona's all tucked up and very nearly asleep,' she announced to Morag before turning to greet Jennifer. 'Miss Jennifer, it's so nice to see you. I'm sorry I didn't get a chance to welcome you when you arrived. No point in standing around in all that rain.'

Morag, not content to take her companion's word, slipped out of the room to check on her granddaughter for herself.

'Thank you for the fire, Miss Tandy, I must say it

66

was a truly welcoming sight. I was expecting the electric fire.'

'Well, you know what your mother's like. I have to battle with her over these things occasionally. She says some dreadful things to me, of course, but having been with her so long, I'm used to her funny little ways. Anyway, I'll go and make your hot water bottle.'

Flora Tandy had indeed been with Morag Sinclair a long while; they'd even gone through school together. To Morag she was simply Tandy, her long-suffering friend and companion. To Jenny she was always Miss Tandy and in turn Jenny was always 'Miss Jennifer'. The two women admired and respected one another.

When Morag reappeared she found Jenny looking through papers in her briefcase. 'So . . . what's this wonderful new idea you have, then? Are you going to show me?'

'No, not tonight. It's far too late and I'm looking forward to sleeping on my own for a change.'

With raised eyebrows Morag shot her daughter a questioning look. Jenny's eyes smiled mischievously in response.

'I've had Fiona sharing my bed for the past two weeks and it's beginning to play havoc with my beauty sleep.'

'Oh!' Morag said lamely. 'You haven't seen Cameron, then?'

'No, Mother! I have not seen Cameron.'

The earlier laughter in Jenny's eyes disappeared at the mere mention of Cameron's name and, snapping shut her briefcase, she rose from the settee.

'Goodnight, Mother, if you'll excuse me.'

Kissing Jenny's cheek, Morag returned to William's

chair and, patting the faded tapestry, she whispered to his photograph, 'Well, William, my dear – I didn't handle that very well, did I?'

Snuggled beneath the covers of the ancient double bed, Jenny stretched her toes searching for the hot water bottle. It took ages for the heat to penetrate and only then was she able to wriggle the bottle up with her feet, until it was within her grasp. Like a mother with a newborn child she clutched it towards her breast, feeling the warmth spread through the voluminous folds of winceyette nightdress.

Cameron had always teased her about the night-dresses she took to Conasg House. But the mere slip of eau-de-Nil silk she wore when he was home on leave did nothing to keep her warm. In Cameron's arms there was no need for winceyette. In fact no need for anything at all. Drawing her knees into a foetal position, Jenny wept silent tears and thought of her past six years as Cameron's fiancée.

Cameron Ross – dashing naval officer and sub-mariner – had literally swept the nineteen-year-old Jennifer Sinclair off her feet at their very first meeting.

'He's a real maiden's dream, the epitome of a romantic hero. Marry him as soon as you you can!' her fellow students urged as she showed off her diamond solitaire . . . but Jenny hadn't wanted to marry Cameron – not then. She was only in her first year at university. It would be better to wait until she finished her studies.

Later, with Cameron away so much, it seemed they'd barely got used to one another again before she was standing with all the other naval wives and girlfriends waving goodbye. Which was why she'd bought the tiny cottage at East Lothian. Far away from Gare Loch and the Faslane naval base, they at least had a bolt-hole where they could be together and she would still be near enough to Sinclair's when they did eventually marry.

'A maiden's dream,' Jenny cried into her pillow. 'Well, I was certainly the maiden.' But in the last year time spent with Cameron was more of a nightmare than a dream. He'd become so moody and possessive that she'd even begun to question if she wanted to marry him at all. Perhaps there was more to Triona's warning – spoken in jest – than she realized.

In fact only last night, when quite out of the blue Cameron had phoned asking to meet her, his tone had been bitter and scathing.

' "I'm sorry, Cameron," ' he'd mimicked sarcastically. ' "I'm afraid I can't. I promised to take Fiona to Conasg and there's a business proposition I have to put to Mother." '

Unable to believe her ears at his mocking tone and not wanting to disturb Fiona, Jenny had hung up on him, but not before he'd shouted at her.

'Well, bloody well go, then, Jennifer! And to hell with Sinclair's and the whole damn lot of you!'

Closing her eyes, Jenny slept fitfully. In her troubled dreams Cameron's pursuit of her was relentless as he chased her down a seemingly endless corridor hung with Sinclair tartan. Terrified and struggling through swathes of ribbon, she tugged and pulled, desperately seeking escape, and all the time heard Cameron's cruel laughter, ever closer on her heels.

With a last-ditch attempt to free herself from the

tangled, beribboned corridor, Jenny pushed her way ahead against a bale of tartan cloth, only to wake with a large feather bolster clutched against her breast. Finding herself shaking, she switched on the bedside lamp, put the bolster back into position on the bed and brushed her hair away from her face.

Tangled and damp from tiny beads of perspiration on her forehead, Jenny pulled her hair into a ponytail and, moving from the bed to the dressing table, found a stray elastic band to hold it into place. Sitting in the stillness of the familiar room, her gaze fell on the antique rosewood frame containing yet another of Cameron's photos. She sighed, stifling her grief, and with trembling hands removed the photo from its brass fixing clips. From that moment – as far as Jennifer Sinclair was concerned – Cameron Ross no longer existed. Slowly and deliberately she tore his photo into a mass of tiny pieces.

CHAPTER 9

'Come on, Auntie Jen! It's a lovely day, there's porridge and eggs and Grannie says we can go for a walk by the loch and . . .' Fiona's words came pouring out in an endless garbled stream.

'Fiona! Will you leave your Aunt Jennifer to get dressed in peace? Come along now if we're going for a walk,' Morag's voice called from the hallway.

Fiona bounced off the bed and ran to the windows, where she struggled to draw back the heavy chenille curtains. Shafts of watery sunlight came streaming through the window, causing Jenny to blink and shield her eyes.

'What time is it?' Jenny asked, before realizing Fiona was still getting to grips with time.

'Half past something,' said Fiona, running back on to the landing.

Jenny heard her footsteps on the stairs, muffled conversation in the hallway and the slamming of the front door. Anxiously she climbed from the bed, rubbed her eyes and went to the window to see Morag and Fiona setting off down the drive. She need not have worried, Fiona was well wrapped up against the chill of the morning with bonnet, scarf and gloves.

Jenny shivered as her toes touched the gap between carpet and linoleum and tried to wrap the swathe of chenille around her shoulders. Fiona had said it was half past something, but half past what? Looking at her watch, she gasped. Half past nine! She'd overslept, and from the looks of it Mother and Fiona had been up for hours.

Gazing longingly at the bed, she decided against cocooning herself once more beneath its layers, as the hot water bottle was long since cold. There was only one thing for it; a quick dash to the cavernous bathroom with its ancient plumbing . . . and breakfast.

In the kitchen Miss Tandy served her porridge and poured strong tea from a large earthenware teapot. Jenny declined the offer of eggs; porridge was more than enough.

'I expect you know they've already gone out for their walk,' Tandy said in her clipped Argyll accent. 'It will do Morag good having you both here for a wee while. That cold she had left her feeling dreadfully low and I've tried to get her to go to Edinburgh to see Alex McAllister, but you know Morag, she's so stubborn. She says it's just a waste of petrol!'

'She looked fine to me when I saw her walking down the drive with Fiona – which reminds me, I'd better get a move on if I'm to catch them up.' Jenny grabbed her coat and headed for the door.

Fiona was right, it was a lovely day. In fact it was glorious. After the heavy rain and low-lying cloud of recent weeks, there was a brilliant, clear blue sky. The sun shone on the snow-covered peaks of Glen Etive, which in turn were reflected in the still waters of the loch. Jenny gulped in deep breaths of air, filling her lungs and held it until the cold rasped in her chest. Slowly, as she let a narrow funnel of warm breath escape from her lips, she scanned the shore for Fiona and Morag.

In the distance she saw two figures. The eldest walked at a steady pace, whilst the youngest stopped and started, darting to and from the water's edge then back to her companion like a puppy.

Jenny smiled fondly. In a way Fiona was like a puppy. Her thick hair – this morning tied in bunches – hung below the tartan bonnet like the ears of a cocker spaniel. The young 'puppy', seeing her aunt's approach bounced towards her, arms waving and 'ears' billowing.

'My goodness, Jennifer, does Fiona never stop running about or talking? I feel quite exhausted and it's definitely not from the walking.'

Jennifer laughed. 'I have to admit it's been quite an eventful two weeks. Certainly never a dull moment with Fiona around.'

'So I gather,' continued Morag. 'I've heard all about chicken "spots", picnics, Worzel Gummidge and two little girls with unusual names. No wonder you looked exhausted last night.'

Listening to Fiona's catalogue of events, Jenny wondered what the child had in fact told her grandmother. She herself still had to tell Morag about her meeting with Paul Hadley.

Later that afternoon, with Tandy occupying Fiona in the kitchen, Morag took Jenny into the study. Previously William Sinclair's domain, it was here that

Morag now chose to keep an eye on Sinclair business. The dark cabinets and desk remained just as they had in William's time, the only difference being that Morag – unlike her husband – appeared dwarfed behind the vast oak desk with its green and gold embossed leather top.

Handing over Paul's folder, Jenny announced boldly, 'It's all in there, just waiting for you, Mother! I hope, in fact I think you'll be delighted!'

Bemused, Morag looked up noting the radiance in Jennifer's face. Such a contrast from last night. What on earth could be in the folder that Jenny had clung to so possessively?

Jenny watched anxiously as Morag lifted each page in turn. When she reached the detailed picture of the gorse she stopped and stared.

'Gorse,' explained Jenny. 'The Sinclair family emblem. Conasg means gorse. I often wondered why great-grandfather called the house . . .'

'So it does,' mused Morag. 'I remember your father telling me years ago. I wonder why we never thought of using it before.'

'Quite possibly because everyone associates the thistle with Scottish products,' Jenny replied confidently and with enthusiasm. 'That's what Mr Hadley says. His idea is to use the gorse as the emblem for the House of St Claire and change the products to suit the seasons.'

During the next hour Paul Hadley's name was mentioned frequently. Morag couldn't fail to notice the eagerness and excitement in Jenny's voice as she described Paul's proposals for the House of St Claire. Her enthusiastic flow was reminiscent of Fiona's endless torrent of words earlier in the day.

Pausing for a moment, Jenny said, 'I'm sorry, Mother, I haven't given you chance to think or say anything. It's funny, Mr Hadley was exactly the same when he was describing everything to me yesterday.'

'I see that's something you've got in common,' said Morag shrewdly.

'What's that?' Jenny enquired, puzzled by her mother's comment.

'Enthusiasm with a capital E!'

Jenny seemed relieved – but did Morag share that same enthusiasm?

In the hallway Fiona took great delight in banging the heavy brass gong heralding the arrival of tea.

'Four o'clock,' announced Morag. 'Let's go and see what delights Fiona and Tandy have produced for us today.'

Grandmother and aunt watched as Fiona, closely supervised by Flora Tandy, wheeled in the ancient trolley with its carved wooden legs and squeaky castors. It creaked and groaned like some ancient retainer and Jenny wondered just how many times the same trolley had wheeled its way along the hallway at Conasg and into the sitting room. As usual, on the top shelf rested the Sinclair silver tea-set and underneath, Tandy's special shortbread and dainty salmon and cucumber sandwiches. Less delicate, however, were the scones and jam tarts. No doubt made by Fiona, who had skimped neither on the jam for the tarts nor on the sultanas for the scones. Jenny caught Miss Tandy's eye and smiled knowingly. Flora Tandy, ever mouse-like, said nothing. She simply handed Morag a plate and began to pour the tea.

Watching Fiona distribute the thistle-embossed napkins, Morag announced matter-of-factly, 'Let's hope this time next year those thistles are replaced by gorse.'

Tandy and Fiona looked at Morag in complete and utter bewilderment, while Jenny could only stare in disbelief.

'You've decided . . . already?' she asked excitedly. 'Don't you want more time to think? I mean, we could discuss it further this evening.'

'We can,' Morag replied. 'In fact, we can discuss just how soon we can get this project off the ground! I shall need to speak to Andrew as soon as possible of course, and there'll be no more jetting off for a while!'

As if on cue, and while Fiona was trying to fathom out all this talk about flying and getting things off the ground, the telephone rang. It was Andrew. The family had just returned home and he was replying to Jenny's message left on the answerphone.

He said little, other than that he was delighted Jenny was staying with Morag until Sunday and it would be perfectly all right to bring Fiona home on Sunday evening.

'Fine, I'll see you tomorrow, then, Andrew. I trust the family are all well and no broken bones,' quipped Jenny.

'What? Oh, no . . . no broken bones.' Just broken spirits, thought Andrew. He almost added that they could all do with a holiday, but in view of the last time he'd mentioned holidays to Jennifer, he thought better of it.

* * *

'You are sure about the House of St Claire?' Jenny queried, seeking reassurance from Morag before getting into the car on Sunday.

'Positive,' came the reply. 'I suggest you tell Andrew all about it first thing in the morning and get him to ring me. I'll leave it to you to arrange a meeting between Andrew and your Mr Hadley.'

Morag caught the look in Jenny's eye. Had that last statement been an unfortunate turn of phrase? It seemed difficult to tell. It was strange the amount of times Paul Hadley's name cropped up during the weekend, yet Jennifer said little about him personally. One thing Morag had noticed was that his ideas had given Jennifer a new air of vitality. Perhaps the House of St Claire was just what she needed. A sense of purpose maybe. Something to care for, watch over and nurture . . . like a mother.

'Goodbye, Grannie. Goodbye, Miss Tandy. Bye, Hamish,' Fiona called from the car window as Jenny slowly drove away. This time it was the remains of the jam tarts and scones she clutched, a welcome home gesture for the family. 'And you have got my pictures from Cele and Emily, haven't you, Auntie Jenny?'

Jenny reassured her. The drawings, now somewhat dog-eared, having been passed round the family so many times during the weekend, were folded safely in the glove compartment.

'Would you like me to stop and show you?' Jenny asked, slowing down at the end of the drive.

Fiona was thoughtful as she waved a last farewell to Conasg.

'No, thank you, Auntie Jenny, I think they'll be quite

safe there for a while. It's prob'ly better for me to look after these.' She held up the plastic container of jam tarts and scones. 'But you won't let me forget my pictures when we get home, will you?'

Jenny made a mental note; she would not forget. But whether or not there would be any tarts or scones left to take in with the pictures remained to be seen. All that Argyll fresh air had given Fiona an enormous appetite.

CHAPTER 10

The whole family, delighted to see the youngest Sinclair, showered her with hugs and kisses. It was as if they were competing with each other. Who cared for her the most; who had missed her the most; whose present did she prefer? If Fiona was oblivious to the tense atmosphere, Jenny certainly wasn't. Quite what had happened in Switzerland she had no idea, but she also had no intention of asking. It didn't seem appropriate to enquire.

Leaving Fiona to extricate the remaining misshapen jam tarts and scones from a much-handled container, Jenny said goodbye. Andrew walked with her to the door and announced quietly, 'I intend to be at the office early tomorrow. There must be plenty to catch up on. I suppose I ought to give Bill Freeman a ring too. I don't expect you had chance to go to the trade fair, Jenny?'

'As a matter of fact I did, Andrew, but you won't be needing Freeman's. Still, don't let's talk of that now or you'll miss your jam tarts.'

From the kitchen, voices in unison were praising – a trifle over-enthusiastically, Jenny thought – Fiona's grey wedges of pastry, now, after much finger-licking on the journey home, severely depleted of jam.

Something was definitely wrong, Jenny sighed as she walked to her car.

'Thank goodness she didn't stay,' said Andrew. 'For one awful moment I thought she was going to ask us about the holiday.'

Mary said nothing and continued on her way upstairs to run Fiona's bath. As far as she was concerned, she didn't ever want to discuss the past two weeks. The entire holiday had been a complete disaster.

True to his word, Andrew made an early start for the office. His original intention had been to get there at eight o'clock, but, unable to sleep, he rose early and was behind his desk shortly after seven. To his surprise everything at Sinclair's was in its place, with no hint of a single tyre-track in his carpet. Looking into Jenny's office, he saw nothing outstanding: no piles of papers, memos or unanswered mail. Andrew was disappointed; he'd hoped to find something – no matter how small – to criticize. That way there would at least be something to use as an excuse for the anger and frustration he felt. Reluctantly, there was nothing for it but to wait for Jenny to arrive. Why, he puzzled, had she said they didn't need Bill Freeman?

Making a pot of coffee, Andrew caught sight of the postcards he'd sent. Pinned to the noticeboard, they showed chocolate-box chalets nestling idyllically beneath snow-covered mountains and clear blue skies. Who would have guessed the events that had taken place behind those brightly painted shutters? Foolish though it seemed, shutters like that always reminded him of illustrations in children's fairy-tales. But the events of the past two weeks had turned from fairy-tale setting into nightmare reality.

The week had begun badly enough with Mary's fall, followed by her obsession about finding a suitable partner for Gordon King. Then there had been Jean and Iain's constant bickering over Gina and Philippe the ski-instructor, until at last earlier tensions subsided and everyone appeared to relax and enjoy themselves. On reflection, Andrew realized they should have recognized the danger signs. One always did in hindsight. Once the wheels had been set in motion, however, there could be no turning back.

On the last night of the holiday Mary had suggested she and Andrew join Gordon and Phyllis King for dinner. Jean and Iain were going to a disco organized by the ski-instructors.

'We're too old for discos, Andrew; let's leave that to the young ones. After all, it is their last night. It's back to serious studying for them again next week.'

Initially Andrew was dubious; these 'disco things' sometimes got out of hand. He thought Jean and Iain appeared young and naïve compared to some of the other guests planning to go to the disco, but Mary assured him she would insist Jean and Iain remain together. She even ventured to suggest that she and Andrew could have an early night for once.

The look in Mary's eye was one Andrew didn't see too often. It wasn't usual for her to make such proposals. In his subconscious, Andrew knew this was why he'd been so jealous of Jennifer's relationship with

Cameron. Initially his sister and her fiancé had been so alive with their love. Lately, of course, he reminded himself, even all that had changed.

Andrew stirred his coffee thoughtfully. It had never been quite like that for Mary and himself. Instead it had been more the expectation of two sets of family friends, one willing their eldest son and the other their youngest daughter to make the perfect match.

As a consequence Andrew had courted Mary, as was expected of him, and from there they just drifted into marriage. It was even quite an event in the local social calendar. Frequently Andrew told himself it wasn't that he didn't love Mary; he did, deeply. It was just that, seeing Jenny and Cameron together, he wanted some of their early magic. Could Mary provide such magic on that Friday night in Switzerland?

Sadly for Andrew, magic was in short supply and the spell was broken by the shrill ringing of the telephone.

'*Monsieur Sinclair?*' came the voice from Reception. '*Excusez-moi, mais votre fils – euh – il est . . .*'

'What is it? What's wrong?' demanded Mary, as Andrew got out of bed. 'Andrew . . .?' Watching her husband dress, Mary reached for her satin wrap to cover her nakedness. Her earlier boldness now gave way to embarrassment. She was no longer twenty years younger, as she'd imagined only moments ago. 'Andrew?' Mary repeated.

'It's Iain; he's drunk!' said Andrew angrily. 'He's causing a commotion downstairs and the manager has been called. There's no point in you coming, Mary. I'll deal with it and pay for any damage.'

'Damage! What damage? Where's Jean – don't say she's drunk too?'

'They didn't say; I expect she just helped Iain back to the hotel. I'll send her up, then perhaps take Iain for a spot of fresh air to sober him up. You go back to bed, dear.' Andrew looked tenderly at his wife, where she stood trying to conceal folds of pink flesh. Yes, she had tried to provide the magic; in fact they both had. Perhaps later there would still be time to rekindle earlier passions.

Long before Andrew found Iain, he heard his son's inebriated shouting, coming from a corner of the now empty restaurant. The manager was trying to coax Iain into drinking a cup of black coffee.

'Shove off!' Iain shouted, angrily pushing the coffee away, where it spilled all over the crisp white cloth. 'I don't want your bloody coffee! I want Gina! Gina . . . Gina . . . Gina . . .' sang Iain drunkenly, his head resting in the pool of hot coffee seeping across the white linen.

Andrew gathered the cup and saucer together and passed it to the manager. '*Je m'excuse* . . . his language – I've never heard him speak like that before. *Combien pour le* – um – *damage* . . . is there much broken?' Andrew produced his wallet.

'It eez no problem, Monsieur Sinclair. It eez but one broken glass.' The manager declined Andrew's offer of payment before continuing, 'The glass I can replace, *mais ce n'est pas possible pour moi* . . . to mend, 'ow you say, a broken 'eart?'

Andrew looked up, puzzled, as the manager enlightened him.

'The first broken 'eart is always the worst, yes? Especially if it broken by the – er – older woman of . . . shall we say much experience?'

Andrew needed no further explanations; his son's drunken ramblings bore witness to that. Heaving Iain into an upright position, Andrew looked round for Jean.

'You 'ave lost something, Monsieur Sinclair?'

'My daughter, Jean. Wasn't she with Iain?'

'*Mais non, monsieur, votre fils* he eez alone!'

Filled with panic, Andrew shook his son. 'Iain! Where's Jean?'

'Gina?' mumbled Iain.

'No, not Gina! Jean! Your sister! Where is she?'

The force of being manhandled by his father as he was pushed into the lift confused Iain. Why was his father yelling at him, when his head hurt so much and all he wanted to do was sleep? As the lift doors closed and they moved upwards, Iain felt the earth spinning. Where *was* his sister?

The commotion outside the lift prompted Phyllis King to send her son to investigate. Gordon was surprised to see Andrew fully dressed; they'd said goodnight ages ago. Mary stood open-mouthed at the door, watching Gordon and Andrew carry Iain to the bathroom. There was no sign of her daughter.

'Where's Jean?' she enquired anxiously. 'Is she drunk too?'

'I'm afraid it's worse than that,' replied Andrew, at last distinguishing something coherent from Iain's ramblings. 'It would appear she went off with Philippe to his flat.'

'What!' shrieked Mary. 'But she's only sixteen! Andrew, you must do something!'

'I intend to – I'm going right away.' Andrew picked up his coat.

'Wait a moment – I'll come with you,' Gordon said. 'You might need some help.'

Quite what help was needed, Gordon had no idea. He just felt Andrew Sinclair could do with some moral support.

Living life to the full, morals didn't exist in Philippe Boccard's dictionary of life. Eagerly each week he welcomed each planeload of tourists, particularly if they contained fresh dewy-eyed teenagers just ripe for the picking. So what if he had a reputation and his employers had issued strict warnings? They also knew he was one of their best ski-instructors. Besides, most of the time he adhered to company rules, and when he didn't . . . well, he only bent them a little. Wasn't that what made life a little more exciting? Philippe thought, the night he and Gina plotted together. They just hadn't realized how quickly the heat of the disco, plus copius amounts of wine, would affect their chosen victims.

Euphoria and nervous excitement filled Jean's whole being. It was so grown-up being with Philippe in his apartment. Greedily she accepted the wine he gave her, drinking it in large gulps and offering up her glass for more. Her friends would be so jealous when she described being swept into his arms . . . and the kisses . . . oh, the kisses! And if they didn't believe her, well, she already had the photos as proof of Philippe's existence. During the disco she'd even planned how

85

she would persuade her best friend Hazel to return with her at half-term. Money wasn't a problem; she had savings in the post office. As for her parents, well, she'd worry about that later. All she wanted to do now was sink into Philippe's embrace, just as they did in films.

Copying a scene from her favourite video, Jean stretched seductively on the sofa. Philippe responded and drew her into each romantic sequence, first kissing her tenderly, then gently taking her hand and leading her towards the bedroom. Standing, Jean found the effect of the wine made her dizzy, causing her to forget the next sequence. What happened in the next scene? she puzzled. Could she still remember? Ah, yes, the bed! She sighed dreamily and allowed Philippe to pull her down beside him. Then, giggling nervously, she found herself naked between the sheets.

In the street outside, running footsteps crunched noisily. Wasn't it funny, Jean thought, how snow creaked when it got below freezing? Now the creaking continued but this time indoors and it wasn't freezing here. Here it was warm, and Philippe was naked in the bed beside her. Feeling him move towards her, Jean gasped as his tongue drove hungrily into her mouth. She froze; this didn't happen in her video. Aware of the smell of garlic and alcohol, Jean couldn't breathe; in fact she felt sick!

Andrew, hearing his daughter scream, ran along the corridor to Philippe's apartment. Surprisingly, the door was unlocked and he entered to find Jean, clad in only a sheet, being sick on the floor. Philippe, who had grabbed a bathrobe, tied it nervously round his waist.

'I 'ave done nothing,' he exclaimed. 'I 'ave not touched her!'

'You bloody liar!' Andrew shouted. 'Just look at her! Why, I'll kill you – you bastard!'

Before he had the chance, Gordon pushed Andrew to one side where he landed on the bed by his daughter. Looking up just in time, he saw Gordon strike the retreating Philippe squarely on the jaw.

Back at the hotel, with Jean safely installed with her mother, Gordon and Andrew took stock of the situation over a glass of brandy. Nursing bruised knuckles, Gordon asked. 'Will you press charges against him?'

'I'm not sure – what exactly can we prove? Jean's in such a state of shock she doesn't want to talk about it. Philippe swears blind it never got that far but I don't know if I believe him. Mary says she – er – thinks Jean is all right, if you know what I mean. Besides, as we're going home tomorrow, do you think it wise to involve the police?'

'From what little I care to remember,' Gordon replied, 'I would be prepared to say we got there just in time, and at least you didn't kill him, otherwise the police really would have been involved.'

'I have you to thank for that, Gordon.' Looking at his own bulging waistline and Gordon's balding head, Andrew said wryly, 'We don't exactly fulfil the picture of two Sir Galahads, do we?'

'Probably not,' said Gordon rising with a grin, 'and this Sir Galahad had better go and check on his mother!'

Andrew sat alone, wondering whether or not to return to Philippe's flat. But what good would it do now? The door would not be left unlocked a second time and Philippe's face had already taken quite a bruising. He wouldn't look quite so attractive the following week. Perhaps, Andrew pondered, he would even think twice before his next attempt at seduction.

A faint smell of cigarette smoke and heavy perfume met Andrew's nostrils. Someone had come into the bar. Without saying a word Gina sat down and studied him carefully. Inhaling deeply on her cigarette, she sent a controlled circle of smoke in his direction. Andrew turned away.

'Your son, he is all right now?' Gina enquired.

Andrew could only nod. This woman had got his son drunk while her friend . . . Andrew chose not to be reminded of it. He got up to go.

'Don't go,' Gina said seductively, reaching for his hand. 'I thought perhaps we could have a drink together.'

'The bar's closed,' snapped Andrew, still sitting with Gina's hand resting on his.

'Yes, but we do not need the bar, do we?' Gina questioned, and swept Andrew a knowing look beneath long, dark lashes.

Andrew was tired but he was also mildly tempted. All week he'd listened to Iain drooling on about Gina and here she was sitting before him. She really was strikingly beautiful, her skin glowing and taut and her body inviting. Inviting him – Andrew Sinclair – but to what? Something in Andrew stirred, distant memories of the local minister spouting fire and brimstone. 'Get thee behind me, Satan,' came the cry from the pulpit. Andrew thought of Mary and stood up. 'Some other time perhaps.'

Now, sitting in his office waiting for Jennifer, Andrew couldn't help wondering what would have happened if he'd gone with Gina. Doubtless he'd never know, but the prospect had haunted him on the flight back to Scotland and he felt so ashamed. In fact the whole family appeared to be suffering some shame or another: Iain for the trouble he'd caused at the hotel, Jean for her compromising situation with Philippe, and Mary suddenly overcome with guilt at leaving Fiona. She blamed herself for everything. It was after all her constant talk of a family holiday so soon after New Year that had caused Andrew to succumb. This morning, unable to face any more of her self-recrimination, he just had to get out of the house.

A car door slammed. Andrew rose and went to the window to see Stevie negotiate herself from car to wheelchair. Although he'd never admitted it, it never failed to amaze him how she coped with her disability. Running a hand through his thick sandy hair, Andrew sighed. Why hadn't he been that keen on Jenny employing her in the first place? He supposed it was silly things really: her being called Stevie when her real name was Cressida and . . .

'With a name like Cressida Stephens,' he'd overheard her say to Jenny, 'is it any wonder I prefer to be called Stevie? It also drives me mad when people pat me on the head. I always expect them to ask me if I take sugar!'

Andrew made sure he never patted Stevie on the

head. He also knew she didn't take sugar, but that wretched wheelchair of hers made terrible tyre tracks in his carpet!

'Good morning, Mr Sinclair,' said Stevie, wheeling herself into the office. 'Gosh, you're here early. Your holiday must have done you good!'

Arriving at the office an hour later, Jenny chose again not to ask about Andrew's holiday. The atmosphere in the house the previous evening was warning enough. Instinct told her to tread warily; she had after all quite a bombshell to drop before Andrew. That in itself would be a shock, and to find that Paul's plan had Morag's approval was bound to provoke confrontation.

Placing the bulky file on Andrew's desk, Jenny said softly, 'This is the reason we won't be needing Bill Freeman. I suggest you look through it while I deal with the morning's post. I'll pop back in a while for a coffee . . . we can discuss it then.'

Andrew scanned the pages of notes and drawings and the detailed logo depicting the House of St Claire. It seemed totally alien to Sinclair's. What on earth was Jennifer thinking of, and who was this Paul Hadley? He'd certainly never worked with Bill Freeman. Later when Jenny popped her head round the door, Andrew's face was devoid of emotion.

'Have you had long enough to come up with an initial response?'

'Well, you and this – er – Paul Hadley have certainly come up with a plethora of ideas, Jennifer, but I can't say I'm that impressed. It's not Sinclair's style at all.'

'Exactly,' replied Jenny acidly. 'That's the point I've

been trying to make these past months, Andrew. Besides, it's a shame you don't approve – as Mother does! She wants you to ring her this evening.'

'What?' demanded Andrew, his dark eyes flashing angrily. 'You mean to say you've already shown these to Mother?'

'Yes, I took them to Conasg at the weekend when I went with Fiona.'

Andrew was stunned. 'Well, you certainly didn't waste any time!'

'Precisely, because time is the one thing we haven't got if we're going to try and promote the House of St Claire this year. That's why Mother wants you to ring her this evening.'

'Damn this evening! I'll ring her now,' said Andrew, reaching clumsily for the phone. 'How could Mother make a decision like this without consulting me?'

'Quite simply because you weren't here, Andrew – you were on holiday, remember?' Jenny's tone was caustic. Andrew looked up, suddenly reminded of the holiday. In the heat of the moment he'd managed to forget it. Was there now to be an inquest on that as well?

Andrew, given a reprieve, listened as Jenny merely repeated his Mother's request. There was no need to ring now; it would be cheaper this evening. Silently accepting defeat, Andrew turned again to Paul's file. Certainly the gorse design was most impressive . . . and the House of St Claire . . . well, it did have a certain ring to it too. Even he had to admit there were possibilities, but the fact that he'd had no part in its inception only made him resentful.

Listening to Andrew's protestations that evening,

Morag gave her son short shrift for neglecting the family business and said she was glad someone – namely Jennifer – had Sinclair interests at heart. Hurt by the pronouncement; Andrew knew it was pointless remonstrating with his mother. Instead he agreed a change of policy might be a good idea. In truth it hadn't been a difficult decision to make – once he'd recovered from the initial shock – but he didn't want Jennifer to know that. In fact, during the hours preceding his call to his mother, Andrew's mind had sprung into top gear.

As a consequence Jenny couldn't wait for her lunch appointment with Paul. How would he react? He would have to meet Andrew too, of course, later that week if possible. In the meantime there was so much to plan.

The waiter showed her to the table she'd reserved, tucked in a corner by the window. She looked at her watch; no, she wasn't late – they'd said one o'clock, but she was a little disappointed Paul wasn't there already. Still, no matter; from the window she could look out for him.

'Miss Sinclair, do you wish to order?' the waiter enquired.

'What? Oh, I'm sorry, I was miles away.'

'Lunch, Miss Sinclair – are you ready to order?'

Jenny looked at her watch again. It was already one-thirty and she'd hoped to be back at the office by two o'clock. Having spent the past half-hour scanning the lunchtime crowds looking for Paul, she drummed her fingers impatiently. Surely he couldn't have forgotten? 'Luigi, have there been any messages for me – my business appointment, he hasn't telephoned?'

'No, Miss Sinclair, nothing at all.'

Reaching for a breadstick Jenny thought resentfully that at the very least Paul could have telephoned; after all, wasn't she helping him too? At any other time she would have left the restaurant in disgust, but she needed to talk to Paul urgently. There was also the vague possibility that he'd been held up by traffic and would at any moment walk through the door.

Sadly he didn't, and Jenny became angrier and hungrier. Not usually one to eat more than a snack at lunchtime, the bowls of hot soup and aromatic pasta dishes wafting basil and oregano temptingly in her direction only made her feel worse. Ten minutes later, humiliated and enraged, she ordered a lasagne and a glass of red wine.

Paul, if he arrived now, would just have to manage without lunch and return with her to the office! That was if she indeed felt like talking to him!

Slamming the outer door, Jenny strode past Stevie to her own office.

Stevie looked aghast; this wasn't at all like Jenny. She'd been on such a high this morning – what on earth could have happened?

'Mr Hadley . . .' Stevie began.

'I don't want to know and I don't wish to be disturbed!" Jenny retorted indignantly, and closed her door. Sitting down, she flung open her desk drawer and came face to face with a photo of Cameron. Staring into what she'd recently decided were Cameron's mocking eyes, she thought of Paul Hadley's – as she'd last seen them – smiling enthusiastically in her direction.

'Men!' she cried in a fit of pique, throwing Cameron's photo in the waste paper basket. 'Who the hell needs them?' Through tear-filled eyes she reached for her handkerchief and thought of her dead father. 'You always said I was too trusting, didn't you . . . and you were right.'

Jenny sniffed and blew her nose. It wouldn't have been so bad if Paul Hadley's ideas hadn't been so good . . . but dammit, they were! And she'd trusted him implicitly. She didn't know which was worse. She did know, however, that for the rest of the afternoon she would have to avoid Andrew. Even now she could see him gloating over Paul's non-appearance, rehashing Paul's ideas and taking them along to Bill Freeman with that 'I told you so' look in his eyes.

When all attempts at making contact with Jenny failed, Stevie supposed it didn't really matter. They both had plenty to keep them occupied in the meantime and anyway it was probably that time of the month. Usually they joked about their PMT but today was different; they were at daggers drawn. At five o'clock Jenny passed a cursory glance over the memos Stevie had placed on her desk. Paul's name appeared frequently.

'Well, what feeble excuse did he come up with, then?' she enquired breaking the frosty silence, at the same time refusing to look up from the papers she was studying.

The reply was nonchalant. 'Oh . . . only that his children have chicken pox, his wife is still away on

94

holiday and the neighbour who usually helps out is visiting her mother in hospital. So I expect you'll think, as an excuse, that's all rather pathetic!' Stevie eyed Jenny critically, the distinct note of sarcasm in her voice deliberate. Had the message got through? she wondered.

'Did you say chicken pox? Oh, my God! That can only mean one thing . . . Fiona . . . they must have caught it from Fiona!'

'Precisely,' said Stevie sardonically. 'That's just what I thought.'

'But why didn't you tell me?'

'Tell you! Tell you!' Stevie's voice rose to a crescendo as she spun her wheelchair to face Jenny head on. 'Wait a second, Jenny! I've been trying to tell you all afternoon but you didn't want to know! Poor man, I've lost count of the times he's rung through this afternoon and he's at his wit's end what to do about the children. Believe it or not, he just couldn't apologize enough for letting you down.'

Jenny sat ashen-faced at Stevie's outburst. Stevie rarely lost her temper, and the thought of Paul having to cope with Celestina and Emily alone only made things worse. Heaven knew it had been bad enough having to cope with Fiona.

'I'm truly sorry, Stevie – you're right, it's not your fault. I shouldn't have been so pig-headed. It's just that I had such high hopes for the House of St Claire, I'd hate for it all to disappear.'

'There's little chance of that,' Stevie added, wheeling her chair alongside Jenny's desk. 'Mr Sinclair's been working on that all afternoon. The telephone's red-hot, what with phone calls to New York and Geneva.'

'Red-hot like my temper?' Jenny asked with a wry smile.

'Well . . . let's just put it down to the dreaded PMT, shall we? Anyway, I'm not surprised you're tired, coping with the office for two weeks and looking after Fiona. Why don't you go home, forget about Sinclair's and have a nice hot bath and an early night?'

Jenny had already forgotten about Sinclair's, but her thoughts were not on baths and early nights. In her mind's eye she conjured up a vision of Paul trying to cope with the girls. Heaven knew it wasn't going to be easy for him, and she herself felt solely responsible for his dilemma. There was only one thing for it. She must go and help.

'I don't believe it!' she cried, looking in her diary. By Paul's name there was only a telephone number. How could she be so stupid? She didn't even know where he lived! Racking her brain, she tried to remember what he'd said when he'd introduced himself? How did he know about Sinclair's? Alistair Jennings, she remembered – that was it! Jenny found Alistair's number and began dialling.

'Jenny, darling,' came the smooth response. 'Why haven't I seen you? Are you avoiding me? You promised me lunch ages ago, remember?'

Jenny remembered all right, which was why she preferred to forget! Alistair Jennings gave her the creeps. It had been one thing earlier that afternoon making comparisons between Cameron and Paul Hadley, but Alistair Jennings was even worse! She was beginning to wish she'd never rung him. There was only one solution: get rid of him quickly even if it meant agreeing to a lunch date; she could always cancel it later. In the meantime she needed Paul's address and she needed it now. Alistair duly obliged.

CHAPTER 11

Surveying the peeling front door of the large Victorian house, Jenny stood nervously on the doorstep. How would Paul react when he saw her, especially when she'd stubbornly refused his calls all afternoon? Her stomach lurched when she heard the ringing of a distant bell, followed by the sound of quick footsteps.

The door opened, but it wasn't Paul who stood there. Surely this ageing hippy wasn't his wife? Hadn't Stevie said Mrs Hadley was away?

'I'm looking for Paul Hadley. Have I come to the right house?'

'Why, yes,' came the cheery reply, 'he's just away to the chemist's. I'm sure he'll only be a wee while; would you care to come in and wait?'

Jenny introduced herself, then with an air of uncertainty followed the unknown woman – clad in a bizarre array of textiles and colours – through the house to a welcoming kitchen.

'I'm Helen Craig, Paul's neighbour,' she said, extending her hand. 'I try to help Paul whenever I can and in turn he helps me with lifts to the hospital. You see it's a bit too far to go on my bike. He would have taken me today of course, only he had a business appointment.' Helen Craig looked wistful. 'Poor man, he never got there in the end, though; the school rang, you see, and he had to fetch the wee bairns home. Quite poorly they look, too.'

Helen Craig poured two cups of tea and put them on the pine table. She was aware of Jenny's eyes scanning the general disorder throughout the house. 'It's in a terrible muddle, isn't it?' she said softly. 'Mind you, you should have seen it before Gina left; it was even worse.'

'Gina?' queried Jenny.

'Paul's wife. I feel quite sorry for him, you know – she's hardly ever here. You've never met her, I take it?'

Seeing Jenny shake her head, Helen continued sadly, 'As for Cele and Emily, well . . . let's just say Gina wasn't cut out for domesticity, though she does try sometimes, poor dear.'

'How long did you say Mr Hadley would be?' Jenny asked, anxious to change the subject. It didn't seem right discussing people she didn't know.

'Och, not long at all now. The chemist's isn't far. He would have gone earlier, of course, only he was hoping to get a phone call. With me being at the hospital, I couldn't come in before and of course he wouldn't leave the girls all alone. So you see . . . we were all in a right pickle and I've still got Mother's laundry to attend to.'

'If you want to go, I'll stay and look after Celestina and Emily; I've plenty of time.' Yes, plenty of time, thought Jenny to herself, having said goodbye to Helen Craig. Plenty of time to feel guilty about Fiona and chicken pox *and* the phone call – no doubt her phone call – that Paul had been waiting for all afternoon!

'Goodness, you do look poorly,' said Jenny, dabbing Cele and Emily with the calamine lotion she'd bought on her way over. 'I'm so sorry, you appear to have caught Fiona's chicken pox.'

At the mere mention of Fiona's name both girls' faces brightened.

'How is Fiona?' they asked almost in unison.

Touched by their enquiry, Jenny swallowed hard and screwed the lid back on the bottle of calamine.

Consumed by guilt, she studied the two small girls trying desperately not to scratch their chicken pox. Here they were, she thought, looking extremely poorly, largely thanks to Fiona, yet they were more concerned about her niece's welfare than they were about themselves.

'She's much better, thank you, and delighted with the drawings you sent her. She even took them to show her grannie last weekend.'

The girls were impressed, then Cele added softly, 'Our Grannie Hadley is dead but our other Grannie – Grannie 'Tino' – is in Italy.'

While the girls waited for the calamine lotion to dry, Jenny set to remaking their crumpled beds and quite forgot about Paul. It came as a complete surprise when she heard a key turn in the lock and his voice called, 'Helen, I'm back!'

'Helen's gone home,' Cele shouted down the stairs to Paul, 'but . . .'

Two at a time Paul rushed up the stairs, desperate to know why Helen had left the girls so unexpectedly. In his hands was a bottle of calamine lotion and some cotton wool. 'Miss Sinclair!' he exclaimed. 'What are you . . .?'

Jenny held up her own medical supplies. 'Snap!' she cried.

In the kitchen, Paul's profuse apologies for his non-appearance at lunchtime were in turn replaced by Jenny's for inflicting Fiona's germs on the two children, who were now sleeping peacefully.

'I feel extremely embarrassed and responsible for all this.' She was insistent. 'You must let me help in any way I can.'

'Well, Helen's very kind,' said Paul, 'and it won't be so bad if I'm going to be working from home . . .' Paul looked anxiously in Jenny's direction. *Would* he be working from home?

'Speaking of work,' she said brightly, 'that's also one of the reasons I'm here. My mother wants you to proceed with the House of St Claire and I'm pleased to say Andrew didn't take too much convincing either.'

Paul looked at Jenny in disbelief. It was as if a great weight had been suddenly lifted from his shoulders. 'Why, that's wonderful! Are you sure . . . really sure?'

Jenny's face shone with delight as she announced, 'I'm absolutely positive.'

'In that case, when do you want me to begin?'

'Tomorrow. Andrew would like to see you tomorrow if that's possible?'

Paul's heart sank and he ran his fingers through his hair nervously.

Reading his mind, Jenny added, 'Don't worry about the girls. I'll come and sit with them while you discuss the House of St Claire with Andrew.'

Paul sighed and shrugged his shoulders. 'I don't know what to say, especially as I understand from your assistant that you're completely snowed under with work.'

Jenny felt herself colour. So that was what Stevie told Paul when he'd been trying desperately to get through to her. Flicking at an imaginary piece of fluff on her jacket she replied, 'I'm quite sure I can bring some of it with me.'

'Miss Sinclair,' said Paul his face brimming with gratitude. 'I don't know how to thank you enough . . .'

'As we're going to be working together, can I suggest we drop the Miss Sinclair . . . please call me Jenny?' She held out her hand, which he shook warmly.

'Paul,' he said simply, and walked to a corner cabinet. Opening the door, he remarked, 'I really think we should be celebrating but I'm afraid the choice looks pretty dismal . . . unless you like neat vodka or apricot brandy?'

Jenny shook her head. 'Thank you, no – not if I'm driving and especially not on an empty stomach.'

Moments later, when accepting his offer of supper, she politely refrained from mentioning that she'd eaten lasagne once that day already. But there seemed little else in the freezer and she recalled Helen Craig's earlier remarks about Gina Hadley's attempt at keeping house.

Nevertheless, in the warmth of the kitchen even frozen lasagne tasted good after the traumas of the day. Paul managed to find a decent bottle of Chianti classico tucked away at the back of the cabinet.

Allowing herself one glass of wine, Jenny raised it in Paul's direction.

'To the House of St Claire,' she said confidently as her eyes met his across the table.

'To the House of St Claire!' Paul sipped at his wine thoughtfully. 'I feel this should really be champagne – sorry I can't oblige. Next time perhaps?'

'Don't worry,' Jenny replied, placing her glass on the table. 'The champagne will come later . . . and if Andrew has anything to do with it you can guarantee it will be one of the best!'

One of the best, Paul mused after he'd waved her goodbye. Certainly one of the best things that had happened to him in recent weeks had been his meeting with Jenny Sinclair.

CHAPTER 12

A welcome smell of coffee pervaded the house as Paul helped Jenny with her coat.

'I'm sorry I won't be there to introduce you, but Andrew's not too bad really,' she said reassuringly. 'He's just a bit like a mother hen when it comes to Sinclair's. Secretly I think he wishes *he'd* thought of the House of St Claire . . . still, as we're all working for the same team, it doesn't really matter, does it?'

Jenny studied Paul for the first time since he'd opened the door. He looked tired and anxious. Here she was chattering on about Andrew and she hadn't even asked about Celestina and Emily.

'You look tired, Paul – did the girls have a bad night?'

'Afraid so. I seemed to be up and down with them all night. It's the wretched itching; it makes them so uncomfortable.'

'You mustn't worry about them now, I'll take care of everything here and Stevie knows where to contact me if I'm needed.'

With Paul safely on his way, Jenny went upstairs to check on Cele and Emily. Two blotchy faces peered from beneath duvets decorated with Spot the Dog motifs – which somehow seemed strangely appropriate. The girls looked flushed and tired.

They'll need to drink plenty of fluids and get lots of sleep, thought Jenny, and at the same time wondered just when their mother was going to make contact. To date, all Paul's repeated messages to Switzerland asking Gina to call remained unanswered. It was as if she seemed not to care that her children were ill.

Without the constant ringing of the telephone and interruptions from Andrew, Jenny was amazed how quickly she dealt with her backlog of work. Much later, pouring herself a coffee, she hoped desperately for Paul's sake that Andrew wouldn't be too bombastic. Paul's sake, she mused – with her work finished, was there anything she could do for him? The girls had already eaten a light lunch and were sleeping again, but there must be something she could do.

The house, she noticed, was a great deal tidier than before, but if she were to help with some housework it would have to be something quiet. In the utility room her gaze alighted on a basket of clothes, neatly folded and ready for ironing. Jenny found the ironing board and plugged in the iron.

Newly cleaned and descaled, it no longer spewed out sludge. Instead there came a gentle purring sound as steam wafted easily over each freshly laundered garment, and she found the act of ironing in the still of the afternoon strangely therapeutic. Her own was usually a frenetic exercise performed while watching the nine o'clock news.

Humming softly to herself, Jenny studied the neat pile of children's clothes ready for the airing cupboard.

Now there were only Paul's shirts. It seemed an eternity since she'd last ironed a man's shirt, and she didn't even know if she could . . . without thinking of Cameron.

Carefully placing a shirt on the ironing board, Jenny smoothed the back and ran her fingers gently on each pearl button, checking to see they were all secure. Tears pricked her eyelids as she did so and she lifted a newly ironed sleeve against her cheek. It was as if she was seeking solace from the still warm fabric.

In the early days Cameron would hold his hand to her cheek like that before leaving for the naval base, saying, 'No tears, now, I'll be back soon.' Then the problem was coping with his long absences; now it no longer mattered.

Although the room was warm, Jenny felt a shiver run through her body at the memory of her last meeting with Cameron and his ferocious attack on not only herself but all the Sinclairs. It was true, since the death of her father she'd thrown herself into the family business. But they all had, Mother and Andrew too. It was a case of having to or else letting Sinclair's go to the wall. No one – least of all Jenny – was prepared to let that happen. She sighed and wiped away a tear, whispering softly, 'Six years, Cameron – we had six whole years together – yet I'm only just beginning to realize I never even knew you.'

There was a faint stirring at the door and Jenny turned to find a small, sleepy figure. It was Emily holding a toy rabbit unceromoniously by the ear. She looked delicate and frail, like one of the flower fairies in the Cicely M. Barker books Jenny had enjoyed as a child. Those same treasured books were now in Fiona's possession but she could still remember each one. Jenny smiled fondly. Cele, Emily and Fiona would be her real-life flower fairies. What a lovely picture they'd make.

'Can I have a drink, please, Jenny? I'm thirsty.'

'Of course. Tell me what you'd like and I'll bring it straight up.'

Returning to bed dragging the rabbit behind her, Emily waited.

Jenny appeared with a glass of juice and Paul's shirts. 'Perhaps you can tell me where the airing cupboard is, Emily, then I can put Daddy's shirts away.'

Drinking thirstily, Emily pointed to the airing cupboard and watched as a jumble of clothes fell out at Jenny's feet. There might just be room for the girls' clothes, but not for the shirts she'd just ironed so carefully.

With the air of an intruder Jenny sought out Gina and Paul's bedroom. There a heavy smell of stale perfume filled the air and make-up and postcards littered the dressing table. She felt strangely uncomfortable; perhaps she should have squeezed the shirts into the airing cupboard after all.

Anxious to vacate the room as soon as possible, Jenny went straight to the wardrobe, only to discover to her horror that it wasn't Paul's. In fact there was no sign of Paul anywhere. Not even a solitary tie or a stray pair of socks. Every shelf, rail and hanger was filled to over-flowing with women's clothes. Jenny was aghast; even Mary didn't possess such quantities. And the colours! Sheer unadulterated extravagance were the only words to flash through her mind as she stood clutching Paul's shirts, shirts that had undoubtedly seen better days. No wonder Paul had looked so dishevelled at their first meeting.

Without realizing it, Jenny found herself loathing Gina Hadley. She was all for husbands and wives having their own interests, but it seemed Gina's interest was not that of her husband and children, only herself. What kind of woman was she? With the intrusive chirp of the telephone, she found out sooner than expected.

'*Ciao*! Who is that? Is that you, Helen?'

'No, it's Jenny.'

'Jenny? Jenny who? What are you doing in my house?' the voice demanded angrily.

Completely taken aback, Jenny replied without thinking, 'I'm helping Paul . . .'

'Oh, how very interesting – and how are you helping Paul?'

Angered by Gina's menacing tone, Jenny replied tersely, 'What do you mean, how am I helping Paul? Here in the house, of course.'

'Oh, I see . . . then you are a cleaner.'

'No, I am not!' Though her reply was indignant, Jenny knew trying to explain her present situation to Gina could prove difficult. Here she was in Gina's bedroom with an armful of Paul's shirts!

A stream of incomprehensible Italian flooded down the line, followed by a venomous, 'So, this is what he gets up to when I'm away. He has wasted no time!'

Jenny was alarmed; it hadn't taken long to realize that Gina was jumping to ridiculous conclusions and, despite protestations, her accusations continued in vitriolic torrents. It was almost unbelievable.

Determined to command attention and take control, Jenny shouted down the phone, 'I don't particularly care what you think at the moment, Mrs Hadley, but I can assure you I am *not* having an affair with your husband. If you'll just stop yelling at me for an instant and listen, I will explain exactly why I'm here. Your children have been ill and I'm only doing what you should be doing: taking care of your family!'

Apart from background laughter, the line remained strangely quiet.

'Mrs Hadley?'

'*Si* . . . yes, I am here. I am sorry . . . is Paul there.'

'No, he's working,' Jenny replied coldly. 'He will be back this evening.'

'And Cele and Emily?'

'They are in bed. Would you like me to bring them to the phone?'

Gina hesitated, then a voice in the background called, '*Gina! Viens, chérie, nous sommes en retard.*'

'No, it's all right,' Gina whispered hurriedly. 'I must go. Please will you tell Paul I will ring him . . . I will come home.'

'Yes, I'll tell him.'

'Was that *Mummy* on the phone?'

'Yes,' said Jenny, putting her arms round the newly awoken Cele. 'She's coming home; isn't that lovely?'

Cele made no comment. Emily appeared, requesting drawing paper.

'Daddy keeps it in his study, I'll show you where.'

In Paul's study, Jenny discovered where to put Paul's shirts.

'It's all right,' Emily said, sensing her reluctance. She pointed to a pile of paper. 'Daddy won't mind.'

It wasn't taking the paper that bothered Jenny so much, it was seeing the room and all it revealed. A narrow camp bed had been pushed against the wall to make way for a single wardrobe and drawing office desk. Quickly Jenny placed the folded shirts on the bed. She'd opened Gina's wardrobe door but nothing would induce her to open Paul's. She'd ventured too far into his private life already.

On the desk she recognized copies of the designs for Sinclair's, all neatly laid out and numbered. How had the meeting gone today? For everyone's sake, especially Paul's, she hoped it had gone well.

'Mummy rang; she's coming home,' Cele announced unenthusiatically on Paul's return.

The look of elation on Paul's face following the success of his meeting with Andrew was short-lived. Watching the girls run off to find their drawings, he turned to Jenny.

'At least they're looking better. Now, what's this about Gina?'

'She rang this afternoon and . . . I have to confess I was rude to her. I'm sorry, I owe you an apology.'

'I doubt it,' Paul replied bluntly. 'Gina has a knack of upsetting people; that is, when she's not putting on her "charm personified" act.' His tone was bitter and resentful. 'What did she say to upset you?'

'Oh, nothing really. Looking back on it, I think I just over-reacted.'

'Jenny please! I'd prefer to know, what did she say?'

'It's quite preposterous really,' Jenny blurted out.

'She accused us of having an affair. Now tell me, how did the meeting go with Andrew?'

Paul shifted uncomfortably. He could see Jenny was blushing and anxious to turn attention away from her embarrassing verbal encounter with Gina, so he changed the subject.

'It went well, really well, that is after the initial hostilities!' Paul teased. 'In fact, I'm convinced we can work together.'

Jenny smiled with relief. 'Thank heavens for that – and did Andrew tell you what happens next?'

'Next, according to Andrew, we go to the factories. Discuss materials, design possibilities, production and marketing. The initial objective is to produce a House of St Claire range – albeit small – for the summer. Andrew wants to be ready to take New York and Geneva by storm.'

'What?' Jenny asked incredulously. 'You're joking!'

'Not according to Andrew,' Paul replied. 'He's deadly serious. There's a British Week in New York and Geneva and Andrew wants the House of St Claire represented at both. He's already pencilled them in in his diary!'

'In that case I'd better go and do some homework.' Jenny reached for her briefcase. 'Otherwise I shall get left behind by you men.'

'Won't you stay and have a drink?' Paul enquired. 'I bought something especially.' He unwrapped a bottle. 'You see, not the ordinary supermarket plonk.'

Jenny hesitated, 'I don't think I'd better. Your wife might ring and if I'm still here . . . There's a casserole in the oven and I'm sure you'll find the girls sleep better tonight. No doubt I'll see you at the office.'

With a gentle smile of acknowledgement, Paul watched her go to her car. What a day! Perhaps his luck was changing after all. The girls seemed so much better already and there was no knowing where this opening with Sinclair's would lead. Closing the door on the murky winter's evening, Paul was comforted by the welcome smell wafting from the kitchen. For the first time in ages he'd returned to find a decent meal waiting. What a pity, then, that Gina should cruelly burst his bubble by telephoning to announce her imminent arrival at the airport.

CHAPTER 13

In the weeks that followed, life for the Sinclairs slipped back into its usual pattern. Andrew, thankful the skiing holiday was no longer mentioned, committed himself wholeheartedly to the House of St Claire. He and Paul made rapid progress by working long hours, which Gina appeared not to mind and Mary compensated for by involving herself with her numerous committees. For Jean and Iain it meant serious study, and for Fiona, the anticipation of her picnic with Jennifer when the primroses were in bloom.

As the day approached, Fiona was bitterly disappointed to learn that Cele and Emily were unable to come. The picnic wouldn't be the same without them. Paul had given no specific reason but instinct told Jenny that Gina was being difficult and things were best left alone.

'Why do you want to go on a boring picnic, when you can come shopping with me for pretty dresses?' Gina had actually demanded of the girls. Her question was met with silence and, young as they were, the children already understood that it was best not to antagonize their mother or provoke disagreements. They had learnt that from their father since Gina's return from her skiing trip.

Initially full of remorse at her extended absence, she'd surprised them all. Remorse, however, soon gave way to boredom, and a phone call from one of her glitterati friends soon rekindled Gina's feelings of wanderlust. The problem was how to approach Paul and tell him she was going away again.

Gina needed look no further than the morning's post. The promotional package for the forthcoming British Week gave her the opportunity she was waiting for.

'You are going away, Paul? Geneva, New York?'

'I doubt it, Gina; that's more Andrew's line.'

'This Andrew, you enjoy working with him, yes?'

'Yes, strangely enough, I do. I think we make a good team and I've a lot to thank Andrew and Jenny for. At least it's meant we can keep the house.' He was going to add, And keep you in clothes, but Gina had been somewhat restless of late; it was easier to keep quiet.

'Then,' Gina added brightly, 'why don't we invite them to dinner?'

Paul couldn't believe his ears. It had been months since Gina had suggesting inviting people for dinner. Perhaps his earlier thoughts had been ill-founded. Gina was a very good cook when she chose to be; the problem was that she didn't choose to be very often. In a small way the dinner party could perhaps be a gesture of thanks on Paul and Gina's behalf. Smiling with satisfaction, he replied, 'I think that's a wonderful idea, Gina. Perhaps you could ring Jenny at the office and arrange a convenient date.'

To Jenny the invitation was like a bolt out of the blue.

114

The one and only conversation she'd had with Gina was one she chose not to remember. What should she say? Surely Gina must remember their heated exchange of words? She said the first thing that came into her head.

'Well, Andrew and I are very busy at the moment – the House of St Claire, you know . . .'

'Exactly,' cooed Gina. 'This is why we both want you to come a little thank-you to Sinclair's, and of course I never thanked you properly for looking after Celestina and Emily for me.'

Could this be the same woman Jenny had spoken to on that cold winter's afternoon? It must be the better weather, she thought, warming the hearts of her fellow men, or in Gina's case fellow woman.

Surprisingly, Andrew was perfectly accommodating to Gina's offer. Wednesday would be fine, he confirmed; Mary had a committee meeting and Jean could look after Fiona . . .

'I'm not sure, Andrew,' Jenny announced. 'Could we not make it an evening when Mary can go with you?'

'Nonsense,' broke in Andrew. 'Mary's not the least bit interested in discussing trade fairs or the business and there's still a great deal Paul and I have to arrange. I was only saying to Alistair Jennings today . . .'

At the mention of the name, Jenny froze. For weeks Alistair had been pestering her for another lunch date to replace the one she'd cancelled, and she was now running out of excuses. A meeting would be inevitable sooner or later. Andrew had chosen Alistair's company to supply the food for the House of St Claire hampers, and advertizing was already under way.

'I'll tell Mrs Hadley eight o'clock next Wednesday,

then,' she said, anxious to avoid any further conversation that included Alistair.

Andrew made a note in his diary for eight pm. He would take the wine and suggested Jenny took flowers for Paul's wife. Andrew stretched contentedly in his chair. Having spent so many hours working late at the office it would be an evening to look forward to.

When Wednesday came, nothing could have prepared Andrew for the shock of seeing Gina by Paul's side when he opened the door. But if Gina had recognized Andrew, it was certainly well concealed.

As the evening wore on a more composed Andrew – mellowed by wine and a full stomach – could only sing the praises of the excellent meal Gina had prepared. It was one of the rare occasions when she surpassed herself, and also she couldn't thank Jenny enough for her earlier help, when Cele and Emily were ill.

With Andrew extolling at length the virtues of the home-made soup, pasta and *tartufo* Jenny and Paul found themselves in quiet conversation. Delighted with the results from the factory, they were in the process of discussing the merits of the new machine – brought in to create the delicate gorse design – when Gina suddenly exclaimed, 'Your sister! Jenny is your sister? But I thought she was your wife!'

Gina's voice echoed down the table in Andrew's direction. Paul and Jenny looked across the table, where Andrew laughed loudly.

'Gracious, no!' he said with a broad grin, and reached for Jenny's hand. 'Mary – my wife – is almost twice the size of Jenny!'

Flushed with embarrassment as Andrew continued to

laugh uproariously, no doubt aided by copius amounts of wine, Jenny was seriously beginning to wish she hadn't come. And for the rest of the evening she felt Gina eyeing her suspiciously whenever she and Paul were in conversation.

Aware of the atmosphere changing from one of jovial relaxation to one of hostility as the two women studied one another across the table, Paul breathed a sigh of relief when Gina left the room to make coffee. He in turn went to fetch the brandy.

Glaring at Andrew, Jenny excused herself to go to the bathroom. Instinct told her there was trouble brewing. With Andrew so reluctant to leave, she wondered how much longer they would have to remain? Halfway down the stairs Jenny heard voices from the kitchen and through the half-opened doorway saw Gina sidling up to her husband. She had already helped herself to a large brandy.

'Paul, darling,' she whispered provocatively, 'why don't you come to my bed tonight? Wouldn't it be nice to sleep with your little Gina again? After all, it has been such a long time since . . .'

Gina ran her hand up and down the inside of Paul's thigh. Feeling sickened, Jenny watched as Paul pushed Gina's hand aside and walked away. Gina's dark eyes flashed angrily, then, just as she was making a grab for Paul's arm, she caught sight of Jenny on the stairs. In a moment she stifled her look of anger and donned a simpering smile.

'Men,' she said, shrugging her shoulders. 'They never know what they want, do they?' If the smile was sweet, the underlying tone was venomous.

Jenny, desperate to leave, discovered Andrew insisting on yet another large brandy. He hadn't felt this relaxed for weeks and beneath the table he felt Gina's foot rubbing against his leg. Andrew's obvious delight and Gina's blatant attention in Andrew's direction was more than Jenny could bear. There was nothing for it but to insist she take Andrew home. As if rehearsing a school drama she announced woodenly, 'Andrew, your wife will be wondering where you are!' Looking in Paul's direction, Jenny was anxious for support. Would he take the cue?

'Why, yes, Andrew . . . aren't we supposed to be making an early start tomorrow and going to the mill to see Duncan?'

They weren't, of course, but Andrew was so confused it didn't matter. Paul's comment had the desired effect. He helped Andrew to his feet and at the same time acknowledged Jenny's grateful look of thanks.

'Your behaviour was absolutely disgraceful, Gina! What the hell were you trying to prove in there with Andrew Sinclair?' Paul loaded the dishwasher whilst Gina sat slumped at the table with a glass of brandy, sulking like a spoilt child.

'Well, at least he didn't push me away as you did!'

'You're the one who did the original pushing.'

'Me! What do you mean? I didn't push you away this evening; I asked if you wanted to come to my bed tonight.'

'Exactly!' He mimicked Gina's earlier fawning tone. 'Do you want to come to my bed, Paul? Hell! What do you think I'm made of, Gina? You turn me out of our bedroom with some feeble excuse that you sleep better on your own – you don't have that problem when you're away skiing, I gather – then ask me if I want to come to your bed like some bloody slave. Good grief, you've got a nerve!'

The truth was out at last. With the girls in the house Paul felt guilty for raising his voice, but it was no use trying to hide his feelings any more. Things had to come to a head sooner or later and it might as well be now. Gina's ongoing outrageous behaviour was purely the catalyst in their rapidly disintegrating relationship.

If Paul was going to raise his voice, Gina could surely go one better. A verbal torrent of abuse poured forth from her lips – most of which was in Italian – and seeing Paul ignore her made the situation even worse.

With an air of calm self-possession Paul merely turned and walked away, leaving Gina to yell incoherently.

'I'd save your breath if I were you, Gina,' he said softly. 'I've heard it all before anyway.'

At that moment Gina threw her empty brandy glass across the room and screamed, this time in English.

'Yes! I do want you out of our bedroom, I want you out of it for ever, that means always! Do you understand, Paul . . . *always*. You are so . . . so *boring* and I . . . I *hate* you! Did you hear me . . . *I hate you*!'

'Yes, Gina,' Paul replied in a low, soft voice, 'and I'm sorry you find me so boring, but that's possibly because I've tried to accept my responsibilities to my family, which is more than you've done in recent years. Still, that's fine by me, and at least I know where I stand. I could of course add that I find the way you've com-

119

pletely disregarded your role as wife and mother a total disgrace, but I think deep down you know that already. Anyway, if you're not happy here – which you obviously aren't – then I can only suggest you leave.'

'*Don't worry, I shall!*' she said, slamming the door and, storming upstairs, left Paul to sweep up the pieces of broken glass.

That night, none of them slept well. While Paul listened to the banging and slamming of doors until the early hours of the morning, Andrew in his inebriated sleep appeared to be constantly calling for Jean. Quite why he should be calling for his daughter, an extremely tired and irritable Mary was unable to fathom.

Alone in her tiny cottage, Jenny tossed and turned and, closing her eyes, could only relive the sordid scenario of Gina rubbing her body against Paul's like a common whore. By morning, however, Gina's bags were packed and loaded into a taxi, whereas Andrew surveyed his own – dark grey and puffy – in the bathroom mirror. There they stood out prominently, staring back at him from beneath exceedingly bloodshot eyes.

CHAPTER 14

The small green shoots Jenny tended so carefully under the apple tree had long since flowered and died, along with the golden carpets of daffodils that almost overnight heralded the arrival of spring. Only yesterday evening, preparing to leave the office for the weekend, she had noticed that people looked less grey and sombre. Instead of a huddled retreat into shadowy darkness, they strode confident and erect, taking in all nature had to offer, even in the heart of Edinburgh. It wouldn't be long before leaves unfurled completely and dappled shade concealed the castle for yet another summer.

Turning on the radio, Jenny heard a band playing 'The Bluebells of Scotland' and was instantly reminded of Morag and Hogmanay. It was one of the few occasions her mother let her hair down. The transference of thought between bluebells and hair ended with Fiona. The missing front teeth had now grown and the auburn plaits were even thicker and longer. To Cele and Emily they were still a source of fascination, and tireless attempts at creating plaits of their own were in vain.

'I can do most things for them, Jenny,' Paul had said

recently, 'but Cele's hair is far too curly and Emily's so baby-fine, it's impossible.'

'The girls,' Jenny said thoughtfully to herself. 'I wonder how they are.'

It was ages since she'd seen them, and such a pity that they'd missed Fiona's picnic. She'd promised to make it up to them, too, but there always seemed so much to occupy her now that the House of St Claire was meeting with such a positive response. Heartened by its success, she'd even succumbed to lunch with Alistair.

Too late she'd realized her mistake, as barely a week went by now without Alistair's pestering. It always began with an excuse about Sinclair's and ended with an invitation to lunch, dinner or the theatre. At the office Stevie was instructed to take most of Jenny's calls and at home she preferred to use the answerphone.

'That was "The Bluebells of Scotland" for Flora MacIntosh on her eightieth birthday,' the radio announcer said cheerily, and continued, 'Well Flora, you'll not be needing a macintosh today to go picking bluebells; there'll be blue skies and sunshine just for you on this sunny Saturday.'

'Blethers!' retorted Jenny, looking out of the kitchen window. 'Not from where I'm standing there aren't.' Still, perhaps the weather would improve as the weekend progressed. Were there bluebells out already?

Absentmindedly Jenny flicked on the answerphone to play its flashing messages, and recognized Paul's familiar soft tones.

'Jenny, it's Paul. Sorry to have missed you; I was wondering if you'd heard from Andrew. There's some-

122

thing I need to check with him urgently. Perhaps you could return my call?'

The remainder of the tape contained the usual assortment of messages. Alistair was still refusing to give up and Morag and Mary were both enquiring as to Andrew's whereabouts in New York. Like Paul, they needed to speak to him.

To Jenny the fact that Andrew hadn't rung could only mean one of two things. Either the House of St Claire was a complete unmitigated disaster, having no success at all on Fifth Avenue – or it was a roaring success, with Andrew rushed off his feet dealing with prospective customers.

Jenny hoped it was the latter and thought it a shame Paul had been unable to go, but with Gina still firmly absent from her family – and quite likely to remain so – Andrew had been confident he could cope alone. She picked up the phone.

'I'm sorry, are we early? I thought when you rang yesterday you said three o'clock.' Paul stood at the door with Celestina and Emily holding tightly on to his hands.

'I did,' said Jenny, rubbing flour from her hands. 'It's just that Andrew rang me in the wee small hours – three am to be precise – with his news. Then I just couldn't sleep and the inevitable happened. I dropped off just as dawn broke, overslept, didn't hear the alarm, and have spent the rest of the day simply trying to catch up!' She gestured to the marble slab on the table, its surface covered with flour and the trays of scones waiting to go into the oven.

'By the look of things, inviting us to tea hasn't made that task any easier for you,' Paul said apologetically.

'Nonsense,' she replied, opening the oven door. 'Believe it or not, everything's under control, and everyone will tell you I always make a mess like this when I'm baking. Mother and Miss Tandy have long since given up on me when I bake, although they say they prefer my scones to Mary's. Still,' she continued wryly, 'that's not much to my credit, is it, when Mary excels at everything else in the kitchen?'

'Ah, but could she run the House of St Claire?' asked Paul.

'I doubt it – speaking of which, great news from Andrew! Just wait till I tell you! Look, why don't you and the girls make yourself at home? They can play in the garden if they want.' Opening the back door for them, Jenny turned back to the chaos in the kitchen. 'I'll just clear up the debris here, then we can have tea. The scones will be cooked by then. I'll call you when they're ready.'

Jenny watched as Paul led the girls outside, where they peered into nooks and crannies, examining each bush and flower, until gradually they felt confident enough to leave him and ran off to peer over the wall at the far end of the garden.

'They're still painfully shy,' she remarked when he stepped back into the cosy warmth of the kitchen.

'I'm afraid so,' said Paul in a deeply concerned tone. 'Gina's behaviour hasn't exactly done wonders for their self-confidence.'

'Have you heard from her lately?'

'I've had the odd phone call and she sends the girls a

124

postcard now and then. The last one came from Canada.'

'Canada! I thought she'd gone to France. How on earth did she manage to get from France to Canada?'

'Quite easily,' replied Paul bitterly. 'She has so-called friends everywhere, and just in case you're wondering, I gather she's doing a spot of modelling along the way. Goodness knows, I couldn't support that kind of life-style.'

As Jenny turned from the oven with a tray of newly baked scones she saw that his face was full of hurt and anguish.

'I'm sorry, Jenny,' he sighed. 'I've no right to bore you with my domestic problems. Let's change the subject, shall we? Now, what's this great news from Andrew?'

Preparing the scones and filling dishes with golden yellow butter and jewel-red raspberry jam, Jenny told Paul the good news. The reason Andrew hadn't rung was because the whole St Claire range had taken the American market completely by storm. The order books were full!

'Why, that's wonderful, Jenny!' Paul said, crossing the room towards her and without thinking hugging her warmly. Suddenly aware of their bodily contact, he drew back sharply, looking first at the ceiling and then down at her face. Searching for something to say, he said simply, 'You've got flour on your nose.'

Blushing and cursing her pale skin, Jenny rubbed the flour away.

'I think you'd better call the girls in for tea,' she said quietly. 'Everything is ready.'

Cele and Emily ran in from the garden, laughing and giggling, their faces flushed with fresh air and the excitement of new-found adventures. Delighted by the change in their appearance, Jenny watched as without warning Emily suddenly became quiet and withdrawn. The petite golden-haired child whispered in her older sister's ear.

It was Cele who interpreted Emily's inaudible comments.

'Emily doesn't like jam with bits in!' she announced.

For a moment Jenny was confused. Paul was placing a spoonful of jam on Emily's scone and she looked as if she was going to cry.

'She doesn't like jam with bits in!' Cele repeated defiantly.

Jenny smiled good-humouredly. 'No, of course she doesn't. I remember now, Fiona told me. Emily is like Fiona . . . she prefers jelly to jam. Well, that's no problem, Emily. You come with me to the pantry; I've some wee pots of jelly I make especially for Fiona. You can choose one.'

Jenny walked to the pantry, closely followed by Emily, who tugged at her father's hand to come too.

'There you are – which would you prefer?' She pointed to the shelf full of jams, jellies and marmalades. 'Raspberry, bramble or blackcurrant?'

From behind Paul's back a small voice whispered, 'Raspberry, please.'

Unable to reach the top shelf, Jenny fetched a small pair of steps and, stretching towards the back of the pantry, located two small jars.

'Here you are . . . just the thing. Raspberry jelly. No bits, you see.'

At that moment a solitary ray of sunlight pierced the gloom of the pantry doorway and Jenny held the jars up to the light. Now Emily could see for herself – there were no bits. Coaxed gently by her father, she stepped forward and held out tiny expectant hands.

As she did so, dappled afternoon sunshine played on her face and her hair, casting stained glass tints from the rows of jams and jellies lining the pantry shelves. Still standing on the stool, Jenny was transfixed by the radiance and innocence of this gentle child. 'An angel,' she whispered softly beneath her breath. 'Emily is just like an angel.'

At that moment, memories of a brief visit to Paris with Cameron came flooding back. With time at a premium before they headed back to the airport, Jenny had wanted to visit La Ste-Chapelle, whereas Cameron had wanted to visit the Pompidou Centre.

'We can toss for it,' she'd suggested brightly.

'No!' Cameron had replied for fear of losing. 'We'll compromise and split the remaining time between the two.' Grabbing her hand, he'd led her in the direction of the Pompidou Centre.

Not unexpectedly, they'd spent so much time at the Pompidou Centre that there was little time for La Ste-Chapelle. Nevertheless, Jenny knew she would never forget the magnificence of the chapel with its amazing rose window and exquisite stained glass.

'You're the only person I know,' Cameron had chided on the flight home, 'who can drool over two blobs on a doorpost.'

'They weren't blobs on a doorpost, they were cherubs . . . or perhaps angels,' she'd said thoughtfully, 'keeping watch. And they were quite delightful. Besides, what about those wonderful carved saints and those columns decorated in such incredible detail? There's certainly no comparison with that and your collection of biscuit tins.'

Cameron had replied indignantly, 'The Pompidou Centre does not look like a collection of biscuit tins!'

Unaware that Paul was studying her, Jenny sighed wistfully. 'Biscuit tins and angels,' she murmured softly, and stepped backwards.

'Jenny?'

'I'm sorry, Paul, I was miles away, thinking of angels.'

'Well, if you're not careful, perched precariously on those steps you'll be one sooner than you think!' Paul held out his hand and Jenny grabbed it just as the steps tilted sideways.

What was probably only seconds seemed to Jenny like an eternity as Paul clung on to her and held her hand in his. Then with the faintest of smiles he whispered huskily, 'You know, you look quite different today. I've never seen you in jeans and sweatshirt before. You're not at all like the Miss Sinclair of our first meeting.'

Colouring at the memory of that first encounter, Jenny felt her mouth go dry. So much had happened since then, not only with the business but her own life too. Now, for the first time in ages, she felt she had a purpose in life. She was no longer Andrew Sinclair's put-upon little sister or Cameron Ross's long-suffering fiancée, she was Jennifer Sinclair . . . joint founder of the House of St Claire!

With Paul standing so close, Jenny was suddenly

conscious of the warmth of his body while his calm, dignified face studied her own. It was as if he was searching for something to say.

'Jenny, I . . .'

The moment was suddenly lost as a voice piped up, 'The jelly's really lovely and the butter is ever so yellowy, isn't it, Daddy?' Emily was tucking hungrily into the scones.

Grateful for the diversion, Jenny explained, 'That's because I buy the butter from the farm. It's a luxury I allow myself only at weekends. During the week it's low-fat spread and it's revolting. Ugh!' She pulled a face which caused Emily and Cele to burst into ripples of laughter.

Paul smiled too and, watching Jenny entertain his daughters, wondered who would have guessed that the slight, trim figure dressed in jeans and sweatshirt was also an astute businesswoman. From where he was sitting there was no reason at all for her to eat low-fat spread; still, at least it had made the girls smile.

Remembering Jenny's earlier antics, Cele and Emily continued to giggle. They'd also noticed the still faint dusting of flour on her nose. Jenny, completely oblivious to the fact, poured tea from a blue and white china teapot and passed a cup in Paul's direction.

'Thanks, Jenny. I have to say you're a tonic for us all. I'd forgotten what Sunday afternoon tea was like.'

'Then you must come again,' she insisted, 'but I'll make some more jelly first!'

'It doesn't seem right taking Fiona's jelly,' Paul said as Jenny fetched the remaining jars for the girls to take home.'

'Gracious, Fiona has more than enough, and I'll soon be going to Conasg to pick raspberries. Mother keeps us all well supplied with soft fruits thanks to Hamish.'

'Hamish?' Paul enquired.

'Oh, Hamish is like Miss Tandy: he's been with the Sinclairs for years. And very proud of his fruit and vegetable garden is Hamish, which is just as well, as Mother has such fixed ideas about serving only seasonal fruits and vegetables at Conasg.'

Paul stared in disbelief. 'You mean absolutely no tins and frozen food?'

'Let's just say Tandy sneaks in the occasional tin and packet when Mother isn't looking or when the weather is really bad. Which according to Mary is all the time. She's convinced it always rains on the west coast and often wonders how Hamish can grow anything at all.'

'He's obviously a miracle-worker, then,' Paul teased.

'Not exactly, more like Noah protecting his flock – or in this case fruit and vegetables – from the flood.'

'They sound quite an interesting trio, the residents of Conasg House.'

'They are. You must meet them some time.'

Paul laughed. 'I don't think I'm quite ready for that, and in the meantime I must remember to look for jam without bits when I'm shopping. Come along, girls, time to go.'

'I was thinking,' said Jenny, passing the tiny jars of jelly to Paul for safekeeping. 'Life's a bit like that, really.'

Puzzled by her statement, he listened intently as she explained.

'Well, if you think about it life's sometimes clear and

smooth – just like the raspberry jelly. Then at other times it can be really fruitful, offering the occasional whole strawberry, like the House of St Claire.'

'And what about marmalade?' enquired Paul, continuing the theme.

'Marmalade?'

'Marmalade can be pretty bitter, lumpy and unpleasant at times.'

'In that case,' she replied thoughtfully, 'we just have to discard it and find something to take away the unpleasant taste it leaves behind.'

Paul nodded. 'I think perhaps you're right, and I shan't ever view all those jars on the supermarket shelves in the same light again.'

His eyes met hers as two smiling faces gazed up at her adoringly. Jenny took the girls' hands and walked with them to the front gate. There, kissing them both goodbye, she watched Cele run to the car. Emily meanwhile remained behind, and Jenny kissed her again. Fixed firmly by her father's side, she studied Jenny carefully.

'Aren't you,' she faltered, 'going to kiss my Daddy goodbye?'

'I . . . er . . .' Jenny hesitated just as Paul bent forward to save her further embarrassment and brushed his lips gently against her cheek.

'Goodbye, Jenny, and thank you. It's been a truly wonderful afternoon.'

CHAPTER 15

Mary replaced the receiver triumphantly. Shona Munro had just phoned with good news: their recent charity lunch was featured most favourably in the latest edition of the *Edinburgh Review*. Locating the page, Mary was delighted; such prominent publicity was good for her committee. All year the Arisaid Ladies had worked tirelessly for charities they supported, and last month's event had been a tremendous success.

As present chairman, Mary was determined her achievements would excel over even those of her predecessor. She knew Shona didn't mind; they had been friends for too long to worry about things like that. Their main purpose was to raise as much money as possible and turn a deaf ear to the folk who referred to them as 'just a bunch of do-gooders with little else to do'.

Studying each photo and caption in detail, Mary was reassured. The young journalist had kept her promise after all. She had tremendous admiration for Mary's committee, her own brother having had a drug problem himself. In fact he'd been one of the first to be helped by the rehabilitation unit funded by the 'Arrys', as Mary called her ladies.

True to her word, the young woman had produced a long, well-informed article and Mary couldn't wait to show Andrew on his return. There were photos not only of the Procurator Fiscal and other local dignitaries attending the church service before lunch, but also the presentation of the cheque and a later ceremony at the garden party. Everything had gone so smoothly, the weather had been perfect, not a cloud in the sky – and the food was the best salmon and soft fruits Scotland could offer.

The following week, still basking in the success of the day, Mary held her own, personal lunch for the committee. It was to be her gesture of thanks to the 'Arrys' and also her chance to show off the new range of St Claire linen. If Andrew had been to America acting as ambassador to the House of St Claire, why couldn't she do the same at home?

The white tablecloths and napkins edged with the gorse motif in yellow and green were much admired. Such a refreshing change from the ubiquitous thistle, they all agreed, and so perfect for summer.

'I think it's a delightful emblem,' said Shona, 'and so right for this time of year. Andrew must be very pleased for Sinclair's.'

'Oh, yes, thrilled,' replied Mary, 'especially as the Christmas range seems to be exciting interest in the States.'

'Will you be using the same designs for Christmas?'

'Not exactly; the gorse design will remain, but the general idea is to promote green for the grouse-shooting season and red – naturally – for winter and Christmas. The usual Sinclair colours really.'

'How wonderful,' Shona added cheerfully. 'Then I shall have to twist Donald's arm for a new set of linen this Christmas. The Munro and Sinclair tartans are very similar, after all.'

'You'd better not let Donald hear you say that! And . . .' joked Mary, 'don't forget we have our connections with the Comte de St Claire!'

Shona smiled good-humouredly. 'Mary Sinclair, are you not forgetting the Munro connections with the Swedish court and Charles I!' She turned to the 'Arrys', who were always amused by the good-natured banter between the two women, and delivered her piece of history.

'In 1626,' Shona began, 'Robert Munro, the eighteenth chief, joined the army of Gustavus Adolphus in Sweden and in 1634 his brother Hector was created a Baronet of Nova Scotia by Charles I. Now how's that for regal connections?'

The idea of Andrew as a count and Donald as a baronet was the cause of much merriment among the committee. And if the truth were told, they'd probably drunk too much of Andrew's fine wine. But, as Mary reflected later, they deserved it for all their hard work. The 'Arrys' had handed over a five-figure cheque and on a more personal level Mary's luncheon had indirectly promoted the House of St Claire. She couldn't wait to tell Andrew when he came home from his first day back at the office.

On the desk in Andrew's office lay the pile of contracts from America plus the usual publicity blurb gathered along the way. It was amazing how many papers you could collect in a week. They would have to be sorted before he went home this evening. He'd promised Mary he would take her to the theatre and leave the House of St Claire at the office for once. That wasn't going to be easy, as there was still so much to finalize. Winning American contracts was one thing; now Sinclair's must meet the required deadlines.

'You promise you won't let me down,' Sol Sutherland had said to Andrew during brunch in New York. 'If I give you these orders for Saint Clara, you will personally see to it that they're delivered on time, Andy?'

'You have my word on it, Sol. I will see to it personally, but at Sinclair's you'll find we're all involved with the House of *St Claire*.'

Andrew placed special emphasis on the St Claire but to no avail; Sol still insisted on referring to the company as Saint Clara! Not to worry, thought Andrew; the contracts were all that mattered.

'Well,' drawled Sol as the waitress placed a huge plate of steak, eggs, hash browns and grits on the table before him, 'I'm glad you're all involved — even old Morag — but in the States we expect commitment too.'

'Isn't that the same?' Andrew enquired.

Sol surveyed the plate of brunch. 'Not from where I'm sitting, it ain't.'

Andrew, puzzled by Sol's remark, waited for explanation.

'See that plate of steak and eggs?' Sol picked up his knife and stabbed at an egg. The golden orb of yolk split open, sending a stream of yellow in the direction of the steak. 'Well, I'd say the chicken was involved but that

Aberdeen Angus,' continued Sol, 'sure as hell was well and truly committed!'

Andrew laughed. Sol Sutherland, a short, balding man in his mid-sixties, was Andrew's main business contact in New York. Son of a Scottish immigrant father and Jewish mother, he had an uncanny head for business. He was convinced the Americans were just ready for Saint Clara. They loved all things Scottish, didn't they? Why, just look at the success Ralph Lauren had had when he'd produced an autumn collection heavily influenced by the heather and the tartan.

Sol was proud of his Scottish connections and made regular trips to Scotland for the Clan Sutherland Society. It was during one of these visits many years ago that he'd first met William Sinclair. Andrew had only just joined the business, and in him Sol had recognized the determination to succeed, that same determination Sol had himself possessed during his youth.

When William Sinclair had died, Sol felt he'd lost a member of his own family, and Andrew, he considered, was almost like a son, albeit a long-distance one. Following William's funeral Sol determined to keep a watch on Andrew and Sinclair's. After all, there was nothing wrong with watching over your 'family' and keeping your eyes open for business opportunities too.

Andrew placed the contracts in the safe and took one last look at the photos Sol had sent him. They were taken at the House of St Claire stand, where, largely thanks to the kindly American, Sinclair's had one of the prime positions.

There had been the usual displays of Highland

produce, shortbread, smoked salmon and preserves – all superior quality but nevertheless looking pretty tired and jaded by comparison with the House of St Claire. Only one other equalled Sinclair's, thought Andrew, and that was the display from a Skye whisky distillery. There, in the midst of Fifth Avenue, a miniature of the Isle of Skye had been recreated.

Thousands of miles away from home, Andrew had viewed the replica of the Cuillins with emotion and become suddenly homesick. The white-capped peaks shrouded by swirling mists left no one in doubt as to why Skye was called 'The Misty Isle'. They'd even managed to add running water to run through mock valleys and pine woods. All probably made from polystyrene, but Andrew nevertheless insisted on taking photos to show Jenny. The idea behind the whisky display was almost as good as Paul's.

Paul! Was there time to ring him before leaving the office? Possibly not now, not if he wanted to get to the theatre on time. Whatever happened, he mustn't let Mary down.

Andrew dropped the pile of photos on Jenny's desk and left the office. It was only on the journey home that he remembered the one he'd meant to destroy. Remembering it again during the interval, he turned to his wife.

'Mary . . . about the British Week in Geneva – I've been thinking . . .'

'Oh, Andrew! You're barely home five minutes and you talk of going away again!'

'No that's just it, I'm not. Anyway, the Geneva trip isn't until the autumn.'

'Then why discuss it now?' Mary said tersely.

'I thought Jenny could go – she could represent Sinclair's. She worked there for a year before university, didn't she? At least she can speak the language, which is more than I can. Pidgin French is OK if you're on holiday but business-wise I'm not much good.'

'Well, you could always do what you tell the children when they say they can't do something.'

'Namely?'

'Borrow a book or tape from the library or go to evening classes!'

'Gracious, Mary! Don't you think I've enough to do already? You're always complaining that I spend too much time at the office as it is.'

'So I do, Andrew, but I'm only teasing, my dear. And I think it would be perfect to send Jenny. After all, she still has friends in Geneva, and although she hasn't seem them in ages, I know they still keep in contact by letter. Perhaps Paul could go too, as he missed out on the American trip?'

'Sounds even better,' Andrew replied. 'I'll discuss it with Jenny later.'

'Shhh,' Mary whispered kindly, 'the curtain's going up.'

'Jenny, I want you to go to the British Week in Geneva.'

'*What*?'

'I want you to go . . .'

'I heard you the first time, Andrew; it's just that I thought perhaps you might be joking.'

'Never been more serious. You speak the language, know the city, you've even got friends there. What's the

138

name of the girl married to that scientist-boffin laddie?

'You mean Moira – Moira MacCulloch, at least she was until she married Helmut, and for your information he's a physicist.'

'That's it – Moira!' Andrew said chirpily. 'You still write to her, don't you?'

'Well, yes.'

'Good, that's settled, then, you can go and stay with her.'

'Just a minute, Andrew. Moira might be my friend but I can't impose myself on her just like that after all these years. I shall be going out to work and for that I shall need a decent hotel room, not a flat seething with children and a mad scientist!'

'I thought you said he was a physicist,' Andrew teased. 'OK, pick yourself a decent hotel, and don't forget to tell Paul so he can give Gina the details . . . in case she needs to contact him.'

'What's this all to do with Paul and Gina . . . I thought she left ages ago.'

'She did, but apparently she wants to spend some time with the children. She's coming home for a while, so it means Paul can come with you to Geneva. It's really quite convenient when you think of it.'

Jenny did not want to think of it, not at all! When had Gina reappeared? Paul certainly hadn't mentioned it, but then she'd seen so little of him recently. Was that because he and Gina were now reconciled?

Some weeks later, hunting for her passport and Moira's telephone number, Jenny felt a sickening in her stomach. What did Paul think of the whole idea? And why

139

hadn't he rung, if, as Andrew said, everything was arranged? It could mean, she thought anxiously, that if Paul and Gina were together again then he probably wouldn't want to leave her and go to Geneva.

Jenny found the prospect of going away with someone else's husband daunting. What would people think? Andrew had no right, no right at all!

'Kline – Helmut Kline, K - L - I - N - E, Rue de la Prulay,' Jenny shouted down the receiver. The line was appalling. What had happened to Swiss efficiency? '*Non, pas comme ça – K comme Kilo, L comme Léo, I comme Isodore, N –* . . . *Oui, c'est ça.* At last! Moira, it's Jenny.'

'Why do they always have to mess about with people's numbers?' she asked aloud, entering Moira's new number in her address book and slamming the desk drawer shut. Jenny sighed. It wasn't the telephone exchange that had provoked her tetchiness, it was her conversation with Moira. It only served to remind her what she knew already. It wasn't anger she felt . . . it was jealousy!

CHAPTER 16

Paul looked anxiously in Jenny's direction. She'd been strangely quiet from the moment they checked in, yet Andrew had assured him repeatedly that she'd raised no objections to his presence on this trip. In fact she'd even endorsed it – according to Andrew – by saying that, as the creator of the House of St Claire, Paul should proclaim it loudly to the Swiss at every opportunity.

Somehow Paul wasn't convinced, and he discerned a distinct atmosphere as he and Jenny sat side by side on the aircraft, not helped by the fact that they appeared to be wedged in their seats by an overlarge women in the aisle seat. Paul turned to Jenny and whispered, 'Perhaps we can persuade her to move and give us some more room as the plane's only half full . . .'

No sooner had the words been spoken than an airport bus pulled up alongside the plane and hurriedly deposited a delegation of Japanese. Delayed by their connecting flight, they were en route for the United Nations in Geneva. Jenny groaned as cameras and duty-free bags were stashed away in every available inch of space and every seat was filled.

What Paul presumed to be sixteen stone of beached whale by his side flopped back heavily in her seat, propelling him sideways on to Jenny's shoulder. At the proximity of his touch, Jenny started like a terrified animal. Unable to meet his gaze, she turned to look from the window. Grateful for the distraction of lights blinking on the runway, she stared thoughtfully as the airport slipped further and further away and the plane rose higher into the cold October night sky.

'Are you sure you're not scared of flying?' Paul asked, remembering the earlier look of terror in her eyes.

'No, it's ships and the sea that terrify me more.' Her reply was abrupt and the significance of her statement lost on him completely. She couldn't expect Paul to know that Cameron had lost two of his best friends at sea in a freak naval accident; only a miracle had saved Cameron himself.

Paul sat in silence, convinced that he'd upset her, wondering what on earth he could say that wouldn't upset her more. Running his fingers through his hair, he was anxious to find the cause – but the problem was how? Now was definitely not the right time.

Like a video rewinding in his mind, Paul played back Jenny's last sentence, something about ships and the sea . . . Realization dawned. Ships and the sea could only mean one thing – Cameron Ross, Jenny's ex-fiancé.

Paul knew little of Cameron, other than that he was an officer in the navy, and he and Jenny had been together for six years. And quite how their engagement had ended so abruptly was still a mystery. It wasn't in

Paul's nature to ask, either. He knew what it was like having to cope with people prying into one's private life all the while.

Coping was one thing Paul excelled at. He'd had experience of that in vast quantities, particularly following Gina's last turbulent exit from his life. Now she was back he was fed up with the day-to-day uncertainties and the constant speculation of friends as to whether or not they would get back together. For the moment he'd agreed to Gina's moving back, solely for Cele and Emily's sake. But on his return, Gina had assured him, she would be moving into a flat of her own. Quite where, Paul had no idea.

'*Le Grand Passage, s'il vous plaît,*' Jenny called to the taxi driver. Paul climbed in beside her and the taxi wove its way through the maze of early morning rush-hour traffic.

'So this is Geneva,' he said. 'I thought the traffic in Edinburgh was chaotic, but this is horrendous!'

Cars tooted their horns and there was much gesticulation of arms as the taxi driver – oblivious to his fellow road-users – deviated from lane to lane across the bridge.

'That was the Pont du Mont Blanc,' Jenny informed Paul, 'just in case you were wondering.'

Paul noticed the grin on her face as he grabbed for the strap to stop himself sliding off the seat. He was relieved to see Jenny looking more relaxed. At breakfast there was no sign of the anxious woman he'd had as travelling companion the previous evening. Instead there was the old Jenny Sinclair, businesslike and efficient, all ready to go. Orange juice, coffee and croissant were hurriedly dispensed with and the next thing he knew she was hailing the taxi to the department store.

'*Mademoiselle Sinclair, bienvenue à Genève.* I trust your stay will be a happy and successful one. I think you will find we have everything in order for the House of St Claire.'

'I hope so, M. Arnaud. My brother had tremendous success at the British Fair in New York and I am hoping to return home with similar results.'

'You can be sure at Le Grand Passage we will not let you down, Mademoiselle Sinclair. Come, I will show you. *Suivez-moi, s'il vous plaît.*'

Guy Arnaud led the way, closely followed by Paul and Jenny. Large posters proclaimed British Week and Union Jacks hung everywhere. On the third floor they even came face to face with a red London bus!

'How on earth . . .?' Paul asked wide-eyed.

'That is our secret, M. Hadley,' said Guy Arnaud, smiling.

Paul couldn't believe his eyes. Wherever he looked there were pockets of the British Isles stretching from the West Country to the north of Scotland and the Shetland Isles. In the cool of the food hall, traditional cheeses, bacon and sausages sat temptingly on marble slabs, while a chubby, rosy-faced man in striped apron and straw boater balanced jars of Marmite and Oxo cubes.

'Goodness,' remarked Paul. 'I remember seeing a chap just like that when I was a lad. They don't make them like that any more, do they?'

'No', replied Jenny, 'not unless you're lucky enough to live in a village with its own family butcher. Here I

144

think you'll find it's pure nostalgia, and in case you're wondering, pork sausages, bacon, Marmite, Oxo cubes and last but not least Cadbury's chocolate were the most requested items among ex-pats when I lived here.'

'You're joking?'

'No, absolutely serious,' Jenny continued. 'If anyone wanted to come and stay with us, that was their entry permit to the flat. You always knew if someone had visitors from home. I can remember it even now. The smell of sizzling sausages and bacon, how it used to make our mouths water!' Jenny was beginning to wish she'd had more than the croissant for breakfast, with all this talk of food. She moved quickly on. Paul meanwhile noticed the Cadbury's stand and smiled.

The muted sound of bagpipes heralded their arrival in Scotland, or at least the equivalent of. As expected, there was a plethora of tartan and thistles, just as Paul had predicted. The whisky distilleries were there, just as they had been in New York, and there in all its splendour was the House of St Claire.

Borrowing a few ideas from the Isle of Skye display, Andrew had commissioned a studio to replicate scenes from Scottish life through the seasons. The result was a delightful tableau showing to full advantage every range of St Claire merchandise. And against a backcloth of misty mountains and purple heather hung the shield of St Claire.

Jenny stopped and stared. A lump rose in her throat and she wanted to cry. She remembered Paul's original folder and his so-called rough sketch. In recent months she'd witnessed the transformation of the St Claire range coming straight from the production line; she'd also seen Andrew's photos from New York. But some-how this was different; this was special. Months ago Mother had described the House of St Claire as 'Jenny's baby'. Was this what giving birth felt like? Jenny wondered.

In a moment all the pain, frustration and anxieties of the past year appeared to float into the mists as Jenny surveyed her 'child'. No birth could have taken place in a more enchanting setting. Paul took a clean white handkerchief from his pocket.

'Here,' he said gently, 'I think you've something in your eye.'

Jenny blinked and turned towards him, 'I'm sorry,' she said, 'you must think I'm being terribly silly. I had no idea it could look so perfect.'

Paul wiped her eyes. 'You're not silly at all, Jenny, in fact you're quite lovely.'

Pressing the button marked *'troisième étage'*, Jenny felt the lift surge and groan on its way. Years ago, when still a student, she'd lived here in the same appartment block with Moira. Then the flats had appeared modern and new; now they seemed dated and shabby. The familiar smell of French cigarettes permeated the lift shaft and memories of her earlier arrival came flooding back. Moira, who was working at the time as a secretary for CERN (the European Organisation for Nuclear Research), had rung Jenny excitedly.

'Jenny, I know you're looking for something for your year out – why don't you come to Geneva? I've just seen a notice on the board . . . an American couple looking for a mother's help. Do you want me to ring them?'

At the time the conversation had been extremely one-sided. Moira would see to everything; she knew a colleague of the American physicist's and as for work permits, they could worry about that later. 'Just get yourself over here,' Moira had insisted, and Jenny had duly obeyed.

That was years ago, before university, before Cameron, before everything. . . Jenny rang the doorbell and waited.

'Jenny! Just look at you! Och, you look gorgeous, you haven't changed a bit!' Moira flung her arms around her wildly and although enveloped in her friend's embrace, Jenny knew she couldn't say the same of Moira. Her friend had developed a considerable amount of padding since they'd last met, presumably not helped by the birth of three children in rapid succession.

Released from Moira's arms, Jenny handed over her parcel. Howls of delight burst forth as Moira unwrapped bacon, sausages and chocolate.

'You remembered,' sighed Moira in gratitude. 'Just like the old times.'

'How could I forget?' Jenny added, 'I thought I'd be refused entry otherwise. I was only saying to Paul . . .'

'Oh, yes, Paul – where is he?' Moira enquired, peering into the corridor. 'I thought you were going to bring him?'

'He said he didn't want to intrude,' explained Jenny, 'but I expect he was just being polite – the prospect of two women chattering all night about the good old days. Anyway, he wanted to ring his children.'

'He's married, then?'

'You could say that!' came the sardonic reply. Jenny regarded the large open-plan living-room. 'It's very quiet, Moira – aren't the children here?'

'No, children's gymnastics class. Helmut's just gone to fetch them.'

'How is Helmut?'

Moira's face shone. 'Just the same; I still adore him. He's still my gentle giant, Jenny, despite what people said when we first got married.'

Jenny remembered the atmosphere of abject disapproval in the small Scottish community when Moira MacCulloch announced she was to marry a foreigner!

'They're just a load of contemptuous old bigots!' Moira had announced tearfully. 'Anyway, it doesn't matter, we're going to stay in Geneva after we're married. At least there we won't be treated like outcasts!'

Geneva boasted a true cosmopolitan society where nationalities lived and worked alongside each other without fear of disapproval. They even boasted a Scottish society of ex-pats who welcomed Helmut with open arms. Helmut with his red hair and red beard could have stepped straight from the pages of Rob Roy. A true Highlander if ever there was one, he proudly lived up to the MacCulloch name – Son of the Boar. It was just a pity Moira's parents were never to witness their son-in-law's transformation from German to Scot.

Through the closed door Moira recognized the familiar noise as the lift stirred into life.

'Some day I expect that lift to give up the ghost

completely; I just hope I'm not in it when it does. Helmut keeps telling the *concierge*, who in turn tells the *régie*, but as usual nothing happens. The only thing they're good at is increasing the rent!'

'I did notice it all looks a bit seedy in the foyer,' Jenny remarked. 'Not at all like it used to be when M and Mme Sablon were in charge.'

'Ah, yes, dear Mme Sablon – she was a wee sweetie, wasn't she? Such a funny wee soul too; do you remember how she used to let us use the laundry room when it wasn't even our turn? Can you imagine, we only have the use of the laundry room once a fortnight now? Thank goodness we have our own washing machine here . . . an absolute necessity with my wee clan.'

As if on cue, two sandy-haired boys tumbled through the door and a flaxen-haired girl sat cradled in her father's arms.

'Jenny! Why, it is good to see you again,' said Helmut in his low, soft voice. 'You are looking well, I think. Why have you left it so long to come and see us?'

'Pressure of work, I'm afraid, Helmut. Although now I'm back here I wish I hadn't left it so long.'

'Ah, but it is much changed. There is now a drug problem in town and the graffiti . . . I expect you noticed?'

Jenny had, but wasn't it a sign of the times? What city didn't have problems with either drugs or graffiti these days?

The boys, rushing past Jenny to the kitchen for a drink, called loudly, 'Gosh, sausages and bacon, Dad, and chocolate!'

At the mention of chocolate the small girl wriggled down from her father's arms and ran to the kitchen.

'Two squares each,' Moira commanded fiercely.

Presently the youngest boy came in crying. 'It's not fair, Will's had more than me! He always has more than me!'

'Blethers!' Moira cried. 'If you're going to fight over the chocolate, I'll lock it away and you won't have anything.'

'I think you're all missing your manners,' Helmut said sternly, hearing Will groan. 'How about coming to introduce yourself to our guest and saying thank you for the chocolate?'

The three children stood sheepishly in front of Jenny and recited in unison, 'Thank you very much for the chocolate.'

'There, that's better. Now, Jenny, may I present to you my three bairns?'

Jenny bit her lip, trying not to smile, as Helmut introduced each child in turn, instructing them to shake hands with their guest.

Wilhelm-Duncan, Johann-Angus and Gisela-Morag, duly introduced, disappeared down the corridor, where Helmut was running their bath.

'I know,' said Moira smiling, reading Jenny's mind, 'it's quite a mouthful to remember, isn't it? In fact Helmut and I almost came to blows over their names.'

Jenny heard a frantic sound of splashing coming from the bathroom as Moira continued.

'I wanted German names and Helmut wanted Scottish. We ended up with Will, Joe and Gila. I suppose you could say it was a compromise of sorts.'

'I want Jenny to bath me,' came a small voice from the bathroom. Jenny took off her jacket.

'Hang on a minute! I'd better give you something of mine to change into.' Walking to her bedroom, Moira warned wryly, 'It's worse than a wet day on Glencoe in there when they're on form!'

CHAPTER 17

At the hotel Paul sat alone. He'd rung Gina, who'd been extremely civil, and in turn spoken to both Celestina and Emily. Later he telephoned Andrew with the day's progress report and even suggested they take on more staff to deal with increased orders. Andrew was delighted, not only with the day's success but also with the prospect of helping the Scottish job market – if only in a minor way. He remembered his father telling him years ago, 'No matter what you achieve, Andrew, or however high you climb in this life, never forget your staff . . . they are the life-force of a company. Look after them and you can attain great heights; treat them badly and you'll rue the day you were born, laddie.'

Andrew drummed his fingers on the desk. Unemployment figures were high at the moment and only today he'd heard of another firm laying off staff. With only three months to Christmas, redundancy couldn't happen at a worse time. He would, he determined, ring the agencies tomorrow.

* * *

'I rang Andrew and he wants you to give some thought to guest lists for the Christmas party,' Paul told Jenny. 'That's if you have the time.'

The mere mention of Christmas filled Paul with horror. Last year's had been such an unmitigated disaster that he didn't even want to think about this one. Besides, in three months an awful lot could happen.

'You're joking,' cried Jenny. 'Just look at this paperwork! We've two more days at Grand Passage then I shall have to make sure everything is dismantled and shipped safely back to Edinburgh.'

'You'll have your work cut out for you there,' Paul said wryly. 'I wasn't aware there was a shipping route out of Geneva.'

Jenny laughed. 'Don't be so pedantic or I might get my own back!'

'Meaning?'

'Meaning I might take you to the Cochon d'Or and make you eat frog's legs and snails!'

'You wouldn't dare!' said Paul, his face creasing into a smile.

'No, you're right, I wouldn't. I think it's a disgusting practice. I'll take you for a *raclette* instead and show you some of my old haunts. We'll have to get through Friday and Saturday first and the way I feel at the moment, I'm asleep on my feet already. If you don't mind I'll say *bonsoir*.'

Paul watched her walk to the reception to collect her key. What on earth was a *raclette*? And what animal did it come from?

At the end of the week walking across the Pont du

Mont Blanc to the old town, Paul repeated his question aloud.

Jenny laughed. 'Wait and see, although – I'll give you a clue – it's not related to the haggis!'

'Come on, Jenny! You don't expect me to believe the yarn about the "wee haggis with his hairy wee legs running aboot the misty glens". You're talking to a fellow Scot, remember.'

Jenny stopped in her tracks.

'What's the matter? Was it something I said?'

'No, your Dr Finlay impersonation was perfect. It's the Cochon d'Or. It's gone! It's not there any more!'

They found another restaurant but to Jenny it wasn't the same. Paul however, enjoyed the novelty of watching slices of cheese melting on the *raclette* machine.

'The girls would love this and think it great fun,' he said, scraping the cheese on to his plate to have with hot skinned potatoes and pickles.

'Then we must look for a portable machine to take home,' she replied.

After the warmth of the restaurant the cold night air caught them by surprise. Without thinking Jenny huddled close against Paul's side.

'It must be the Bise,' she said, taking his arm. 'It's a north wind and cuts right through you. The only cure for that is a *chocolat danoise*. Come on, I'll race you back to the hotel for one; it's too cold to walk round the lake now.'

Paul watched as she scooped up spoonfuls of chocolate-laced whipped cream, below which was a steaming cup of hot chocolate.

'I don't know how you can, Jenny, not after all that *raclette* and flan.'

'You should try it. It's just the thing to beat the cold.' She held the spoon in his direction.

Paul leaned forward and, holding her hand to steady the spoon, opened his mouth. Their eyes met and Jenny drew back. 'Perhaps not,' she said, 'you'd probably find it too sickly; best stick to your coffee.'

Walking Jenny to her room, Paul realized this was to be their last night in Geneva. Tomorrow it would be back to Edinburgh and . . . what? Gina being charming with her obsequious grin or Gina the snarling tigress, pacing the floor like a caged animal. Neither prospect appealed to him. He turned to look at Jenny who, relaxed by the local wine, was chattering excitedly about the success of St Claire and still extolling the virtues of *chocolat danoise* on such a cold night.

With Jenny by his side the last thing Paul felt was cold. Struggling to keep his tone casual, he thanked her for the *raclette* and arranged a time for breakfast. Then, watching her take the key-card for her room from her pocket, could contain himself no longer. He had to say something . . . do something. With his subconscious opting for the latter, Paul reached forward and drew Jenny into his arms.

'Oh, Jenny, my dear sweet Jenny,' he murmured as his lips found hers.

Swept into his embrace, Jenny found herself curiously unresisting. The moment was so predictable. It was why she'd been wary of this trip, why she'd not taken him to see Moira and why she'd avoided being alone with him. Even during the meal their body language had said it all.

Now, alarmed by the situation, she was helpless. She didn't know what to do. Her heart said one thing, her conscience another. Her mind was in turmoil and Paul was talking softly . . . but what was he saying? Something about the week being wonderful and going back to Edinburgh. Going back to Edinburgh . . . but that was tomorrow!

'Jenny,' Paul whispered, stroking her hair as he held her close, 'when we get back to Scotland can we . . . I mean . . . would it be all right if we . . . Gina told me . . .?'

Gina! From the wonderful sense of wellbeing locked in Paul's embrace, Jenny felt panic rise inexorably inside her. In her mind's eye she saw Gina Hadley on the night she and Andrew had gone to dinner. Saw scarlet fingernails encircling Paul's inner thigh, dark curls tossed in Andrew's direction and, last but not least, dark eyes flashing at her suspiciously. Jenny shuddered and pulled away from Paul's arms.

Seeing the shuttered look on her face, Paul asked anxiously, 'Jenny? What's wrong . . . what is it? I thought we . . .'

'So did I, Paul,' she sighed wearily, 'but aren't you forgetting something – Gina?'

'How could I forget Gina?' Paul said bitterly. 'But that's what I'd started to tell you. Gina's moving out when I get back to Edinburgh. She says she's moving into a flat.'

Nervously Jenny flicked her thumbnail against the key-card in her hand. 'It's not that simple, though, Paul

. . . she's still your wife, and there's the girls too, of course.'

'But Celestina and Emily adore you! You've only got to see the way they look at you. They'd be delighted if you and I saw more of one another.'

'Exactly,' Jenny replied lamely, 'and can you imagine Gina's reaction to that? Goodness I can still hear her outburst on the phone when the girls had chicken pox, and the way she looked at me when she realized I wasn't Andrew's wife. Why, even you said only the other day how unpredictable she is. I'm sorry, Paul, I can't . . . risk putting the House of St Claire in jeopardy.'

Jenny turned away sadly, only to feel Paul's hands forcefully on her shoulders. 'The House of St Claire – is that all that matters to you? Is it . . .?'

Compelled to look up into his face, Jenny noticed that his eyes had changed from being loving and warm to a cold, steely blue. Then with a sigh his arms fell dejectedly to his side and she was released from his grasp.

'You haven't answered my question,' he whispered.

Moving away, Jenny slipped her key-card into the door. Her hands were trembling and the lock wouldn't turn. Silently Paul stepped forward and opened it for her. She nodded and stood hesitating in the doorawy.

'Paul.' Her voice was barely audible. 'It's been a lovely evening and I have enjoyed working with you this week but I really feel we need to discuss our feelings if we . . .'

'Do we really need to discuss them? Don't you think we already know how we feel? Surely you must know how much I've wanted you these past months? I thought you felt the same.'

She lowered her eyes unable to look at him. 'Yes,' she whispered, 'I know, but as I've already said, it's not that simple, is it?'

'It is from where I'm standing,' said Paul, 'and if you really want to discuss the situation – our situation – then isn't it best we discuss it inside and not out here in the hotel corridor?' Reaching for her again, Paul cupped her face in his hands. 'Jenny?' he questioned.

There were tears in her eyes as she turned back towards the door.

'Please understand,' she begged, 'or at least try to. I can't ask you in, even if I want to. You're still married to Gina and I'm . . .'

Staring blankly through tear-filled eyes, Jenny saw not Paul but Cameron. Cameron with his mocking eyes and scathing retort.

'You're what, Jenny?' Paul urged kindly.

'I,' she said, her voice faltering to a soft whisper, 'according to my ex-fiancé, am married to Sinclair's.'

'Of course you're not,' he remonstrated, 'you're just . . .' He got no further; his words, he realized, had fallen against a closing door.

Aware of his murmured goodnight beyond the locked door, Jenny sought sanctuary in her lonely hotel room. It would be so easy to call him back but there was no denying where that would end. Moments ago it was what they both wanted and for any other couple it would have been so easy to walk into this room, with its romantic setting of satin and lace, and declare their love. Only they weren't any other couple, were they? Like the lyrics from the song, they were 'lost and alone'. Paul lost in a loveless marriage with Gina, and Jenny alone, still mourning the loss of six years of her life spent with Cameron.

A feeling of complete and utter desolation swept over her. She needed someone to talk to, someone to confide in. The trouble was she was hundreds of miles from home and even there who could she turn to? Morag and Mary were family, Stevie too closely connected to Sinclair's and, following her engagement, Cameron had discouraged her from keeping in contact with her university friends.

'Besides,' she said tearfully looking at her watch, 'it's half-past midnight. I can't ring anyone at this time of night, can I?' The phone sat temptingly on the side table. Jenny dialled and waited.

'Hello?' a voice answered sleepily.

'Moira, it's Jenny. I'm sorry . . . I need to talk to someone . . .'

Moira sat on the bed cradling Jenny in her arms like a child, trying to decipher through the deep sobs the reason behind the phone call.

'It's all right, Jenny,' she murmured, stroking her hair, 'you go ahead and have a jolly good cry.'

'But Helmut and the children . . .?' came the muffled voice.

'Och, don't you worry about Helmut and the children. Once my family are in bed they don't sleep like logs, they sleep like Scots pine!'

Jenny smiled through her tears and sat up.

159

'I'm sorry, I've made your shoulder all wet. Let me get you a towel.'

'Don't bother with a towel, but if that wonderful state-of-the-art object just happens to be a hairdrier, I'd be grateful for that.'

Jenny watched in amazement as Moira directed a warm blast from the hairdrier on to her sodden shoulder.

'You see,' she said, 'works a treat every time!'

'Wherever did you get such an innovative idea?'

'Jenny, my dear, when you've had three children in rapid succession, you invent all sorts of tricks. Otherwise you'd be changing your clothes umpteen times a day. Now, as I managed to get past the night porter and into these opulent surroundings dressed like a Michelin man, am I to be allowed to stay a little longer? Do you still want to talk and tell me what's the problem? Or should I change that to *who* is the problem?'

'The problem,' said Jenny, watching Moira remove her padded ski suit to reveal red and white spotted pyjamas, 'is that I think I'm in love with Paul and I'm totally racked with guilt for feeling the way I do. I shouldn't be in love with Paul, should I? I mean, he's married, and after Cameron I don't know if I . . .'

Replacing the hairdrier, Moira reached for a box of tissues and patted the luxurious satin quilt. 'Come on,' she said kindly. 'Tell me all about it.'

Just as they had in their earlier Geneva days, the two women sat snuggled beneath a duvet, munching chocolate and pouring out their souls. The only difference now was that Moira did the munching and listening, while Jenny did the talking. Moira, perceptive as ever, listened intently and then turned to her friend.

'I'm not going to tell you what to do, Jenny, and I expect you're sick to the back teeth of people telling you you'll soon get over Cameron.'

'But I really thought I loved him,' Jenny replied wistfully. 'Only now I'm not so sure.'

Moira placed a comforting arm around Jenny's slim shoulders. 'The trouble is, everyone has a different perception of the word "love". I adore Helmut – even after all these years – love him to my very soul, in fact, and if he even has to go away on a convention I hate it. When we're together it's magic and when we're apart it's gut-wrenching. God knows what I'd do if he ever walked out of my life.'

Moira cast an anxious sideways look in Jenny's direction. 'Gosh, I'm sorry,' she remarked apologetically, 'that was extremely insensitive of me. By the way, why did that bastard Cameron walk out on you?'

'Because I wouldn't set a date for our wedding.'

'And can I ask why you wouldn't?'

Jenny shrugged her shoulders. 'I don't know really – the time never seemed right. I had my studies to finish, then Father died and Mother needed my support . . . and of course I've been so involved with Sinclair's. Last Christmas Cameron even accused me of being married to Sinclair's, but there's so much to do with the House of St Claire . . .'

'Hang on a minute. Correct me if I'm wrong, but I thought you said you didn't meet Paul until January, yet you and Cameron split up at New Year.'

'Yes,' Jenny nodded, 'but I knew I had to do something for Sinclair's.'

'Hmph!' Moira retorted. 'Do something for Sinclair's by all means, but not at the expense of your own personal happiness. You know what they say; all work and no play, etc. etc.'

'So you think Cameron was right, then, I am married to Sinclair's?'

Moira reached for Jenny's hand. 'Jenny, I've known you an awful long time, so do you mind if I speak my mind?'

Shaking her head, Jenny buried her head in her hands and waited.

'Well, Jennifer Sinclair, for what it's worth, I don't think you would ever have married Cameron Ross. Even if you'd waited a million years, "the time", as you called it would never have been right; whereas, with this Paul . . .'

At the mention of the name Jenny looked up, her red-rimmed eyes in her pale, wan face, framed by a curtain of sleek strawberry-blonde hair.

'God, I'm so jealous of your gorgeous hair,' said Moira tugging at her unruly mousy curls. 'Do you know I'm even going grey in places – at my age, can you believe it? I reckon it won't be long before my hair looks like a Brillo pad that's been left on the sink for too long.'

Jenny smiled weakly and dabbed at her eyes. 'You started to talk about Paul. What were you going to say?'

'I was going to say that from what I've heard tonight – and the other night too when you came to the flat – I'd be prepared to stick my neck out and bet you feel far more for Paul than you ever felt for Cameron.'

'But I've only known him for about nine months!'

'And we all know what can happen in nine months, don't we?' Moira patted her generous stomach.

'You're not, are you?' Jenny gasped wide-eyed.

'No, more's the pity, I just look permanently pregnant, that's all.' Passing Jenny a chocolate, Moira announced. 'Anyway, I digress; the point I'm trying to make is, you spent six years with Cameron . . .'

'Yes, but don't forget he was away a great deal.'

'Och! Jenny, do shut up!' Moira chided good-naturedly. 'Can't you see I'm trying to be serious for once? I thought I was the one with VD – *and* before you say anything, that's verbal diarrhoea! What I was going to say before I was so rudely interrupted was . . . you spent six years with Cameron and never felt the time was right to marry him and you've spent one week here in Geneva with Paul. So tell me, after just one week how do you feel about him now?'

'Totally and utterly bereft at having rejected him. If only you'd seen the look in his eyes, Moira. They looked so haunted, yet earlier this evening when he smiled at me and held my hand in his, it was like . . . like hands joined together in prayer . . . just like a dream, in fact.'

'Whew!' whistled Moira, reaching for a tissue. 'Trust you to be so poetic,' she said kindly. 'I talk about gut-wrenching and you talk about prayers and dreams!'

CHAPTER 18

Bad dreams woke Jenny from yet another night of troubled sleep. She'd slept badly since returning from Geneva and last night was no exception. Her immediate reaction on rising had been to ring Moira again, but that would have been totally unreasonable. Instead she would have to make do with recalling their conversation on that last night in Geneva.

Jenny turned and looked at her bedside clock. It was just after half-past six. She sighed. There was no point in trying to go back to sleep, she was already wide awake. Besides, if she left early, she could avoid the rush-hour traffic and even look at the window display of some of the stores before going to the office.

With her thoughts still on Paul and Geneva, Jenny found herself in the centre of town. She walked towards the kerb.

'Jenny! Jenny Sinclair!' A hand clutched at Jenny's shoulder.

Dazed and alarmed, she turned to see Helen Craig, whose bike lay at the kerbside, wheels spinning.

'My goodness, Jenny, you gave me quite a fright! I thought you were going to step right off the kerb into

164

the road. Thank goodness there's not much traffic about. Are you all right, my dear? You look as if you'd seen a ghost!'

To Jenny, Helen's choice of words couldn't have been more appropriate. All week she'd felt haunted by thoughts from the past. She shivered and looked at Helen standing there in an array of rainbow-coloured garments. Her appearance was somehow strangely comforting and reassuring.

'Helen, how lovely to see you. I must have been daydreaming. Goodness, isn't it cold this morning?'

'I'm not surprised you're feeling the cold – just look at you! The suit you're wearing – fine as it is – might be all right for a nice warm office but it's hardly the thing for such a cold morning!' Helen went to her bike, where she rummaged in the basket strapped to the handlebars and returned with a brightly patterned shawl.

'Hardly the House of St Claire, my dear,' she said, draping the shawl over Jenny's shoulders in motherly fashion, 'but it will at least keep you warm until you get to the office. Whatever are you doing in Princes Street at such an early hour?'

'I heard there were some particularly good window displays just now. I thought I ought to see them for myself before the streets got too crowded and perhaps see what our competition are up to!'

'I don't know,' replied Helen, 'talk about dedication to business. You out and about in the early morning and Paul working away in the wee small hours, all for the sake of inspiration.'

'Paul?'

'Yes, my dear, his light has been on most mornings at

half-past two and when I asked him about it he said almost the same as you. I gather the Geneva trip was a great success.'

Jenny gave Helen a puzzled look. She responded with a loud chuckle.

'I expect you'll be thinking what a nosy old busybody I am, but I seem to wake most mornings about half-past two – trouble with getting old I'm afraid – and I see Paul's light from my window.'

Jenny, anxious to refrain from further conversation about Paul, looked at her watch. 'Look, Helen, I really must dash – get these ideas down, you know. Perhaps we could have lunch together one day? Oh, and what about the shawl?' She began to unwrap the welcome layers of crochet squares from her shoulders.

'I've a better idea,' said Helen, 'you come and have tea with me one day instead, then we can have a nice chat. As for the shawl, don't worry about it, I took it along for Mother this morning – I like to check on her first thing. She told me not to mollycoddle her and sent me away with a flea in my ear!' Helen chuckled loudly again and mounted her bike.

Jenny noticed her leg warmers; they were made from the cut-off sleeves of some long-since-discarded sweater. Jenny smiled. Helen Craig would doubtless get on extremely well with Morag and Miss Tandy!

In Geneva Paul had mentioned the Christmas party and there on her desk Jenny found a memo from Andrew. Morag, as usual, wanted their proposed guest lists asap! It was Sinclair custom to hold an annual staff dinner-dance and this year it was to be extra-special. Even Morag was thrilled at the prospect of the House of

166

St Claire's first Christmas. In recent years she'd only attended the dinner, but this year she told Andrew to book extra rooms at the hotel; she and Tandy would stop over. It should be a night to remember; she might even let her hair down!

Jenny compiled her list and took it to Andrew's office where she found his, already complete and ready to send to Morag. She scanned the two lists of names. For the most part they were identical. The two additions on Andrew's left Jenny with mixed emotions.

Naturally Paul's name should appear on both lists, but seeing 'Mr and Mrs Paul Hadley' written in Andrew's bold script caused her to question the reason why. Was Andrew being polite, not wishing to offend Paul by including Gina's name, or did Andrew know something Jenny didn't?

Paul had spoken of Gina's return as being purely to see the children. In Geneva he'd even implied she would be leaving again on his return. Hadn't there been mention of a flat too? Perhaps Helen might know? Jenny chided herself for her curiosity. It was none of her business. Nevertheless she still couldn't forget the scene between Gina and Paul the night she and Andrew were invited to dinner, nor the situation last week when she'd found herself willingly drawn into Paul's arms. She swallowed hard and looked again at Andrew's list and his second addition. Nothing would ever induce her to be drawn into the arms of Alistair Jennings!

'I love the shawl,' Stevie quipped. 'Is this the equivalent of Dior's New Look for the House of St Claire?'

'No, it isn't!' Jenny replied tetchily. 'I forgot my coat this morning and was given this by a friend. I intend to return it next week.'

'Thank goodness for that,' said Stevie, staring at the garish-looking crocheted squares. She grinned wickedly. 'Heaven knows what Mr Sinclair's going to say when he sees you; it quite lowers the tone in the office.' Stevie smiled and pointed to the outer door. Andrew had just arrived.

'Jenny, don't forget to let me have your list for the Chris . . . Good grief! What on earth is that you're wearing?'

Stevie spun her wheelchair to hide her face from Andrew, then, taking out her handkerchief, tried desperately to suppress the giggles.

'Don't you like it, Andrew?' Jenny's voice was in mock-earnest. 'It's a sample. I thought we might use it for next season.'

'No, I don't, I think it's bloody awful! It looks like something from a jumble sale!'

No longer able to keep up the charade, Jenny's face broke into a grin. Surprisingly for once, Andrew didn't share her sense of humour.

'If that's your idea of a joke, Jenny, then I don't find it very funny!'

He left the office, slamming the door behind him.

'Goodness, what's eating him?' Stevie asked. 'Last week when you were away he was like a dog with two tails!'

'Perhaps I'd better go away again, then,' suggested Jenny. Later, pondering Andrew's behaviour, which was so out of character, she was surprised to receive a phone call from Mary.

A lunch invitation from Mary was extremely rare. Lunches and dinners at the Edinburgh house with the family maybe, lunch in a restaurant hardly ever, and at the Pompadour restaurant of the Caledonian Hotel, never! Jenny was intrigued. Could there be some connection with this and Andrew's earlier outburst?

'The mystery deepens,' said Jenny, preparing to leave the office to meet Mary. 'Whatever you do, Stevie, don't tell Andrew I'm meeting Mary for lunch. If he asks just tell him I've gone shopping. He'd have a fit if he knew we were going to the Pompadour!'

'Wow!' Stevie exclaimed. 'It must be the French connection.'

It took Jenny a few moments to make the link between Louis XV's favourite mistress and the House of St Claire.

'I think my sister-in-law would prefer to be compared to Lady Stair rather than Madame de Pompadour,' Jenny added. 'Mary's far too strait-laced to be a king's mistress!'

Mary sat waiting at a corner table, looking unusually tired and ashen-faced. Not what you'd expect from someone sitting in such opulent surroundings with the prospect of a superb meal ahead. Eating surprisingly little, Mary picked at her food like a sparrow. Jenny was amazed. Mary usually attacked her meals with refined gusto.

'Is there anything wrong, Mary? The whitebait – is it all right?'

Mary looked up from where she'd been unconsciously decapitating a tiny silver fish on her plate.

On one side there was already a small pile of heads. Jenny was puzzled; Mary knew only too well that whitebait were always eaten whole.

Without warning, Mary's eyes filled with tears. 'It's Andrew,' she blurted out. 'I think he's having an affair.'

'*What?*' Jenny gasped loudly.

Mary's pronouncement and Jenny's response were swallowed up by the music playing in the background. Mary sat with fork poised, ready to sever another head.

'Andrew? He can't be!' gasped Jenny, thinking of her staid brother. 'Are you sure, Mary? Do you have any proof?'

'No, not really,' whispered Mary, placing her fork on the table and reaching for her handkerchief. 'Let's just say,' she said dabbing at her eyes, 'it's woman's intuition – he's different.'

'Different?'

'Yes . . . different.'

'But how do you mean, different?'

Jenny waited for an explanation, and when it came she wished she hadn't asked.

'When we're alone together . . .' Mary continued, her face crimson with embarassment. 'When we're alone together . . . in bed . . . he's different; he wants to do things we've never . . .'

Jenny reached for Mary's hand. 'It's all right, Mary, don't say any more, I think I understand.'

She didn't really – not at that precise moment – it was just the thought of Andrew and Mary in bed together. Even Cameron had passed comment on more than one occasion about Andrew and Mary's sex life, or quite possibly the lack of it. It was common knowledge that teenagers found it repugnant to think of their parents having a loving sexual relationship, but for Mary to raise the subject made Jenny feel distinctly uncomfortable.

'What am I going to do, Jenny?' Mary clung on to Jenny's offered hand. 'You're the only person I can talk to. I daren't mention it to Shona. She's a very good friend, I know – but within days it would be all round the committee. I . . . I thought, as Andrew's your brother and you work together . . . you might have some idea what's going on.'

'No,' said Jenny reflectively. 'Andrew's in the office every day. You know how busy we are with the House of St Claire, everything is going so well and . . .'

'I know,' broke in Mary, 'and Andrew's been working such long hours.'

Hesitantly Jenny enquired, 'Mary, I don't like to suggest this, but do you think if Andrew is seeing someone, working late is just an excuse?'

'Oh, no!' Mary's voice was adamant. 'He rings me from the office, you see, just before he comes home, and I always recognize the chime of father-in-law's old clock, plus of course the hum of the terminal on Andrew's desk.' Mary continued guiltily, 'I have to confess I've even tried to catch him out sometimes. I've rung him with some excuse or other . . . but really it's just to check up on him . . .'

'And?'

'And he always answers the phone, but . . .'

'But what?' The conversation was taking an age; Jenny knew she ought to be getting back to the office. She couldn't leave Mary yet – not in this state.

171

Mary's eyes filled with tears once more. 'It's the perfume, you see – sometimes he smells of a very heavy perfume. He got so angry when I asked him about it this morning and insisted it was his new aftershave.'

At least that explained this morning's outburst, thought Jenny. 'And has Andrew got a new aftershave?'

'Why, yes! I've seen it on the bathroom shelf, only it doesn't smell quite the same – not so . . . sickly.'

Something stirred in Jenny's head. What was it Stevie had said only that morning? Last week Andrew had been like a dog with two tails. Last week when she and Paul were away in Geneva! Jenny felt her mind go into overdrive. Gina wore a heavy perfume, a heavy sickly perfume. Jenny remembered it vividly. She also remembered Gina's eyes positively devouring Andrew across the dining table. No! It was all too preposterous. Andrew and Gina together – never in a million years!

With the seed of doubt sown, a chill ran through Jenny's veins.

'Look, Mary, I'm sure you've nothing to worry about. Perfumes and aftershaves smell differently on each individual. Remember the Christmas Mother bought us both the same scent, yet the fragrance was different on each of us.' Jenny held her breath. Had she sounded convincing enough?

Mary was quietly thoughtful. Yes, she had remembered. For the moment at least all doubts and suspicions could be cast aside. She even managed a weak smile.

'Right, then,' said Jenny some time later, finishing

her coffee. 'Off you go and don't worry.' She kissed Mary goodbye. 'We'll meet again soon, my treat next time, but it will have to be somewhere far less grand!'

Returning to the office, Jenny's earlier suspicions made an unwelcome return. From now on she determined to keep a surreptitious watch over Andrew. No one, not even Stevie, must suspect a thing. Managing to evade all Stevie's questions relating to lunchtime, she would say only that Mary was planning a Christmas surprise for Andrew. Jenny hoped and prayed it wasn't going to be the other way round.

'OK,' said Stevie, 'if you won't tell me about Andrew's surprise, you can at least tell me where you got that hideous shawl?'

She seemed disappointed when Jenny explained it was from Paul's neighbour.

'Oh! I thought you'd got it from the bag lady; she tried to sell me something equally revolting like that the other day.'

The bag lady, Stevie explained, frequented the square at lunchtimes and for some reason or another seemed fascinated by the corner chemist's shop. Jenny wasn't interested in bag ladies and chemist's shops, only Andrew.

During the following weeks Jenny left her office door open deliberately in the hope of keeping a watchful eye on Andrew and listening for any suspicious phone calls he might make or receive. It was easier for Stevie to wheel her chair in and out of the offices when they were busy, she'd lied, especially with the build-up to Christmas.

Andrew accepted this without comment and work continued as before, to the extent that Jenny was beginning to think she and Mary had become paranoid over his movements. All this was to change one Thursday afternoon.

Answering what Jenny believed to be a routine call, Andrew's expression altered dramatically. Even from this distance she thought he looked embarasssed and uncomfortable. Jenny quickly picked up a file and made her way to his office. Almost immediately he hung up, but not before she heard him say, 'I'm not sure. No! Definitely not tonight – Monday at eight-thirty.'

'Problems, Andrew?'

'What? Oh, no, just someone at the golf club wanting a game.'

Jenny bit her lip and, returning to her office, suspected Andrew was playing a different sort of game. Halting at the door, she said nonchalantly, 'By the way, how's Mary? I thought she was looking strained the last time I saw her? I get the impression she's worried about you working all these late nights. You're not overdoing things, are you, Andrew?' She waited to gauge his reaction.

'What *do* you mean?' he snapped. 'I have to work late, Jenny. You of all people should know that . . . all these new products to launch and Christmas rapidly approaching.' His gaze rested on the House of St Claire file she was holding.

'I appreciate that, and I'm sorry to be the cause of your problems.'

'What do you mean?' he asked suspiciously.

'Well, if I hadn't introduced you to Paul Hadley, you wouldn't have to work all these late nights.'

The meaning of her statement was twofold. Turning slowly, Jenny left Andrew to ponder on its interpretation.

CHAPTER 19

Saturday and Sunday were what Jenny had come to call 'marmalade days'. Days of decision-making and problem-solving when if nothing went right, she only had herself to blame. The phrase had sprung from all those months ago when Paul and the girls had come to tea.

Turning away from the window where rain lashed against the pane in torrents, Jenny studied the two boxes on the table. One to be filed away, the other to be discarded. The former contained her personal collection of papers, newspaper cuttings and photos relating to the House of St Claire and the latter an assortment of letters, postcards, theatre tickets, programmes and the like, all connected to the six years she'd spent with Cameron.

With firm resolve she took one last look at them, peeled open a black bin-liner and deposited the box's entire contents inside. Knotting it securely, she then dumped it unceremoniously by the dustbin at the far end of the garden. At that moment a gust of wind heavy with driving rain lashed against her back, long before she had time to reach the shelter of the cottage.

Soaked to the skin, she filled the kettle before hurrying upstairs for a change of clothing and ten minutes later, dressed in warm leggings and an over-large Arran sweater, drew the curtains on heavy rain-clouds. Picking up her tea tray, Jenny took it to the fire and, nestling against a pile of cushions, poured deep gold, fragrant rose pouchong tea into a fine china cup.

'Mmm, roses and warm summer days,' she sighed nostalgically, breathing in its sweet scented aroma.

Placing her cup by the hearth, Jenny ran her fingers along the shelves she'd had built into the alcoves.

'Goodness,' she murmured as her hands swept across the rows of books and photo albums, 'you could all do with a jolly good clear-out.' Examining the pad of dust that had collected on her finger, she added, 'Not today, though, I'm far too tired. I've already done enough clearing out for one day.'

As she absent-mindedly rubbed the dust from her finger, Jenny's gaze alighted on a brightly patterned photo album decorated in garish colours. That must be an old one, she told herself; she'd never buy anything like that nowadays. Curious as to its contents, she slipped the album away from its neighbours and turned page after page of photos encased in clear, though slightly brittle and yellow cellophane.

'Why, it's that wonderful summer we had at Conasg just before . . .' She stopped herself. She was going to say, before Father succumbed to what he'd referred to as 'the indignity of a wheelchair'.

Through tear-filled eyes, Jenny turned each photo-laden page. It had been such an idyllic, carefree summer. A summer when she'd walked the shores of Loch

Etive, run barefoot through deer-hair grass, laughed in unison with the tumbling brooks that cascaded down the hillsides and then, exhausted, spent endless hours just talking and arguing playfully with her father in the gardens at Conasg.

There a multicolour of rhododendrons had created their own Impressionist painting against a backdrop of clear blue skies. Clear like the jelly favoured by Fiona and Emily, not unpleasant and lumpy like the marmalade preferred by Andrew or the grey clouds she'd so recently shut out.

Andrew, she mused. What would he be doing today? There would be no golf. The rain had been relentless and the damp chill that accompanied it pervaded to the very marrow. Andrew, she thought, would be assuming the role of dutiful husband and father. Carving the Sunday roast, reading the newspapers, helping Jean and Iain with their homework and later discussing the forthcoming week's activities with Mary before they said goodnight.

Jenny felt sickened. Time and time again she'd tried to dispel from her mind the picture of Mary at the Pompadour but it refused to go away. Mary clutching on to her hand, her eyes filled with tears, struggling to say, 'When we're in bed he's different.'

'Poor Mary,' whispered Jenny, thinking of the clandestine meeting Andrew had arranged for the following night. It now seemed strangely ironic that she and Stevie had made comparisons between Mary and Lady Stair, while talking about the Pompadour. Mary, like Lady Stair, would be the perfect hostess, but would Gina be the perfect mistress?

Andrew's mistress! It all sounded so cheap and sordid. Was that what Gina was? She had to be. What else would you call her? Tart, whore, bit on the side? Jenny shuddered. It certainly had been a marmalade weekend. A weekend for contemplating the recent arrivals and departures in her life.

Closing the photo album, Jenny placed it back on the shelf and gave a sardonic smile. 'Arrivals and departures,' she whispered solemnly, remembering a scene from a spell with the local amateur dramatics group. 'I suppose you could say Paul and Gina Hadley have now entered centre-stage, whereas Cameron's made his exit via the back door and the dustbin!'

On the Monday morning, Jenny realized that her immediate problem was how to act normally throughout the day and what to do once she left the office at five-thirty. If she stayed on after work Andrew might become suspicious. No, she must get in her car and go through the motions of leaving to go home, but first she needed to make a phone call and secondly she must remember to leave a file on her desk. If she was to going to return to the office after hours, then she would need a genuine reason for doing so.

Footsteps clipped down the hallway and the door was suddenly thrown open to reveal Helen Craig looking like what Jenny could only describe later as a liquorice allsort! Gone was the familiar woollen hat and red hair. In its place was a neat black bob even Mrs Bertie Bassett would be proud of. Horizontal stripes began at Helen's neck and continued to her ankles in layers of pink, white, brown and orange all interleaved with

179

black. Only the flat blue aniseed-flavoured sweet was missing.

'Thanks for inviting me, Helen; sorry I've kept this for so long.'

'Away with you,' said Helen, 'it's nothing; I've been hoping you would ring. As for the shawl, you could have kept it.'

Jenny hesitated, but Helen, eyeing her neatly tailored suit added quickly, 'Although I expect it's not really your cup of tea, is it my dear? Far too colourful for you. You probably only wear two or three shades at a time, whereas I, as you can see, go for the whole caboosh!' She laughed loudly, her merry chuckling seeming to bounce off the weird collection of furniture and ornaments in the hallway.

'Now come and sit yourself down by the fire, throw off your shoes and make yourself at home,' Helen insisted. 'You must be fair worn out.'

Too tired to argue, Jenny followed instructions. The relief when she slipped off her high heels was wonderful. She wriggled her toes in the deep rag rug.

'Gosh I haven't seen one of these in years,' she said. 'Did you make it?'

'Aye, like most things here, if you haven't already guessed.' She waved her arm to encompass the array of rugs, blankets, runners, curtains and antimacassars, each one stamped with Helen's trade mark of bright colours.

'My grannie taught me to sew and knit when I was a wee lassie. Times were hard and mother had to work. We saved and collected everything and ne'er a scrap was wasted. The trouble is, Jenny, if you've been brought up to be frugal the habit sort of sticks. Not like some I could mention!'

Jenny immediately thought of Mary, but Helen didn't know Mary, did she? The kettle sang out from the range in the kitchen and Helen reappeared pushing a trolley laden with high tea.

'Goodness, Helen, just how many people are you expecting?'

'Just you my dear, just you,' said Helen, lifting the teapot.

Refusing another slice of Dundee cake some time later, Jenny patted her stomach. She'd eaten far too much already, despite Helen's protestations that she'd eaten barely enough to keep a sparrow alive.

'I can understand why Celestina and Emily like coming here so much, Helen. It's all so welcoming.'

'Thank you, Jenny. I like to think so and I shall miss them terribly when they go. It won't be the same without them.'

'Go! Go where? I didn't know they were leaving, Paul never said. Where are they going?' There was a distinct note of panic in Jenny's voice.

'Oh, not Paul, just Gina and the girls. She's threatening to take them away if Paul doesn't buy her a flat in Edinburgh. She's even talking about taking them back to Italy to live with her parents!'

'But she can't. That's outrageous, Paul won't let her . . . will he?'

Jenny looked to Helen for reassurance. Whatever would Paul do without the girls? He'd given up his career to remain at home with them; they were his whole life. Of course he had the House of St Claire now, but that was different . . .

'Let's just say she can and she will, if she's a mind to,' Helen said angrily, 'but as I said to Paul, it's all blethers. It's just Gina trying to get her own way. I've seen it so many times before, Jenny. There's no way Paul can afford to buy her a flat . . . not unless he sells the house, and I know he doesn't want to do that. However, if her latest boyfriend comes up with the goods – the flat, I mean – then no doubt Gina will just pack her bags one day soon and go. Once and for all, I hope, for Paul's sake! Poor man. If you only knew the half of it, Jenny.'

Not usually one to pry, Jenny realized she needed to know the half of it, particularly Gina's half, especially if it included her new boyfriend. If she played her cards right she had the distinct feeling Helen would tell her.

'What about Gina's boyfriend, then,' she enquired casually, 'how long has she known him?'

Helen smoothed her recently dyed black hair and gave a wry smile.

'Let's just say she saw plenty of him when Paul was away in Geneva. I know that not from peeping out behind the curtains but because Gina asked me to babysit. As for the boyfriend, well, he's not like her usual selection of young men. He's no spring chicken is this one, in fact he's more like an old broiler, and he'll have his work cut out for him keeping up with Gina Dintino!'

'Gina who?'

'Gina Dintino. Didn't you know that's Gina's professional name?'

Jenny shook her head sadly. There was so much she didn't know, and there was still the problem she had to deal with later this evening. At any other time it would have amused her to hear Andrew described as an old broiler. This evening it just seemed sad and pathetic.

Waving goodbye to Helen, Jenny called back that she wouldn't forget the wool. Somewhere in the cottage was a bag of half-finished knitting and endless balls of wool. She'd started knitting every time Cameron went offshore and never finished a thing, mainly because on his return he'd tease her about the pairs of odd sleeves and dropped stitches.

Jenny smiled reassuringly. In Helen's capable hands the assortment of fronts, backs and sleeves would be transformed. It would also give her an excuse to see Paul and find out if Gina's threats were serious or just a form of blackmail. It wouldn't be just Paul and Helen who would be heartbroken to see Celestina and Emily taken away. Fiona too would be devastated, not to mention Jenny herself. Switching on her ignition, Jenny saw Paul standing at his window. He beckoned and went to the front door, only to see her car pull hurriedly away.

Driving back to the office, Jenny's mind was in turmoil. She couldn't pretend she hadn't seen Paul; foolishly she'd even acknowledged his wave. But how could she say, 'Sorry, Paul, I can't stop, I'm pretty sure your wife is having an affair with my brother and, as I'm about to prove it, would you like to come too?'

What would his reaction have been? Come to think of it, how was she going to react herself? She hadn't even thought of that until now.

Apart from the usual security lights Sinclair's appeared to be deserted, but there in the car park was

Andrew's BMW with its personalized number plate and distinctive cream leather upholstery. Up on the second floor a light shone in his office. Jenny breathed a sigh of relief. At least he'd had the presence of mind to draw the blinds.

Reaching for her handbag, Jenny stepped from her car. Already her throat had gone quite dry and her hands felt clammy. Bracing herself, she took a deep breath and whispered to the enveloping darkness, 'I must keep perfectly calm and behave as normal . . . nothing must seem out of the ordinary.'

'This is normal!' a voice echoed inside her head as she walked along the dimly lit corridor towards the stairs. She never used the lift at night in case it got stuck. It had once, years ago, and the poor cleaner trapped inside had become quite hysterical until help arrived.

With each step Jenny's heart began to pound and the dull thumping in her ears appeared to echo in the stairwell. Jenny panicked. Surely Andrew and Gina could hear it too, or was it just a figment of her imagination? One thing she had not imagined however was Gina's presence. The heavy scent of her perfume in the air was proof enough.

Removing her white-knuckled hand from the bannister rail, Jenny lifted it to her face and grimaced. Even the bannisters were impregnated with the same cloying perfume. No doubt Gina's hands had confidently clasped the same handrail as she'd ascended the stairs to join her lover. Small wonder Mary's suspicions had been aroused. Wanting to wash all trace of Gina from her hands, Jenny realized she must first confront Andrew.

In Andrew's office, Gina finished her whisky and

watched Andrew walk to to the now familiar cupboard. Unlocking the door, he reached in and produced a tartan rug, which he placed on the carpet.

'And just what is that for?' Gina teased with a knowing look.

'I thought we could . . . well, you know,' Andrew said nervously.

Gina sidled up to Andrew. 'But you said we would discuss my flat; you promised me you would look at the estate agent's details and give me a cheque for the deposit.'

'I will, Gina, later . . . but can't we just . . .?' Andrew reached out for Gina, grabbing her around the waist, and drew her roughly towards him.

Gina flashed her dark eyes and shook her curls brazenly in Andrew's face. 'My goodness, Andrew, how desperate you are. Just as you were in New York, my darling. Am I to understand by such a display that Mary has not been performing her wifely duties to your satisfaction?'

At the mention of Mary's name, Andrew was overcome with a surge of guilt, and for a brief moment he hesitated as Gina's mocking eyes searched his face. Sensing that she had perhaps spoken out of turn, Gina swiftly remedied the situation by reaching for Andrew's hand, guiding it sensuously under her skirt until it reached her buttocks.

Touching bare flesh, Andrew gasped. 'But you're not wearing . . .'

Gina laughed with mocking eyes and moved his hand between her thighs.

'Why so shocked, Andrew'. Am I not being just like the typical Scotsman?'

Andrew, momentarily bewildered, felt Gina's body writhe against his hand. 'You see,' she announced playfully, 'I am just following Scottish tradition. I am wearing nothing under my kilt!'

'Your kilt!' Andrew gasped. 'What you're wearing could hardly be described as a kilt! Why, there's barely half a metre of fabric in your skirt. Do you have any idea how much material goes into a kilt?'

'No,' Gina replied, 'and I don't much care either, I'm far too interested in other things.' Gina wriggled away from Andrew's grasp, smoothed down the woollen bouclé fabric of her skirt and moved towards his desk where she'd left the brochures from the estate agents. Andrew meanwhile gazed longingly at the tartan rug spread out on the famous Sinclair carpet. Gina caught his gaze and read his thoughts.

'No! Not the rug,' she pouted. 'Here . . . here on the desk.'

'But . . .!'

'But what, Andrew? Come, now, don't be a spoil-sport, I never had to persuade you in New York.'

Andrew felt himself going hot under the collar at the memory, and also of Mary's reaction on his return, when he'd tried to . . .

'Oh, what the hell?' he sighed, seeing Gina's firm buttocks spreadeagled across his desk.

Bending over to enter her, Andrew's eyes alighted on the estate agent's details and all thoughts of passion deserted him.

'Bloody hell, Gina, I said a small flat, not Holyrood Palace!'

With Gina still wedged beneath him, Andrew

reached angrily for the papers containing photos of penthouse flats and luxury apartments.

'You've got to be joking! I can't afford a place like that!'

Gina wriggled sideways. 'Well, in that case, Paul will just have to sell the house!' she snapped angrily.

'That's hardly fair . . .'

'Fair! *Fair*! And have you been fair with me, Andrew, considering what you promised me in New York . . .? Why, only last week . . .'

With his trousers round his ankles, Andrew felt strangely vulnerable.

'In view of the circumstances,' he began, unaware of his office door opening quietly.

'In view of the circumstances, from where I'm standing I would suggest you've some explaining to do,' Jenny's voice echoed.

'Jenny! What on earth are you doing here? I thought you left ages ago.' Andrew grabbed frantically at his trousers, panic and guilt written all over his face.

'I did,' said Jenny, feeling the colour rise in her cheeks, 'only I forgot this file for tomorrow's meeting. It was incredibly stupid of me, I know, but I decided to come all the way back for it.'

At that moment Andrew looked like a frightened junior schoolboy discovered smoking in the dorm. His clothes and hair were dishevelled and his face a profusion of pink. Gina meanwhile was tucking her blouse into what Jenny presumed to be a skirt, but what Miss Tandy and Mother would no doubt describe as a belt.

Clutching the property papers, Andrew announced feebly, 'I was just helping Gina choose a flat.'

'Oh, I see,' said Jenny with a sardonic smile. 'And I suppose when I came in just now you were about to give her the key to the door!'

Not waiting for Andrew's reaction, Jenny clutched her file tightly to her breast and fled hurriedly down the stairs into the late November night.

Behind her she could hear Andrew calling her name and Gina's screams. Whether Gina's hysterical ravings were directed at Andrew or herself Jenny wasn't sure, and she didn't intend to find out. She'd seen enough and said enough. Now all she wanted to do was go home.

CHAPTER 20

Leaving Sinclair's car park with her heart still pounding, Jenny couldn't wait to get on to the open road where she could relax and take stock of the situation.

'Just concentrate on the DVLC – don't let your mind wander, Jenny.'

Like a mantra she kept repeating the same phrase over and over again. It was her way of describing her route home to the friends who questioned the sanity of such a long journey, i.e. Dual carriageway, Village, Lane and Cottage.

Just before exiting from the dual carriageway, Jenny noticed a car approaching from behind at breakneck speed. Passing her, it came to a halt on the road ahead. Braking hard, the driver slammed the car into reverse but stopped abruptly when flashed from behind.

'Bloody idiot,' said Jenny to herself, switching on the radio cassette. 'If you've missed your turning you go ahead to the next one. You don't reverse back down a dual carriageway! Mind you, you've a long way to the next exit.'

With the strains of Schubert's 'Trout Quintet' echoing softly in the car, Jenny breathed a sigh of relief as her headlights picked out the village signpost. There remained only the lane and the narrow driveway to the cottage.

Knowing the end of the tape signalled the approach to the little-used lane, Jenny's thoughts turned to a welcoming cup of hot chocolate, hot water bottle and bed. It therefore came as a surprise to discover in her rear-view mirror that she was being followed.

With every minute the pursuing car came closer, its lights flashing angrily, until Jenny found herself blinded by pure terror and headlamps on full beam. Panicking, she accelerated hard and swung the wheel sharply; never had the lane seemed so full of twists and turns and never was she more relieved to discern the welcoming silhouette of her cottage roof.

With a squeal of tyres, narrowly missing the gatepost, Jenny slammed on her brakes, sending a shower of gravel ricocheting against the garage door. Then, grabbing her handbag and briefcase, she ran for the safety of the porch.

'Keys! Keys! Where are the bloody keys?' she cried as beads of perspiration appeared on her forehead and a beam of light swept across the hedgerow at the bottom of the lane. With trembling fingers she forced the key into the lock but with her hands shaking and palms sweating so much, the doorhandle just wouldn't budge.

At that moment the sound of metal hitting the gatepost and wheels skidding on gravel filled Jenny's whole being with terror. 'Turn, damn you!' she cried, pushing so hard that she jerked open the door and found herself in a heap on the floor.

'Oh, thank God!' she sighed, turning to slam the door

shut. But relief soon gave way to fresh terror when she saw a man's foot wedged in the doorway and felt strong arms firmly grip her shoulders. Opening her mouth to scream, she emitted one loud shriek before her mouth was clamped tightly shut.

'Jenny, for God's sake shut up! It's me, do you hear, it's me, Andrew! It's all right, it's not some bloody rapist . . . it's your brother!'

'Andrew . . .? *Andrew*!' she cried, still trembling in fear. 'What the hell do you think you were *doing*? You gave me the fright of my life! Do you mean to say it was you driving like a maniac scaring me half to death?

'I'm sorry, but I need to talk to you.'

'Talk to me! *Talk to me*! Well, all I can say to that, Andrew Sinclair, is that you picked a bloody stupid way of doing it!'

'I know, I realize that now, but at the time . . . Look, I've said I'm sorry, so now will you please stop shaking and get up from the floor and let me in, or are we going to wait here and see if the people who live in this Godforsaken place have done the neighbourly thing and called the police?'

'You don't think they have, do you?' she asked, rising shakily to her feet.

Andrew steadied her and helped her into the sitting room before gathering the strewn papers from the porch. 'And what did you want to talk to me about?' she asked coolly.

'My God! Isn't that obvious? I want to talk to you about this evening. But first would you mind if I poured myself a drink? I need it; in fact I think we both do.'

She motioned to the decanter on the sideboard and

watched Andrew pour two large whiskies. He looked and felt distinctly uncomfortable. Where to begin was the problem.

'How much do you know, Jennifer?'

'Let's just say, Andrew, until this evening it was all pure speculation.'

'So you weren't at the office by accident? I guessed as much . . . Then when, may I ask, did you begin to . . . er . . . speculate?'

'The day I had lunch with Mary and she told me she suspected you were having an affair.'

Andrew groaned at the mention of Mary's name. 'Mary knows? Oh, God!'

'No, she doesn't know for certain, she was merely guessing. I told her it wasn't possible you'd do such a thing and that she must be imagining it.'

Her voice was sarcastic, but Andrew seemed relieved and took a deep gulp of whisky.

'Nevertheless,' continued Jenny, 'from that moment I decided to keep an eye on you.'

'You mean spy on me!'

'Call it what you like, but I didn't want to see you make a fool of yourself with Gina. You do realize you're just one of many to join her list of conquests? And when you embarked on your sordid little affair with her, did you have no feelings at all for Mary and your children or even Paul and his for that matter?'

'Oh, come on, Jennifer, you know as well as I do that Paul and Gina's marriage broke down long ago. You can't accuse me of splitting up the family home.'

'That's precisely where you're wrong, Andrew. Did you know Gina was threatening to take the children away from Paul . . . if he doesn't comply with her wishes and sell the house? Doesn't that split up the family home?'

Andrew looked sheepish. 'Gina did mention something of the sort, and I thought at the time it didn't seem particularly fair to Paul, so . . .'

'So?' Jenny demanded.

'So I just happened to mention I might be able to find her a flat.'

'And you think that was being fair to Paul? Well, I don't – I call it downright stupidity!'

How long they sat and talked Jenny didn't know, but it came as a relief to hear Andrew agree – albeit reluctantly – to sever the relationship with Gina once and for all.

'Please believe me, Jenny,' he begged. 'In fact I've already tried to finish with her once before but she's . . . she's like a drug, you have no idea!' Andrew sat down and buried his head in his hands.

'Just like a drug,' Jenny heard him whisper, 'you try it once – just for kicks – then get swept along by the excitement and euphoria of it all. Before you know where you are, you're hooked.'

'I hardly think we can get you a place at the Arisaid Ladies' Drug Rehab Unit, though, Andrew,' said Jenny sarcastically, reminding him of the tireless work the 'Arrys' put in with Mary at the helm.

Andrew grunted. 'I don't think that's very funny.'

'It wasn't meant to be. Now, can you tell me one thing please? Why Gina? Was it because she was Paul's wife, or did you see it as a challenge?'

Andrew laughed wryly. 'No, Paul had absolutely

nothing to do with it. When I first met Gina I didn't even know Paul. Gina and I met in Switzerland and later in the States at the British Fair in New York.'

Had Jenny heard correctly? She knew the Swiss holiday had been a disaster and Iain had been infatuated with an older woman. Was that woman Gina? But New York had that been planned? There was no need to ask . . .

'Before you ask, I can quite categorically say no,' Andrew continued. 'It was *not* planned. Gina had been in Canada when she was offered a job in New York by a friend and quite by chance we found ourselves together at a reception.'

Jenny vaguely remembered the New York photos. There had been a woman on one of them but it hadn't seemed significant at the time. Jenny frowned; something bothered her. Something Helen had said earlier that evening. Only now it seemed like an eternity away.

'Geneva!' Jenny asked. 'What about Geneva, then? Whose idea was it to send Paul and me to Geneva together?'

Andrew hung his head. 'Gina's, I'm afraid. She said with Paul away there was less chance of him finding out. Also with you in Geneva . . .' he hesitated '. . . it would be easier for me to tell Mary I was working late.'

'Oh, Andrew, how could you? Don't you see? You fell into Gina's lap just like a ripe plum!'

Andrew sat slumped dejectedly in the armchair. He'd been a complete and utter fool. Even he'd begun to realize the relationship couldn't last, and this evening, when Gina had produced the list of flats for sale, he'd suddenly begun to panic. He couldn't admit it now but he was beginning to feel grateful for Jennifer's untimely intervention, even if it meant he had been discovered literally with his trousers down!

'You know, Jennifer, you're going to think this a feeble excuse but in a way I suppose I've always been jealous of the relationship you had with Cameron. I thought having an affair with Gina would bring some excitement into my life.'

Jenny looked up, puzzled that Andrew should suddenly mention Cameron.

'You were both such free spirits,' Andrew explained. 'Mary and I were so staid by comparison. Then, when Father died, there was the business to see to and . . .' Andrew looked towards the window. He'd heard a car and voices in the lane.

'That can't be Gina, can it?'

'Surely not? I sent her home in a taxi.' Andrew walked anxiously to the window and saw a police officer coming up the drive. Groaning inwardly, he opened the door.

'Good evening, sir, sorry to trouble you, but someone reported hearing a young lady scream.'

Andrew invited the officer into the sitting room where Jenny sat. She was still surrounded by the contents of her handbag and brief case.

'That was me, Officer. A bat flew out of the porch as I was trying to open the front door. It gave me and my brother quite a fright. He said I'd probably disturbed the whole neighbourhood. I can only apologize for wasting your valuable time . . . I'm most dreadfully sorry.'

'That's quite all right, madam; we have to check these

things, you know. Can't be too careful these days.' Standing in the hallway, the young officer turned to face Andrew. 'You won't be driving tonight, I take it, sir . . . seeing as you've been drinking?' He nodded towards the half-empty decanter of whisky.

'Phew,' Andrew said after he'd gone. 'That was quick thinking, Jennifer. Jennifer?'

Jenny sat sobbing uncontrollably, tears streaming down her face, her whole body shaking. Andrew drew her close. 'Whatever is it? What's the matter?'

Through her sobs Jenny explained. Seeing the young policeman in uniform had reminded her of the time the navy sent their own officers to break the news of the accident when Cameron's friends had been killed. Memories of that day still haunted her even though she and Cameron were no longer engaged; she had been so shaken by how nearly it would have been him. Then of course there had been the week in Geneva with Paul and tonight . . . confronting Andrew and Gina – it was all just too much.

Cradling Jenny in his arms, Andrew stroked her hair just as he did with Fiona when she was unwell. 'My poor, poor Jennifer,' he whispered. 'I had absolutely no idea. Perhaps you need a break, a holiday away from the business.'

'No!' Jenny was adamant. 'I don't need a holiday, that would only make things worse. I need Sinclair's; I need the House of St Claire. Don't you see, it's the only thing that's kept me going since Father died . . . since Cameron and I . . .? Without it I don't know what I would do.'

'I could suggest you try eating a bit more. You know,

there's nothing of you!' Until Andrew held his sister in his arms he hadn't realized just how thin she'd become. She seemed little more than a child, and her limp, distraught body reminded him of the old rag doll Fiona insisted on dragging everywhere.

'I do eat,' Jenny cried feebly, 'it's just that perhaps I don't eat as much as you or Mary and . . .'

'Mary!' Sitting here all this time, he'd quite forgotten Mary. Andrew strode to the phone. 'I must ring Mary and tell her I'm spending the night here with you. Tell her we've been having a business meeting with too much of the hard stuff.' He looked to Jenny for reassurance. Nodding in Andrew's direction, Jenny watched him pick up the receiver.

'I'll tell her I'm in no condition to drive,' he continued, 'and if you speak to her as well, who knows, maybe we'll convince her!'

The next morning Andrew studied his car. The damage was extensive.

'I shouldn't be too upset about it if I were you, Andrew,' Jenny said reassuringly, slipping her arm into his. 'After all, cars can be mended – broken marriages hardly ever.'

Andrew regarded his sister with a knowing look. 'You're dead right,' he said, 'but then you nearly always are. Just think how right you were about the House of St Claire.'

Bending, he kissed her on the cheek and squeezed her hand. 'Are you going to be OK now?'

Jenny merely nodded and thought longingly of Paul.

CHAPTER 21

'Is Mr Sinclair moving house?' Stevie breezed chirpily into Jenny's office with the morning's post.

'Moving? No . . . not that I know of. Why do you ask?'

'Oh, it's just there's a pile of details from estate agents on his desk.'

Jenny froze. Was the enquiry purely innocent or did Stevie suspect something? 'Oh, those,' she said, thinking quickly. 'I think they're for a fellow Andrew met in the States. He wants to spend some time in Edinburgh testing the water, so to speak, for a new business venture, and naturally doesn't want to be stuck in a hotel for months on end. Andrew suggested renting.'

'Well, I'd certainly like to meet him,' Stevie added, 'that's if he's not already married. Anyone who can afford properties in the vicinity of the Royal Mile must have plenty of money!'

Desperate to change the subject, Jenny turned to examine the bulky envelope on her desk. She didn't like lying to Stevie, and how foolish of Andrew to leave the property details in his office. Though to be fair he probably hadn't given them a thought once he'd realized she was in the building. Anxious to divert Stevie's attention and recognizing Morag's handwriting, she opened the envelope.

'Well, Mother certainly hasn't wasted any time. It's the guest list for the Christmas party, all signed and sealed with her approval. Can I suggest you send the invitations asap, Stevie, then contact the hotel and caterers with the provisional numbers?'

'Speaking of wasting time,' Stevie announced, wheeling her chair forward to take the list, 'that new GP of mine certainly hasn't. I've already received my appointment to see the specialist at the hospital. It will mean me having to take the whole morning off for tests and X-rays at the hospital . . . will that be OK?'

'Of course. You know you don't even have to ask. This new doctor . . . what exactly did he say when you saw him?'

'Not a lot really. But he thinks I should see a specialist again. Apparently there's some new treatment I could try . . . physiotherapy and different painkillers as the others upset me so much. That's why I stopped going to the hospital.' Stevie looked thoughtful. 'I know it's never going to be a case of "take up your bed and walk, Stevie" and that I'm stuck with this wheelchair and crutches for the best part of my life . . . but you never know, do you?'

For a moment Jenny forgot all about Andrew and Gina. Studying Stevie, she caught sight of the wistful gaze in china-blue eyes framed by close-cropped dark brown hair. 'Is the pain still bad?' she enquired.

Stevie shrugged and gave a wry smile. 'Well, you know what it's like. Some days it's OK and others I could quite cheerfully jump out of the window – that's if I could jump. Perhaps I should change that to wheel myself out of the window.'

Placing a comforting hand on her shoulder, Jenny teased, 'Promise me you won't do anything like that – at least not until after you've organized Sinclair's Christmas bash. In the meantime, of course, take advantage of the fact that you've got a decent GP, and no more cancelled hospital appointments. Do I make myself clear, Miss Stephens?'

Spinning the wheelchair to face Jenny head-on, Stevie gave a mock salute and grinned broadly. 'Yes, ma'am!'

'Good! Now I'd better go and have a word with Andrew. He mentioned having a disco as well as a band this year.'

In Andrew's office Jenny picked up the property brochures and threw them into the bin just as he walked into his office. He seemed surprised to see her there.

'Just doing some tidying up. Stevie thought you were moving.'

Andrew's face filled with alarm. 'It's OK,' Jenny assured him. 'I told her you were looking for a friend. Mind if I open the window?' She didn't need to explain why. There was still a distinct underlying smell in the office . . . Gina's perfume.

The sudden gust of cold November chill took them both by surprise. Leaning from the window, Jenny breathed in deeply, sensing in the air the distinctive smell of autumn days. Days that heralded bonfires in the garden and tea in front of the fire.

Satisfied that Gina's presence had evaporated like some ghostly spirit, she closed the window, noting as she did so a gentle flurry of leaves falling from the trees.

'Everything all right with Mary and the family?' she asked, watching the familiar shadowy outline of the castle reappear through skeletal branches.

Andrew, having decided to call home for a change of clothes before coming to the office, had been dreading awkward questions from Mary and the children. He was highly relieved when none came. Iain, however, couldn't resist the opportunity of chiding his father about having to stay with Auntie Jen as a result of over-imbibing.

He reminded Andrew of the previous weekend when he'd reprimanded Iain and his friend Callum for drinking more Douglas Scotch Ale and Gordon's finest Gold than he thought wise for boys their age.

'Fancy not being able to hold your drink, Dad!' Iain had teased, watching his father pour yet another cup of strong black coffee.

'Yes, everything's fine.' Andrew said, turning to Jenny. 'It looks as if you did a good job of convincing her we'd overdone it with the malt. She was more interested in telling me about last night's committee meeting. Oh, yes, and I'm to ask you something. Do you know what you're going to wear for the Sinclair dinner? Both Mary and Jean want to know.'

Jenny smiled to herself. Thank goodness for Mary; at least she could be relied upon. Any suspicions of her husband's infidelity could be forgotten if there was a committee meeting to attend or a new dress to buy.

'Jennifer, about last night. I want to thank you . . .'

'I'd rather you didn't, Andrew. Let's just forget it, shall we – or at least try to – as long as it's over. No inquests, no recriminations.'

Relieved, Andrew pushed his waste-paper bin with the incriminating evidence under his desk. He knew he'd been stupid to leave it lying around but last night, after Gina left, his main concern had been to catch up with Jennifer. For one dreadful moment he'd thought she was going to go straight to Mary. No one could have been more relieved when he saw her heading away from the city.

'Yes, it's over,' he sighed. 'I've been a bloody fool, I realize that now. When I returned home this morning and saw Mary and the children having breakfast together, I couldn't help but think of Paul and his two girls.'

Jenny watched Andrew swallow hard and rub his chin thoughtfully.

'To think,' he continued, 'Gina actually wanted him to sell the house and threatened to take Cele and Emily away from him. I ask you, Jenny, what kind of mother could do such a thing?'

'Not a very nice one, and certainly not one worth losing sleep over.'

'I know,' murmured Andrew under his breath, 'and I'm quite prepared to try and forget all about Gina, but will she be prepared to forget all about me?'

'In time, perhaps,' mused Jenny, 'but not until after the Sinclair Dinner. You've obviously forgotten, Andrew . . . you invited Gina as well as Paul!'

Andrew groaned. 'Surely you don't think Gina will come?' He remembered Gina's volatile display the previous evening. There was no telling what she would do. Jenny, sensing her brother's concern and sharing his anxieties, tried in vain to think of something reassuring to say.

'The way I see it, the dance is weeks away, so let's not think about it now. We can only hope that by December something – or someone – will divert Gina's attention elsewhere.'

Jenny's statement only served to remind Andrew that, though just another diversionary plaything in Gina's life, he'd come so close to losing the people and business he cared so much about. In the moments that followed he prayed desperately for a shift in Gina's attention away from himself and Sinclair's. Looking up, Jenny's eyes met his. They were warm and understanding. How strange – in all the years they'd spent together as older brother and kid sister, the past twenty-four hours had somehow drawn them closer together.

'Jennifer . . .'

'Shh,' she whispered, putting her fingers gently to her lips. 'No inquests, remember? Just tell Mary I'm going out hunting for something to wear this week and I promise to let her know what I end up with. Now, if I don't get on with some work there won't be time to go shopping and I shall end up like Cinderella with nothing to wear!'

Andrew watched her go. No matter where she went or whatever she wore, there was no danger of Jennifer looking like Cinderella before the ball. She was a truly wonderful ambassador for the House of St Claire.

Nodding ruefully, he recalled her emergence from timid, shy student into the feisty young businesswoman of today. Their father would have been so proud of his only daughter. Father! How he missed him.

Andrew swallowed hard and banged his fist on the desk. Life could be bloody cruel, yet at the same time he was glad his father hadn't lived to see how Cameron Ross had dealt with Jennifer's dedication to the family business.

CHAPTER 22

Jenny halted Stevie's wheelchair in front of yet another shop window. Despite her promise to Mary of finding something to wear, her search had so far been in vain. Repeated phone calls from Mary and Jean had done nothing to improve the situation. Announcing that they had both found dresses for the dance, they advised Jennifer to find something quickly before there was nothing left to choose from!

'The trouble is, they're all too fancy for my liking,' said Jenny, eyeing the window display with its froth of lace and frills. 'I mean, just look at them, Stevie, I'd be just like the fairy on top of the Christmas tree in most of those!'

'They're certainly not like the fairy we used to have on our Christmas tree!' Stevie giggled, turning to look at Jenny. 'Mum spent ages making an elaborate white satin dress for ours and trimmed it with silver tinsel all the way down the back. The thing was, when Dad fixed the doll to the tree you couldn't see her handiwork. He solved the problem however by lifting the skirt up and fixing it to the tree to show off Mum's efforts. It certainly looked effective – but as Mum forgot to make any undies for it – I took great delight in telling anyone who came to the house that our Christmas fairy had a bare bum!'

'Cressida Stephens,' Jenny said mockingly, 'what a frightful child you must have been. If I'd known I would never have employed you.' Turning the wheelchair away from the window she pointed it in the direction of Princes Street and bumped into an elderly woman laden with bags of shopping.

'I'm terribly sorry,' said Jenny apologetically, 'I'm afraid I wasn't looking where I was going.'

'Och, dinna yae trouble,' said the woman as she picked up the scattered shopping. She patted Stevie on the head and looked sorrowfully at Jenny. 'Poor wee thing – it's very sad, isn't it?'

Watching the woman go on her way, Stevie didn't know whether she should laugh or scream? Why was it just because you were in a wheelchair people thought you were completely brain-dead? Jenny, seemingly unaware of Stevie's sensitivity, carried on pushing the chair through the milling crowds.

'Lunch, I think,' she said, 'before we die of starvation. I'm not looking at another frock until we've had something to eat.'

'Sorry to be the cause of so much aggro,' Stevie apologized, as Jenny negotiated the busy restaurant and tutting diners, trying to locate a suitable table.

In the end a kindly waitress intervened and directed them to a corner table where she brought two menus and took their orders. Stevie breathed a sigh of relief. 'Well, that makes a change. They normally presume I can't read either and ask my mother for my order. It really is like the radio programme, you know . . . *Does He Take Sugar?* Sometimes I get so cross!'

'The way you did when the woman patted you on the head?'

'So you did notice.' Stevie shifted uneasily in her chair. 'Was it that obvious, Jenny?'

'No, it's just that I know you so well now. I appreciate it must be infuriating and thought it was best just to get away.'

'Thanks, boss!' Stevie replied good-naturedly. 'Now, let's hurry up and eat so we can carry on dress-hunting.'

For Stevie, finding something to wear wasn't a problem. It was a simple choice of black evening trousers and a patterned silk blouse. The muscle wastage in her legs meant she only ever wore trousers and brightly coloured tops to lighten her sallow complexion. She reminded Jenny of her one mistake – years ago at her first Sinclair Christmas – when she'd worn black all over.

'Do you remember, Jenny? Gracious, I must have looked like a black widow spider all ready to pounce from her wheelchair. I'm not surprised no one asked me to dance,' she joked, referring to her inability to trip the light fantastic.

'Mmm,' mused Jenny, 'not a very good move, was it, especially as black widow spiders kill their mates? We can't have you making the same mistake this year. By the way, don't forget you can invite that young man of yours to the Sinclair dinner.'

'I can't do that . . . I hardly know him . . . besides, he's not my young man, he's my nurse! Well, not my nurse exactly . . . but one of the nurses from the physiotherapy department.'

Stevie was looking flustered. Jenny looked quizzically in her direction. 'Oh, I see. But I thought you said he'd taken you to the theatre a couple of times . . .'

'Only because his friend couldn't go at the last minute,' Stevie retorted, 'and I expect he feels sorry for me as I make such a fool of myself struggling with these new exercises. Now, are we going to try and find you something to wear or stay here and discuss my love-l . . .?'

Pushing Stevie to the far corner of the store's dress department, Jenny pondered those last words. Stevie had almost said love-life! So her suspicions were well founded after all. The young male nurse she'd seen on more than one occasion waiting outside the office on a Friday evening had perhaps more than just a clinical interest in her personal assistant. Warmed by the prospect, Jenny sorted through the rails of silk, taffeta and velvet.

'You could try this one,' Stevie suggested. 'You've certainly got the figure for it and the colouring.' She waited for Jenny to emerge from the fitting room.

As expected Jenny, looked stunning. With her ivory complexion and strawberry-blonde hair, the bias-cut black crêpe hung beautifully, showing her figure to perfection.

'Wow,' said Stevie, 'Alistair will love you in that!'

'You're joking!' Jenny retorted. 'That's the last thing I want. Why did you have to go and spoil things, Stevie? I'd quite forgotten about Alistair Jennings. Besides, I thought you said he hadn't replied to his invitation.'

'He hadn't, that is until this morning. His reply came in the same post as Mrs Hadley's.'

'What! But Paul told me Gina couldn't come.'

'Apparently not. According to her note, a last-minute change of plan means she can come after all. Now, what about that dress – you are going to have it, aren't you?'

The magic Jenny felt when she'd slipped on the dress rapidly disappeared with Stevie's announcement and talk of Alistair and Gina. What had made Gina change her mind? Not wishing to draw attention to the subject, Jenny turned her thoughts to the dress instead. 'You don't think it's too short or too fancy?'

'Good heavens, no! How can a simple black crêpe dress be too fancy? As for being too short – are you sure you feel all right, Jenny? *That's* what I call too fancy and too short!' Stevie motioned to the garish red velvet dress on a nearby stand – or at least what was supposed to be a red velvet dress. From where Stevie was sitting, neck and hemline almost joined together as one. And although the dress might have looked cheap, the price tag tucked discreetly away revealed otherwise. Her eyes widened in amazement. 'Tell me,' she asked incredulously, 'how can you pay so much for so little? It looks like something you'd wear to the Vicars and Tarts disco they're holding at the local community centre!'

The sombre-faced, blue-rinsed assistant, packing Jenny's dress carefully between layers of tissue, raised only an eyebrow at Stevie's outspoken comments. Even if she agreed with her, it was more than her job was worth to say so. Passing the bag to Jenny, she added casually, 'Could I suggest madam looks in the next department? We've just taken delivery of some exquisite lingerie . . . ideal for such a dress as yours. Silk crêpe needs the right foundation garments, you know, otherwise you get all those unsightly lines.'

Jenny followed the woman's eyes, where displays of glamorous satins and lace beckoned.

'Of course,' the assistant added, failing to notice Jenny's finger devoid of a wedding ring, 'Madam could always suggest her husband buys them as a Christmas present.'

'But I . . .' Jenny changed her mind. Now wasn't the time to enlighten the assistant as to her marital status.

Misinterpreting Jenny's hesitation, a voice broke in, 'Oh, but I can assure you my colleague is very discreet and used to dealing with embarrassed husbands.' She acknowledged a heavily rouged woman standing adjusting a rail of black lace underwear.

Jenny thanked the woman politely, nodded to her friend and, placing her bag on Stevie's lap, wheeled her chair in the direction of the French knickers, camisoles and suspender belts. Eyeing the expensive displays of satin and lace with envy, Stevie sighed longingly. 'If only . . . gosh, it must feel wonderful to wear something like that. It's all looks so luxurious and feminine. Can't you just imagine the reaction you'd get from a man, wearing something like that?'

'I could, and I did once – but I don't any more!'

'Me and my big mouth,' blurted Stevie in response to the wistful reply. 'Sorry, Jenny, I wasn't thinking. After today you'll definitely be wondering why you ever took me on.'

'I doubt it, and for your information I'm jolly glad I did,' replied Jenny, bracing herself to do battle in

Princes Street once more. 'You know you're probably the only person I can rely on.'

Returning to the office, Jenny pondered. Should she tell Andrew now of Gina's decision to attend the dinner, or wait until later? What good would it do at this stage? she thought. Besides, knowing Gina, she could quite easily change her mind again, and Andrew would have worried in vain. No, she decided, it was best to say nothing at all. Nearer the date, if she thought there were going to be problems she could always mention it then.

In the meantime Andrew and family appeared settled once more, and with no further lunch invitations from Mary, Jenny assumed all was well. These days Mary was more concerned with organizing a trip to the pantomine for Fiona and her friends – Celestina and Emily included.

'You know, Stevie,' Jenny said as she prepared to leave the office that evening, 'there's nothing to stop you from wearing sexy underwear. It doesn't always have to be cotton knickers and sports bras.'

'I know,' she replied, 'but I would have a job getting them on.'

'What do you mean, the camisoles or the French knickers?'

'Neither, Jenny,' grinned Stevie, lifting a trouser leg. 'I'd just have the devil of a job trying to hook the suspenders on to my pop socks!'

At home Jenny hung her new dress on the wardrobe door. She would try it on again later after her bath. It seemed such a wildly extravagant purchase, but not nearly as ludicrously priced as the red velvet.

Besides, she told herself, it would be equally suitable

for Christmas and New Year. This year she would be doing things differently. There would be no celebrations with Cameron's family, just Christmas and New Year at Conasg House with Mother and Miss Tandy.

When she'd last spoken to Flora Tandy on the phone, she'd even been surprised to discover Morag was already making plans for Burns Night, and that was months away. Sinclair's dinner-dance, Christmas, New Year and Burns Night, Jenny thought as she lay submerged beneath a layer of sweet-smelling foam. There was still a great deal to arrange.

Relaxed and recovering from her arduous shopping expedition, Jenny surveyed the range of gorse-decorated bottles and containers standing on the bathroom shelf. They were yet another idea of Paul's and one they'd been able to get into production quickly, made easier by the unanimous decision to keep the packaging simple. With Christmas approaching, it was proving to be an extremely popular line.

Today, with so much money wasted on excess packaging, the beauty of the St Claire products was their simplistic and unique design. Cut down the packaging and cut down the costs, Andrew had insisted, but not to the extent that the products inside the bottles suffered.

The task of finding the correct oils and perfumes had fallen to Jenny and she and Stevie had had a wonderful time testing and sampling all manner of wonderful fragrances. There was only one strict criterion as far as Jenny was concerned: nothing in the House of St Claire range must be heavy and cloying or reminiscent of the scents favoured by Gina!

Thoughts of Gina invariably turned to thoughts of

Paul as Jenny slipped into the black crêpe dress for the second time that day. It was strange how certain garments gave you the feeling of being just right. This dress was one of them, she told herself. She sighed. She no longer felt like Cinderella.

CHAPTER 23

'Andrew, can you just give this your seal of approval? It's the seating plan for the Sinclair dinner. Stevie's had to make some last-minute alterations but I think for the most part it's satisfactory.' Jenny placed the revised plan on Andrew's desk.

His eyes scanned the table layout, noting the diplomatically placed circular tables, each seating ten guests. Last year they had been rectangular, prompting disgruntled comments of 'being stuck on the end'. Andrew scrutinized the Sinclair table.

'You were going to be outnumbered by females,' Jenny explained, 'until Morag suggested inviting Dr McAllister and Mary thought it might be a good idea if Callum – Iain's friend – came along to escort Jean.'

'I haven't got time to read the name of every guest at every table, Jenny, and I'm sure Stevie's done a good job, so perhaps you can just reel off who's on our table and who's in the immediate vicinity?'

Jenny duly obliged. 'Apart from us Sinclairs – that is you, Mary, Jean, Iain, Morag and myself – there's Miss Tandy, Alex McAllister, Duncan and Callum. I think you'll find that makes ten.'

Andrew looked puzzled. 'And do you think that's fair on Paul? I know Duncan's worked flat-out to get everything off the production line and into the stores but after all it is Paul who's made this past year so successful. I'm surprised, Jennifer, I thought you of all people would have wanted Paul on our table. Surely Callum could sit elsewhere?'

Jenny hesitated, then realized Andrew hadn't studied the seating plan as well as she'd hoped. She pointed to the adjoining table.

'I thought it better if Paul sat there . . . next to Gina.'

'Gina! Surely not!' Andrew said in alarm. He studied the table plan in greater detail. 'But I thought you said she wasn't coming; even Paul said she was going to be away.'

'She was,' acknowledged Jenny, unfolding Stevie's neatly executed plan, 'but apparently she's changed her mind. She sent a letter of acceptance and even rang Stevie to make sure it had arrived.' She was going to add 'you know Gina' but felt in the circumstances it was wholly inappropriate.

Andrew looked panic-stricken, his eyes filled with horror. 'My lord! What are we going to do, Jennifer? What do you think she's playing at?'

'I suggest you do nothing, Andrew, just behave as normal. Gina won't be on our table, and as for what she's playing at, let's just hope she's playing at being the dutiful wife for once. Who knows, she might even have a conscience after all. Perhaps she now feels she should be by Paul's side and save him from any further embarrassment.'

Secretly they both thought this unlikely, but with the

dance only days away there was little either of them could do now. Jenny leaned forward to pick up the plan. 'There is one thing I could do,' she added thoughtfully. 'What if . . . when I see Paul – we have a meeting arranged for tomorrow – I explain the seating arrangement? I'll try and think of an excuse between now and then.'

'Wait a minute!' Andrew cried, stroking his chin. 'I've an idea. Move Alistair from that table to Paul and Gina's table; he and Paul have known each other for ages. That way it won't look so odd.' He looked towards Jenny for a positive response and discerned abject disapproval. 'Oh, I was forgetting, you really don't like Alistair Jennings, do you?'

Jenny shuddered. 'No, quite frankly I don't, Andrew. Oh, I realize his marketing of the House of St Claire hampers was superb – particularly those for the glorious twelfth – but he just makes my flesh creep!'

Dejected by Jenny's disapproval of his suggestion, Andrew sat in silence. It had seemed such a good idea, the perfect solution in fact. Alistair, who was so full of himself, would probably keep Gina entertained for most of the evening and thus reduce the risk of Gina straying in Andrew's direction. If only he could persuade Jennifer to change her mind.

'Oh, all right,' she replied. 'If you think it will do the trick I'll tell Stevie to make the necessary alterations. Only don't forget I have absolutely no desire to be in close proximity to Alistair.'

'Thanks, Jennifer,' said Andrew, putting his hand on hers. 'I'll try and make it up to you some time.'

'There'll be no "try" about it, Andrew Sinclair – just

216

make sure you do!' Jenny threatened jokingly as she left the office.

Stevie listened to yet more alterations to the seating plan without comment. Hers was not to reason why, yet she knew Jenny loathed Alistair Jennings and suffered him purely as a business colleague. He didn't quite make Stevie's flesh creep, but she had the distinct feeling there was an ulterior motive behind Alistair's constant attention where Jenny was concerned. What was he trying to prove, or, more to the point, what was he after? The more Stevie saw of Alistair – which was too much just lately – the more convinced she became of his intention to wheedle his way into Andrew's good books. Did he perhaps hope for a place on the Sinclair board or, worse still, have serious designs on Jenny?

With the photocopier whirring in the background Stevie's imagination gave rise to flights of fancy. Smiling, she picked up one of the copies. Yes, she'd done as instructed and placed Alistair at the adjoining table – but sitting with his back to the Sinclairs! That way she could also seat him next to Gina Hadley, whom she also didn't much care for, thus making it possible for Paul to be facing in Jenny's direction. She congratulated herself on her cunning.

Later her mother would accuse her of playing with fire. Stevie however saw it differently; Jenny deserved some happiness in her life. She'd wasted six years of it on the moody Cameron Ross, spent endless hours at Sinclair's, and with Paul perhaps . . . OK, so Paul was married to Gina, Stevie conceded, watching her mother peel vegetables, but in name only, and, if rumours were to be believed, not for much longer. Why then, argued Stevie, couldn't Jenny and Paul just be good friends?

'Because,' insisted Mrs Stephens, 'I don't think being good friends is going to be enough for either of them, and you'd best not interfere, Cressida.'

Stevie felt disheartened. She should have known better than to discuss the situation with her mother. Still, she had kept one thing from her. Gina might be sitting on one side of Paul but Stevie would be on the other! There, from her vantage point, she hoped to gauge the atmosphere between Jenny and Paul. They got on so well and there had been the Geneva trip too. Stevie was desperate to discover what had happened in Switzerland. Something had, she was sure of that. It showed in the way Paul looked at Jenny when he came to the office. Stevie smiled. She was prepared to bet Paul Hadley didn't make Jenny's flesh creep.

'That meeting went far better than I imagined,' said Paul brightly as they left the buyer's office. 'Just think – a whole window given over to the House of St Claire. What a great start for the New Year.'

Jenny was thrilled at the prospect; she couldn't wait to tell Andrew, and Morag too, of course. Morag would be arriving in a few days with Tandy. Andrew had offered to go and fetch her but she'd declined, insisting Hamish bring them in the Bentley instead. Covered for so long under dust sheets, it was about time it was taken out for a run, and what better than the journey from Argyll to Edinburgh? With Hamish driving at a leisurely pace she would at least see some of the scenery. When Andrew drove, she told him, the countryside simply whizzed by like some speeded-up film. Small wonder he'd crashed his car into Jenny's gatepost.

'Do you have time for lunch, Paul?' Jenny enquired. It would be easier to explain about the dance over lunch as opposed to standing outside the buyer's office.

Paul hesitated; they hadn't lunched together for ages. Prior to the Geneva trip, working lunches had been a familiar practice; since then . . . Since then what? Neither of them had spoken of it; it was like an unseen barrier between them. Paul bit his lip thoughtfully. Lunch together might put things right – give him chance to explain his feelings.

'Well?' she asked gently. 'Do you have time?'

How long had she been watching him? Paul studied her face, her ivory complexion and such gentle questioning eyes. He wanted to reach out and hold her again, to feel her respond as before. Sadly he remembered that the response had been oh, so brief; he couldn't risk upsetting her again.

'Lunch sounds like a great idea, but only if I'm paying.'

Jenny opened her mouth to remonstrate but he continued, 'I have an ulterior motive – I need to ask you something.' Feeling herself tense, she wondered if perhaps this was such a good idea after all. Since Geneva she'd consciously avoided being alone with him.

Sensing her unease, Paul added quickly, 'Don't look so worried. I only want you to help me choose something for Celestina and Emily. I've promised them new dresses for Christmas. As you're used to buying clothes for Fiona, I hoped you might be able to help me.'

Relieved, Jenny followed him to the restaurant where she prepared herself mentally to broach the subject of the forthcoming dinner. If Andrew had been shocked to learn of Gina's intention to attend, Paul's reaction was one of total disbelief and anger. 'But Gina told me,' he insisted, 'she was going away, she couldn't be bothered to attend some silly company Christmas dinner!' The words had already escaped from his lips before he realized whose company it was Gina had been referring to.

'I'm sorry, Jenny, I shouldn't have spoken like that about Sinclair's.'

'You didn't, you merely repeated Gina's opinion, and I dare say it's one we've all shared over the years. Some company dinners, even Sinclair's, can be a bore. I just hoped – we just hoped,' she added quickly, 'this year would be special.'

Aware of her slip of the tongue, Paul reached for her hand. 'Let's hope it will be,' he said earnestly. 'After all, the House of St Claire has a lot to celebrate.'

In the children's dress department Jenny recognized the assistant who'd served her on the previous shopping trip with Stevie. She graced Jenny and Paul with a sweeping smile before continuing on her way to lunch. There her friend from the lingerie department was already waiting.

'Someone you know?' enquired Paul, staring in disbelief at the blue rinse.

'Company stalwart,' Jenny explained. 'She's been here years, so Morag tells me. Sadly she's a dying breed – nothing's too much trouble, unlike this one,' and she nodded in the direction of the young assistant whose attention they were trying to attract.

'Thanks, Jenny,' said Paul, almost an hour later. 'I'd no idea I was going to take up so much of your time. I'm extremely grateful, it's a great weight off my mind. The colour will be just perfect for them both.'

He smoothed his hand against one of the midnight-blue velvet bodices.

'I wasn't so sure about the colour at first but the broderie anglaise at the neck and hem makes a pretty contrast. As you say, if Fiona's new dress is bottle-green, we can't have the identical colour. I think red is a bit too garish, especially on young children. It always reminds me of Red Rhoda.'

Jenny sought an explanation as the reluctant assistant laboriously folded the two dresses.

'Red Rhoda,' Paul grinned, 'was the local "lady of the night" when we were lads. Her real name was Rhonda but her father kept chickens – Rhode Island Reds to be precise – and some wag, seeing her strut her pitch, called her "Red Rhoda". She always wore a lot of red, you see, and somehow I always associate the colour red with her.'

With both dresses wrapped, Paul accepted Jenny's offer of keeping them at the cottage until Christmas. The temptation for Cele and Emily to refrain from hunting for Christmas presents would be far too great. Particularly if they saw him arrive home with two large department store bags. Out in Princes Street he quickly bent and kissed Jenny's cheek before saying goodbye.

'Looks as if you've had a successful shopping expedition,' came a voice.

221

Paul and Jenny turned to see the two assistants returning from lunch.

'I'm sure your little girls will love their dresses,' said the blue rinse. 'I saw you looking at the delightful velvets and taffetas.' She turned her attention to Jenny with a knowing smile. 'And did madam show her husband the lingerie?'

Not waiting for Jenny's reply, she directed her next remark to Paul.

'It's just what her dress requires, you know. Even the most exquisitely cut garment, although worn by the most perfect figure,' here she looked at Jenny and winked knowingly at Paul, 'needs the correct foundation garments. The perfect Christmas present, if you ask me.'

Jenny said nothing; she was far too embarrassed. Paul meanwhile was transfixed by the blue hair set into rigid waves. Somewhere in the back of his mind he remembered an elderly aunt who'd been a hairdresser. What was it she used to say? Something about the beauty of Marcel waving. Was this what she meant? As a boy it had meant nothing.

In his mind's eye he'd just conjured up a picture of a Frenchman. And quite how a Frenchman waved beautifully, Paul had been unable to fathom! The blue rinse was addressing him once more. 'Of course my friend here will be only too pleased to help if you're not sure of madam's size.'

Paul roared with laughter as the blue rinse was led away by her friend.

'Do you know, Jenny, I'm convinced they've been drinking. Obviously a pre-Christmas tipple in the local wine bar if you ask me. What on earth was she on about?'

'Oh, just something she suggested to go with a dress I bought when I was with Stevie. Look,' she said hurriedly, anxious to get away. 'Let me know when you want the dresses. I must dash. Thank you for lunch and for being so understanding about the seating arrangements.'

With that she was gone through the bustle of early afternoon shoppers, leaving Paul to ponder on the bizarre conversation he'd just been part of. Later, waiting outside the girls' school, realization dawned.

'You fool, Paul Hadley!' he said to himself. 'That woman thought Jenny was your wife! No wonder she looked so embarrassed and left in such a hurry! How could you be so blind?'

To the sales assistant they must have seemed like any other happily married couple. She'd probably seen them lunching together and then shopping for the girls' dresses. What then could have been more natural than for Paul to kiss his wife goodbye?

With Paul's imagination getting the better of him, he pictured what it would be like going home to Jenny. Preparing dinner together, they would discuss the day's events and later help Celestina and Emily get ready for bed . . .

A flurry of children appeared at the school gates, to be met by mothers with welcoming arms. Even through the window Paul could hear their animated conversation. Talk of Mary and Joseph, donkeys and shepherds filled the air. 'Goodness,' thought Paul, 'can Christmas be so near?'

'Are you sure Cele is coming?' he asked as Emily sat with her nose pressed against the car window looking for her sister.

'Yes, but first she's got to see her teacher. It's about angels.'

'Angels,' Paul replied. 'Oh, I see.' He didn't, but it must be something to do with the school nativity play and doubtless Cele would tell him.

The last trickle of children and mothers with pushchairs came into the playground. At the back, holding the hand of a young classroom helper, was a very sorrowful-looking Cele. Paul noticed she had been crying.

'I'm very sorry, Mr Hadley, Cele appears to be very upset. It's about the school nativity play.'

Paul bent down to be on the level with his daughter, leaving Emily to watch from the car window.

'Now, Cele,' he coaxed kindly, 'what's this all about?'

'Mrs Edwards won't let me be an angel. She says my hair's too dark and curly! I can only be an angel if I've got hair like Phillipa Blair.'

Paul sighed and lifted Cele into the car. 'Well, I'm afraid not everyone can have fair hair. Can't you be something else instead? I'm sure there must be lots of other parts to play.'

Cele stuck out her bottom lip. 'Mrs Edwards said I can be the innkeeper's wife . . . but I don't want to be.'

'Why's that,' Paul asked, dreading the reply.

'Because Darren Hendry is going to be the innkeeper and he smells!'

Switching on the ignition Paul sighed. 'This,' he said quietly under his breath, 'is going to be one of those evenings!' Instead of going home to the tranquil domestic scene he'd imagined earlier, there was Gina to contend with and a distraught innkeeper's wife.

For some reason known only to herself, Gina had stormed out of the house only minutes before Paul left to fetch the girls, announcing that there was a tin of ravioli in the cupboard and fish fingers in the freezer!

Removing his jacket, Paul hung it on the door and ran the girls' bath, adding two capfuls of sweet-smelling bath gel to the water. He watched as the thick layer of bubbles rose slowly and parted them to test the temperature. The water took on a rosy glow and for the second time that afternoon he found himself thinking of Jenny. What was it she'd said in the summer when she'd held the rose-tinted jars of raspberry jelly and spoken of angels . . . something about marmalade days?

Paul's own would-be angel stood at the bathroom door with the remnants of ravioli and dry tears on her cheeks.

'Better now?' asked Paul as he helped her into the bath. Cele nodded and waited for her father to lift Emily in beside her. In doing so, he caught sight of the official manilla envelope in his inside jacket pocket.

The contents of the letter stated clearly that Gina was perfectly agreeable to a divorce. The problem was that that had been last week, when Gina was calm and co-operative and could be reasoned with. Now, given today's state of mind, anything could happen, and before the first court hearing they would have to face the Sinclair dinner – together as man and wife.

Emily piled bubbles on to her head and announced brightly, 'Look! I'm a Mr Frosty ice cream.' Cele, for once not amused, turned to Paul. 'Anyway, I'm having a new teacher, 'cos Mrs Edwards is having a baby like Mary and Joseph and she's got to leave *really soon*! *Hurray*!'

'I 'spect that's 'cos it's a long way to Bethlehem,' Emily announced.

Smiling fondly at them both, Paul lifted a towel from the radiator.

CHAPTER 24

With the tables cleared and the band playing, Andrew allowed himself a moment to relax and view the proceedings. He glanced only briefly at Gina, who with her back to him sat in animated conversation with Alistair. Paul caught his eye. Andrew smiled and nodded acknowledgement. He'd been dreading coming face to face with Paul and Gina, yet their arrival had passed without incident. Paul had paused only briefly to speak to Morag and introduce Gina before joining Alistair at their table.

Once out of earshot, Morag and Flora Tandy found themselves discussing Gina's dress – or what little there was of it. The red velvet with its short skirt and low neckline, which only days before had adorned a store's model, was now tightly moulded over Gina's curvaceous body. Paul had disliked it on sight but had refrained from voicing his disapproval, deciding, as he'd so often done in the past, that it was better to remain silent. Tonight was not a good time to provoke Gina. For the moment she appeared calm and was enjoying the attention of Alistair and the other male guests at their table. As at the airport almost a year ago, female sympathies lay with Paul.

'Wow!' gasped Callum, as Iain explained about their skiing trip, quite forgetting he was here as Jean's escort. Jean and Mary just looked at each other in disbelief. Andrew and Jenny had both mentioned Gina before, but to them she was Mrs Gina Hadley, not the Gina Dintino of their ill-fated skiing holiday. The questions Mary now wanted to ask would have to wait; Andrew was leading her to the dance floor.

Chatting enthusiastically about the latest piece of Sinclair machinery, Duncan turned to address Jenny.

'It's quite amazing, really – you must come and see it some time. I expect there's no time before Christmas, but in the New Year perhaps?'

Jenny wasn't listening; her attention was elsewhere. She was watching Gina leaning heavily on Alistair's shoulder. Whispering something in his ear, she gave a deep, throaty laugh and held her glass in his direction to be filled. Paul's quiet entreaties to take it easy were ignored.

'I don't want to take it easy, I want to dance! But you don't want to dance, do you, Paul?' Gina addressed the entire table. 'He's such a bore, not like Alistair. We've had great times together, haven't we, Alistair?'

Alistair looked about the table, where their fellow guests sipped their drinks uncomfortably and averted their eyes.

Jenny watched as Alistair withdrew from Gina's grasp. No longer was he the self-assured Alistair Jennings she was familiar with. Instead there was anxiety written all over his face, prompted by Gina's revelation.

'Jenny,' he called nervously. 'Why don't you come

and join us? Perhaps you can persuade Paul on to the dance floor?'

All eyes from the top table were now on Jenny. She met Morag's gaze, and was surprised to hear her mother say, 'You go and dance, my dear – forget about us oldies. Who knows, perhaps I might even take to the floor myself later, that is if Alex and Duncan ever stop talking about machinery and golf!'

Allowing herself to be led by Paul through the group of people already dancing, Jenny stood in the middle of the floor. Gina glared at her angrily, emptied her glass and turned her attention once more to Alistair.

'Sorry to drag you away from your family,' Paul said as the band began to play a slow waltz. He slipped an arm around her waist. 'I'm afraid I'm not much of a Fred Astaire, or even a John Travolta come to that.'

Jenny smiled, remembering Callum's earlier gyrations on the dance floor with Jean. The band's attempt at playing Stevie Wonder's 'Woman in Red' had been a bad choice, with Callum failing miserably to impress either Jean or Gina. Jean had been acutely embarrassed by his display and Gina had only roared with laughter when Callum, trying one fancy step too many, had retreated across the parquet floor on his bottom.

'Frankly I was only too glad to get away,' Jenny replied. 'Duncan's very sweet but I'm afraid I can't quite share in his enthusiasm for every piece of equipment we purchase for Sinclair's.'

'Ah, yes,' said Paul. 'Duncan is a prime example of man's love of machinery, but he does tend to go into every nut and bolt – or should that be microchip? However, I must confess I find him an extremely personable fellow, and I expect you already realize he's performed wonders at the factory? In fact, Andrew maintains we would never have got the St Claire range into the stores in time if it hadn't been for Duncan.'

Feeling Paul's eyes meet hers, Jenny nodded in agreement and smiled warmly. 'In that case I'd better take back all I said about him. I stand duly corrected.'

Forgetting her earlier anxieties when Paul and Gina had first arrived, Jenny found herself relaxing in Paul's arms. She'd not felt like this since . . . Sadly, all too soon her spell was broken, the last strains of the waltz faded away and Paul and Jenny stood apart.

'Now,' announced the bandleader, moving to the edge of the stage, 'moving on from our earlier rendering of Stevie Wonder's "Woman in Red", we shall now play Chris de Burgh's "Lady in Red", and I think we have our very own lady in red here tonight . . . so where is she?'

All eyes, including Andrew's, were on Gina standing by Alistair's side.

'Perhaps we could make this a ladies' excuse me?' said the bandleader in Gina's direction. 'Would you like to lead the way?'

Jenny could only watch in horror as Gina, her eyes sparkling with delight, made her way in Andrew's direction. His face filled with panic, and grasping Mary's arm, Andrew remained frozen to the spot.

Turning to Paul in desperation, Jenny pleaded, 'I don't care what you do or how you do it, Paul, but just get Gina away from Andrew and out of here – now!'

Alarmed by the sudden change in Jenny's voice, Paul

230

looked first at Gina and then at Andrew. All too soon he recognized in Gina's triumphant glow and Andrew's state of panic another clear case of betrayal. But this was no time to ponder where or when, or even for how long. For Jenny's sake he must act quickly.

Striding positively towards Gina and stopping only inches away from Andrew, Paul announced convincingly, 'Where I come from, for the first "Ladies' Excuse Me" of the evening, the ladies must always dance with their husbands or partners first.' So saying, he nodded to the bandleader to strike up the opening bars and Gina was led open-mouthed across the floor.

What seemed like an eternity to Andrew and Jenny was in fact only moments but it was long enough for Mary to recognize a familiar scent. The same heavy perfume she'd noticed months ago on Andrew.

Twisting away from Andrew's grasp, Mary scanned the room, searching for Jenny, only to see her crossing the floor in the opposite direction. Feelings of hurt and disgust filled Mary's whole being. She wanted an explanation and she wanted it now. What had Jenny been keeping from her?

Realizing a showdown with Mary was inevitable – but not now and not in full view of the Sinclair family and staff – Jenny took the only available means of escape. Under the watchful eye of Morag and Flora Tandy, Jennifer Sinclair invited a bemused and delighted Alistair Jennings to dance.

She shuddered as Alistair's warm clammy hands clasped her body tightly against his own and discovered to her horror that dancing with Alistair had not quite the same effect as dancing with Paul. To begin with Alistair had been drinking heavily, and secondly he persisted in running his hands up and down the black silk crêpe, while continually fondling her buttocks. Sickened, she wanted to run, but first she must try to discover if Paul and Gina had left the room.

Where was Paul – had he managed to get Gina away? Horrified, Jenny caught a glimpse of red velvet through the crowds. Surely they weren't still here? Couples were beginning to change partners and panic rose inexorably in Jenny's breast – what would happen now? Briefly Paul's eyes met hers, but they showed no flicker of emotion.

Stony-faced and tight-lipped, Paul led Gina into the cold December night, where she tried to slip from his grasp.

'Paul, let me go! What are you doing? Where are we going?'

'*We* are going home, Gina!'

'But they're playing the song for me! I wanted to dance with And . . .'

She stopped short as Paul opened the car door and forced her inside.

'You wanted to dance with Andrew, I know. But this is one time, Gina, when you are not having your own way, and I refuse to be made a fool of, particularly in front of the Sinclairs.' Paul fastened Gina's seat-belt as she tried to struggle from the car.

'You're hurting me, Paul – let me out or I shall scream!'

'You can scream all you like, Gina,' said Paul, switching on the ignition. 'As for hurting, I suggest you sit still, then the seat-belt won't cut into you. You could also try covering up some of that bare flesh. In that outfit you look just like a common . . .!'

Sickened and disgusted, Paul watched Gina clutch the straps of her dress where they'd fallen from her shoulders to reveal a bare breast. She then tried pulling at the material to cover her knees. Angrily she glared in Paul's direction, but he said nothing and stopped only briefly at the car park entrance. There he reached into the rear passenger seat for a rug and threw it across her lap.

The journey home was spent in silence, which from experience Paul knew to be the calm before the storm. He was only thankful Cele and Emily were spending the night at Helen's. They would at least be spared the ensuing vitriolic scene.

Gina, still swathed in the travel rug, emerged from the car docile as a lamb. Once indoors, however, she turned on him like a wild animal ready for the kill. Her dark eyes flashed as torrents of abuse poured forth from her cruel, scarlet-painted mouth.

Weary from so many months of her unpredictable behaviour, Paul stood quietly by the fireplace, his hand resting on the mantelpiece. He'd decided on the way home that he wasn't going to be drawn into yet another of Gina's screaming bouts. Everything that needed to be said had been gone through already; their marriage was at the point of no return.

Furious at failing to draw Paul into verbal combat, Gina changed tactics by loudly proclaiming her liaisons with Alistair and Andrew, but to no avail. Paul would not be provoked. It was only when Jenny's name was mentioned that she perceived a flicker of emotion in his face.

'Rant and rave all you like, Gina, but I refuse point-blank to subject myself to one of your slanging matches.' Paul's voice was calm and unemotional as he continued coolly, 'Earlier you spoke of being hurt, physically hurt, but you've only yourself to blame, for wearing that ridiculous dress.'

Gina had discarded the rug, but she picked it up again and covered herself as if she were naked. Warily she waited for Paul to continue, convinced he was going to say something she really didn't want to hear.

'Have you thought of the hurt you've caused everyone?' Paul asked in a dignified tone. 'Have you, Gina? The emotional hurt to our children or to me, your husband? No, of course you haven't, you've been far too busy thinking of yourself and having a good time at everyone else's expense!'

Gina slid nervously into an armchair. She'd never seen Paul like this before. He seemed so cold and distant and so . . . so alien. Usually she never had any trouble provoking him into argument so she could add fuel to her next tirade. This time none was forthcoming.

Reaching into his breast pocket, Paul drew out his wallet and, removing his personal papers, placed it on the mantelpiece.

'In there, Gina, you'll find more than enough for where you intend to go. Take what you need, as I understand you've already decided against spending Christmas with us. And if you haven't yet made your excuses to Celestina and Emily, I shall tell them you've had to visit your parents in Italy. There's no point in spoiling their Christmas further. For your information, I now intend to return to the hotel to make my apologies to the Sinclairs, but when I get back I expect to find you gone. Do I make myself perfectly clear?'

Panic-stricken, Gina stared after him in disbelief. Her throat felt dry as she opened her mouth to speak. Paul couldn't leave her, not like this. No, he couldn't possibly just walk out on her!

'Aren't you even going to say goodbye?' she called lamely.

With his hand on the door, Paul stopped and slowly turned to face her.

'Gina,' he said with a sardonic smile, 'I appear to have spent the best part of our married life saying goodbye to you; I'm sure I don't need to say it again. Let's use your phrase, shall we . . .? *Ciao*, darling!'

CHAPTER 25

Returning to the hotel, Paul was surprised to find many of the older guests departing or in the process of saying goodbye, leaving the younger members heading for the disco. Morag, perceptive as ever, decided she'd had enough excitement for one night and summoned Tandy, who had been dancing with Alex McAllister, to accompany her to her room.

'No doubt Andrew and Mary – and Jennifer too if she can tear herself away from the clutches of that Alistair fellow – can see to the rest of our guests,' Morag announced tersely.

'What about Miss Stephens?' Tandy enquired. 'Do you think she needs to be helped back to her room? She looks quite lost and all alone at that table in her wheelchair.'

'I doubt it. I expect she's only too glad she's not had the likes of Duncan trampling over her feet all night. She's an extremely capable young woman, you know, but if it makes you feel any better, Tandy, then I suggest you go and ask her if she needs any assistance.'

Stevie, acknowledging Morag's departure and touched by Flora Tandy's concern, expressed her thanks but said she intended to remain a little longer; she enjoyed watching people dance.

'I expect she'll go away feeling sorry for me,' whispered Stevie to herself, not wishing to divulge her real reason for staying. Jenny had been dancing with Alistair for ages, or at least Alistair had been monopolizing Jenny for ages. Stevie's intention was to remain until Paul returned. She wanted to see Jenny and Paul dance together again, but where was Paul?

Like Jenny, Stevie's eyes were constantly on the door, watching as each cool gust of air from the outer corridor heralded the entrance or departure of another guest. And she only had to look at Jenny's face to know Paul had arrived. Without warning Alistair found himself alone on the dance floor, and he turned to see Jenny hurrying to Paul's side.

'Well,' she asked anxiously, leading him to a quiet corner, 'has she gone?'

'Oh, yes, she's gone, Jenny. I don't think you or Andrew need worry any more.' There was a note of solemn finality in Paul's voice.

'Thank God!' she sighed, taking his arm. 'I'm so grateful, Paul.'

'You don't have to be. In fact I can only apologize for the trouble she's caused.'

Paul looked in Andrew and Mary's direction. There was a distinct frostiness between husband and wife. 'I just hope,' he continued, 'that Mary has a forgiving nature.'

'You knew . . . you knew about Andrew and Gina?'

'Not exactly,' Paul said ruefully. 'Let's just say I suspected. You get used to recognizing the signs. It wasn't until tonight that I knew for certain Andrew had been Gina's latest victim.'

'I'm so sorry . . . so sorry,' Jenny whispered. 'I know Andrew bitterly regrets betraying your trust and friendship.'

'Then tell him not to worry; if it hadn't been Andrew it would have been someone else – though she's already had Alistair, in case you hadn't already guessed!' He looked up to see Alistair making his way towards them, only to find his way barred by Stevie, who ran her wheelchair deliberately into Alistair's foot.

Ignoring Alistair's cry of pain, Paul leant forward and reached across for Jenny's hand. He held it gently, caressing her fingers, and looked earnestly into her eyes.

'Jenny, there's so much I need to say to you, I just don't know . . .'

His statement remained unfinished as Alistair came limping over.

'Damned woman!' Alistair muttered under his breath. 'I'm sure she tripped me up deliberately. Don't know what the hell she's playing at.'

He froze as he came across Jenny and Paul deep in quiet conversation. Paul was even holding Jenny's hand! Alistair had absolutely no intention of allowing this delightful *tête-à-tête* to continue.

'Ah, Jenny, there you are. Fancy leaving a fellow standing alone like that on the dance floor without explanation.'

Jenny remained seated and made no attempt to remove her hand from Paul's. Nothing would induce her to return to Alistair's lecherous grasp. Sitting down uninvited, Alistair turned his attention to Paul.

'Got Gina home all right, did you? She's a wild one, that wife of yours, not like our sweet Jenny here.' Alistair leered in Jenny's direction and put his hand on her knee.

Paul's fingers tightened on to Jenny's. He would not be drawn on the subject of Gina, least of all with Alistair, and definitely not in front of Jenny. Why didn't Alistair just go and leave them alone?

'Well,' said Alistair, 'I was going to ask you to continue our dance, Jenny, but I see Paul wants you all to himself. I'm not surprised really – when he was so desperate for work and I suggested he came to see you, I told him you were a real soft touch. From where I'm sitting it looks as if he's already found that out for himself. Aren't I right, Paul?'

Stunned, Jenny looked at Paul. She was waiting for some show of denial on his part but none came. Was Alistair correct? Was that all she'd been – a real soft touch and Paul's passport to security?

Calmly Jenny released her hand from Paul's grasp and rose from her chair, showing no sign of emotion to either man – Alistair who made no secret of his designs on her, or Paul who had played on her trust.

'If you'll both excuse me, I really must go and see to Stevie. She appears to be having trouble with her wheelchair.'

'Come back soon, Jenny. Don't forget the last waltz,' Alistair called.

Swallowing hard and choking back tears, Jenny forced herself to walk away slowly in Stevie's direction. She had to behave as if nothing had happened. 'Last waltz indeed! Who the hell does Alistair think he is?'

'Pardon?' Stevie said raising an eyebrow. 'I didn't quite catch that. Are you all right, Jenny? You look dreadful. It's not your feet slowly coming back to life after all Duncan's trampling, is it?'

Jenny forced a flicker of a smile. 'No, not Duncan's feet, but you could say I feel well and truly trodden on. Look, I don't feel like staying here any longer. Andrew and Mary can see to all the farewells. Are you coming too?'

Stevie hesitated; she wasn't ready to leave. What had happened in that far corner? One moment it seemed Paul and Jenny were getting on so well and the next . . . that idiot Alistair had to go and spoil things. It was a pity she'd only managed to bruise his foot and not put him out of action for the rest of the evening. 'What about the last waltz?' she asked feebly. 'Won't you even stay for that?'

'Stevie! As I consider you a true friend, I'm too polite to tell you what you can do with the last dance; however if Alistair asks for me you have my permission to tell him to go to hell!'

Dumbstruck, Stevie watched Jenny turn sharply and leave the room. Were there tears in her eyes? She couldn't be sure, of course, but how was she going to find out? Anxiously searching the room, her gaze rested on Paul sitting at a corner table. He looked distinctly ill at ease, while Alistair forcefully pushed a large glass of wine in his direction with a loud, 'Cheers, Paul, and here's to absent friends.'

Dejectedly Stevie reached for her own glass and sipped at her wine. What an evening! What a truly awful evening it had turned out to be, especially when she'd had such hopes.

240

'Damn you, Gina Hadley!' she hissed under her breath. 'This is all your bloody fault. And as for you, Alistair Jennings, what a pity I wasn't driving a double-decker bus instead of a wheelchair. Then you wouldn't be looking quite so smug.'

In desperation swinging round to have another look at Paul and the obesquious Alistair, Stevie caught her elbow against the sugar bowl, left from when the waiter brought coffee. 'Damn!' she cried, watching the silver bowl resound solidly against her wine glass where it sent a pool of deep red wine trickling into a drift of sugar. 'That's all I need!'

Mopping up the wine, Stevie surveyed the red stain as it seeped into the white damask cloth. From there she ran her forefinger into the residue of unsullied sugar. Red against white, she mused, and in her present state of melancholy she associated the red with Gina's ridiculous dress and the white with Jenny's ashen face as she'd rushed from the room.

241

CHAPTER 26

Sitting in her hotel room, a tearful Jenny sat in front of the dressing table and viewed her reflection in the mirror.

'You fool, Jennifer Sinclair, you complete and utter fool! How could you let yourself be taken in by such a man?'

With fresh tears welling in her eyes, she remembered her first meeting with Paul and his dishevelled appearance. Had that been a ploy to make her feel sorry for him? Perhaps he'd even encouraged Gina to make a pass at Andrew too – and Geneva! What about Geneva? Had Paul and Gina planned that deliberately? Tears streamed down her face. The more she tried to think about events of the past year, the more confused she became.

'No!' she cried aloud. 'Andrew told me the Geneva trip had been Gina's idea – Paul had no part in it.'

Now, however, she wasn't so sure and, spying the complimentary basket of St Claire products on the dressing table, she picked it up and threw it across the room in the direction of a champagne bottle. 'You and your bloody clever ideas, Paul Hadley. How I wish I'd never met you!'

Unzipping her dress, Jenny became aware of a bottle of bath gel wedged precariously against two champagne glasses and, walking over to retrieve it, dislodged a gift card edged in Sinclair colours.

Smiling ruefully, she read Andrew's message, written earlier in the day.

'Let's drink to the House of St Claire and a wonderful year. Many thanks for all your help (particularly with you know who!). Sorry you've got to suffer Alistair this evening. Love, Andrew.'

How typical of Andrew, Jenny thought bitterly, and how simple it was. Just send your sister a bottle of champagne to ease your guilty conscience. But would Mary be so easily won over? If Mary didn't know before this evening the full truth behind Andrew's affair, then she would certainly know by now.

'Poor Mary,' Jenny sighed, uncorking the champagne. Filling her glass to the brim, she returned to the dressing table to toast her reflection in the mirror. What was it Andrew had said on the card? 'A wonderful year'.

Had it been a wonderful year? It certainly should have been, and it had often seemed that way when they went from store to store. In fact at every stop the House of St Claire was highly acclaimed, and Paul's name was always greeted with glowing accolades.

'Paul Hadley,' Jenny whispered to her reflection as she emptied her glass and poured another. 'How could you be so cruel?'

Though Alistair was certain of Jenny's return, Paul was of a different opinion. He'd seen Jenny approach Stevie; witnessed their brief conversation and watched her leave the room. Furious with Alistair for coming out with such a ludicrous comment, Paul was even angrier with himself for not denying it.

What made it even worse was that he couldn't ever remember Alistair describing Jenny as 'a soft touch'. Paul ran his hands anxiously through his hair. Knowing Alistair, it was possible, and if it had been said, then it had been at such low ebb in his life. With the inception of St Claire, a vastly improved work situation and the girls settled at school, there'd never been any need to dwell in the past.

Alistair wandered off drunkenly in search of another bottle, leaving Paul with only one thought in mind. He must find Jenny and he must find her quickly. He must try and explain – that's if she would listen – and also apologize for any offence caused. With firm resolve Paul placed his glass on the table and stood up. There had been no ulterior motive behind his friendship with Jenny! Surely she would believe that?

'Stevie, where's Jenny? I need to speak to her.' Paul, looking tired and drawn, waited for Stevie's reply.

Tracing her finger in the spilt sugar, Stevie thought carefully. What was it Jenny had said? 'Tell Alistair to go to hell!' There'd been no mention of Paul. Nevertheless she must tread warily . . . Jenny was her boss, after all.

'Stevie!' Paul began earnestly. 'I *must* speak to her. There's been a terrible misunderstanding and if it's not resolved tonight then . . . it may all be too late.'

Hearing the desperation in his voice, Stevie motioned Paul to sit by her side. She was getting a crick in her neck looking up at him and she didn't want to shout.

Besides, Alistair, having found yet another bottle of wine, was searching the room for a drinking partner.

'Oh, no!' Paul groaned. 'Not Alistair again! This is all his fault. Alistair and his big mouth!'

'He's got big feet too,' Stevie added, smiling at the memory of crushing Alistair's foot.

'As I don't think you'll be able to get away with that twice, will you please tell me where I can find Jenny?'

Stevie knew she had to act quickly. Alistair had already spotted Paul and was weaving his way across the floor. Without explanation she dropped her handbag on the floor and watched bemused as the contents scattered at Paul's feet.

'It's more than my job's worth to give you Jenny's room number, Paul, but as her room's next to mine, when I do see her I'll tell her you're anxious to speak to her.'

Giving Paul a knowing look, she enquired, 'Before you go, do you think you could help me with my bag, please?'

Although desperate to leave, Paul painstakingly collected the contents together and extended the bag in her direction.

'Can you just check to see if my room key is still there? I don't want to disturb Jenny when I go back, do I?'

Paul frowned. What on earth was wrong with Stevie? Why did she keep looking first at him and then at her open handbag? When realization dawned he gave a broad grin. The penny had dropped at last, or at least the key fob did . . . right into Paul's hand as he realized the significance of Stevie's previous remark. No, she couldn't possibly give him Jenny's room number, but she could give him her own! And twice she'd already mentioned Jenny was in the room next door!

'Stevie, you're an angel,' Paul said, kissing her on the cheek and, placing the key back in her bag, murmured, 'Wish me luck!'

'That's right, I'm an angel on wheels, and I wish you all the luck in the world, Paul.' Stevie grinned wickedly. 'Now, where's that Alistair Jennings? Do you think he's about ready for a second onslaught from my tyres?'

Paul didn't wait to find out – he was already running down the corridor to find Jenny's room. Stevie meanwhile sighed contentedly; perhaps there was hope after all. Glancing towards the table with its wine stain, she discovered she'd been subconsciously drawing the letters C and S in the scattered sugar granules. Anyone else would have thought Cressida Stephens had been writing her own initials. Stevie, however, knew otherwise.

In her hotel room at the far end of the corridor Jenny sat on the bed with unfocused eyes, a half-empty bottle of champagne by her side and a scattering of St Claire products at her feet. In the street outside, a car horn tooted noisily. Startled by its sudden discordant notes, she rose and walked to the window.

Late-night revellers from the Sinclair dance waved and shouted their farewells to each other. Glad someone had enjoyed themselves, Jenny closed the curtains and, looking in the dressing table mirror, discovered she not only felt awful, she looked awful too.

Slumped on the dressing-table stool, she tugged first

at her hair then at the shoulders of her dress and forced her mouth into a sultry pout. She frowned. There was something about her freshly tousled appearance that just wasn't right.

'No, Jennifer, you just haven't got it!' she announced, contemplating her dishevelled hair and newly acquired off-the-shoulder effect. 'You'll have to try harder than that if you want to emulate Gina Hadley!'

With a deep sigh she reached for Andrew's card. What was it he'd said – something about the year being wonderful? Well, Andrew might have thought so, but from Jenny's point of view it had also been extremely tiring. Her pale, wan face and eyes heavy with exhaustion now bore witness to the fact. Unlike Andrew, she hadn't even had a holiday this year, but – she brightened – she did at least have the remains of his champagne!

'That's it! That's just what I need! Another glass of champagne and perhaps some colour in my cheeks.'

Walking back to the dressing-table with another full glass, Jenny tipped out the contents of her make-up bag. Unlike Gina, she had no bright scarlet lipstick, but if she applied her own burnt copper over and over again the effect should be almost the same. Humming the tune of 'Woman in Red' while applying mascara, she was startled by a knock at the door.'

'Jenny, it's Paul,' the muffled voice murmured. 'Please, I must talk to you.'

'No! Go away! Go home to your wife, Paul, and compare notes on how you both made complete and utter fools of us Sinclairs.'

'Jenny!' Paul pleaded. 'It isn't like that at all. You've

got to let me explain. Please! If the House of St Claire means anything to you – anything at all – then you must let me in.'

Spying the remains of the champagne, Jenny gave a wistful smile. Yes, the House of St Claire. Why not invite Paul in to share a toast to its success and her stupidity? Purposefully she strode to the door and unlocked it.

'Jenny!' Paul cried, aghast at her appearance. 'What on earth have you been doing to yourself?'

Ignoring his question, Jenny reached unsteadily for the bottle and poured him a glass of champagne. 'Here you are, you see, you're just in time for a drink, Paul. Oh, dear, I'm afraid it's rather full . . . but you don't mind, do you? After all, you like doing things to excess. Cheers!'

'Jenny, please!' begged Paul. Taking the dripping glass from her hand, he watched her walk with wavering footsteps to the edge of the bed and drink thirstily from her own.

Taking in her unusual state of disarray, her tousled hair and stained orange mouth, Paul shook his head sadly. Any moment now her dress was in danger of slipping even further from her shoulders, and if she wasn't careful she was going to spill her drink all over that exquisitely cut black crêpe. He hadn't failed to notice either, as she'd staggered to the bed, that it was completely unzipped at the back.

'Be careful of your dress!' he warned as Jenny slipped sideways. But it was too late, the champagne spilled from the glass all over the fine silk fabric. Quickly he passed her a box of tissues but she pushed them away.

'I don't need them,' she cried drunkenly. 'And I don't need my dress either because I'm going to bed. Besides, as you probably don't like my dress, then it really doesn't really matter if I take it off . . .'

'Jenny,' whispered Paul, 'I think it's a lovely dress, so please . . .'

'No, you don't!' she snapped bitterly. 'You don't like it at all. For a start it's not short enough or low enough for you, is it? And it certainly isn't red!' So saying, she hitched the skirt well above her knees and dropped the bodice to reveal her new set of black silk lingerie. 'There now – surely you think it looks better like this?'

Stunned, Paul walked towards her and took her firmly by the shoulders.

'Stop it! Jenny, stop! You don't know what you're doing!'

Struggling against him, Jenny fell back on to the bed where she lay quiet and still against the pillows. Paul sat down beside her and with trembling fingers raised the shoulders of the dress back into place. Aware of her turning on her side, he buried his head in his hands. This was all his fault, he thought sorrowfully – he'd reduced her to this.

In desperation Paul reached for his own full glass of champagne and swallowed deeply. Instinct told him he should leave, and leave now, before the situation got out of hand. But how could he leave her? It was obvious Jenny wasn't in a fit state to be left.

Feeling a hand on his arm, Paul watched in silence as Jenny took his glass, drank the remainder and then slipped seductively out of her dress.

'Come along,' she whispered, holding out her arms.

'Isn't this what you want, Paul? I'm a real soft touch, you know. Why don't you give me your hand, then you can feel for yourself. You don't really want to go home to Gina, do you? Won't I do for tonight? Just think, you can tell Gina you've made it a Sinclair double!'

Mention of Gina caused Paul to snap and, grabbing Jenny by the shoulders, he shook her angrily. 'Gina might act like a whore, Jenny, but I will not have *you* behaving like one! For your information I have *never* thought you a soft touch.' Paul's voice was desperate, 'Believe me, Jenny! I can't even remember Alistair saying it in the first place. You've really *got* to believe me!'

Rising dejectedly from the bed Paul walked towards the door. 'You're right, I do want you, but not like this. I want you because I love you, but you probably won't believe that either. In which case I'd better leave . . .'

Placing his hand on the door, he heard a muffled cry behind him and, turning, saw her face filled with tears.

'Please don't go, Paul,' she sobbed. 'I don't want you to go. I'm so sorry . . . but Gina and Andrew and then Alistair . . .'

'Hush,' he whispered, returning to take her in his arms. 'It's all right. Everything will be all right, you'll see.'

Long before dawn broke through the heavy December darkness Paul fumbled for his jacket. From the dim light of the bedside lamp he watched Jenny sleeping peacefully, her tears long since dried and all trace of the vulgar make-up gone. Cradling her in his arms earlier, she could have been a child; then he'd wanted nothing more than to console her and hold her close until she fell asleep.

As she slept, Paul studied the dim outline of their surroundings. Jenny's dress lay in a heap on the floor amidst a scattering of House of St Claire products and an empty champagne bottle. Moving uneasily, he wondered how he could leave without disturbing her.

Jenny stirred. The room felt suddenly cold and her head ached from the champagne. Shivering, she puzzled why she was on the bed and not beneath the covers where it would be warm and cosy? And why was she still in her underclothes? She would never sleep in her underwear and certainly not in her expensive new black silk.

'I'm cold,' she murmured, and, feeling a strong pair of arms lift her gently beneath the covers, urged softly, 'Please come back, come back and keep me warm . . . Cameron always . . .'

Paul held her in his arms and said nothing. If Jenny's thoughts were of her ex-fiancé, then in this soporific state she must surely be thinking she was with Cameron. Kissing her gently and caressing her face and hair, he realized it would be so easy to pretend he was Cameron . . . he wanted her so much.

Angry with himself for even thinking such things, Paul moved to the edge of the bed, but he felt a restraining hand on his shoulder. A whispered voice pleaded, 'Don't leave me.'

'Jenny, I mustn't stay . . . it's not Cameron, it's Paul . . .'

'I know, and it's because you're not Cameron that I want you to stay. Cameron was so . . . he said such cruel

251

things . . .' Jenny's arms reached towards him and, drawing him into her arms, she sighed deeply.

For Paul it was all too much of a temptation, and without thinking further he found himself undressing and slipping into the bed beside her.

CHAPTER 27

Christmas lunch at Conasg House was a sombre affair. In true matriarchal fashion Morag presided over the head of the table and surveyed each member of the family. An unhappy Mary was sitting next to a very subdued Andrew. Jean and Iain were casting each other furtive glances and there was Jenny looking what Tandy had described as 'decidedly strained'. Only Fiona remained unchanged.

Andrew in turn regarded his mother fearfully, expecting her at any moment to raise the subject of the dance. She'd said nothing, which was strange, as usually she and Tandy would spend hours having a post-dance discussion. They would then praise or criticize everything from the food and band to the clothes people wore. It was a standing family joke. Morag and Tandy were like hawk and mouse on such occasions, vying with each other in their opinions.

No one need wonder what their opinion was of Gina's dress. Their expressions on the night in question had made that perfectly clear. Prior to the discovery of her husband's infidelity, even Mary had voiced her thoughts openly while declaring her sympathy for Paul.

'Poor man,' she'd repeated over and over again, 'and those poor wee girls of his. I'm so glad Fiona suggested we take them to the pantomime, Andrew. Can you just imagine having a mother like that?'

At the time Andrew chose not to, and merely shook his head.

On Christmas Eve, however, Mary had not been so benevolent in her feelings towards Cele and Emily when Fiona raised the subject of the forthcoming pantomime.

With the family preparing to go to church, it was a wonder the whole household hadn't heard Mary and Andrew arguing. Only the celebration of Midnight Mass had drawn a veil over hostilities. And even now, with the natural flow of conversation resuming, Andrew still felt uneasy.

Fiona meanwhile chatted merrily away to her grandmother and her aunt, reminiscing about her chicken 'spots' and their summer picnics. It was inevitable therefore that the names of Celestina and Emily, and even Paul, should crop up time and time again.

At the mere mention of his name Jenny felt herself blush and reached for her glass of water. Since that fateful night of the dance she'd been unable to face him, not even to hand over the girls' dresses. She'd made some excuse to Stevie and left them with a note in the office.

Puzzled, Stevie had simply followed instructions and the dresses were duly handed over. In return a subdued Paul left a small package – Jenny's Christmas present – which as yet remained unopened in her room upstairs. Anxious to change the subject, Jenny asked Fiona about the pantomime.

'It's going to be Cinderella,' Fiona said eagerly, and in one breath, 'She has a wicked stepmother and a fairy godmother and goes to a ball and wears a pretty dress and there's a glass slipper and a handsome prince and I'm going to wear a pretty dress too . . . only mine is green but I 'spect Cinderella's will be white or gold.'

'Not red?' Iain asked sarcastically, joining in the conversation. From beneath the table, Jean kicked his ankle hard. Mary and Andrew glared in his direction and sat daggers drawn.

'No, of course not red, silly!' Fiona said defiantly. 'Red's a horrid colour!'

Glaring at her brother – who was pulling a face at her – Fiona continued angrily, 'Only nasty stepmothers wear red, or sometimes witches with frizzly black hair and big red mouths.'

'Sounds like someone we know,' muttered Iain beneath his breath, this time moving his ankles out of Jean's reach.

'But I wear red sometimes, Fiona,' Mary reminded her youngest daughter.

'Yes, but you're different, you're a kind mummy and you love me.'

With all eyes directed at Fiona, Mary produced a white lace handkerchief from her pocket and blew her nose. Even the stoic Morag swallowed hard.

Thank heavens for Fiona, thought Jenny to herself.

Aware of her new-found attention, Fiona addressed her audience.

'My mummy's a nice mummy, she lets me have my friends to tea and we're all going to the pantomime. But I can't go to Cele and Emily's house 'cos their mummy's a whore and anyway,' sighed Fiona, 'she's gone away again.' Puzzled, Fiona turned solemnly to face her grandmother. 'What is a whore, Grannie?'

'*Fiona*!' gasped Mary. 'Go and wash your mouth out with soap and water this instant!'

Fiona stared at her mother in disbelief – the mother whom only moments ago she'd described as loving and kind. Her eyes welled with tears as she climbed down from the table and made to leave the room.

'Just a moment,' said Morag kindly, as she held out her hand to her grandaughter. 'Now, Fiona, you come and sit on Grannie's knee and tell me all about it. I expect there's been a wee bit of a misunderstanding.'

Through tear-filled sobs Fiona explained.

'Last night I heard Daddy talking to Mummy about fetching Cele and Emily for the pantomime. When I asked if I could go with him, Mummy said no,' here Fiona looked at her mother, 'but she did say Cele and Emily could still come to tea.' Fiona's face turned red as she continued, 'Later Mummy and Daddy were shouting. They thought I was in bed but I listened at the door and Mummy said she didn't want me to go with Daddy to see his whore. I only wondered what it was, Grannie, I didn't know it was rude.'

'Goodness!' announced Tandy. 'Is that the time? If we don't hurry we shall miss the Queen's speech. Shall I go and switch on the television?'

Andrew coughed and wiped his scarlet face with his napkin before placing it on the table, while Mary sat folding and unfolding hers on her lap.

'What a good idea,' replied Morag, thankful for the diversion. 'We musn't forget Her Majesty. Now, Fiona

256

dear, just run along and put Grannie's stool in front of her chair, will you?'

Fiona hesitated. 'It's all right, dear,' Morag said softly, 'I'm sure Mummy didn't mean it about the soap and water. Let's just say what you overheard,' here she looked at Mary, 'wasn't very polite and it's best not to say it ever again.' So saying, Morag left the room without uttering another word and the rest of the family followed in silent procession.

Boxing Day, unlike Christmas Day, began in more relaxed fashion. Jenny woke to the smell of kippers and Fiona bouncing all over her bed.

'Daddy says you're a lazybones, Auntie Jenny. He was up ages ago and has even had his breakfast.'

'I know, I can smell it. How your father can eat kippers for breakfast never ceases to amaze me. Is everyone up, then?' Jenny enquired.

'Everyone 'cept Iain. He wasn't very nice when I tried to wake him up.' Fiona turned to the door for fear of being overheard, then whispered softly, 'He even said something rude – not the same thing I heard Mummy say, but I don't think Grannie would like it either.'

Jenny, amused by her niece's wide-eyed innocence, laughed good-naturedly.

'Well, I expect Iain didn't take very kindly to being bounced on. Now, perhaps you can tell me what's for breakfast apart from kippers and what everyone is planning to do this morning?'

'Mummy and Daddy are going for a walk. Miss Tandy's going to teach Jean to crochet, so I thought I'd go with you and Grannie to the grave.'

Fiona made it sound so matter-of-fact and clinical that for a brief moment Jenny felt angry. Her anger however was only fleeting. She couldn't possibly expect Fiona to understand how bereft the family had been following William Sinclair's untimely death.

It had been Morag's suggestion to visit William's grave when they'd left the church following Midnight Mass. 'We'll slip out quietly together on Boxing morning,' she'd said, unaware that they would have Fiona for company.

Jenny and Morag stood, each with their thoughts, in silent contemplation, while a cold wind stirred stray tufts of grass that had escaped the final autumn mowing. Fiona, sensing the solemnity of the occasion, remained at the far end of the churchyard searching for treasures. On a recent visit, when she'd found the skeleton of a leaf, Hamish had shown her how to press it flat between the pages of an old gardening encyclopaedia.

'The wee lassie has come back with her own skeleton from the churchyard!' Hamish had announced chuckling to Tandy, who'd quickly dispensed him from her kitchen with a broom, unable to share his macabre sense of humour.

Watched by Morag, Jenny placed three small sprigs on her Father's grave, one each of gorse, purple heather and rosemary. The rosemary from the herb garden at Conasg was for remembrance. The heather and the solitary sprig of gorse she'd found in a secluded spot were from the amenity land close by where she'd often walked with her father when he was alive.

Jenny felt a pang of guilt and remorse. Until she met

Paul, the only association with the yellow gorse was her father. Now, touching the golden petals, she kept seeing Paul's face full of enthusiasm when he'd first shown her the beautifully executed emblem for the House of St Claire.

Morag, aware of Jenny's desire to be alone, joined Fiona on the main footpath. Kneeling, Jenny traced the writing on the headstone with her finger. 'Oh, Father, if only you hadn't died, if only you hadn't left us. I need you to help me . . . will you . . . can you?'

Closing her eyes, she tried to visualize the last time she'd seen her father, remembering how he'd waved from the window as she'd reversed her car to Conasg's main gates. Had he known then that he was so close to death? Through misted eyes the picture became blurred and a distant squeal of delight from Fiona caused the memory to fade completely. Footsteps sounded on the gravel and a solitary tear falling on the gorse glinted in the wintry sunlight.

'Look! Auntie Jenny, look, I've found a lucky stone.'

Excitedly, Fiona held up a small round stone with a hole in it.

'I'm sorry,' said Morag breathlessly, following her in pursuit. 'I tried to stop her interrupting your conversation with your father. She was a bit too quick for me today, I'm afraid; I must be getting old.'

'Nonsense, Mother! You're not getting old – why, you've got more energy than most of us put together.' Nevertheless, she contemplated thoughtfully, turning to take her mother's arm, Morag had looked decidedly tired of late. There was, however, nothing wrong with her eyesight. Even from the far end of the churchyard

259

she'd not missed Jenny's 'conversation' with William.

Fiona reverted to her earlier habit of running round them in circles.

'A lucky stone, a lucky stone,' she sang, opening her hand slowly and peering into the palm of her hand.

'Grannie,' she asked earnestly, 'do you think this is like the stone Coinneach Oddar found?'

'Gracious, child! What a memory you have. Fancy you remembering the Brahan Seer.'

Puzzled, Jenny enquired, 'Who on earth is the Brahan Seer?'

'Coinneach Oddar,' Morag explained. 'He lived in the seventeenth century and was famous for his Highland prophecies. Folk say he fell asleep on a hillside and when he woke he was clutching a stone with a hole in it.'

'A stone just like mine?' Fiona broke in, holding it up to the sky.

'And like Coinneach Oddah, can you see the truth and the future in your stone?' teased Morag.

'No,' Fiona said sadly, 'but I can see the sun. Still,' she said after a pause, 'I 'spect that's 'cos this stone is special too. You can't see the future but you can wish for it!' Cheered by her own response, she darted off along the footpath, leaving mother and daughter to walk arm in arm.

Hearing Fiona chattering merrily away to herself, Jenny smiled warmly.

'Talk about old head on young shoulders. No doubt she's making her own wishes for the future.'

'I expect so,' acknowledged Morag with a deep sigh, 'and what would you wish for the future, Jennifer?'

Completely taken aback by the question, Jenny shrugged her shoulders.

'To be honest, Mother, at this precise moment I honestly don't know.'

Returning to Conasg in pensive mood, they saw Mary and Andrew walking ahead of them, hand in hand and deep in conversation.

'Thank heavens for that,' murmured Morag. 'Well, that's one wish granted. Fiona's stone must be lucky after all!'

In the hallway Tandy stood waiting to greet them. 'I'm glad you're all home,' she said. 'They say the weather's going to change. Snow is forecast and I've just heard on the wireless that there's been a dreadful avalanche in the Italian Alps.'

CHAPTER 28

Not wishing to be bounced on again by Fiona, Jenny made a point of rising early the next morning. She knew even before drawing back the curtains that it would be as Tandy had predicted. There was a perfect stillness about the landscape, a stillness only associated with heavy falls of snow. Ben Cruachan, completely enveloped in a mantel of white, was like a scene from *The Snow Queen*. Perhaps later, to give Andrew and Mary more time together, she would tell Fiona the story of Kay and Gerda.

Before then there would doubtless be the obligatory building of a snowman. Even Iain would get up for that if it meant being able to bombard his two sisters with snowballs, once the ceremonial placing of Hamish's old hat, three pieces of coal and a carrot had been duly adhered to.

'In that case,' Jenny said aloud, imitating Flora Tandy, 'you'd best be getting a decent breakfast inside you.' She determined to eat hers before the dreadful smell of Andrew's kippers pervaded the entire house.

Tying back the heavy curtains, she heard whistling in the drive and looked down to see the paper boy struggling through the snow back to his bike propped against the gates. There had been no cycling up to the large oak door and aiming at the letterbox today! Morag would be pleased; she hated papers with chewed up edges.

In the kitchen, alone and ashen-faced, Flora Tandy stood stirring the porridge. 'Oh, Miss Jennifer,' she cried, 'there's been a terrible accident.' She pointed to the front page of the newspaper. 'Those poor little girls – it is their mother, isn't it?'

'Little girls? Miss Tandy, I'm afraid I don't understand.'

'Fiona's friends. Mr Hadley's wife? Isn't Dintino her professional name?'

Jenny sat down slowly on the hard kitchen stool and picked up the paper. The stark black headline – 'THEY WERE WARNED NOT TO GO!' – glared out at her. 'Yet another party of skiers refusing to heed avalanche warnings chose to ski off-piste . . .' ran the story.

Scanning the paragraphs avidly, searching for Gina's name, Jenny was convinced Miss Tandy had been mistaken. The accident had happened in the Italian Alps and although Gina was Italian, there must be numerous Italians with the same surname? Surely, too, Gina wouldn't leave the children at Christmas – but something Fiona had said yesterday niggled away in her mind. Something about Gina being away? She'd paid scant attention to it at the time; it was bad enough listening to Fiona's account of Mary and Andrew's argument.

Jenny's eyes rested on the third paragraph. '. . . a party of eight experienced skiers . . . three killed, two injured and two still missing . . . a search party out looking for survivors.' Miss Tandy had not been mistaken; Gina – described as model and socialite – was one of the two skiers found injured and airlifted to hospital.

'Thank God,' Jenny whispered.

Flora Tandy, surprised at Jenny's benevolence, continued stirring the porridge.

Running through the hallway to the study, the only thought in Jenny's mind was to ring Paul. He would need help . . . and if she left straight away . . . It was only when she heard the dialling tone that she realized she'd not seen Paul since the night of the dance. What must he think of her?

Jenny shuddered at the recollection of that night. It was almost too embarrassing to recall; she'd behaved just like a common . . . In the gloom of the ice-cold study with its heavy curtains still drawn against the chill of early morning, Jenny felt a wave of panic sweep over her. What on earth should she say to Paul? Perhaps she should even hang up?

Numbed by shock and cold and transfixed by the large painting of Princes Street hanging above the fireplace, she discerned an exasperated voice at the end of the line.

'Hello! Hello?'

Wanting to say so much, she could only whisper feebly, 'Paul, it's Jenny, I've just seen the newspapers.'

There was a long pause before he replied with a sigh, 'Jenny! Thank God it's someone I know. I've been inundated with phone calls from Gina's friends and the Press. I'd almost decided to leave the phone off the hook . . . but just in case the hospital . . .'

'Is there any news from Italy?'

'None, other than that Gina's still in intensive care.'

Down the line Jenny heard the ring of the doorbell and a man's voice.

'Jenny,' continued Paul, 'I'm sorry, I must go, it's the taxi.'

'The taxi?'

'The taxi to take me to the airport. I managed to get a seat on the next plane to Milan. I didn't feel like driving myself in all this snow.'

Remembering the weather, Jenny pulled back the study curtains. The brilliant white dazzled her eyes. Her reason for ringing was to offer her help – to leave right away – but how could she in such conditions?

'I was wondering if you needed help,' she said numbly, 'only there's so much snow here and it could take me ages to get to Edinburgh.'

'It's kind of you, Jenny, but . . . look, I really must go. Perhaps you could give Helen a ring . . . the girls are staying with her.'

A car horn tooted impatiently in the background.

'What –? Oh, yes, all right, I'll ring Helen. Have a . . . safe trip.' She couldn't say good. In the circumstances it didn't seem appropriate. 'And Paul – thank you for the present.'

Replacing the receiver, Jenny looked up to see Morag wrapped in layers of thermals and woollens. She seemed surprised to find her daughter in the study so early in the morning.

'I'm sorry, my dear, I didn't mean to startle you. I just thought I'd sort through some paperwork ready for Andrew to take back to the office.'

Morag walked towards the desk, where she placed a

bulky pile of papers and fastened the curtains with their heavy gold tassels. 'Do you feel all right, Jennifer? You look quite pale? Perhaps it's the cold. Let me switch on the fire.' Stooping low, Morag flicked the switch of an ancient brown socket and a thin, feeble red twist of heat shone dimly in the hearth.

'It's all right, Mother, it's not the cold, it's shock. I've just been on the phone to Paul Hadley. His wife was one of the survivors of yesterday's avalanche and I just can't help thinking of Celestina and Emily.'

Morag was tight-lipped, as if waiting for Jenny to continue, but Jenny said nothing. 'Well,' Morag asked tersely, 'and what is the situation regarding Miss Dintino?' It was strange how she refused to acknowledge Gina as Paul's wife.

'She's in intensive care and Paul's flying out to Milan. The girls are with a neighbour.'

'As a Christian I suppose I should be sorry for the woman,' Morag replied. 'However, if she'd been doing her duty as a mother, none of this would have happened.'

Jennifer took the accent on the word 'none' to encompass the situation between Andrew and Gina as well. Please God, Morag wasn't going to ask for all the sordid details!

She was saved by a discreet tapping on the door. Tandy appeared with a tray of coffee. 'I just thought I'd let you know, Miss Jennifer, Hamish says they are clearing the road. It should be open again in a couple of hours.'

'Then if you don't mind, Mother, I'll leave today instead of tomorrow. Can I suggest,' she said warily, 'you try to conceal the papers – or at least the pages referring to Gina – from Andrew and Mary? I'm sure they'll find out sooner or later but for the moment perhaps . . .'

Nodding understanding, Morag gave instructions to Tandy to remove the telltale pages from the paper. 'You can use them for lighting the fire and you'd better make sure you've none of your silly magazines lying around too, Tandy. They always appear to document Miss Dintino's exploits in words and pictures!'

Flora Tandy looked embarrassed. Until today she'd no idea Morag knew of her weakness for such publications. Much as she enjoyed being Morag's companion and living at Conasg, the magazines with their celebrity interviews and photos of exotic locations and lifestyles were her only form of escapism. Not for those beautiful suntanned creatures was there one bar of an electric fire and plain arrowroot biscuits.

Then Tandy frowned thoughtfully. How did Morag know Gina had featured in so many of them . . . if she hadn't read them too?

In her room Jenny quickly packed her suitcase and gathered the smaller items left on the dressing table into her vanity case. Only one thing remained: the present from Paul. Remembering their telephone conversation, she felt guilty. She'd even thanked him for his gift, yet it still remained unopened. Only once during the Christmas holidays did she get as far as untying the simple gold ribbon, then her courage had failed her. The simple act of unwrapping Paul's gift would be like opening her very soul.

Unlike Pandora, Jenny was afraid, not because of its

hidden contents but because it served only to remind her of the moments spent in Paul's embrace, moments when humiliation and anger had turned to a shared passion. Later on that fateful morning, unable to respond to Paul's gentle questioning, she'd listened to his murmured apologies and let him depart without explanation while she shed silent tears.

Even now, with tears pricking her eyelids, there could be no escape from her feelings. She'd acted disgracefully, practically called Gina a whore and then behaved like one herself. Jenny's mind was in turmoil. She'd actually encouraged Paul into her bed.

But he said he loved me, she remonstrated with her conscience.

Ah, yes, but aren't you forgetting, came the stern reply, Paul's married. He's married to Gina.

Gina! Jenny gave a strangled cry. Gina was alive and within a few hours Paul would be at his wife's bedside. She must stop thinking about Paul. She would open his gift and that would be that!

'Think about Celestina and Emily instead,' she said aloud, slipping her thumb beneath the Sellotape. 'After all, they will need you.'

The narrow package in Jenny's trembling fingers revealed a slim black box and a letter.

My dear Jenny,

I am writing this letter as I fear – by not returning my calls – you are avoiding me. If I've hurt you I can only apologize but I beg you, give me chance to explain. After what's happened between us we must talk. Even you must realize it's something we can't discuss on the phone. Have lunch with me one day before Christmas – PLEASE! If however you feel that's impossible, then I shall try to understand. As you know, my contract with Sinclair's lasts until the New Year. If I don't hear from you I shall assume you no longer wish to speak to me and I shall endeavour to keep out of your way – seeing Andrew if there is a problem. Please don't let things end like this, Jenny. I love you. Will you ring me?

Paul

Examining the date on the letter, she saw it had been written on the morning after the dance. Later, when she'd been too embarrassed to face him or even speak to him on the phone, Stevie, angry and exasperated with her and her feeble excuses, had wheeled herself into the office like Boadicea on her chariot, placed the small package on her desk and passed on Paul's impassioned instructions to, 'Open it now!'

The command had met with negative response and the atmosphere throughout the day had worsened. Never had Jenny and Stevie been so hostile, and by the end of the evening their farewells were civil and coolly polite.

CHAPTER 29

'Jenny dear, how kind of you to come. Paul was very touched, especially as it meant leaving your family at Christmas.' Helen Craig took Jenny's coat and led her through to the sitting room. Pausing at the foot of the stairs, she held a finger to her lips. 'I think the girls are asleep at last. It's been a terrible time for them; you wouldn't believe the amount of people they've had ringing and calling at the door. These dreadful tabloid newspapers! Mind you, I soon got rid of them once Paul left!'

'How is he? Have you heard from him?'

'No, not yet, which makes the waiting even worse. Every time the phone rings, Celestina and Emily jump like startled rabbits. They didn't really want to go to bed but I insisted, poor wee things. I told them you were coming and you'd read them a bedtime story. I hope you don't mind?' Helen looked in Jenny's direction. 'I gather you're very good at it. They still remember how you looked after them when they were poorly.'

Jenny sighed wistfully. 'Yes, I seem to be quite good at looking after other people's children, Helen. Do you think I should go up now?'

'Let's leave them for a while, shall we? But if they wake then of course you must go up. Can't break our promises, can we? Now let me get you something to eat, you must be starving.'

Helen produced the familiar trolley laden with food but Jenny, despite Helen urging her to eat, wasn't hungry. The food only stuck in her throat. Like Cele and Emily, the not knowing and waiting was all too much to bear. 'I'm sorry Helen,' she said, looking at the carefully prepared trolley, 'I'm really not hungry, I expect I'm still recovering from eating too much at Christmas.'

'Never mind, perhaps later when you've got over your long journey. I gather you had quite a bit of snow on the west coast. What were the roads like?'

Describing the road and weather conditions, Jenny was glad to be sitting in the warmth and comfort of Helen's sitting room. She wanted desperately to ask about Paul and Gina but where to begin, that was the problem. She remembered that the last time she'd been here was when Helen had talked about Gina's latest man friend. She'd been convinced then that Helen hadn't known about Andrew, but had she learnt about him since, and if so, from whom? Paul, or Gina herself perhaps?

An assortment of clocks all set at different times ticked and whirred quietly away, creating a hypnotic effect. Jenny dozed momentarily, only to be woken by the shrill ringing of the telephone. Immediately Helen leapt from her chair to pluck at the receiver.

'Hello? Paul! Thank goodness you've arrived. Yes, the girls are fine, they're sleeping and Jenny's here too. Where are you calling from?'

271

There was a pause and Jenny strained to hear the one-side conversation.

'I'm sorry, Paul,' Helen shouted, 'the line's really bad – I can hardly hear you. Perhaps I could try ringing you back. Give me the number quickly just in case we get cut off.' Helen reached for a pen. 'Damn!' She called, looking in Jenny's direction, 'It's run dry. Do you have a pen, Jenny?'

Reaching into her handbag, Jenny brought out the slender gold-nibbed fountain pen in Sinclair colours. It had been her Christmas present from Paul. She watched anxiously as Helen noted down the number and redialled. Paul answered almost immediately.

Most of Helen's replies were monosyllables until she mentioned the children. 'Oh, yes, the girls are fine, Paul. They're sleeping and I got rid of those dreadful reporters; I was only saying to Jenny . . . Yes, she's here, would you like a word?' Helen beckoned Jenny to the phone.

Jenny took the receiver, not knowing what to say. Thankfully Paul did most of the talking, explaining the situation at the hospital.

'Well, promise you'll ring if there's anything I can do,' Jenny said before replacing the receiver. Turning to Helen, she shook her head.

'Oh, dear! Is she . . .?'

'No, she's still on a life-support machine but the scan shows extensive brain damage. The result of the injuries sustained in the accident.'

'And can they do anything?' Helen enquired.

'They're not sure. They want to do another brain scan and Paul will see the doctor tomorrow. He said

272

he'll try and ring about lunchtime so he can speak to Cele and Emily. It all sounds very serious, Helen.'

Helen looked towards the stairs, half expecting movement, but there was none. 'Those poor wee scraps,' she said, 'as if they haven't had enough to contend with.'

'Can I go up and see them? I promise not to wake them.'

Jenny stood in the doorway of Helen's bedroom and saw where the dark hair of the unwilling innkeeper's wife was entwined with that of the angelic Emily.

Cele's arms were wrapped protectively around her younger sister as they lay in the sprawling double bed, completely enveloped by a patchwork quilt in autumn colours.

'I always let them sleep in my bed when they stay,' whispered Helen, leading Jenny back downstairs. 'They get frightened if they're not together. When I see them curled up like that under the quilt they remind me of Babes in the Wood under a carpet of leaves.'

Jenny supposed there was a similarity, particularly with the autumn-coloured squares of fabric made from Helen's long-since discarded clothes and scraps of fabric. She didn't want to mention the other similarity that came to mind at the mention of last year's pantomime, or the totally naïve comment that had sprung from Fiona's mouth about mothers leaving their children. Jenny yawned and put her hand to her mouth.

'Look at you,' said Helen. 'You're quite worn out! Now I'm not going to take no for an answer. You are going to stay here tonight, Jenny.'

'But . . .'

'There's to be no buts, and in case you're wondering,

I will sleep on the settee. First of all, though, I'm going to make us some supper. You must build up your strength for tomorrow.'

'Tomorrow?'

'Aye, tomorrow. I have a feeling when Paul rings he's going to need you.'

Jenny lay in bed with a deep sense of foreboding. Staring at the plain wooden cross on the opposite wall, something told her she should be praying. The difficulty being, since the night of the dance, the simple act of prayer she usually found so comforting had completely eluded her.

What had Helen meant by Paul's needing her? Had Helen already thought that far ahead? Was Gina so seriously ill that there was no hope? There seemed to be so many unanswered questions. Heavy with sleep, Jenny closed her eyes and waited for morning.

Unlike Fiona, Cele and Emily were late sleepers and quiet risers. Jenny awoke in unfamiliar surroundings with the sound of Helen humming 'Onward Christian Soldiers' as she attacked the dusting. Every item of china, glass, wood and brass was lovingly picked up, dusted with a flourish of brightly coloured sheepskin and replaced carefully.

'I must keep myself busy,' Helen announced. 'I've a feeling we've a long wait until lunchtime.'

'Then you must let me do something, Helen.' Jenny insisted, spreading honey on to thick wholemeal toast. A vivid china orange with dark green leaves rested in the middle of the table. Jenny found her attention drawn by the garishness of the colour compared to the dreary weather outside.

'There's homemade marmalade in there; the leaves form the lid and you just lift it off,' Helen instructed, dusting the ears of a china spaniel guarding the hearth.

'I'm afraid I don't much care for marmalade. That's usually Andrew's favourite.'

The spaniel was returned to its resting place with a heavy thud. Helen said nothing, but in the silence that followed, Jenny realized Helen knew about Andrew and Gina. Presently Helen rose from the hearth and moved towards the table, picking up the china orange dish.

'Well, in that case,' she said brightly, 'I'll put this away. The girls don't like marmalade either.'

Marmalade days, Jenny thought to herself, seeing the orange disappear into a stripped pine cupboard that in another life had probably been a wardrobe.

Leaving the house with Helen's old-fashioned wicker basket and a shopping list, Jenny cast a cursory glance towards Paul's front door. There was no sign of journalists today, nor of course was there any sign of Paul. But wouldn't it be lovely, she thought, to see the door open and find him standing there?

The curtains in the house next door were still drawn. Helen said she would go in later once the girls were up and Jenny had returned with the shopping.

'Perhaps there'll be no need,' Jenny murmured. In Latin countries they still kept curtains drawn in times of sorrow, didn't they? Gina was, after all, Italian. There was something else she remembered about Italian law, but for the moment it escaped her. She must concentrate on the shopping or they would have nothing for lunch.

Jenny crossed off each item on the reverse of the used

envelope Helen had given her. The pen moved easily and silently. This morning in panic she'd hunted for it everywhere, only to find it by her breakfast plate. She'd quite forgotten that Helen had borrowed it the previous evening to take down Paul's number.

Now it seemed ironic to use the pen Paul had given her to write down his number. Biting her lip, she remembered the pen from their week in Geneva. They'd noticed it – or at least Paul had – in the window of an extremely upmarket stationer's window. It was the type you used to see years ago in all reputable stationers. Now, sadly, they had mostly been replaced by plastic biros and rainbow coloured felt tips.

'Gracious, a St Claire pen,' Paul had teased, recognizing the familiar Sinclair colours. 'Our fame must be spreading, Jenny!'

Knowing she always used a fountain pen, Jenny could only presume Paul had returned to the shop later when he was on his own.

Celestina and Emily sat at the breakfast table finishing off their breakfast. Helen was wiping the remains of egg yolk from Cele's chin and Emily toyed with the remaining two bread and butter soldiers left on her plate.

'There,' announced Helen, hearing the door open. 'I told you Jenny had only gone shopping for your lunch. Now will you believe me, and perhaps, Emily, you'll finish your soldiers?'

Jenny was warmed to see the girls' faces light up when she entered the kitchen. 'Perhaps those soldiers will disappear if they have this on them,' she said, placing a jar of bramble jelly in front of Emily and,

276

unscrewing the jar, she scooped a spoonful on to the plate.

Emily beamed. 'Did you really stay the night?'

'Yes, I saw you both under your blanket of leaves *and* I heard Helen snore!'

The girls giggled uncontrollably and Helen, who was tidying up at the kitchen sink, turned and gave Jenny the thumbs-up sign. It was ages since she'd heard the girls laugh like that.

Cele became suddenly thoughtful. 'Helen's bed isn't really made of leaves, is it?'

'No', Jennifer replied. 'It just reminds us of a story about two children who slept under a bed of leaves, that's all.'

'Will you tell it to us?' Cele asked. 'And will you help me with my letters, please? Daddy says I should practise my "d"s and "b"s.'

Some time later Cele had produced a large sheet of 'b's and 'd's and Emily tried writing out her own name in large letters.

'I'm glad I have Grannie Hadley's name and not Grannie "Tino"s,' she said concentrating hard on the curly tail of the 'y'. 'I don't like writing letters . . . drawing is best.'

Jenny passed Emily a sheet of drawing paper and crayons and continued with her own writing. A brief note to Morag thanking her for Christmas and apologizing for her impromptu departure from Conasg, and a copy of the text she'd found hanging beneath the wooden cross in her room.

When lunch was ready there was no Fiona to bang the gong to summon them all to lunch, just Helen clapping her hands together, briskly rounding them up like stray sheep. She sent the girls off to wash their hands and eyed the array of clocks nervously. 'Paul said he'd ring at lunchtime. I just hope, for their sake, he rings after and not during.'

When the phone rang, Cele and Emily ran to it eagerly.

'That's right,' said Helen, 'you speak to Daddy, then let Jenny have a word while you come and help me with the dishes. I have this amazing washing-up liquid that makes the most amazing bubbles. Let's see who can make the biggest.'

Helen motioned to Jenny to close the door behind her, while watched curiously by the two girls, she squeezed an enormous quantity of thick green liquid into the washing-up bowl.

Celestina and Emily stood wide-eyed as Helen whisked the water frantically with her fingers and produced copious amounts of lather. Then she clasped thumb and forefinger together and blew. The girls were entranced.

Standing in the doorway, Jenny saw the girls' hands cupping snowball-sized bubbles. Gracious! Was it only the other day Jean and Iain had had their snowball fight? It seemed like an eternity ago. Helen looked up with questioning eyes and Jenny shook her head.

'Your Daddy's coming home; he's asked me to meet him at the airport.'

A shower of bubbles filled the air as the girls clapped their hands and danced about the kitchen. They did not see Helen wipe away her tears.

CHAPTER 30

From the window of the taxi, Paul stared with unseeing eyes at the heavy grey clouds and swirling mists sweeping across the tarmac at Milan airport. First reports had indicated flight delays because of fog.

'Please God, let them be wrong,' he said, taking his suitcase from the puzzled driver.

'*Signore?*'

'What? Oh . . . nothing. *Grazie.*'

In bewilderment the taxi driver examined the handful of lire notes Paul had thrust into his hand. '*Grazie, signore!*' he called, but Paul was already out of earshot, running towards the main entrance.

Relieved to be allocated a window seat and ignoring his fellow passengers, Paul closed his eyes. It was only when the plane was above cloud level and the bright rays of morning sunlight pierced his eyelids that he opened them again. In the seat in front of him, an American was chattering excitedly about the magnificent view they would find once they flew over the Alps.

Feeling a tremor run through his body, Paul forced himself to look from the window at the mountainous spectacle below. There, row after row of crested peaks dusted with fresh snow glowed with a rosy hue.

'Say! Just look how the sunshine has painted it all pink,' the American announced to his travelling companion.

'Yeah, sort of welcoming yet at the same time awesome,' came the reply.

'Welcoming', thought Paul sadly. Had Gina found it 'welcoming'?

Shielding his eyes from the sun-dazzled peaks, Paul scanned the mountains and snow-fields still in shadow. Smooth and white, they reminded him of the starched cotton sheets covering Gina's body at the hospital. Momentarily trying to shut the picture from his mind, Paul closed his eyes again. But it was no good – the scene, like Gina's poor battered body when they found her, was frozen.

'She was one of the lucky ones, Signor Hadley,' the junior doctor had announced excitedly just after Paul arrived. 'They managed to find your wife within the first hour . . . so there is a chance.'

Later, of course, when the neurosurgeon appeared and the junior doctor was despatched with a flea in his ear, there was little cause for excitement. The prognosis was grim, Paul discovered, sitting amidst a tangle of machines, tubes and wires at Gina's bedside. In anguish and despair he'd watched both the afternoon sun and his wife fade away.

Waiting for Paul at the airport, Jenny studied the milling crowds. Her heart leapt when she saw him and she decided, for the moment at least, that events on the night of the dance had to be forgotten.

Looking haggard and drawn, Paul stood motionless

at the barrier. Jenny walked slowly towards him; she wasn't even sure if he'd seen her.

'Paul,' she whispered, taking his arm.

He said nothing until they reached the car park and she put the key in the ignition.

'Can we sit here for five minutes? I don't think I'm ready to face the girls just yet.' He groaned softly and placed his head in his hands.

Jenny put a reassuring hand on his shoulder. 'Would it help to talk about it . . . tell me what happened?'

'It was awful, simply awful. She looked so . . . all those wires, all those machines. When I first arrived some idiot said there was hope, but you only had to look at her to see . . . to see . . .' Paul swallowed hard and reached for Jenny's hand. Then, taking a deep breath, he continued.

'She'd sustained such horrific injuries . . . the brain was damaged. It was irreparable, you see, the monitor line was completely flat, and they told me . . . I would have to take the decision to switch off the machine. I couldn't do it, Jenny!'

As his voice trailed away Paul looked at her, his eyes haunted by events and, squeezing her hand even tighter, whispered almost inaudibly, 'That was until this morning.'

'What happened this morning?'

This time when he spoke it was as if Jenny wasn't there, as if she didn't exist and he was addressing an empty space. 'They showed me the results of another scan which confirmed the same irreparable brain damage – only this time they told me there was also a tumour. A tumour that must have been there for some time.'

Suddenly aware of Jenny's presence, Paul turned his anguished face towards her. 'And do you know what they asked me?' he enquired bitterly.

Jenny shook her head.

'They asked me if I'd noticed any change in her behaviour recently! What do you think of that?'

'But you weren't to know, Paul. You couldn't have known. You can't blame yourself!'

'Can't I?' he said lamely. 'Well, her family certainly does. They've even accused me of killing her!'

'What! Killing her! But how . . . why?'

'Because I gave the doctors permission to switch off the machine. You can in Italy, you know, as long as the brain itself is dead.'

It all came back to Jenny now. The death of Ayrton Senna – the Brazilian racing driver. He'd been injured during one of the Italian Grand Prix. His family had been faced with the same agonizing decision.

'What happens now?'

'I have to arrange the funeral. We shall have to go back tomorrow.'

'Tomorrow? We? I don't understand.'

'Yes, I must take Celestina and Emily with me.'

Jenny looked up in alarm. 'But aren't they too young to cope with all that? The funeral, I mean.'

'I don't know. I shall have to explain Gina's death to them. And whether or not they understand the full implications of the situation remains to be seen. They know about going to heaven when you die. But how they'll react when they see Gina's coffin – well . . .'

'Oh Paul, that sounds dreadful.'

'I'm sorry, Jenny, that's the way I feel at the moment.

I mean look at us. In a couple of months the shops will be full of Easter eggs – that's if they aren't already! We'll then be telling the children stories about the Easter bunnies and wonder why they look so puzzled at scenes from the crucifixion. Besides,' he said, crestfallen, 'Gina's parents want her buried in Italy and say they want to see their grandchildren. Who knows, they might even try and take them away from me!'

'You don't really think that!'

'I don't know, Jenny,' he replied dejectedly. 'Quite frankly I don't know what to think any more.'

With a profound sense of longing, Paul reached out and drew her into his arms.

'Jenny . . . the night of the dance, I thought we . . . Why wouldn't you reply to my calls?'

Choking back a sob, there was a murmured. 'Oh, Paul, I'm so terribly sorry,' before she found his lips on hers.

In the confined space of her car they clung to one another, both unable to speak and oblivious to the car pulling up behind them. In that brief shared moment of grief they let the tide of emotion sweep over them.

Hearing a car's horn close by, Paul started and wound down the passenger window. There a gesticulating driver in a quilted ski-suit yelled cheekily, 'Sorry to break up such a romantic scene, only me mates and I woz wonderin' if you were leavin'? There ain't no other parking places left, see. We've got a plane to catch, goin' skiing – if you haven't already guessed – in the Italian Alps. And we don't want to miss out on all those bonnie Italian lassies, do we . . .?'

Jenny didn't wait to for him finish his sentence. Amid

283

a hail of cheers from the occupants of the battered Cortina, she reversed the car at speed out of its narrow parking space.

The next day, quite by chance, she found herself parked alongside the very same car and spied a solitary ski boot, wedged in the corner of the rear seat.

'Oh, well,' she remarked, eyeing the empty lager cans strewn on the car's floor. 'I expect whoever it belongs to will survive without it!'

The journey to the airport had been fraught. Paul looked numb and grey like the weather and the children remained totally bewildered. Travelling in torrential rain, they discovered there'd been an accident on the motorway holding up all the traffic. By the time they reached the airport their flight was already being called.

Jenny, desperate to buy the girls something for the flight, if only to remember her by, left them briefly. She still couldn't come to terms with the fact that she might never see them again. Could their grandparents really fight Paul for custody? She knew nothing of Italian custody law. Surely they were only bluffing?

Leaving Paul to check in the luggage, she hurried towards a kiosk selling soft toys and, snatching two rabbits with long floppy ears, fumbled in her purse for the money.

'Keep the change!' she called to the astonished assistant, and ran back to where Paul stood anxiously searching for her. He and the girls were in the queue at passport control. Thrusting the furry animals towards two bewildered and tired-looking faces, she turned to Paul just as a man in uniform stepped forward.

'Hurry along, sir, you're holding up the queue.'

Amidst much murmuring from onlookers Paul reached out, grabbed Jenny by the shoulders and kissed her full on the mouth. Then he was gone.

Numbed and with silent tears pouring down her face, she watched the back of his head as the forlorn trio were ushered through the doorway. Minutes later, a lone, desolate figure with aching heart and racked with despair watched the Alitalia plane taxi down the runway into the enveloping mist.

Clutching their toys, Cele and Emily cried too. They didn't like airports – people always cried at airports. It was barely a year since they'd been here at this airport, saying goodbye to their mother.

This journey, their Daddy had explained, was to bid her a last farewell. On either side of him Paul felt tiny hands reaching reassuringly for his. Swallowing hard, he forced a smile and closed his mind to the harrowing days that lay ahead.

CHAPTER 31

'I like your pen. It's very House of St Claire, isn't it?' Stevie was watching Jenny sign the day's correspondence.

'Thank you. I must say it writes beautifully, and just in case you're wondering, Stevie, it was a present from Paul. That's what was in the box you kept pestering me about.' Jenny smiled and handed the letters back.

'Oh, I see,' said Stevie with an air of disappointment. She'd been hoping the box contained jewellery, not just a pen. Although, as she'd had to admit, it was a very nice one. 'Has Paul rung again?' she asked.

Jenny screwed the cap back on the pen. 'Yes, he phoned last night. He's coming back the day after tomorrow and I shall be going to the airport to meet him. He has some legal business to attend to first.'

'And what about the children – are they coming too?'

Jenny shook her head sadly. 'I don't know, he didn't say . . .'

'Well, I think it's disgraceful,' Stevie broke in. 'Surely they can't take the girls away from Paul just like that?'

'If you don't mind, I'd rather not think about it; the

whole situation is all too depressing as it is. Let's just wait and see, shall we?'

Stevie wheeled herself from the office, leaving Jenny alone with her thoughts. If the girls didn't come back, what was she going to tell Fiona? Mary had been on the phone constantly. Fiona was distraught at losing her friends and not even the prospect of a trip to Conasg for Burns Night celebrations consoled her.

Burns Night! Jenny had quite forgotten all about Burns Night. After such a disastrous Christmas, Morag was summoning them all to Conasg to let their hair down. She planned to have quite a gathering.

Andrew was already complaining about going. There was too much to do in the office, he argued – meetings to organize and business trips to arrange. And with Paul away it meant an even busier workload. At least this year Mary hadn't even suggested a skiing holiday.

'We must go, Andrew,' Jenny announced. 'We can't let Mother down. You know how much she's looking forward to it. After all, Christmas wasn't exactly a roaring success.'

Andrew turned in Jenny's direction. There was no need to say any more; her look said it all.

'You've heard from Paul, I expect? How did the funeral go?' Andrew mumbled the last five words. He felt duty bound to ask, but the last thing he wanted to discuss was Gina's funeral. It had been bad enough trying to evade the issue at the weekend. On one side he had Fiona pestering him for news of Celestina and Emily, and on the other Mary throwing him furtive glances.

Giving the barest details of the funeral, Jenny reassured Andrew that Paul had every intention to 'knuckle down to business' on his return.

'You needn't worry about Paul, he's totally committed to St Claire.'

Her words 'totally committed', reminded Andrew of his meeting with Sol Sutherland in New York and a train of thoughts chugged into motion, picking up Gina along the way. Andrew remembered every stop en route. It had been an exciting and perilous journey, but one which he always knew would end in disaster and tragedy.

Studying the arrivals board, Jenny watched the black and white letters and numbers click into place. With each passing minute they moved slowly upwards until at last she recognized Paul's flight. A surge of relief swept through her body.

Like the prophets of doom, the morning papers had been full of disasters: plane crashes, earthquakes and floods. It was true what they said – everything came in threes.

Before leaving for the airport she'd emptied her handbag and discovered the three pieces of paper, which she'd picked up the fateful morning she'd left Helen and the girls. Until now they'd been forgotten. One was a drawing, the other a child's letter and the third, the text Jenny had copied out using Paul's pen. Three pieces of paper each with three possible courses of action: to show them to Paul; to keep them until the appropriate time; or simply to throw them away. The first two Jenny folded neatly and put in her drawer, the third she put back in her handbag.

Waiting for Paul to clear customs, she studied the words of Cardinal Newman once more.

May He support us all the day long
till the shades lengthen, and the evening comes,
and the busy world is hushed,
and the fever of life is over,
and our work is done!
Then in His mercy may He give us
a safe lodging, and a holy rest,
and peace at last.

Wiping a tear from her eye, she thought perhaps she should give the text to Paul. After all, it would be a great deal more comforting than Emily's picture of Gina, bloodied and broken in a pile of snow, or Cele's short note, 'mummy, i hop you get detter soon.' Poor Cele, she still needed help with her 'b's and 'd's.

From out of nowhere two floppy-eared rabbits dropped into Jenny's lap. She looked up in surprise as Cele and Emily hugged her tightly while at the same time warm tears fell on to pink felt noses and shiny button eyes.

'How? What happened?' was all she could say as Paul lifted her from her seat into his arms.

Driving from the airport with the girls asleep in the back of the car, she asked him again, 'I still can't believe it. What happened? Didn't Gina's parents make any claim on the girls after all?'

Paul gave a sardonic smile. 'Oh, yes, they tried very hard at first, but it was just a ploy. You see, they saw it as a way of trying to extract some money out of me . . . as if Gina didn't take enough!'

Paul thought bitterly of the night he'd taken Gina home from the Sinclair's dance. Having left his wallet for her on the mantelpiece, he hadn't expected to find on his return that she'd taken every penny! 'Quite frankly, Jenny,' he added, 'it was horrendous.'

'I'm not surprised Cele and Emily are so tired – they look exhausted, poor things.'

Looking in her rear-view mirror, Jenny glimpsed children and rabbits belted in together. Turning to check on his sleeping daughters, Paul added solemnly. 'You know, I don't think they slept the whole time we were away. There was always so much noise. Gina's parents' flat was on the corner of a busy street and they are such an excitable family. In fact the girls were convinced they were arguing all the time. They weren't, of course, it's just their manner.'

'Poor Gina,' Jenny said compassionately. 'No wonder she wanted to get away from it all.'

Paul hesitated. 'You're very forgiving, Jenny . . . especially after all the pain Gina caused your family.'

'Perhaps . . . but the dead can't defend themselves, can they? Anyway, Andrew and Mary appear to have called a truce. Christmas, as you can imagine, was very strained, and they've thankfully decided against going away for a skiing holiday this year. We've all been summoned to Conasg instead.'

To deflect attention away from Gina when the girls stirred, Jenny told Paul about her mother's plans for Burns Night. He found it hard to think of Morag Sinclair enjoying herself. He'd met her only briefly, of course, and then not in the most auspicious of circumstances.

'Don't be fooled by her outwardly fragile appearance,' Jenny informed him as she pulled up outside the familiar Victorian house. 'There's strength and determination in that steely gaze of Mother's – in case you hadn't already noticed.'

Paul nodded. He hoped never to cross swords with Morag Sinclair.

'Won't you come in for a coffee, Jenny?'

'If you don't mind, Paul, I'd better get back to the office. Besides, I know Helen is anxious to welcome you back. She's been making casseroles and pies for the past twenty-four hours!

'Then will you have lunch with me one day? I think we've some unfinished business to discuss.'

Jenny felt herself go both hot and cold at the thought. It was something she'd been trying to forget. 'Yes, of course,' she replied hastily, 'but it will have to be after Burns Night. Still I shall see you in the office before then? Andrew's got heaps of work for you, you know, so don't let him bully you!'

Kissing the girls goodbye, she nodded in the direction of the garden path and smiled. There Helen Craig came running with arms outstretched, a welcoming splash of colour in an otherwise dreary day.

CHAPTER 32

At Conasg House, Andrew sat at the breakfast table removing bones from his kippers like a surgeon. Tandy appeared with fresh toast and searched the room for Jennifer.

'Oh! Is Miss Jennifer still not down for breakfast? I thought I heard her on the landing and I've made her some toast. I know how much she hates kippers.' She turned to Fiona. 'Fiona dear, will you go and tell your Aunt Jennifer?'

Morag sat contentedly reading the morning paper. The previous evening's celebrations had gone well, in fact very well. She couldn't have hoped for a better Burns Night supper, and Alex McAllister had brought with him a superb malt whisky. She would look forward to this evening's 'wee dram' with pleasure.

'Boo!' shouted Fiona on entering Jenny's bedroom and was disappointed to find the bed empty. Hearing a noise in the nearby bathroom, she went to investigate, peeped in and promptly ran downstairs.

'Auntie Jen's being sick!'

'Fiona!' Mary looked up from where she was spreading butter thickly on to her toast. 'Really, dear, do you have to? What a thing to say. People are trying to eat their breakfast.'

Fiona's announcement appeared not to bother Andrew as he lifted his second kipper on to the plate and deftly removed the backbone. Mary continued. 'Well, it certainly couldn't have been the food; Jenny ate so little last night. Why, she only picked at her food and had hardly anything to drink.'

Unlike you, my dear, thought Morag, watching the contents of the butter dish rapidly diminish. 'Tandy, go and see if Jennifer needs any help. Tell her to stay in bed and I'll be up later.' Morag folded her newspaper. The crossword would have to wait.

Knocking on the bathroom door, Tandy found Jenny rinsing her mouth with water. Her face was ghostly pale and she was shivering.

'I'm sorry to be so late for breakfast, Miss Tandy. Tell them I'll be down in a minute.'

'By the look of you, Miss Jennifer, I think not. Your mother says you're not to come down and I'm to help you to your bed.'

Like a sick child Jenny allowed herself to be led back to her bed where Miss Tandy plumped pillows and smoothed sheets. Somehow she hadn't the will to resist.

'There, now, I'll draw the curtains and you can sleep. It's not a very nice day to look at, is it?'

Silently Jenny agreed. Prompted by the smell of Andrew's kippers wafting up the stair-well, she'd seen the view from the window only briefly before dashing to the bathroom. It was a typical Conasg day. The rain fell down in sheets and the cloud hung heavy over Ben Cruachan and the loch. Jenny closed her eyes and slept.

How long she slept she wasn't sure. It was only when she sensed the smell of lily-of-the-valley that she realized her mother was in the room. Morag sat on the bed studying her daughter's pale, wan face.

'My goodness! Tandy was right. You poor thing, you do look quite green about the gills. Have you any idea what's caused it?'

'No,' came the feeble reply. 'It must have been something I ate last night at supper. All I know is that Miss Tandy has made me so comfortable I hardly feel like getting up at all.'

'Then don't,' Morag said kindly. 'I suggest you have the day in bed and if you don't feel better when you return to Edinburgh, make an appointment to see Alex McAllister. You've been looking a bit peaky just lately; you probably need a tonic. I shall have a word with Andrew, he's probably been driving you too hard.'

Morag pulled the covers up to Jenny's chin. Like Tandy, she was unable to resist the urge to tuck Jenny in just as they did with Fiona.

'Something she ate, indeed,' Morag said tersely, going back downstairs to join the others. 'All the food served at Conasg is fresh; you'll find none of your supermarket heat-and-serve rubbish here!'

Andrew looked up from his chair, wondering what all the fuss was about.

'I trust that's not my crossword puzzle you're doing, Andrew?'

In a profusion of guilt Andrew laid down his mother's paper.

* * *

Sponging her face, Jenny returned to her bedroom. Everyone had been so kind at Conasg and taken such good care of her, but she was relieved to be home. There was nothing worse than being sick in someone else's house, even if that someone was your mother.

'Make sure you drink plenty of fluid,' Morag had insisted. 'You mustn't let yourself become dehydrated.'

The words echoed in Jenny's ears. The trouble was, she didn't really know what to drink. She'd been sick after her last cup of coffee and prior to that the tea she'd tried earlier had tasted so bitter.

Catching sight of her ghostly appearance in the mirror, she unhooked her bathrobe from the bedroom door and went downstairs to hunt in the cupboard. Perhaps if she was lucky she might find the remains of the lemon squash she kept for Fiona.

With barely a drop left, Jenny dropped the plastic bottle in the bin with a sigh. There must be something else she could try. On the shelf below the jams she found the box of fruit teas Stevie had bought her for Christmas. They sounded so peculiar at the time. Blackberry, raspberry and mixed fruit. Which one should she try?

Deliberating over the brightly decorated sachets, she recalled Emily standing in almost exactly the same spot, deciding on her jam without bits. Pouring boiling water into the cup, Jenny smiled at the memory of the two girls tucking into scones and jam.

Almost immediately a strong smell of raspberries filled the air and Jenny clasped her hand to her mouth. There was no time to run to the bathroom. Instead she made straight for the kitchen door and the garden.

After ten minutes of being sick and standing in the early morning drizzle, she soon began to shiver just as she had at Conasg and quickly returned to the kitchen. Rubbing her arms and shoulders briskly in an attempt to get warm again, she found – not for the first time that day – the pressure against her breasts strangely uncomfortable.

Puzzled, Jenny reached for the offending cup of raspberry tea and emptied it down the sink. How long was this queasiness going to continue? It was only then that alarm bells began to ring in her head and she looked about the kitchen for a calendar.

'Damn,' she muttered, looking at Emily's offering of a paper plate, decorated with pasta shapes and a tiny calendar stuck on to two thin strands of red wool. That's no good, it's still only January . . . I need last year's.'

Searching frantically in the kitchen drawer, she found what she was looking for. When was the dance and when had she last had a period? Some time towards the end of November was all she could remember. Since Cameron had broken off their engagement there'd been no need for telltale red circles on the calendar. And with the trauma at Conasg during Christmas she hadn't even given the missed period a thought.

Working backwards from Christmas, Jenny counted the days to the dance.

'Oh, God! It can't be . . . I can't be, it's not possible!'

The words of Vera McDougall – one of her mother's elderly neighbours and local gossip – rang in her ears. Following the discovery that the deputy head girl of the academy was pregnant, Vera had proclaimed knowingly to all and sundry, 'Only good girls get pregnant. Bad ones don't, you see. They know how to look after themselves!'

Giving a low moan, Jenny sat slumped at the kitchen table. If she, Jennifer Sinclair, was pregnant with Paul Hadley's child, was that good or bad?

CHAPTER 33

'Hello,' said Stevie. 'How was Burns Night? Andrew said you had a stomach upset. What was it, the haggis or the whisky?'

Jenny declined to comment. Her mind was already racing back to the morning. She'd been sick again and forced herself to go for a walk before leaving for the office. If nothing else it had at least put colour in her cheeks.

Being absent from the office meant there was a backlog of mail and paperwork needing her urgent attention, thus enabling her to avoid Stevie each time she appeared with a cup of coffee. The mere smell of the coffee machine turned her stomach, and as for drinking it . . . Not taking too much notice, Stevie put Jenny's unusual behaviour down to sheer conscientiousness. Unlike Andrew, Jenny was hardly ever away from the office.

Friday, apart from being the end of the week, was significant in two ways. It was the day Stevie fed and tended all the office plants before the weekend and it was the day she and Jenny allowed themselves the treat of cream cakes or Danish pastries. Having seen to all the plants in the outer offices and corridors, Stevie called in on Jenny, Danish pastries in one hand and Baby Bio for the plants in the other.

'Mmm, just smell these, Jenny – almond, our favourite. It's just as well I asked Maggie in the bakers to save these. One of the chaps at Freeman's has a birthday today and he specifically asked for Dan . . . ish.'

Her words petered out as Jenny made a dash for the door, sending the Baby Bio flying. Retrieving the bottle of plant food and manoeuvring her wheelchair to the plant stand, Stevie examined the contents in detail.

What on earth had happened to Jenny's plants? They looked incredibly sickly, and all this damage in just a week! OK, so it was only early February and daylight hours were still short, but last weekend everything had been positively blooming in this plant trough. She'd even told her mother about the magnificent display of caladiums.

Now sad and wilted, they no longer looked anything like the angel's wings loved by Fiona, nor did the weeping fig resemble the healthy plant Stevie had been nurturing since her arrival at Sinclair's. Stevie could have wept herself. These plants were her 'children'; and like children they had suddenly become very sick. Who or what was the culprit? She intended to find out.

Stevie perceived there were two immediate possibilities: the dreaded vine weevil or Daphne the new cleaner. She shook her head – surely not. She'd even teased Daphne and threatened to run her over with her wheelchair if she so much as added a drop of water to any of the plants. In Jenny's absence Stevie scooped up the pot containing the 'rosebud' caladium and peered at the layer of brown sludge at its base. This was no vine weevil damage, she discovered; the culprit here was coffee, and on close examination of all the neighbouring pots she saw cups and cups of it!

How many cups of coffee had she taken in to Jenny during the past week and how many had been poured on to these plants? If Jenny hadn't wanted the coffee she only had to say so. Why try and pretend otherwise? Stevie watched Jenny come back into the office, her face a sickly yellow.

'Goodness, you do look rough, Jenny. Are you sure you're better?'

'It's this stupid tummy bug. I just can't seem to shake it off.'

'In that case,' Stevie announced, 'I think you should see a doctor even if it does mean offending your mother. You could have a dose of food poisoning, in which case you're going to need some proper medicine.'

Jenny felt herself go cold. There was no medicine for this condition and quite how she was going to remedy the situation she had no idea. For the moment her only concern was to get rid of the offending Danish pastry glistening on its white shiny plate!

'Stevie, your luck's in,' she said picking up the plate. 'Thanks to my misfortune it's double Danish for you today, so can you please just take it away?'

Puzzled, Stevie found herself pushed forcibly from Jenny's office, once more in possession of a Danish pastry and bottle of plant food.

At the weekend, in between bouts of sickness, Jenny found herself absent-mindedly drawing up a chart.

Marking the date of the dance and circling it in red, she then made a line for each following week, coming to the conclusion that she could be at least seven weeks pregnant. There was nothing for it but to get a pregnancy testing kit. That, she decided, was out of the question locally where people knew her. It would have to wait until Monday and the anonymity of an Edinburgh chemists.

It seemed an eternity to wait with no one to confide in, and even then, with the result, who could she tell? She could hardly tell Mary and Andrew. And Paul, what about Paul? He'd been put out to learn she'd changed her mind about going to the cinema with them, particularly as Cele and Emily were so looking forward to her company. In fact he'd been quite brusque with her on the telephone.

How could she explain that the thought of sitting with hordes of people devouring huge buckets of popcorn was enough to turn her stomach, let alone tell him she thought she was expecting his child? More to the point, how would he react? He'd barely had chance to recover from the shock of Gina's death and the near financial ruin caused by her selfishly extravagant lifestyle.

Andrew's timely intervention with the bank manager on Paul's behalf had prevented that. Now, with Paul keeping his freelance options open, he'd assured Andrew that Sinclair's would always come first. Nevertheless he must also consider any other viable commissions to come his way.

On the grapevine Jenny discovered there would be more than enough work coming Paul's way. For the most part she was happy for him, but when Hendry and Co. became interested, Jenny was not so sure. Bruce Hendry and his father were well respected but Marina Hendry hadn't got her nickname as 'man-eater Marina' for nothing.

It had been bad enough for Jenny seeing Marina and Paul lunching together before she discovered she was pregnant; now she felt even worse. Still, as she reminded herself, checking her diary, in two weeks she was due to have lunch with Paul herself. That meant two weeks in which to decide what to tell him. For the moment she would try to remain calm.

When Monday lunchtime came, Jenny waited for Stevie to leave the office and then set off in the opposite direction. Like a criminal she skirted the far end of the square, anxious to avoid meeting anyone she knew until she came to the small corner chemist's. Inside, to her relief, she found only one other customer, an elderly woman extolling the virtues of the purchase she held in her hand – a box of bicarbonate of soda.

'Best thing for stomach upsets, this is,' she proclaimed loudly, looking at the fancy array of packaging on the shelves. 'Better than all yon' modern potions any day. One big burp and you're better,' she added crudely, waving her arm in the air, and, as if to illustrate her point, belched loudly.

At any other time Jenny might have found the old woman amusing, only she realized 'one big burp' wasn't going to make *her* stomach any better. Nor was the other old-fashioned remedy favoured by kitchen sink dramas – a hot bath and a bottle of gin!

'So sorry about that,' the assistant whispered politely. 'Meg can be a bit – well, you know, at times – but we're used to her.'

'She's a regular, then?'

'Oh, yes! She comes in practically every day. Hardly ever buys anything, mind you. She just likes looking at the shelves. Mr Frazer thinks she knows our stock better than we do ourselves. He assures us she's perfectly harmless and just lonely . . . Now, how can I help?'

Jenny was relieved to leave the shop. Normally she would have welcomed so friendly and helpful an assistant but today was different. Why hadn't she realized there would be more than one type of pregnancy testing kit? She'd come here for anonymity and ended up with an agony aunt!

Clutching the small rectangular package, she hurried back in the direction of Sinclair's, passing a greengrocer's along the way, where bunches of bright yellow bananas caught her eye. Like golden crescents they hung against a backdrop of lush artificial grass and posters advertising fruit from the Cape. In the office Jenny put the fruit on her desk and slipped the chemist's bag into her drawer.

'I could have saved you a journey. Didn't you hear me say I was going for my horsepills?'

Stevie's 'horsepills' were part of the new treatment suggested by the doctor. Why, she thought tetchily, had Jenny chosen to ignore her?

Jenny felt her cheeks colour. She'd known Stevie so long, she didn't want to lie or make excuses. Instead she picked up the bananas.

'Here,' she said, breaking one off, 'have a banana. They looked so tempting and reminded me of summer. I just couldn't resist them.'

Stevie shook her head and watched Jenny peel back the thick, yellow, fibrous skin. This was Jenny in a new dimension. Jenny, who'd never before brought so much as an apple into the office, tucking into bananas. Jenny pouring cups of coffee into the plants and furtively trying to conceal chemist's packages. And why, thought Stevie, recognizing the logo on the bag, had it been the chemist's at the other end of the square, when there was one just round the corner?

Shrugging her shoulders, Jenny said somewhat too brightly for Stevie's liking, 'Well, if you change your mind you can always have one later. Now, are you going to tell me about your weekend with Charles?'

'He prefers to be called Charlie.'

'Sorry! I stand corrected, and did you have a good weekend?'

Stevie looked downcast. 'As a matter of fact I didn't see him at the weekend.'

'Oh, but I thought . . .'

'So did I, Jenny. But little did I realize, when Charlie Stuart said about us meeting up with some of his friends, it meant an activity weekend.'

Jenny raised a quizzical eyebrow.

'Hillwalking, rock-climbing, badminton and table tennis. I mean,' protested Stevie, looking down at the smooth white tyres of her wheelchair, 'I'm hardly equipped, am I?'

'But you're brilliant at table tennis; why, you even won . . .'

'I know,' Stevie interrupted, 'and Charlie said while the others walked, he would have pushed me along . . .'

'Then why didn't you let him?'

'I don't know,' sighed Stevie. 'He's such a nice chap, but what on earth does he want to get involved with a cripple like me for?'

'Rubbish!' snapped Jenny, glad to have her mind taken off her own problems. 'Cressida Stephens, you are not a cripple and I will not have you behaving like one, do you hear? Hasn't it occurred to you the reason Charles – sorry, Charlie – wants to get involved with you is because he likes you? In fact I'd go so far as saying – if the flowers he sent you are anything to go by – he's extremely fond of you.'

A rare flush of colour rose in Stevie's cheeks as she thought of the wonderful bouquet delivered to the office only last week.

'So,' enquired Jenny, 'when are you going to see him again?'

'I'm not.'

'*What*?'

'I told him I thought it would be best if we didn't . . .'

'Stevie, you must be mad . . .!'

'I know,' she sniffed moving slowly towards the door, 'but in the circumstances it seemed the only way.'

Jenny sighed. In the present circumstances, what was *her* own only way?

CHAPTER 34

At home and alone, Jenny took the pregnancy kit into
the bathroom, studied the enclosed leaflet, followed the
instructions and waited. The result was almost instan-
taneous. Numbed, she found herself wandering downstairs, where she switched on the television. It didn't
matter what was on, she just needed a diversion.

Close to Valentine's Day, the programme she'd
tuned into was all about romance and loving relation-
ships, and, switching channels, even the natural history programmes showed animals mating and giving
birth to their young. Reaching for the off switch, she
dislodged a magazine Mary had passed on. The headline glared at her. 'HOW TO UNDERSTAND,
CARE FOR AND PLEASE THE MAN IN YOUR
LIFE.' Jenny cried tears of desperation. She had no
man to care for but she was pregnant! What on earth
was she to do?

'Dr McAllister's office, how may I help you?' the
clipped, efficient voice enquired.

'It's Miss Sinclair. I'd like to make an appointment
with Dr McAllister.'

'I'm afraid Dr McAllister's fully booked this week. I can fit you in next Tuesday.'

Tuesday! But that was another eight days away. Another eight days of waiting and deciding what to do. She'd hardly slept a wink last night once the dreaded word 'abortion' crept into her head. If that was to be the answer, then time was running out.

'Miss Sinclair, are you still there? Will Tuesday at ten o'clock be all right.'

'What? Oh, yes,' Jenny replied lamely. 'I just hoped for something sooner . . . you see, we're very busy at the moment.'

'Can I have your Christian name, then, please, Miss Sinclair?'

Jenny obliged, remembering that Morag, despite living so far away, was, like her daughter and daughter-in-law, also Alex McAllister's patient.

'I'm not surprised you're so busy, then,' came the reply. 'The shops are full of the House of St Claire range right now, aren't they? I was only saying to my fiancé, we must put some on our wedding present list.'

Jenny wasn't listening. She was thinking that this woman would probably read her notes, know she was Morag Sinclair's unmarried daughter, and even type the letter to the gynaecologist Alex would no doubt refer her to. Why hadn't she thought of this before picking up the telephone? Heavens! This was going to be worse than she thought.

The clock struck the quarter-hour. Having waited until nine o'clock to ring the practice, she would be late for work again, which meant more excuses. The only saving grace was that for the past few mornings she hadn't been sick. A sure sign, according to the book she'd bought, that the pregnancy was progressing normally.

Andrew eyed both the clock and Jenny's flustered appearance.

'I had a phone call from Mother last night. She's coming to Edinburgh to see the accountant – wants to get a few things sorted out before the end of the financial year catches up with us.'

'But Andrew, it's only February!'

'I'm perfectly aware of that, Jennifer, but you know Mother. Besides, she also mentioned something about her summer wardrobe. Mary says that probably means leaving off her thermals!'

Morag had indeed mentioned her summer wardrobe to her son and also to Tandy. But her companion's puzzled expression at the mention of a summer wardrobe in February had been answered with the retort, 'I need to go to Edinburgh to keep them all on their toes. I'll not have them thinking I'm sitting here waiting to die!'

Who'd mentioned dying? Tandy certainly hadn't. She'd been reading her magazine – the one that used to feature Gina so regularly. She'd half expected Morag to voice her usual disapproval at the magazine's presence. Instead she talked about dying and went on to admire the twin set and tweeds some dowager duchess was wearing in the 'Welcome to my Home' feature.

Morag looked tired, but it was more than Tandy dared mention. The last time she'd enquired after Morag's health, she'd almost had her head bitten off. She'd later been informed about the appointment with the accountant and also thought she'd overheard a low and whispered conversation with Alex McAllister.

Munching her way through another banana, Jenny remembered Andrew hadn't told her when Morag was coming.

'A week Friday, and as usual she's invited herself and Tandy to tea at your place on the Sunday. She says you make better scones than Mary!'

Stevie smiled; she was looking forward to seeing Morag Sinclair again. They hadn't spoken since the night of the dance and she was convinced that in her time Morag Sinclair must have been quite a girl! The phone rang on Jenny's desk.

'Answer that for me, will you, Stevie?' Jenny requested, dropping the banana skin in the bin. 'I must just pop to the loo.'

With furrowed brow, Stevie placed the message on Jenny's desk and at the same time caught sight of the banana skins. Like Jenny, she'd been doing some calculations of her own. After all, you couldn't work with someone for ages and not know when something was wrong. The hazy puzzle in Stevie's mind was beginning to fit together, and if her assumptions were correct, then she held herself partly responsible.

Indirectly she'd given Paul Jenny's room number and, while not aware of him entering the room, she had certainly heard him leave. It was a night when her back had been playing up and, combined with the awful hotel bed, even strong pain-killers hadn't helped. Contemplating events of the past few weeks, Stevie considered the introduction of bananas as a daily addition to Jenny's diet, her surreptitious visits to the chemist's and more recently her frequent visits to the loo.

Surely they could only mean one thing? Jenny was pregnant! But had she told Paul? Was he angry? Was that why Jenny looked as if she'd been crying the other day? Come to think of it, she'd hardly mentioned Paul or the girls for a while. Yet weren't they due to have lunch soon? Stevie became suddenly angry. Today was Valentine's Day. Why hadn't Paul sent Jenny flowers?

'I've put the message on your desk, Jenny, only if you check your diary you'll see you were supposed to be having lunch with Paul at the same time.' Stevie made an excuse and left; she didn't want to be around when Jenny read the message.

'Dr McAllister's receptionist called to say, Dr M. has a seminar to attend on Tuesday but will see you tomorrow at one o'clock if that is convenient?'

A flood of relief swept through Jenny's body. She wouldn't have to wait until next week after all. It would mean cancelling lunch with Paul, but Stevie could tell him she was still suffering from her stomach upset – which in a way was true, wasn't it?

'Jennifer, it's lovely to see you; I always say I never see enough of you Sinclair ladies – you're always so fit and healthy.'

Alex McAllister extended his hand and showed her to a chair. He was a kindly man with thinning grey hair, twinkling eyes and the softest of voices. What Mother always referred to as a 'real bedside manner', only Jenny wished he hadn't, it only made the situation more difficult.

310

'Now,' said Alex, fixing her with concerned eyes, 'what's the problem?'

'The problem,' Jenny blurted out, 'is that I'm pregnant!'

There was no flicker of emotion in Alex's face as he put down his pen.

'I see,' he said raising one eyebrow slightly. 'And what do you feel about being pregnant, Jenny? Are you happy or sad, and what does your partner, the father, feel . . .?'

'I don't know,' Jenny replied brusquely. 'I don't know what to think. How do I know if I'm happy or sad? As for the father, he doesn't even know I'm pregnant!'

Alex passed her a box of tissues and waited. 'I'm so sorry,' she apologized, 'I shouldn't have snapped at you like that.'

'Nonsense, my dear, it's very common in your condition: those ubiquitous hormones we doctors are always talking about. Now you have a good cry and when you're feeling better I'll examine you. In the meantime I'll just take a few notes.'

Returning to his desk, with Jenny's suspicions confirmed, Alex McAllister continued, 'It's obvious from what you say, Jennifer, that this has come as an unexpected surprise. So it looks as if it's completely up to you to make the necessary decision if – as you say – you don't intend to tell the father.'

She thought his choice of words somewhat bizarre but said nothing as he continued thoughtfully, 'The fact that you didn't come in here demanding an abortion leads me to think you want to keep this baby. You're a

311

very healthy young woman, you know, and I can refer you to an excellent gynaecologist.'

Jenny remained silent. Alex McAllister was also extremely perceptive.

'I don't know,' she whispered, screwing the bundle of soggy tissues in her hand into a ball. 'I just don't know.'

'And you won't discuss it with the father?'

'No, I can't!' For some reason the picture of Marina Hendry and Paul lunching together filled her mind. Jenny shook her head firmly.

'Well, in that case . . . I suggest you come and see me towards the end of next week and we'll take things from there.'

Deciding against returning to the office, Jenny stopped in the square where a watery pool of sunlight – heralding another spring – bathed one of the benches in a pale golden glow.

Sitting down, she searched in her bag for a proper handkerchief. Her nose felt sore from constant rubbing with Alex's paper tissues. An old woman shuffled down the path with an array of carrier bags and joined her on the bench.

'What's up, lassie? Got yourself in the family way and he won't marry you?'

Jenny looked up in complete shock and disbelief. How could a total stranger know she was pregnant?

'Dinnae ye fret now, being in the club's no problem these days, you know. They're all at it round my way. As my old mother used to say, "it 'aint no picnic but worse things happen at sea."' The old woman rummaged in her bag, belched, adjusted her hat, then went on her way.

Where, Jenny puzzled, had she seen the old woman before? Suddenly it came back to her. Old Meg from the chemists! Hadn't the chemist's assistant said she spent most days there, studying the shelves until she knew all the stock? Presumeably she'd still been around when Jenny bought the pregnancy kit. Seeing her now with red eyes, it probably wasn't too difficult to put two and two together, was it?

Jenny recalled Meg's unfortunate turn of phrase. Yes, worse things did happen at sea. Cameron had lost two of his best friends at sea and hadn't been the same since. Through misted eyes she watched a sparrow pecking amongst the leaves, revealing a clump of brightly coloured crocuses. Spring was coming – spring and a time for new growth. Jenny felt a stirring in her breast. She had something growing within her. She didn't need to wait until the end of next week. She knew what she wanted to do now. She still wouldn't tell Paul, but she would keep his baby.

CHAPTER 35

Relieved to be home, Jenny kicked off her shoes and unbuttoned her waistband. The last week had dragged, and during this afternoon her pencil-slim skirt had become increasingly uncomfortable. Now, looking in the wardrobe, she searched for something loose and less restrictive.

Deciding to abandon her nightly ritual of eating at the dining table, she prepared an omelette and salad and took it into the cosy sitting room on a tray. There she was able to contemplate matters needing her mother's urgent attention. Morag, she knew from experience, would be in the office at eight-thirty sharp.

For the moment, however, she need not worry about such things. The cottage was tidy – she'd had a blitz at the weekend – and, no longer suffering from morning sickness, she was able to enjoy her meal. The main problem now, she realized, would be coping with the excessive tiredness.

Yawning and stretching wearily, she decided on half an hour's rest before checking the fridge and pantry for tomorrow's lunchtime shopping trip. That way every-thing would be fresh, leaving only the Victoria sponge and scones, which could quite easily be made on Sunday morning.

Relaxed in the armchair, Jenny rested her hands on her stomach. There was no bump as yet, just the usual bloated feeling she got before a period. If she was lucky she could conceal the pregnancy for another month or two, but after that – what then? She counted the months on her fingers. By May or June the weather would be on her side. Warmer temperatures meant looser clothes. Softer styles – as opposed to the tailored ones she favoured in autumn and winter – would then hopefully hide her secret.

Jenny bit her lip thoughtfully. Was it a secret she was hiding or was it guilt? What would people think when they knew? Would they compare her with Gina? That night in the hotel room she'd called Gina a whore. Would Paul see her in exactly the same way?

In melancholy frame of mind she caressed the soft warm curve of her stomach through her wrap, thinking how only yesterday evening she'd been positively ecstatic. Sitting in this same armchair, she'd looked through magazines and catalogues of prams and baby clothes, ticking item after item and even managing to knit half the back of a white matinee jacket.

Holding her handiwork in the air to examine it, she'd proclaimed to the four walls the words she'd always longed to say. 'I'm pregnant! I'm going to have a baby! I'll take my knitting in and show it to Stevie!' Stevie would understand and be so pleased, wouldn't she? Together they would share the wonderful news.

Only this morning, in the cold light of day, last night's euphoria had gone into hibernation, as did the baby magazines and the dainty knitting. Remembering that she was expecting company for the weekend, she'd collected all the telltale evidence and hidden it beneath her bed.

Feeling her eyelids close for the umpteenth time, Jenny rose reluctantly. There would be no knitting tonight and she still had to write her shopping list and check the pantry. Why had she let supplies get so low? Andrew no doubt would take great delight tomorrow lunchtime seeing her return so heavily laden, and she would invariably have to suffer his familiar jibes of 'living in the sticks away from shops and civilization'.

Climbing the stairs, Jenny recalled recalled Fiona's bewildered questioning when she'd first heard her father's phrase.

'I thought Auntie Jenny lived in a cottage – so how can she live in the sticks? Is she like Eeyore from *Winnie-the-Pooh*?'

She smiled fondly. Dear Fiona – at last, and much to Mary's relief, the missing front teeth had finally put in an appearance.

Fiona? Something stirred in Jenny's head as she reached the landing. Should she have done something for Fiona? She'd already placed in a box the long-discarded fashion jewellery of brooches and bracelets she'd promised, and even found a pair of high-heeled shoes for her to dress-up in, yet something still niggled.

'Oh, well,' she sighed sleepily. 'Whatever it is, I shall probably remember in the morning.'

At two-thirty am, waking with a start, an inner voice

announced jam. *Jam!* That's what she'd been trying to remember – or at least in Fiona's case jelly. Was there any of Fiona's jelly left? Groaning at having to leave the warmth and comfort of her bed, Jenny ran downstairs. It was far better to look now; by morning she would probably have forgotten again.

With the stone-flagged floor of the kitchen and pantry ice-cold against her feet, Jenny shivered. Was this hunt for jam without bits really necessary at such an ungodly hour? She was convinced she still had some jars of jelly left . . . but on the other hand, her conscience niggled – what if she hadn't? She couldn't possibly disappoint Fiona.

Wriggling her toes back to life, Jenny stood on tiptoe and peered up at the top shelf. All that was needed was a quick look, then she could hurry back to the warmth of her duvet and hot water bo . . .

'Damn!' she murmured. 'From here I can't even see the top shelf. I shall have to get the steps.'

The steps. Where were the steps? Why weren't they in their usual place? Remembering she'd taken them upstairs when she'd cleaned the windows, Jenny looked about the kitchen. If she stood on one of the chairs that should do just as well . . . on tiptoe she could just reach and . . . yes, there were two small pots of jam nestling in the top corner of the pantry.

'Thank heavens!' She sighed with relief. 'That's one thing less to carry back with me tomorrow.'

With the jars in her hand Jenny turned to balance herself on the chair and, leaning heavily against the back support, suddenly felt it tilt. In a moment of panic she reached forward to steady herself but this time there was no Paul to save her. Here, in the wee small hours, cold and alone, she just slipped and fell.

As expected the following morning, Morag was the first to arrive. Hamish having exchanged his role of gardener to that of chauffeur delivered her to Sinclair's at eight-thirty sharp. Duly dismissed, Tandy was then taken to have coffee with a distant cousin.

At her desk a bemused Stevie watched Morag's hawk-eyed gaze scan the offices for signs of change. Not one to miss anything, Morag nodded approvingly at the new photo of Mary and the children gracing Andrew's desk. Presuming she would still find her husband's photo on Jenny's, Morag was therefore taken aback to find the late William Sinclair obscured by a bunch of bananas!

'If it's not too pertinent a question to ask, Miss Stephens, what is a bunch of bananas doing in a filing tray on Jennifer's desk?'

Without looking up from a pile of letters, Stevie replied nonchalantly, 'Oh, they're Jenny's; she's very much into bananas these days.'

'Is she indeed?' enquired Morag, casting a quizzical eye in her direction.

Later, with everyone assembled in the boardroom, Morag pronounced her delight with the developments of the past year and suggested they all stop for coffee. Andrew and Jenny smiled knowingly and averted their gaze while Morag surreptitiously added a wee dram to her coffee.

'Jennifer, my dear,' she said, sipping her coffee appreciatively. 'You look a bit peaky – are you all right?'

'Yes, I'm fine, thank you, Mother. It's just my back; I foolishly fell off a chair.'

'And what were you doing perched precariously on a chair?'

'Hunting for Fiona's jelly at half-past two in the morning!' came the reply.

'Hmph! Did anyone ever tell you, you spoil that youngest grandchild of mine?'

'That's rich coming from you, Mother,' Andrew retorted. 'Why Fiona tells me you're taking her to lunch tomorrow – at McDonald's, of all places!'

Stevie, coming in with a fresh pot of coffee, was highly amused to think of Morag in a burger bar with not a china cup in sight. She whispered in Jenny's ear, 'Paul's on the phone again, wants to know if you're recovered enough to have lunch with him next week?'

'Tell him yes,' replied Jenny, anxious to avoid mention of Paul in front of Morag. She felt the familiar stirring in her stomach when she thought of him. She would have to face him sooner or later.

With the meeting closed, Hamish returned with Tandy to take the two elderly women to lunch at their favourite Edinburgh haunt. There, at the old-established family hotel favoured by Morag and her generation, they could lunch in peace.

Away from the hubbub of yuppies and what was it Jean called them . . . Gothics and Grunge, they were at liberty to eat what Morag called 'proper food' and watch the comings and goings of ladies impeccably dressed in finest tweeds and woollens. Although Morag would be the last to admit to it, there was also the

319

chance of hearing just the merest hint of the latest gossip.

'Will you be wanting to go and look for your summer wardrobe directly after lunch?' equired Tandy.

'No!' Morag said abruptly. 'I have to see the bank manager.' She had to make some excuse for seeing Dr McAllister.

'Blethers!' hissed Tandy.

In astonishment Morag dropped her knife and looked up in surprise.

'You don't have to lie to me, Morag Sinclair! I know you're not going to see your bank manager. You are going to see Alex McAllister about these dizzy spells you keep having!'

Morag said nothing as Tandy continued boldly, 'You Sinclair women, you think you can keep your secrets from everyone, but you can't fool me!'

'Whatever do you mean?' Morag asked defensively, dabbing at her mouth with a napkin.

'I mean,' said Flora Tandy, 'you are worried about your health, Mary and Andrew have had difficulties with their marriage, and as for Miss Jennifer . . .'

'What about Miss Jennifer?'

'Isn't it obvious? You as her mother should know that, Morag Sinclair – your daughter is pregnant!'

Morag's hands gripped the table. So her worst suspicions were confirmed. 'Well, Flora Tandy, as you seem to be such an old witch, perhaps you will be so kind to tell me who the father is?'

'Well,' mused Tandy thoughtfully, 'at first I thought it might be that dreadful Alistair Jennings . . . you know he paid Miss Jennifer a great deal of attention

320

at the dance . . . but I've since changed my mind and I'm convinced it must be that nice Mr Hadley. I'm surprised you didn't see it yourself. Didn't you notice how they looked at one another when they were dancing?'

Morag was silent. Never had Tandy been so outspoken. She was right, Morag had noticed Jenny and Paul together. She had also been gravely concerned for her daughter's welfare. At the time Gina was still alive and there had also been that dreadful scene at the dance.

Of course it could have been far worse if Jenny hadn't managed to persuade Paul to take Gina away. Morag, in fact, had missed nothing. Poor Jennifer, thought Morag. How could she say to her only daughter, 'Jennifer, my dear, I know you're pregnant and please will you let me help?'

'You're quite correct, Flora,' Morag sighed wearily, 'correct about everything . . . but what do you suggest we do about it?'

'For the moment, nothing,' came the simple reply.

Flora Tandy reached across the table for Morag's hand. She patted it reassuringly and continued, 'Don't do anything – that is, not until you've seen Dr McAllister. Best wait to see what happens this afternoon. Besides, the family are all gathering for dinner tonight, aren't they? Perhaps you can gauge the situation from that.'

Nodding assent, Morag prepared herself for her afternoon appointment. She already feared the worst and would have nothing but the truth from Alex McAllister.

CHAPTER 36

Once more sitting at opposite ends of a dining table with her son, Morag Sinclair studied her immediate family. Mary, with her eldest children on either side, sat on one side of the table with Jenny, flanked by Fiona and Flora Tandy, sitting on the other.

Casting a furtive glance in Tandy's direction, Morag turned her gaze back to Andrew. Although his waistline had begun to thicken, he was becoming more and more like his father as he got older; he even had the same telltale white streaks appearing at his temples.

Morag swallowed hard. In his younger days William had been such a fine figure of a man and it pained her still to think of him wasting away before her very eyes. Why was life so cruel?

If what Alec McAllister had told her that very afternoon was correct, there would be no such wasting away for Morag. It would be one fell swoop if she didn't heed his advice, and then gone – just like that – snuffed out like a candle! With a shudder Morag tore her bread roll in half.

Mary Sinclair, oblivious to her mother-in-law's secret torment, served the soup with an air of satisfac-

322

tion. As usual she had surpassed herself: the table was laid with the finest House of St Claire linen and the crystal and silver sparkled and shone in the candlelight. She smiled lovingly at her husband. It was, she told herself, just like old times. Although if she was to be perfectly honest, wasn't their relationship perhaps now better than it had ever had been before? Mary felt two blobs of colour rise in her cheeks.

That, thought Morag, watching Andrew's eyes meet Mary's, was at least one thing less for her to worry about. Who could tell, maybe that little blip with Gina had done some good after all? But what of her daughter? What had the past few months done to her?

Jennifer's face was still strained from the morning. How badly had she hurt her back? Compared to Mary she looked painfully thin, but not for much longer, Morag reminded herself. And how to broach the subject of Jennifer's pregnancy she had no idea.

With dinner completed and at a knowing look from Morag, the ever-discreet Tandy withdrew from the table, using the Friday night concert on the wireless as her excuse. Meanwhile the pensive Morag watched the younger members of her family in silence.

Iain chatted earnestly about his studies in such an animated way that it could have been a younger William sitting by her side. Certainly he had his father's looks and Mary's colouring, but the mannerisms were those of his grandfather. Had Jennifer begun to recognize such similarities in her nephew? Jennifer, she noted, was deep in conversation with Fiona.

'Are you coming to watch me ice-skate tomorrow, Auntie Jen? I'm going to practise for my medal.'

To everyone's surprise Morag interjected, 'No, she's not! She needs a rest. Do you realize your Auntie Jennifer fell off a chair while hunting for your jars of jelly?'

Alarmed at her mother's outspokenness, Jenny put a reassuring arm around Fiona's shoulder. It wasn't Fiona's fault she'd fallen, it was her own stupidity for being too tired to fetch the steps. In an attempt to make Fiona feel better, she added, 'I think Grannie's right – perhaps I should rest my back. But I'm sure she will watch you carefully and tell me all about it when you come for tea on Sunday. Mummy says you've been practising really hard.'

Fiona's face brightened. 'Yes,' she beamed, 'I want to skate just like Jayne Torville.'

'In that case,' teased Iain, 'you'd better find a nice young man to partner you.'

'Speaking of nice young men . . .' Morag had found her opening at last '. . . how's that nice young man, Mr Hadley?' She cast a quick sideways glance at Jenny to gauge her reaction. To her dismay Andrew responded to the question.

'Oh, he's very well, Mother – he's really done us proud.'

'Quite recovered from the death of his wife, has he?'

For a brief moment Andrew felt all eyes turn in his direction.

'Er – well, yes, sort of; he seems much better now. Mind you, he should be grateful to Jennifer,' he added quickly to cover his slip of composure.

'Why should Paul Hadley be grateful to me, Andrew?' Jenny demanded tetchily.

Andrew shifted uneasily in his chair. He'd discerned that distinct tone in Jenny's voice that meant he was treading on dangerous ground.

'Well,' he said slowly, taking a deep breath, 'it's largely thanks to Sinclair's that Paul's got a string of freelance contracts to look forward to.' Andrew's tone was smug. 'And as you were the one to give him a job in the first place, Jennifer . . . I mean, where would he be now without you?'

Instead of easing the situation, Andrew had only succeeded in making it worse. Jenny sprang defiantly to Paul's defence.

'Where would he be? *Where would he be*! Well, isn't that obvious? If I hadn't found Paul Hadley when I did – and thank goodness I did, as we were in danger of being stuck in the same old rut and swallowed up by our competitors to sink without trace – Paul would no doubt be being fêted by another company similar to our own.'

Andrew sat in stony silence as his sister turned on him angrily.

'You of all people, Andrew, should be the first to admit that Paul's idea for the House of St Claire has completely revolutionized the business, so I think it's us who should be grateful to Paul Hadley and not the other way round!'

Iain cheered and clapped loudly. He loved it when Auntie Jen put his father down. Fiona in her innocence clapped too. Wasn't that what people did when they liked something? She certainly liked Auntie Jenny and Iain was shouting for more. It was just like the panto-mime at New Year when Iain had encouraged her and the timid Cele and Emily to hiss, cheer and boo to their hearts' delight.

Suddenly aware of her appreciative audience, Jenny lowered her eyes and took a sip of water. 'I'm sorry, Andrew, perhaps I was a bit too outspoken. You must excuse me, it must be this wretched backache. I could probably do with some of Stevie's "horsepills".'

'Nonsense,' said Mary kindly. 'Andrew needs to be taken down a peg or two sometimes, don't you, dear?' She smiled lovingly in her husband's direction as he walked downcast to the cabinet, fetched a bottle of Courvoisier and poured brandy into his mother's glass.

At the same time Morag watched her daughter's every gesture. Even in the candlelight Jennifer's face and eyes shone with such magnificence in her defence of Paul. Morag smiled knowingly; she now had all the evidence she required. Jenny must be carrying Paul's child.

'Well,' she acknowledged, raising her brandy glass, 'in that case here's to Mr Hadley, and long may he remain with Sinclair's!' Morag looked Jennifer straight in the eye as if to say, That's the best I can do for you, my dear – you have my blessing; the rest is up to you!

CHAPTER 37

Bathed in dappled winter sunlight, Jenny stretched contentedly in bed.

'Mmm, Saturday.' She sighed appreciatively. 'The cottage is tidy, the shopping done and I can have an utterly lazy day all to myself for once.'

Filled with a sense of wellbeing, she plumped up her pillows and lay back. As the sun rose higher and its rays stronger, rosy patterns danced on the walls and ceiling and from the corner of her eye she caught sight of yesterday's list of things to do. How wonderful to know each and every item had been ticked off and tomorrow there would only be tea to prepare for the family.

Tracing the design of a full-blown rose on the duvet cover, Jenny's mind wandered back to happier times and Cameron's teasings.

'You're like a wild bird, suddenly set free from your nest amongst the roses,' he'd said one day, jumping out of bed and encircling her in his arms. 'Why on earth did you choose all these roses? Roses on the curtains, roses on the walls – it's worse than Sleeping Beauty in this room! Thank goodness they don't have thorns otherwise I'd never get to you. When we're married I shall change it all to . . .'

Her memories, like rose thorns, were still painful as she opened the bedside drawer and brought out a creased snapshot of Cameron.

'Well, we'll never be married now, Cameron, so I can keep my roses and you can keep your blue stripes!' Smoothing down the corners of the photo, she whispered softly, 'and I wonder what you'd think about your ex-fiancée now that she's pregnant. Not a great deal, I expect . . . but then it wouldn't have happened if you'd been . . . been . . .'

Been what? she asked herself. Less possessive, less demanding, less moody. Looking back on it, Cameron had always been possessive and demanding, but at the time she'd been blinded by love. Not wishing to be reminded of his black moods, she tore the snapshot into tiny pieces, reached out to drop them in the rose-covered bin and disposed of Cameron with a smile.

Ignoring the dull pain in her back, Jenny leapt from the bed, opened the windows wide and breathed in the soft morning air. If the forecast was good she thought she might even be able to potter in the garden. Miss Tandy always loved to wander round the garden when she came, and there was a magnificent clump of *tête-à-tête* daffodils to show her. A true herald of spring blooming in East Lothian.

Blooming. What a wonderful word . . . blooming like the golden daffodils and . . . Jenny placed her hand gently against her stomach.

'Blooming just like me,' she murmured. 'Isn't that how they describe expectant mothers? Apart from this

328

stupid niggle in my back, I certainly feel blooming. In fact I feel wonderful.'

With her mind racing on the tiny being growing inside her, her own baby – Paul's baby – to love and cherish and care for, Jenny walked purposefully to the bed and turned back the duvet. Poised with her hand in mid-air, she froze, and all sense of well-being and euphoria vanished without trace. In panic and alarm she rang Dr McAllister's surgery.

Relieved to find him there and not on the golf course, she described the telltale stain on the pale sheet that filled her heart with dread. Alex McAllister's voice was as calm and reassuring as ever.

'I shouldn't worry, Jennifer. It is very common in first pregnancies, you know. Have you been doing anything to upset things?'

'I've been doing some early spring cleaning. Morag's here – did you know?' He did, of course, only too well, but declined to comment.

'Then, of course,' Jenny continued, 'there was the fall . . .'

'Fall?'

'I fell off a chair.'

It seemed some time before Alex spoke again. 'Jennifer . . . if you've decided to keep the baby, then I suggest you stay in bed and rest. If not, then perhaps . . .'

Jenny had already decided there were to be no 'if nots' about it.

'I'll go back to bed straight away,' she announced.

Unused to spending all day in bed, it wasn't long before she became bored. She'd already looked through a whole gamut of magazines and designed the baby's nursery at least half a dozen times. The box-room next door to her bedroom would make an ideal nursery, then, when a bigger room was needed, she could transform the guest room at the far end of the landing. But, she mused, picking up one of the magazines, will it be pink candy stripes or pale blue gingham?

In the afternoon following a light lunch of salad and a glass of milk Jenny returned to bed and continued with her knitting. With nothing else to do it was amazing how quickly the tiny matinee coat took shape and after five more rows she could even begin to decrease for the armholes. Thrilled with her efforts, she announced to the well-loved teddy bear propped against her dressing table mirror, 'Well, Mr Bear, this is one garment I do intend to finish! And if I carry on making such rapid progress I can even go and buy those pretty mother-of-pearl buttons I've seen.'

Remembering her shopping trip to buy dresses for Emily and Celestina, Jenny longed for the warmth of Paul's embrace. Eventually drifting into a fitful sleep, she found herself pushing a pram through skeins of wool that twisted and wound themselves about her, while at the same time she tried desperately to reach Paul. Paul who was waiting for her and the baby with open arms. With one last push through the tangled strands, Jenny gave a groan and woke with a start.

Disentangling herself from the winter-weight duvet that had somehow left her feeling like an Egyptian mummy, Jenny struggled to the bathroom and splashed her face with cold water.

'Too much sleep, that's your trouble, Jennifer Sinclair,' she said, addressing her flushed reflection in the bathroom mirror. 'Goodness, just look at the state of you! A refreshing shower is just what you need, and maybe a brisk walk.'

Remembering Dr McAllister's instructions to rest, she hesitated and changed her mind. Perhaps not a brisk walk, more a gentle stroll, then an evening lounging in front of the television or perhaps listening to the Saturday night play on Radio Four. 'How simply wonderful,' she whispered, turning on the shower. 'Surely that won't exhaust me too much.'

The pine-scented shower gel that usually left her feeling invigorated and reminded her of the walk she'd taken with Paul and the girls to look for fir cones, smelt sickly and strangely intoxicating. Jenny studied the green decorated bottle carefully. Surely the company hadn't changed the formula? This wasn't yet another of those 'new improved products', was it? Why couldn't they leave things alone – and why did her head ache so much?

In a daze, and mesmerized by the slow trickle of dayglo shower gel oozing silently and monotonously to the floor of the shower cubicle, Jenny realized all too late the danger of the situation. Startled by what appeared to be a pool of green slime spreading between her toes, she drew up sharply and, reaching forward to close the nozzle on the upturned bottle, felt herself slip.

Much later, wrapped in her bathrobe and slumped against the bathroom door, Jenny wept deep uncontrollable sobs for the pain that now racked her body and the anguish at losing the thing she yearned for most. Numbed by despair, her fingers plucked absent-mindedly at the soft white pile of the towelling robe.

'Soft,' she sighed through fresh warm tears, 'soft like the hooded towel we wrapped Fiona in as a baby . . . soft and sweet-smelling like the mass of copper-coloured baby curls I used to press against my face.'

Reaching for a clean towel, Jenny rolled it into a bundle and drew it close, visualizing as she did so her own sweet-smelling bundle with rosebud mouth fresh from her breast. So many times today as she lay in bed she'd imagined what it would be like to hold her own precious baby in her arms . . . and now it was no more.

Unable to cope with her loss and wondering how she would fill the deep void that now beckoned, Jenny forgot all about Morag's visit. All she wanted to do was sleep. What was it Cameron had said about her bedroom? Rising to her feet and reaching for the bottle of paracetamol, she walked to her bedroom in a daze. Just like Sleeping Beauty, she would go to her own bed amongst the swathes of entwining roses and with luck sleep for a hundred years.

CHAPTER 38

With scones and a Victoria sponge to prepare, Jenny found her attention diverted only briefly from the previous evening. Her gaze rested on the bottle of tablets. How many had she taken before falling into a deep sleep? At least this morning the pain wasn't quite as bad. With a shrug of her shoulders she screwed the top back on the bottle and placed it back in the bathroom cabinet. It wouldn't do to leave such things lying around with Fiona in the house.

At three o'clock Fiona came bouncing to the front door and insisted on taking Miss Tandy into the garden immediately. There were the daffodils to see, she called excitedly, plus of course her own promised plot where Auntie Jenny said she could grow some seeds.

'But first I must wait until the soil becomes warmer,' Fiona explained to a bemused Miss Tandy.

Jenny smiled, seeing Fiona pat the rich brown soil expectantly with the palm of her hand. Sadly, it was not yet warm.

A jaded-looking Morag declined to go into the garden, choosing to remain indoors by the fire instead. Turning from the window, Jenny was surprised to see her mother rubbing her chest. 'Jennifer, do you have any bicarbonate of soda? I didn't like to say anything in front of Fiona for fear of upsetting her. You see, I've had the most dreadful indigestion since eating that burger yesterday. Andrew and Mary did warn me that it wouldn't be quite like Tandy's cooking, but the child was so looking forward to our outing.'

Jenny recalled old Meg in the chemist's and her comments about bicarb.

'I'm afraid not, but I think I might have some liver salts in the bathroom. Why don't you go and rest on my bed, Mother? It will be more comfortable, and I'll see what I can find.' Surprisingly, Morag was led upstairs without a murmur.

'Actually,' said Jenny rearranging the pillows, 'if it is indigestion you're probably better sitting propped up. There, is that better?'

Morag nodded weakly.

'Right, then, I'll go and fetch the liver salts.' On her return Jenny became anxious. In those few short moments Morag's face had turned quite ashen. 'Perhaps I'd better go and fetch Miss Tandy; you do look poorly, Mother.'

'I'd rather you didn't, Jennifer – you know how the woman fusses and I can't stand fuss. However, if you could get me a bowl . . . I'm so sorry but I think I'm going to be sick!'

Deciding to fetch Miss Tandy even if it meant upsetting her mother, Jenny ran into the garden.

'Oh, my God!' cried Tandy in alarm. 'It must be her heart.'

'Her heart! But what's wrong with Mother's heart?'

Explaining as they ran into the kitchen, Flora Tandy stopped abruptly as she heard a resounding thump coming from the room overhead. In Jennifer's bedroom, the last thing Morag saw as she reached for the bowl was a pair of knitting needles and some delicate white knitting.

In the ambulance Jenny clung grimly to her Mother's hand while a shocked and white-faced Tandy remained at the garden gate, comforting a tearful Fiona.

'For goodness' sake, Flora, tell the child to stop crying,' Morag commanded feebly. 'I am not going to die!'

The ambulance man closed the door and Flora Tandy, wiping Fiona's eyes, pondered on the fact that in little more than forty-eight hours Morag Sinclair had twice used her Christian name. Her old friend was either mellowing in old age or else was going to . . . 'No!' Tandy cried under her breath in the direction of the disappearing ambulance. 'Morag Sinclair, you've always had your way and I refuse to let you die first!'

Alex McAllister sat by Morag's bed and watched her open her eyes.

'Morag, my friend,' he whispered softly, 'you are a very lucky lady.'

'Meaning I'm lucky to be alive?' she asked faintly.

'Meaning, I had just finished my game of golf and was able to come rushing to your bedside!'

Morag grinned weakly. 'Alex McAllister, you always were a rogue, you know. And there was me thinking you were concerned for my health.'

'As a matter of fact I am, and when you're discharged

from hospital and return to Conasg, I want you to promise me you'll follow all my instructions . . . perhaps Jennifer could even go home with you for a few days?'

There was something in the way Alex spoke Jennifer's name, something in the way he looked at her as she stood in the outer corridor.

'Alex,' said Morag trying to wriggle up on her elbows, 'tell me, is Jennifer pregnant?'

'Morag Sinclair,' he admonished kindly, 'you should know better than that . . . Fancy asking me about one of my patients!'

'She might be your patient, Alex, but she's also my daughter!' Morag didn't like being put down. Jennifer had been pregnant, she and Tandy were convinced, yet today Jennifer looked different. Her eyes were dull and tired, not glowing as they had been on Friday evening, and she'd spent an unusually long time in the bathroom not long after they arrived for tea. The fall from the chair . . . Jennifer's backache – had it all ended so tragically?

'I'll just say, then,' Morag continued, determined to get to the truth, 'I'm convinced Jennifer was pregnant and . . . that perhaps she isn't any longer. Now, shall I wait for you to contradict me, Alex?'

When Alex McAllister remained silent, Morag wept silent tears.

'Flora Tandy, will you please stop fussing! How many more times? I can assure you I feel fine; I've come back to Conasg to rest, not die!'

Watching her companion retreat with an armful of

cushions and yet another rug, Morag turned to her daughter. 'Gracious, if she's not careful she'll kill me by suffocation!'

'Don't be too hard on her, Mother. You know she's been fraught with worry over you this past week.'

'I know, dear,' Morag sighed, 'but the last thing I need right now is to be treated like an invalid. I just want to forget all about this silly heart business.'

Jenny wanted to say, 'This silly heart business nearly killed you,' but thought better of it.

Dr McAllister had advised against any undue excitement or unnecessary confrontations and it had been bad enough trying to keep Andrew and Mary from fussing round Morag's bedside. Eventually it was agreed that only Jenny would remain at Conasg, and Andrew was sent away with a briefcase full of instructions and the command from his mother not to come again unless called for!

'Now, Jennifer,' Morag said, patting the bed, 'come and sit here and we'll discuss the holiday.'

Bemused, Jenny sat down on the burgundy satin quilt. Holiday – what holiday? No one had mentioned a holiday. Surely Mother wasn't planning a trip to convalesce? And was Jenny to go with her as travelling companion and nurse, leaving Miss Tandy behind?

'I'm sorry, Mother, I wasn't aware you were planning a holiday. Was it something you discussed with Andrew or Dr McAllister?'

'Yes and no,' Morag replied with a twinkle in her eye. 'I'm not going on holiday, Jennifer. You are. Andrew is arranging it all.'

'What? But I don't understand . . .'

'It's quite simple: I think you could do with a break. Shall we just say I think you've got some soul-searching to do? You've not been very well just lately, have you?'

Aware of Morag's penetrating gaze, Jenny lowered her eyes. How much did her mother know? If she knew about the baby then had everyone else known too? Perhaps it hadn't been such a well-kept secret after all?

'How did you . . . when did you . . .?'

Morag reached for Jenny's hand. 'Hush, my dear. I don't really know anything for certain, do I? Shall we just say an old woman's intuition?'

Swallowing hard, Jenny laid her head gently against her Mother's shoulder.

'Cameron hurt me so much, you know. He accused me of being married to Sinclair's and said such cruel things about the family. After he broke off our engagement, there were times when I didn't know what to do. Then, when I discovered I was pregnant I just thought . . .'

'Ssh,' Morag whispered stroking Jennifer's hair. 'I know, my dear – believe me, I do understand. In a way perhaps Cameron was right; after your father died we all expected far too much from you . . .'

'No, Mother, that's just not true!'

'. . . and look at how much you helped Mary when Fiona was a baby.' Morag shook her head angrily. 'In fact, not only when Fiona was born but for the past seven years! And as for Andrew . . .'

'You mustn't be too hard on Andrew,' Jenny pleaded. 'It wasn't easy for him when Father . . .'

Morag reached for her handkerchief. 'You know, the trouble with you, Jennifer, is that you're too soft and far too sweet-natured for your own good sometimes, which is why I think it's time you laid your ghosts to rest.'

'Ghosts! But I don't have any ghosts!'

'Don't you?' Morag asked wryly. 'Well, I can think of two for a start, namely Cameron and Gina.'

'But Cameron's not dead!'

'Maybe not, and, much as I dislike the way he treated you, I wouldn't wish that on him just yet. Anyway, that's enough talk about Cameron. Aren't you going to ask me where I'm going to send you?'

Puzzled by all this intrigue, Jenny shook her head. If her Mother's present state of mind was anything to go by, she could end up being sent anywhere.

'Venice!' Morag announced triumphantly. 'And before you say anything, I'm not taking no for an answer, and Andrew has Sinclair's all under control!'

'Venice – but why Venice? I haven't been there for years, not since Moira and I . . .'

'Exactly and that's why I'm sending you. If I recall, you and Moira never stopped talking about the wonderful paintings and art treasures. The two of you were always saying how much you wanted to go back.'

'Yes, but Moira went to Switzerland and married Helmut.'

'And you got yourself engaged to Cameron, who wouldn't even recognize a decent picture if he saw one!'

'Mother! You said you didn't want to talk about Cameron.'

'Quite so,' Morag acknowledged, 'so let's discuss your plans first, then you go and have a rest. Perhaps you could also send Flora to see me with some tea. Tell her she can stay if she's quiet and can even bring one of those awful magazines of hers to look at if she likes. I can't abide them myself, you know!'

Smiling, Jenny left the room. Morag was obviously getting better!

CHAPTER 39

The office felt strangely empty and quiet. Stevie was used to Andrew darting in and out but it was unusual for Jenny to be absent for days at a time. She had therefore been surprised to receive Jenny's phone call announcing her intention to have a short holiday.

'Going anywhere nice?'

'Italy,' had come the reply.

When anyone mentioned Italy, Stevie immediately thought of Gina and then, through thought-transference, Paul. Had Jenny remembered her lunch appointment with Paul?

'What about Paul? You haven't forgotten your lunch date, have you? You've already cancelled twice.'

In the confusion of Morag's heart attack and the subsequent return to Conasg, it had completely slipped Jenny's mind.

'To be honest I had, Stevie, but don't worry, I won't get you to make excuses for me this time. I'll ring Paul myself.'

The caladiums, despite being completely drained of coffee and dosed with Baby Bio, still looked pretty sickly. Stevie sat contemplating drastic action. Should she cut them right back and hope they would spring into new growth or simply drop them into the bin and send them on their way to the great garden centre in the sky? She had a few days to decide before Jenny returned. At least the weeping fig had perked up, but there was still a terrible smell somewhere in the office. Reaching down behind the desk, she found the remains of Jenny's last bunch of bananas, their skins blackened and the fruit mushy.

'Goodness, they don't look too healthy. Where is everyone?' Paul stood in the doorway, smiling.

'Paul! What are you doing here?'

'I'm having lunch with Jenny, remember? Third time lucky by my reckoning.'

'But she's not here; didn't she ring you?'

Paul looked dejectedly about the office. 'No, and there's been no message left on the answerphone.'

'You haven't spoken to Jenny, then, so you won't have heard the news about Morag Sinclair . . . She had a slight heart attack the Sunday she was with Jenny.'

'No, I haven't! What a dreadful shock – is she going to be all right?'

'Apparently so. Jenny went back to Conasg with her once she was discharged from hospital. She's been looking after her, but now . . .' Stevie was going to add, she's going to Italy, but decided against it.

'Anyway, I'm surprised Andrew hasn't told you. Didn't you see him last week?'

Paul was thoughtful. 'Mmm, yes, I should have, but I cancelled that meeting; Marina Hendry telephoned me with a business proposition which seemed too good to refuse.'

'And was it?' Stevie asked sardonically. 'Too good to refuse, I mean?'

'Actually, no. Wait a minute, Stevie! What are you getting at?'

Stevie eyed him suspiciously. 'Well, you know what they say about Marina Hendry – "Man-eater Marina" and all that. I was just wondering.'

'Come off it, Stevie, you can't be serious! Surely you don't think Marina Hendry has got designs on me?'

'Not me necessarily, but I know Jenny thinks so!'

Paul couldn't believe his ears. 'You've got to be joking,' he remonstrated. 'Jenny – surely not! Wait a minute – is this why she keeps putting off having lunch with me? Is that what this is all about?'

Stevie didn't know what to say. They were getting into dangerous waters. 'No, that's not it at all,' she added quickly. 'She really has had tummy troubles.' That wasn't a complete lie, was it? she told herself.

'Well I'm not surprised if that's what she's been eating.' Paul studied the blackened bananas in the bin. His gaze then took in the sickly caladiums and the slowly recovering weeping fig. 'Mind you, most things in this office seem to be looking pretty sickly at the moment. Even you don't look your usual chirpy self.'

'That's probably because they've been on a diet of coffee.' She gestured to the plant trough. 'And I suppose I've been worried about Jenny and Morag.' She refrained from mentioning how much she missed Charlie Stuart, yet time and time again she'd refused his dinner invitations.

Paul's face brightened. 'Stevie . . . as you look like a

lost soul in here all on your own, how about joining another lost soul for lunch?'

'That sounds like a super idea; the only problem of course is getting into some of the restaurants with my wheelchair. However, if you don't mind, we could buy some baguettes from the deli, take them to the square and eat al fresco.'

Paul nodded in agreement. Fresh air seemed like a good idea. Maybe it would clear his head. He'd been thinking of Jenny so much lately – it was as if she was trying to avoid him and she always seemed so ill at ease. With luck perhaps Stevie could throw some light on the situation.

Manoeuvring Stevie's chair through Sinclair's main doors, Paul was convinced she was hiding something from him. It wasn't just Marina Hendry that had brought about the change in Jenny; she was too intelligent a woman for that.

Once in the square, where sunlight flickered through branches packed tightly with buds ready to unfurl in a profusion of blossom, Paul prepared himself to broach the subject. With Stevie remaining in her chair he found a bench bathed in sunshine and handed over her baguette.

'OK, Miss Stephens, now I have you as my prisoner and you can't escape, I want you to tell me what's going on. What have I done to upset Jenny?'

Through Paul's attempt at humour Stevie recognized the desperation in his voice and very nearly choked on her pastrami and salad. In some ways it was an unfortunate turn of phrase on his behalf. How could she answer that? Feebly she replied, 'Well, you didn't send her any flowers on Valentine's Day.'

'No, you're right, I didn't, which I suppose was extremely remiss of me in the circumstances. But to be honest, Stevie, I just had the impression Jenny was trying to avoid me, in which case flowers wouldn't have helped very much, would they? Anyway, did Jenny actually say she expected flowers from me?'

'Well, no,' continued Stevie, 'I just thought . . . as you were both getting on so well together . . .'

'So did I,' Paul murmured sadly, 'and I'd do anything to put things right between us. Any suggestions . . . apart from buying her flowers?'

Stevie shook her head; she was getting out of her depth. Other than to suggest Paul wait until Jenny returned from her holiday, it was difficult knowing what to do. In the end she was grateful to change the subject and exchange trivial pleasantries instead. The baguettes and fruit tarts demolished, Stevie handed Paul the wrappers to place in the nearby bin.

'Thank you for the banquet – now, Sir Galahad, can you do the honours and return me to the office in my steely charger?'

'Why, certainly, m'lady.' Paul grinned broadly and with a sweeping bow turned the chair in the direction of the office.

Back at Sinclair's, Stevie studied Paul's face. It had now lost its earlier cheerfulness and it was obvious he was thinking of Jenny. Bending to kiss her on the cheek, Paul whispered softly, 'Thanks for your company, Stevie. I'll bear in mind what you said and next time when I see Jenny . . . if I see Jenny . . . I'll take her some flowers.'

Watching him turn and walk away Stevie felt so utterly helpless. She wanted to run after him and tell him about Jenny and the baby but how could she, confined to this heap of rubber and metal?

'Paul!' she cried in desperation. 'Please, you don't understand – Jenny, she . . .'

Stopping by his car, Paul turned back and heard Stevie call.

'About Jenny – she . . . she . . . loves you . . . you know.'

With the words ringing in his ears, Paul ran back to Stevie's side. He thought he'd heard her correctly the first time but he just wanted to make sure. Helping her into the lift, neither of them saw the slim figure standing in the shadows.

'Yes, Mother, I understand. Yes, I will tell her . . . the moment she comes back from lunch. I promise!'

Hearing Andrew's exasperated voice from the corridor, Stevie and Paul exchanged enquiring glances.

'Stevie – thank heavens! My mother's been plaguing me for the past three quarters of an hour. Will you please ring her?'

Stevie shot Paul a puzzled look and excused herself to wash the remains of fruit tart from her fingers.

'Andrew, I was truly sorry to hear about your mother. Stevie says she's on the mend,' Paul said as she left.

'Yes, and don't I know it! Gracious, Paul, she sent me away from Conasg with a list of instructions as long as your arm. There's even a letter for you somewhere. Now let me see . . .' Andrew rummaged through a pile of papers in his briefcase and handed Paul a slim white envelope.

'Now, if you'll excuse me, I must dash. I'm late for an appointment. Just remind Stevie to ring Mother or my life won't be worth living.'

He smiled as he closed his briefcase and headed for the door. 'Oh, and by the way, Paul, don't worry – Mother won't eat you! We're all very fond of her really, you know.'

Paul was leaning against the desk studying the contents of Morag's letter. 'The mystery deepens,' he said to Stevie as she came back in, folding the creamy white vellum. 'Morag Sinclair has summoned me to Conasg House. What do you make of that?'

Stevie was as mystified as Paul. What on earth had been happening at Conasg? And why the urgency for Stevie to ring Morag? The whole business was becoming increasingly bizarre.

Placing the letter in his pocket, Paul left the office to make arrangements for the girls to stay with Helen and Stevie reached anxiously for the phone.

Moments later, leaving Jenny's office where she'd been spraying air-freshener, Stevie was startled to find Charlie Stuart standing in the corridor.

'Charlie! But what are you doing here? I thought I told you it was better if we didn't see . . .'

'Aye, I know, and until about an hour ago I thought I might be able to change your mind.'

'An hour ago? What happened an hour ago?' she enquired nervously.

'An hour ago . . . I just happened to see you in the park with your new boyfriend.'

'Oh! You mean Paul! But I thought you knew Paul was . . .'

'Obviously I didn't, Stevie, but I have to admit he's a handsome-looking guy and I can't blame you for falling for him.'

'You can't?' Stevie asked in disbelief.

'Why, no. I have to admit he's far better-looking than I am . . . and he's got more hair than I have . . .'

Stevie studied Charlie's receding hairline and nodded thoughtfully.

'And what about his eyes – don't you think he's got nice eyes?'

'Aye, from what I could see he's got nice eyes too; at least he doesn't have to hide them behind John Lennon spectacles like me.'

'Then of course there's his teeth,' she teased, re-membering Charlie's two front teeth, lost during a savage encounter on the rugby field.

Charlie pushed his tongue against his false teeth as if to make sure they were still there and caught the wicked glint in Stevie's eye. 'Hey, what is this?' he cried. 'Do you intend to go through all my physical attributes – or should I say lack of them – and make me feel even worse?'

Moving her chair to where Charlie now sat slumped discontentedly at her own desk, Stevie ran her hand over his close-cropped hair.

'Charlie Stuart,' she said softly, 'I think you've got lovely hair, lovely eyes and a lovely smile. Yes, you're right about Paul, I do think he's smashing,' she watched Charlie's face drop, 'but Paul's just a very good friend.'

'But he kissed you and you said you loved him . . . I

heard you . . . outside the office when he brought you back from lunch.'

Stevie thought long and hard. 'No, I didn't! That's where you're wrong, you see – I said "she loves you". I don't love Paul Hadley – which is just as well really as he's in love with Jenny . . . my boss.'

For what seemed like an eternity Stevie studied Charlie's solemn face while the significance of what she'd just told him clicked into place like a computer program.

'Then why did you say you didn't want to see me any more?' he begged, reaching for her hand. 'I thought we were getting along great together.'

'We were . . . but I thought . . .'

'You thought what, Stevie?'

'I thought it wasn't fair on you and your friends being lumbered with an invalid.'

'Blethers!' Charlie protested. 'If you're an invalid then I must be a haggis!'

A faint flicker of a smile curled at the corners of Stevie's mouth. She began to remonstrate with him but Charlie held up a hand.

'Why, Cressida Stephens, you've got far more energy and personality than hundreds of people I know!'

Releasing her hand from his grasp, Stevie ran her fingers over the white-walled tyres of her chair. 'It's kind of you to say so, Charlie, but aren't you forgetting my legs?' she whispered sadly.

'No, dammit, I'm not, 'cos I'll be your legs, Stevie. Besides,' he quipped, 'what with your legs, my hair, eyes and teeth, I think between us we'll make a bonnie couple!'

349

Charlie grinned a toothy smile and, stooping forward, kissed Stevie full on the mouth.

'You know something?' she giggled, gazing into his eyes. 'I don't think you should be comparing yourself to a haggis. According to all those wee furry creatures in tourist shop windows they have much more hair than you!'

CHAPTER 40

Tandy ushered a nervous Paul into the study with a gracious smile.

'Morag will be with you in a moment,' she said kindly. 'I'll just go and make some coffee.'

It was a large room, Paul noted, with dark oak panels that smelt strongly of beeswax. Books lined the walls and dark green drapes hung heavily at the casement windows. Alone in the room, he walked to the fireplace and, lost in thought, studied the large painting hanging above the solid oak mantelpiece.

Although it was set in Princes Street at the turn of the century, Paul's thoughts nevertheless turned to Jenny and the day they met to buy the girls dresses. The day the slightly inebriated shop assistant had talked about underwear. Paul felt a stirring in his body; doubtless that was the underwear Jenny was wearing the night of the dance. The night he'd gone to her hotel r . . .

'You are admiring Mr Geoffrey's picture, I see,' said Morag quietly entering the room. 'He's recreated the atmosphere perfectly, hasn't he, which I think is extremely clever for a contemporary painter? He used to live locally, you know, but went south of the border a few years ago. Such a shame, I always say. I only hope wherever he is he's appreciated.'

'It reminds me very much of Atkinson Grimshaw,' remarked Paul, stepping back to study the carriages and dimly lit streets.

Morag's face brightened, pleased that Paul should appreciate one of her pictures. 'So you're a Grimshaw fan too, are you, Mr Hadley? How nice.'

Morag sat down behind the desk that had once belonged to her husband and his father before him. In her hand she held a bulky brown envelope. Brown envelopes, Paul thought warily. He'd taken a distinct dislike to thick brown envelopes; they reminded him of the divorce papers. The divorce papers that in the end he'd never had to use.

Recalling they were still in his desk drawer, Paul resolved to destroy to them on his return to Edinburgh. After all, what purpose did they serve? They were now only a grim reminder of Gina's irrational behaviour, and since her tragic death, surely it was best to try and forget . . .

Paul's gaze fell on Morag dwarfed behind the uncluttered desk. Apart from the thick brown envelope there was just a row of pens nestling in a shiny brass inkstand, a leather bound sheet of virgin blotting paper and two photographs in antique silver frames. Morag motioned Paul to a chair.

'Mr Hadley, I must thank you for answering my summons at such short notice.'

So this was a summons, he thought. His earlier assumptions had been correct, and whatever crime he'd committed, he was hoping Morag Sinclair would be a lenient prosecutor and judge. Paul sat in silence. Was he expected to respond to Morag's statement or wait for her to continue?

'I'm afraid I haven't spoken to you since the death of your wife, Mr Hadley. It must have been a very painful time for you and your children. I understand from Mary the girls are well; they had tea with Fiona last week?'

'Yes, quite well, thank you, Mrs Sinclair. Mary has been very kind. Fiona's company has helped the girls immeasurably.'

'Good, I'm pleased to hear it. It's nice that the family are able to do something in return.'

'Return?'

'Yes, I don't think I've ever really had the chance to thank you properly for the new lease of life you injected into Sinclair's. We owe you a great deal, you know.'

Overcome with embarrassment, Paul was sure this wasn't the reason he'd been brought to Conasg.

'I have to confess I was slightly dubious when Jennifer showed me your first draft for the House of St Claire, but her positive faith in you . . .' Morag glanced at one of the photographs on the desk '. . . allayed any earlier doubts I might have had.'

Morag wanted Paul to follow her gaze to the photo. Unconsciously he responded. It was Andrew and Mary's wedding photograph with Jenny as brides-maid, radiant and smiling in ivory silk. Paul thought of the contrast between Jenny and Gina. There was a pregnant pause.

'Have you seen much of Jennifer lately, Mr Hadley?'

Paul shook his head. 'Unfortunately no, not since my

wife's . . .' He didn't really want to mention Gina, especially as he was convinced Morag must have known of Andrew's dalliance with her. He continued quickly, '. . . Jenny helped out enormously with Celestina and Emily, you know, and the girls adore her.'

'So I understand,' replied Morag.

What was she waiting for him to say? Paul thought nervously. This sparrow of a woman, dwarfed behind the vast oak desk. What was it Andrew had said about her? 'She won't eat you!'

'Jenny and I were due to have lunch together but I understand she's had a stomach upset.' He refrained from adding Stevie's comment about the Burns Night haggis lying in the field for too long! Stevie's Sassenach comments would doubtless not meet with Morag Sinclair's approval.

Morag got up from her chair and walked round the desk. She wanted to see Paul's face more clearly. With the study facing north and its dark oak panelling, it wasn't that easy.

'A stomach upset? Mmm, I suppose you could call it that,' said Morag, drawing back the heavy curtain to let in some light from the steely grey skyline. 'I've sent Jennifer away for a rest, you know, Mr Hadley . . .' Morag's tone was abrupt as she turned to face him '. . . and I want you to go to Italy and accompany her home!'

All manner of thoughts flashed through Paul's head, including the mere mention of Italy. The last time he'd gone to Italy was for Gina's funeral.

'Is Jenny ill?' he enquired anxiously. If Jenny had been able to fly out to Italy on her own, why couldn't she come back on her own? What on earth could have happened?

Morag, sensing concern in Paul's voice, was relieved to find he hadn't balked at her suggestion. 'No, Jennifer's not ill,' she replied. 'Let's just say she needs some care and support from someone she trusts. So will you go to Venice for me?'

In total bewilderment Paul studied Morag's questioning gaze. Why Venice, when he'd been led to believe Jenny was in Scotland? Stevie hadn't said . . . 'Venice,' Paul whispered softly to himself. Well, as far as he was concerned Venice wasn't Italy – at least not Gina's Italy.

'If it's not too impertinent a question, Mrs Sinclair, why me and why Venice?'

Morag opened her mouth to speak but was interrupted by the gentle knocking on the door. Flora Tandy entered with a tray of coffee and chocolate digestive biscuits. Morag looked at her companion with a wry smile. Flora was taking liberties. Chocolate biscuits was it now, instead of the usual arrowroot?

'Now, where were we?' enquired Morag, pouring the coffee.

'Venice?' said Paul, still waiting for explanation.

'Ah, yes, I have your tickets here,' and she picked up the envelope.

Declining cream, Paul stirred his coffee. He decided he needed his strong, sweet and black. Morag hadn't finished with him yet and he watched her brush biscuit crumbs from her tweed skirt in preparation for her next salvo.

'Jennifer has gone to Venice to lay a ghost – well, three, to be precise.'

Paul looked up and waited for an explanation.

'The first is that of her ex-fiancé, and the second that of your wife.'

'My wife! You mean Gina? But what's that got to do with Jenny? Since Gina died I've hardly seen Jenny.'

'Precisely,' acknowledged Morag. 'And that's why, you see . . .'

Paul didn't, but he saw no reason to interrupt Morag. He gulped at his coffee and waited for her to enlighten him.

'You might think me a selfish old woman, Mr Hadley but I want Sinclair's to have a future as much as I want Jennifer to have one. And as far as my daughter is concerned that will only be possible once she's laid her ghosts and shed her tears.'

'Shed her tears – but I don't understand what you mean.'

'Perhaps not – and you can tell me to mind my own business if you like, but I think you not only understand my daughter but love her as well. Am I right?'

Morag, suddenly frail and vulnerable, waited for his reply.

'Yes, I do, very much, and I've been wanting to tell her so for weeks but it wasn't easy after Gina died . . . and then Jenny kept avoiding me.'

'I know,' Morag said softly.

'You do . . . then will you please tell me why?'

'You have absolutely no idea, then?' Morag enquired. She had now reached the moment she was dreading. She only hoped she and Tandy had been correct in their assumption. Clasping her hands together until her knuckles grew white, Morag offered up a silent prayer.

'If you recall, I mentioned three ghosts, Mr Hadley, but named only two.'

Paul nodded for her to go on and watched Morag swallow hard.

'Sadly, the third ghost had no name . . . you see, it was the baby Jennifer was expecting . . . your baby, I think, Mr Hadley?'

Paul sat in stunned silence and ran his fingers through his hair. After a while he turned his anguished face towards Jenny's photograph.

'But I didn't know Jenny was pregnant! Oh, Jenny! Why didn't you tell me?'

'You're not denying it then?' Morag asked quietly.

Paul thought back to the fateful night of the dance. Of course he couldn't deny it. They'd made love, hadn't they? Only, in the true sense of the word, could you really describe it as such? The situation that night in the hotel room had hardly been conducive to conceiving a child.

Paul shook his head sadly, remembering Gina's outrageous behaviour, followed by that idiot Alistair Jennings' insensitive remarks and Jenny in her room so distraught and suffering the effect of too much champagne . . . and begging him to stay with her.

Suddenly Paul gave out a deep sigh. Like a veil being lifted from his eyes, everything fell into place now. All the cancelled lunch dates and talk of tummy upsets . . . Jenny's 'tummy upset' was a baby – his baby!

'You said *was* expecting? What happened – you don't mean to say she had an abor . . .'

'No!' broke in Morag. 'Definitely not!'

'Thank God! I just couldn't bear it if she had.'

'Jennifer had a miscarriage the same weekend as my heart attack.'

'But why could she tell you and not me!'

'She didn't tell me, in fact apart from the doctor she didn't tell anyone, not even Stevie. It was Tandy who first mentioned it and I just put two and two together.'

Resting his head in his hands, Paul remembered Tandy bringing in the tray of coffee. If Morag Sinclair was to be his judge, then would Flora Tandy have been his executioner? He thought not; after all, she'd brought chocolate biscuits. Condemned men didn't warrant chocolate biscuits, did they?

'As for Jennifer's not telling you, don't be too upset. Try to put yourself in her situation. So soon after your wife's death, it wouldn't have been easy for either of you.'

'Perhaps,' Paul replied. 'But I should have been with Jenny! She shouldn't have had to shoulder this burden all on her own!'

'I know,' Morag said kindly. 'But she doesn't have to now, does she, if you go to Venice to bring her home?'

'Mrs Sinclair, I would do that willingly – it's just my . . .'

'Your children? Yes, I know – Celestina and Emily. Don't worry, it's all arranged. Stevie has helped me to sort it all out.'

'Stevie?'

'Well, let's say Stevie has arranged it with Helen Craig – is that her name? And then of course Mary's offered to have them too.'

At any other time Paul would have been furious with people organizing his life without prior warning. Turning, he managed a weak smile in Morag's direction. 'Well, it looks as if you've thought of everything.'

'Let's just put it down to Sinclair efficiency, shall we, Mr Hadley?'

'I do wish you'd call me Paul.'

'Then you must call me Morag,' she urged, handing him the brown envelope containing his airline tickets and hotel booking. 'Stevie, as I've already mentioned, has made all the necessary preparations for Celestina and Emily, but I left the travel arrangements to Andrew. He likes doing things in style. He assures me the hotel is ideal for – shall we say a reunion? It's off the Riva degli Schiavoni – do you know it?'

'I'm afraid I don't know Venice at all. Gina's family came from Abruzzi. But at least I speak the language a bit.'

'Well, then, I'll wish you good luck, Paul.' When Morag held out her hand, he noticed a distinct twinkle in her eyes.

CHAPTER 41

As the plane circled over the lagoon Jenny began to have misgivings. Perhaps this wasn't such a good idea after all. She should never have let them persuade her into coming away. It wasn't so much leaving Mother so soon after her heart attack, but more a case of being here in Venice alone.

Dr McAllister had assured her Morag was perfectly well enough to be left; there was Flora Tandy after all. Even Hamish had taken to coming into the house more and more. Fussing and clucking like an old mother hen, he'd even offered to help with the cooking and housework, annoying Tandy no end, until eventually Jenny had been glad to escape and leave them all to it.

With the plane touching down on the runway she found herself being swept off the plane with the mêlée of post-carnival tourists and elegantly tailored business-men.

'Please,' she wanted to say to the stewardess, 'can't I just stay on board and fly back with you?'

'The stewardess, flashing a brilliant smile, exposing exquisite dentistry in an immaculately made-up face, said, 'Enjoy your trip, madam,' and Jenny found herself on Venetian soil.

In the Arrivals hall a young woman stood holding a placard bearing the name 'Miss Gennifur Sinclair.' Jenny stopped. Mother had told her Andrew had arranged a water taxi. Such extravagance, she'd thought at the time, remembering how she and Moira had arrived by train and stepped straight out of the station on to a water bus with homeward-bound Venetians.

'Signorina Sinclair, I am Francesca Vitti – you follow me pliz. My brother, 'e wait with taxi.' The young woman picked up Jenny's suitcase and was gone. With no time to deliberate, Jenny had little choice but to follow. A blast of diesel fumes from the row of water taxis met her nostrils as she scanned the bustle of navy-blue-raincoated couriers for the one familiar face. Francesca turned and waved. 'Signorina Sinclair, come, Giovanni 'e will take you.'

Giovanni grinned and reached forward. With one hand grabbing hold of Jenny's arm he swept both herself and her suitcase on board and into her seat. Switching the taxi first into reverse, he manoeuvred his way from the busy quayside then settled into a steady forward direction across the lagoon and into the maze of canals leading to the hotel.

Breathing in deeply, Jenny watched as the refreshing breeze caught at Giovanni's curls. He looked little more than a boy but presumably was old enough to hold a taxi licence. In Britain, she thought, you associated getting older with young policeman. Perhaps here in Venice Venetians felt the same about taxi drivers.

Arriving at the hotel, Francesca appeared agitated and, jumping on to the jetty, ran to a short balding man with a large moustache. There she snatched a violin case from his grasp and scurried away.

'Signorina Sinclair, welcome to our 'otel. You must excuse Francesca, she play in orchestra and eez late for rehearsal. This way if you pliz. *Giovanni, bagaglio!*'

Giovanni duly obliged and Jenny found herself ushered from a lift through pale marble corridors and windows hung with turquoise silk. Her suitcase was placed outside a polished mahogany door.

Signor Vitti stopped purposefully, drew a large key from his pocket and slid it into the lock. As the door swung back, Jenny stood open-mouthed and silent.

Registering the look of shock on her face, Signor Vitti's anxious voice broke the silence. 'But you do not like?'

Jenny turned to him in disbelief. 'Yes, I like . . . I like it very much, but I'm sorry, there must be a mistake – this room can't be for me. It's far too big. I'm on my own, you see.'

'No mistake, *signorina*,' he replied, breathing a sigh of relief. 'Your brother Andrew say 'e want the best room for you, you are very special sister – yes? This room eez very special. It once belong to the *marchesa* and now while you are 'ere it belong to you. Now would you like tea?'

Jenny smiled. '*Si*, Signor Vitti, tea would be lovely.

When he'd gone, Jenny sat on the bed and laughed for the first time in weeks. Here in this hotel – that had once been a palace, no less – she was sitting in the *marchesa*'s bedroom waiting not for her lover, fine champagne or sweetmeats, but a tray of tea!

Roused from a deep slumber by the sound of fog-horns echoing across the lagoon, Jenny climbed from the bed and walked barefoot to the window, aware of cool marble beneath her feet. How strange it felt after the deep pile of Sinclair's and the berbers and rugs of her cottage.

The windows, she discovered, were still shuttered from her arrival. She had declined Signor Vitti's offer to open them, saying she would first prefer to have some tea and then rest before dinner.

'*Si*, that eez good, Signorina Sinclair – *riposarsi*. Eet eez better after the travelling, give you appetite for dinner. Andrew 'e say you must eat, and my wife Carla make the best pasta in Venice.'

Pasta, Jenny said to herself. I can't eat pasta – I must find Kenny's.

Taking her raincoat from the panelled sliding ward-robes of polished mahogany, gilt and glass, Jenny avoided using the lift and slipped quietly down the stairs to the side entrance where Giovanni had moored the taxi only hours earlier. Water lapped effortlessly at the brightly painted mooring posts and in the back-ground she heard Signor Vitti extolling the virtues of his wife's pasta to some unseen guests.

'Kenny's' – could she remember where it was? Doubtless Signor Vitti would have thrown up his hands in horror to hear her ask directions to the burger bar! Burgers in Venice, when there was all the glorious seafood and pasta. It would be too difficult and too complicated to explain why; she would just have to find her own way there.

Through the tight maze of alleyways and narrow bridges she criss-crossed her way behind the hotel away from St Mark's Square towards the Rialto. Delicious smells wafted forth from restaurants and behind closed shutters came the sound of laughter, excited chatter and, even in this magical city, the noise of television.

Standing alone on a corner where canals and alleyways led in every direction Jenny felt suddenly lost and alone. The arrow she'd last seen certainly showed the Rialto as being this way. But which way that was the problem? In the distance she heard the sound of the foghorn once more and waited as a faint echo of footsteps drew ever nearer.

'Jennifer Sinclair,' an inner voice whispered. 'This wasn't such a good idea after all, was it? And if that sea mist sweeps across the lagoon to St Mark's you really will be lost.'

Weary and cold, Jenny tightened the belt of her raincoat. On her previous visit with Moira they'd got hopelessly lost almost every day. Then it had been fun as they'd giggled their way across bridges and down dark alleyways. Tonight, however, it didn't feel quite the same.

Turning round aimlessly, she wondered whether she should press onwards or attempt to find her way back to the hotel. Suddenly, when she was at the point of panic, shrill girlish laughter met her ears and three teenage girls dressed in jeans, ankle boots and warm jackets met her head on. In their hands they carried Kenny's burgers!

'*Scusi, signorina,*' called the tallest girl, moving to let

Jenny pass, her large brown eyes smiling apology.

Pointing to the containers they were holding, Jenny replied in turn, '*Scusi*, Kenny's *per favore?*'

'*Dritto, sempre dritto*,' said the young girl, indicating behind her before running off to catch up with her friends.

Jenny breathed a sigh of relief, walked to the end of the narrow street and joined the straggling queue.

Clutching the warm box, she then made her way to the Rialto bridge and sat down to watch a solitary gondolier help two elderly tourists on to the landing stage. She wasn't hungry, least of all for a cheeseburger, but she forced herself to take one bite of the meat and cheese.

'Moira,' she whispered, gazing at the stonework in front of her. 'Do you remember all those years before Helmut, Cameron, Paul and . . . my baby?' Tears filled her eyes as she placed the remains of the burger back into its polystyrene container, recalling as she did so how on their last night in Venice they'd sat on the Rialto bridge eating like this. It was all they could afford, having spent almost all their money on ridiculously expensive fashion shoes.

Leaving one of her 'ghosts' on the Rialto, Jenny walked back along the Grand Canal to the Mercerie and St Mark's, politely brushing aside the lone gondolier still searching for custom. At opposite ends of the square two street traders stood selling umbrellas. With their careworn faces and feet lost in a swirl of mist drifting across the vast empty space, they made a sombre and gloomy contrast against the brightly lit windows of Venetian glass, jewellery and linen.

The exquisite linen, with its delicate hand-drawn work and self-embroidery, directed Jenny's thoughts to the House of St Claire, yet not a single yellow gorse graced these windows.

'Oh, Paul,' she cried as tears pricked her eyelids. 'If only things had been different, if only I'd been able to tell you about the baby.'

Thoughts of Paul turned to thoughts of Celestina and Emily as she moved along the arcade and saw a shop full of brightly decorated glass animals. Creatures of every size and description filled the windows and *millefiore* pendants and brooches hung suspended in every available space. With Moira there'd been no money left for presents but this time there would be no excuse. There would be glass for Mary, *millefiore* for Jean and Fiona and quite possibly a family of glass rabbits for Celestina and Emily.

A lump rose in her throat. Cele and Emily – how were they, she wondered, and had they forgiven her for cancelling the proposed cinema trip? Paul had said they'd been terribly disappointed; she'd even detected the slightest hint of exasperation in his voice.

She would try to make it up to them on their return – if they would let her – and now she was no longer pregnant it might even be easier. But, she thought, choking back more tears, she also knew Paul had been seen with Marina Hendry. Despite telling Stevie otherwise, she had not rung Paul to cancel their lunch appointment. Perhaps if she felt brave enough in the morning she might even ring Paul and Stevie to apologize.

CHAPTER 42

In the Edinburgh house there was great excitement. Fiona, freshly bathed and her hair newly plaited in thick coils, jumped up and down at the bedroom window.

'I can see the car, Hamish is driving it and Grannie is there too! You see, I told you she would come, she promised.'

She ran to where Celestina and Emily stood in white broderie anglaise petticoats, waiting to be dressed by Jean and Mary.

'Fiona! Will you stop bouncing about like that? Your ribbons have already come undone once. Be a good girl now and find Cele and Emily's shoes and tights while I go and welcome Grannie and Miss Tandy.'

In the hallway Andrew was helping his mother with her coat. Apart from looking a trifle thinner, Morag's eyes sparkled with excitement.

'Do stop worrying, Andrew! Alex McAllister says there's a good few years left in me yet and I've really been looking forward to this outing.'

'Yes, but do you not think you'll find it all too tiring, Mother, after the journey and . . .?'

'For goodness' sake, Andrew! Stop fussing and take

your mother and Miss Tandy into the sitting room. She *will* be tired if you leave her standing in the hall like that.' Mary bent and kissed her mother-in-law, taking in the delicate smell of lily-of-the-valley. Morag's hair, she noticed, was newly permed; she was also wearing a new tweed suit.

'Are the girls ready?' Morag enquired, aware of much giggling coming from the upstairs landing.

'Almost,' replied Jean, 'but they're also terribly excited. Fiona's been standing at the window since lunchtime and all three girls hardly slept a wink last night. I'd better warn you, though, Cele and Emily can, believe it or not, be a little bit quiet and withdrawn at times.'

Mary cast a cursory look towards the door. 'They haven't quite got over . . . well, you know.'

Morag nodded in understanding and allowed Flora to lay a rug across her knees.

'What of Mr Had . . . I mean Paul?' she asked. 'Have you heard from him yet?'

'Yes, he telephoned Andrew to say he'd arrived safely. His flight was delayed . . . surprisingly by fog in Venice and not here for once.'

'Well, that makes a change, I suppose. Right, all we have to do now is gather our trio of small girls together and go and collect Miss Stephens.'

Fiona led Cele and Emily downstairs where they stood nervously at the sitting room door.

'Hello, Grannie,' said Fiona, skipping forward. Seeing Morag's knees swathed in a rug she stopped short, a worried look upon her face.

'We are still going, aren't we? You're not poorly again, are you?'

'Yes, we're still going, Fiona. When your Grannie makes a promise she keeps it! Although I think your Daddy thinks I'm totally incapable of taking three wee girls out to tea. He forgets he was young and once,' she grinned wickedly, 'he and your Auntie Jennifer were so naughty!'

Fiona's eyes opened wide at the thought; she would ask Grannie all about it during tea. But first she must remind her of something. She leant forward and whispered in Morag's ear, while everyone looked on.

'No, it's all right, Fiona,' Morag whispered in reply. 'You don't have to worry, dear, I haven't forgotten. Now Celestina and Emily, are you going to come and introduce yourselves? I don't want to get you mixed up, do I?'

Jean and Mary watched from the doorway as Hamish helped Morag into the front passenger seat of the Bentley before putting the three girls in the back. Andrew meanwhile assisted Miss Tandy into the Jaguar and checked the boot, making sure there would be space for Stevie's wheelchair.

'I'd love to be tucked in a corner to see them all arrive,' said Mary, turning to her elder daughter. 'Can you just imagine? I expect your father is glad he's only acting as chauffeur and hasn't got to stay with them for the entire afternoon!'

Jean smiled warmly. 'I think it's lovely, all this plotting and planning on Gran's behalf. Mother,' she said wistfully, 'I do hope it all turns out right for Auntie Jen. Do you think it will?'

'I'm sure it will, Jean,' said Mary, closing the front door. 'If not, your Grandmother is going to want to know why!'

'It's all so romantic,' sighed Jean.

'Don't worry, dear, there'll be plenty left in the world for you, just you wait and see.' Mary put a comforting arm around Jean's shoulders. 'Now how about us having a nice cup of tea? With Iain at the rugby match we can have some Earl Grey without his rude comments about smoky dishwater. I've made us some smoked salmon sandwiches and éclairs, so if you'll just slice the lemon and find the House of St Claire napkins, we can pretend we're at the Ritz!'

A bemused silence fell as the party of six – comprising an elderly lady leading three small girls, followed by her equally elderly companion pushing a young woman in a wheelchair – were led to their table by the head waiter.

Soft murmurings of approval emitted from the on-lookers as the three girls, dressed in velvet with white lace tights and black patent shoes, took their places at the table. Morag acknowledged her audience with a gracious smile; she was already beginning to enjoy this.

'Are you quite comfortable there, Miss Stephens?' Flora Tandy manoeuvred Stevie's chair nearer the table. 'Will you be needing a rug?'

Stevie smiled kindly in her direction and shook her head.

'Of course she doesn't, Flora,' said Morag sharply, 'and don't you dare go asking me if she takes sugar or you won't have any cream cakes!'

Morag winked at Stevie and Fiona giggled gleefully. As if on cue Cele and Emily giggled too. They were beginning to like Fiona's grannie. Perhaps she wasn't quite so frightening after all, and hadn't Fiona said they could share her? With Grannie Hadley dead and Grannie 'Tino such a long way away, it would be nice to have a grannie again.

'Young man!' Morag called to the waiter. 'We will have our tea now, if you please. That will be five cream teas – no, make that six,' she said, looking at Flora with a mischievous glint in her eye.

The waiter walked away only to be summoned back immediately. Morag's clear, clipped voice echoed across the packed tea-room as all eyes turned in her direction. What was it Fiona had whispered to her before they'd left? 'Oh, yes! And remember to make that special jam. We want jam without bits, please!'

CHAPTER 43

Francesca knocked gently at the bedroom door and entered with the tray. Jenny stirred sleepily and watched the slim figure draw back heavy brocade drapes, fixing them with ornate silken tassels.

'Shall I open the shutters, *signorina*? It eez cloudy at the moment but will be a beautiful day, I think.'

Jenny nodded and surveyed the tray of fresh rolls, fruit juice and tea. Apart from the meal on the plane, the one mouthful of cheeseburger and the odd piece of fruit, she'd eaten practically nothing at all for the past few days. Could she even stomach breakfast? Two nights ago she had shed tears for Cameron; today she must lay another ghost to rest. Wasn't that what her mother had advised?

'Signorina Sinclair, I excuse myself. The day you arrive, I leave you quickly with Giovanni. I 'ave orchestra practice with my violin. If I can 'elp you today . . . take you sightseeing?'

'Thank you, Francesca, it's very kind of you, but I already know where I am going today. I intend to visit the Frari's Basilica and La Fosca.'

Francesca might think it an odd choice, the sharp

372

contrast between the ornate Frari and the small church on the island of Torcello, but Jenny had her reasons.

'My father 'e say you must eat. We do not see you at dinner since you arrive and my mother eez very worried.'

'Tell your parents not to worry, Francesca – tonight I will eat, I promise.' As the girl left the room Jenny's eyes took in the opulence of the *marchesa*'s bedroom. Trust Andrew! All this luxury but what a waste.

Dreamily she ran her hands along the white linen sheets and reaching upwards felt her fingers slide over the carved wooden posts of the bed.

'What pure unadulterated luxury,' she sighed studying the pleated silk canopy above her head. 'I doubt very much if the *marchesa* got much sleep in this bed!'

Feeling her cheeks redden at such thoughts, Jenny turned on her side and clutched at her pillow, trying desperately to remember what exactly had happened on the night of the Sinclair dance. 'Or should that be morning?' she whispered into lace-edged linen. 'Oh, Paul. If only you were here now, if only things could have been different. This bed isn't made for one . . . it's made for making love . . . made for making . . . babies.'

With a stifled sob, Jenny leapt from the bed. Goodness, what had she been saying? No doubt the lack of food was beginning to play tricks in her head. She looked at the breakfast tray. First she would have a shower, then she must force herself to eat some breakfast. However, she must also leave soon if she was to reach Torcello before the tourists arrived.

* * *

373

Hopelessly lost, Paul was beginning to regret not taking a water taxi direct to the hotel. He'd been so sure that with his knowledge of Italian he could find his way easily enough, but Venice, he discovered to his dismay, was not Abruzzi. Convinced Jenny would have already left the hotel, he realized it could mean waiting an entire day before catching up with her.

'Perhaps I should have telephoned,' he cried in anguish, turning into another blind alleyway, but at the time Andrew had assured him everything would be all right. Late last night, leaving for the airport, it had seemed such a wonderful idea. Today in this dreary grey light he wasn't so sure.

'Oh, Jenny,' he sighed, 'where are you? Will I ever find you?'

Hearing his desperate plea, a woman scrubbing white stone steps looked up with questioning eyes. '*Signore?*'

Running in her direction, Paul showed her the name of the hotel.

'*Si*,' she cried, grinning a toothless grin, and pointed. '*Si – dritto attraverso la piazza e poi a destra.*'

He repeated the instructions and she nodded enthusiastically, leaving Paul to wonder if dentists were in short supply on Venice. Then he ran, in fact he ran as he'd never run before, straight on and to the right. He'd been near the hotel all along but had been walking round in circles.

The hotel was almost empty, with a lone waiter clearing the remains of the breakfast buffet bar and laying tables for lunch.

'*La Signorina Sinclair?*' Paul enquired. The surly young man shrugged his shoulders and pointed in the direction of the enclosed courtyard. Did that mean Jenny was there? Paul stopped dejectedly; there was no sign of Jenny but a young woman was playing part of Schubert's string quintet in C major. Laying down her violin, Francesca looked up. '*Signore?*'

'*Scusi, la Signorina Sinclair, per favore.*'

'Ah, *si*, she 'as gone.'

'Gone? Gone where – *dovè*? You mean left the hotel for good?' Paul's heart sank. Could Jenny have left so soon and decided not to stay in Venice after all?

'No, *signore*, she 'as gone to sightseeing. Signorina Sinclair tell me she go to the Frari and Torcello. Perhaps eez best you try Torcello first. But she must be very 'ungry, *signore*, she eat nothing for days, I think she only cry.'

Francesca remembered collecting Jenny's breakfast tray. The rolls and tea untouched, the glass of juice half full and *la signorina* with red eyes. Red eyes, she'd said to her mother . . . from so much crying.

'Torcello. *Grazie.*'

'*Prego, signore*,' announced Francesca, picking up her violin, and watched Paul disappear almost as suddenly as he'd arrived.

Approaching Torcello on the water bus, Jenny cast her mind back to the time she and Moira had fallen in love with the island's isolated position in the middle of the lagoon. Earlier, having marvelled at the magnificence of Titian's *Assumption* in the Frari, they'd then found themselves in the octagonal church of Santa Fosca. Standing together in silence, admiring its melancholy beauty, both young women had been lost for words.

There were only two other tourists leaving the bus and she breathed a sigh of relief seeing them head in the direction of Sainte Marie de Genetrix. Presumably those remaining would be travelling on to Murano and Burano for their glass and lace.

Glass and lace were the last things on Jenny's mind as she made her way to the church and, tying a black silk scarf around her head, slipped in quietly through the wooden door. Years ago she'd read that someone had once described Santa Fosca as looking more like an Alpine refuge then a church. How very appropriate, she thought.

Also appropriate were the two mosaics, one representing the Last Judgement and the other the Madonna. The first reminded her of the sad, tragic Gina and how only months ago Gina – judged by the Sinclairs – had been the victim of all their hatred and anger.

Hatred and anger, Jenny thought to herself – how dreadful even to think of such emotions in this deeply hallowed place. No, she must no longer feel hatred towards Gina . . . Gina had been ill. Weeping silent tears, Jenny turned her face to the Madonna's own tearstained cheeks and, drawing solace and comfort from the gentle hands raised in blessing, lit a candle and prayed. It was now, she decided, that she must say goodbye to the child who had been so very nearly hers.

A scraping of chairs told her she was no longer alone. It was the couple from the bus. The woman talked noisily, pointing upwards to the cupola. Through misted eyes Jenny watched her candle slowly burn away and left the building with heavy heart.

Once outside in the cool freshness of morning she

became suddenly dizzy and overcome with hunger. Until now she hadn't wanted any food and with her head in such a whirl, her stomach knotted and churning at so many painful memories, food had been the last thing on her mind.

Thinking back to the morning's breakfast tray, Jenny thought longingly of the untouched home-baked rolls and golden cubes of butter. 'Gold,' she murmured softly, 'just like the burnished gold squares of mosaic decorating La Fosca.' Faint with hunger, she reproached herself for not having the sense to bring the rolls with her.

You must eat! an inner voice urged. I know, she whispered in reply.

Stepping on to the footpath from the grass, still damp with morning dew, she announced to a startled local, 'I'll go to the restaurant on the corner, but first . . . first I must go to the bridge . . .'

The bridge, still fresh in her memory from her visit with Moira all those years ago, was just as she remembered. Completely devoid of parapets, it spanned the narrow expanse of water with an air of simplistic solitude. It was the perfect setting for a last farewell.

From the shadows, Paul watched in horror as Jenny approached the bridge. At least he thought it was Jenny, but the slim, pale figure with head and shoulders draped in a black headscarf couldn't be Jenny, could it? The eyes looked so haunted and the face so . . . so full of sadness and despair.

A mixture of desolation and anger surged through Paul's veins. Had he done this to Jenny, was he the cause of all her pain? Frozen to the spot, he relived the night of the dance and saw Gina's taunting face, the obsequious fawning of Alistair and Jenny . . . his own beautiful Jenny, reaching out to touch him.

Overcome with guilt, Paul banged his fist angrily against a stone wall and, aroused from his melancholic stupor, looked up just as Jenny reached the centre of the bridge.

'My God!' he whispered in horror. 'The bridge has no parapets, she's in a complete daze and walking too close to the edge . . . there's nothing to save her!'

His voice was soft and his grasp firm as he reached out to stop her from falling. 'Jenny . . . My dear sweet Jenny.'

'Paul? Paul! But I don't understand what are you doing here . . .?'

'At the moment,' he said nervously, 'trying to prevent us both from falling in the water!'

'What!' Jenny looked down to where their feet were edging dangerously close to the edge of the bridge. 'But how did I get here? I don't remember coming this far; I was in the church and the Madonna was crying and . . .'

Fresh tears fell from Jenny's eyes as Paul held her close. Then, loosening her headscarf and stroking her hair, he murmured softly, 'I'm so sorry . . . so sorry about the baby. Why didn't you tell me? I've only just found out.'

'Who told you?' she whispered, unable to meet his gaze.

'Your mother, in fact it was her idea that I come and take you home; she made Andrew see to all the arrangements. I . . . we were all so very worried about you, you know.'

'We?'

'Yes, me, Morag, Miss Tandy, Mary and . . .'

Jenny broke away from his embrace. 'You mean they all know about the baby . . . they know everything?'

'No, don't worry.' Paul said reassuringly. 'They can't know everything, can they?' He lifted her face to look into her soulful eyes. 'Jenny, I love you, you do see that, don't you? But the night of the dance . . . it wasn't exactly the ideal way to conceive a child, was it?'

Her voice was almost inaudible as she looked down into the blue-grey water flowing away under the bridge. 'I wanted that baby – our baby – so much. I had nothing, you see. Cameron said . . .'

At the mention of Cameron's name, Paul felt her tremble in his grasp and, brushing away a stray tear, he urged her to continue. She swallowed hard and forced herself to go on. 'Mary and Andrew have their children, Moira has hers, you have Cele and Emily . . . even Mother has Miss Tandy!' she said, smiling weakly.

Paul brushed his lips gently against her cheek. 'Jenny, you have me – that's if you want me . . .?'

'Oh, yes . . . I want you, Paul. I want you so much.'

'Thank heavens for that,' he sighed. 'Then you have Fiona and the girls, we all love you . . . surely you must realize that, and as for Stevie, well, she's been frantic with worry.'

'Stevie! Is she in on this conspiracy too?'

'I'm afraid so,' he said, smiling, and bent down to where a bouquet of pink rosebuds lay at his feet. 'Stevie told me I should take a leaf out of Andrew's book and buy you some flowers. Gracious, she gave me a real ticking off for forgetting Valentine's Day!'

Jenny took the flowers and, carefully removing a single bloom, tossed it lovingly into the water. 'For the baby,' she whispered huskily.

Paul thought for a moment then slowly removed a stem for himself.

'For Gina,' he murmured.

There was no need to explain. Jenny knew that without Gina she and Paul would never have met. Alone and in silence they watched the two rosebuds drift slowly away while high in the sky above them, clouds like wispy curtains parted to reveal the first sunshine of the day.

'Now it's something to eat for you, I think,' said Paul, taking her arm and leading her towards the restaurant. 'And after that . . .'

'After that?' Jenny enquired.

'I thought perhaps we could go on to Burano or Murano to buy Stevie a wedding present.'

'What? But Stevie's not even engaged!'

'There I have to correct you, Miss Sinclair,' Paul teased.

'You mean Stevie and Charlie . . . but when? Are you sure?'

'Let's just say a little bird told me before I left for the airport, although on reflection I hardly think describing your brother as a little bird . . . But yes, it would appear a certain modern Charles Stuart has found his own Henrietta Maria.'

'But that's wonderful!' Jenny cried. 'I can't wait to congratulate them both. I wonder if there's a flight back to Edinburgh this evening?'

Paul looked up in mock alarm. 'Not so fast, Jennifer

Sinclair, I've been given strict instructions to keep you here for a few days longer yet. Andrew mentioned something about a . . . certain *marchesa*'s bedroom.'

A flush of colour dusted Jenny's cheeks as Paul reached across the table for her hand.

'*Luna di miele*?' enquired the waiter with a smile as he poured the coffee.

No, thought Paul to himself, no honeymoon on this trip . . . but one day soon, perhaps?

CHAPTER 44

With memories of Paul's Edinburgh house and Jenny's pantiled cottage behind them, Jenny stood in the doorway of Paul's study. It had been the right decision to move to the new house after all. Here, not only had they begun a new life together, but it also meant Paul had a proper place to work.

Jenny watched him now, taking comfort from his very being as he sketched away in earnest. Gone was the strained and anxious-looking Paul she'd first met, and in his place was a man at peace with himself. Feeling a surge of contentment sweep through her body, Jenny watched the dappled late afternoon sunshine dance on Paul's head, picking out the stray silver hairs at his temples and the fine laughter-lines around his eyes. Sensing her presence, he turned to face her.

'Everything all right?' he enquired softly.

'Yes, fine – it's just so quiet without the girls. Would you mind if I sit here for a while? I promise not to disturb you.'

'Of course. I won't be a moment, I just want to finish this sketch.'

Listening to the soft scratching of pencil on paper, Jenny thought fondly of Celestina and Emily. Now old enough to go to school summer camp, they had both grown in confidence during the past five years. Cele of course remained the ever-protective older sister, but Emily was no longer the shy, nervous child Jenny remembered. Aware of Paul laying down his pencil, she asked casually, 'What's that, a new idea for the House of St Claire?' From where she sat it was impossible to distinguish.

Paul stood up and walked towards her, holding out a piece of paper.

'There,' he said, 'what do you think of that?'

Jenny looked puzzled. 'What is it supposed to be?'

'What does it look like?'

'Well . . . it looks like a tartan pram, with the House of St Claire emblem on the side.'

'And what do you think of it?'

For a moment Jenny said nothing; she didn't want to hurt his feelings, yet for the first time ever she thought the design to be in appalling taste.

Paul waited patiently for her reply. 'Well – what do you think?'

'I'm sorry, darling, I really don't like it at all, in fact it's . . .'

She looked up, expecting to see a hurt expression on his face, but instead he was smiling at her.

'I quite agree with you.' He grinned. 'So you won't be wanting one like that for our baby, then?'

Jenny hesitated. 'How . . . how long have you known?'

Paul took her in his arms. 'Oh, Jenny! I live with you

and work with you, we've been married for five years and you think I don't know everything about you? I've been waiting for weeks for you to tell me about the baby . . . why haven't you?'

Jenny's eyes filled with tears as she clung to him. 'Because we've had so many false alarms, I just couldn't bear to disappoint you again.'

Comforted by the warmth of his embrace, she thought back to all her previous miscarriages and the dark empty nights she'd lain in his arms, totally bereft, as they'd mourned the loss of yet another baby.

'Well, take it from me, this is no false alarm,' Paul said confidently, tearing up his drawing, 'and as our baby is going to need a proper pram, I'd better get cracking on a decent design both worthy of our son and the House of St Claire. In the meantime, Mrs Hadley, may I suggest you go and ring your mother?'

Watching her walk down the hall with a spring in her step, Paul sighed contentedly and turned to the familiar painting of Princes Street hanging above his desk. Morag had given it to him as a housewarming present.

'You take it,' she'd insisted. 'I want you to have it – I know it reminds you of Jenny . . . and hopefully you can . . .'

Reluctantly he'd accepted the gift, offered with her frail and wrinkled hands, then he'd noticed the twinkle in her eye.

'Morag?' he'd asked quizzically. 'And hopefully I can what?'

'Give me a photograph of your son to hang in its place alongside those of my other grandchildren.'

Smiling, Paul had kissed her on the cheek and murmured softly, 'Bless you, Morag. You're just as perceptive as ever, I see . . . and don't worry, I'll make sure you get your photograph.'

⬛ THE EXCITING NEW NAME IN WOMEN'S FICTION!

PLEASE HELP ME TO HELP YOU!

Dear *Scarlet* Reader,

As Editor of *Scarlet* Books I want to make sure that the books I offer you every month are up to the high standards *Scarlet* readers expect. And to do that I need to know a little more about you and your reading likes and dislikes. So please spare a few minutes to fill in the short questionnaire on the following pages and send it to me.

Looking forward to hearing from you,

Sally Cooper

Editor-in-Chief, *Scarlet*

QUESTIONNAIRE

Please tick the appropriate boxes to indicate your answers

1 Where did you get this Scarlet title?

Bought in supermarket ☐

Bought at my local bookstore ☐ Bought at chain bookstore ☐

Bought at book exchange or used bookstore ☐

Borrowed from a friend ☐

Other (please indicate) _____

2 Did you enjoy reading it?

A lot ☐   A little ☐   Not at all ☐

3 What did you particularly like about this book?

Believable characters ☐   Easy to read ☐

Good value for money ☐   Enjoyable locations ☐

Interesting story ☐   Modern setting ☐

Other _____

4 What did you particularly dislike about this book?

_____

5 Would you buy another Scarlet book?

Yes ☐   No ☐

6 What other kinds of book do you enjoy reading?

Horror ☐   Puzzle books ☐   Historical fiction ☐

General fiction ☐   Crime/Detective ☐   Cookery ☐

Other (please indicate) _____

7 Which magazines do you enjoy reading?

1. _____

2. _____

3. _____

And now a little about you –

8 How old are you?

Under 25 ☐   25–34 ☐   35–44 ☐

45–54 ☐   55–64 ☐   over 65 ☐

cont.

9 What is your marital status?
   Single ☐   Married/living with partner ☐
   Widowed ☐   Separated/divorced ☐

10 What is your current occupation?
   Employed full-time ☐   Employed part-time ☐
   Student ☐   Housewife full-time ☐
   Unemployed ☐   Retired ☐

11 Do you have children? If so, how many and how old are they?
   _____
   _____

12 What is your annual household income?
   under $15,000   ☐   or   £10,000   ☐
   $15–25,000   ☐   or   £10–20,000   ☐
   $25–35,000   ☐   or   £20–30,000   ☐
   $35–50,000   ☐   or   £30–40,000   ☐
   over $50,000   ☐   or   £40,000   ☐

Miss/Mrs/Ms _____
Address _____
_____
_____

Thank you for completing this questionnaire. Now tear it out – put
it in an envelope and send it, before 31 December 1997, to:

Sally Cooper, Editor-in-Chief

USA/Can. address   *UK address/No stamp required*
SCARLET c/o London Bridge   SCARLET
85 River Rock Drive   FREEPOST LON 3335
Suite 202   LONDON W8 4BR
Buffalo   *Please use block capitals for*
NY 14207   *address*
USA

MASIN/6/97

Scarlet titles coming next month:

SWEET SEDUCTION Stella Whitelaw
Giles Earl believes that Kira Reed is an important executive. She isn't! She's been involved in a serious road traffic accident and is in Barbados to recover. While she's there she decides to seek out the grandfather who's never shown the slightest interest in her. Trouble is – he's Giles's sworn enemy!

HIS FATHER'S WIFE Kay Gregory
Phaedra Pendelly has always loved Iain. But Iain hasn't been home for years. Last time he quarrelled with his father, Iain married unwisely. Now he's back to discover not only has Phaedra turned into a beauty . . . she's also his father's wife.

BETRAYED Angela Drake
Business woman Jocasta Shand is travelling with her rebellious niece. Sightseeing, Jocasta meets famous soap star Maxwell Swift – just the man to help her get even with Alexander Rivers. But Maxwell already has a connection with Alexander . . . and now Jocasta is in love with Maxwell.

OUT OF CONTROL Judy Jackson
Zara Lindsey stands to inherit a million dollars for the charity of her choice, *if* she is prepared to work with Randall Tremayne for three months. Zara can't turn down the chance to help others, but she thinks Randall's a control freak, just like the grandfather who drove her away from home ten years ago. So *how* can she have fallen in love with Randall?